Talking to Tesla™

AN ARTIST'S DREAM JOURNAL

The Mirror That Is The Door
Alex Bigney

Quadro Creative Development™

An original publication by Quadro Creative Development, LLC™
www.talkingtotesla.com

Copyright © 2004 by Alex W. Bigney

All rights reserved. This book may not be reproduced or utilized in any form or by any means, electronic or mechanical, including photocopying, recording, or by any information storage and retrieval system, without permission in writing from the publisher.

Jacket painting, *Identity*, Kent Wing, *www.kentwingart.com*
Jacket design, Jack Hadley, *www.clarityworx.com*
Text design, Gavin Jensen, *www.gavinjensen.com*

Printed on acid free paper in the United States of America

First hardcover edition printing January, 2009

ISBN 978-0-9821797-0-3

Dedicated to my dear children
Falcon, Miriam, Simeon, Samuel, Alex, and Siro
And to children everywhere.

Contents

Preface   i

ONE

1 – Believe and Make Believe   3
2 – Coming of Age   15
3 – An Unexpected Visitor   23
4 – A Lecture   33
5 – What Is a Pattern?   45
6 – Comedies and Earthquakes   55
7 – The Source and the Wasteland   65
8 – At the Brink of an Abyss   77
9 – The Empty Stage   91
10 – Butterfly Hunting   101

TWO

11 – Dreams Within Dreams   115
12 – Free Falling   135
13 – The Infinite Degrees of Santa Claus   153
14 – Touching the Veil   165
15 – Like a Tangle of Something (How It Is)   183
16 – Line and Circle   201

17 – Talking to Myself	221
18 – Frequencies	229
19 – Talking to Tesla	241
20 – You Or Me?	253
21 – Black Rock, White Rock	261

THREE

22 – Concerning My Moons	279
23 – The Poetics of Pegasus	293
24 – A Quickening	305
25 – Daydreams	319
26 – The Two Keys	327
27 – Awakening in Italy	335
28 – Music and the Bonfire	347
29 – Pietà and Compianto	365
30 – The Rudiments of Electricity	379
31 – Of Compound Things and Complexities	389
32 – Birth and Rebirth	405
33 – Where All the Stories Come Together	423
A Final Note	445
Acknowledgments	447

"…there is an influence which is getting strong and stronger day by day, which shows itself more and more in all departments of human activity, an influence most fruitful and beneficial—the influence of the artist."

—*Nikola Tesla, 1897*

Preface

We met about two years ago, although it might have been fifty, a hundred, or even thousands—as that limitation and many others are less important to me now. Our first meeting was one of those events from which life seems to happen in all directions, as much a part of what preceded as what follows. So I keep looking back, picking through the clutter of my life for clues, hoping to stumble upon something that suggests a beginning to this story—my childhood and youth, life as a painter, my travels in Italy; all motifs in the complex pattern that led me here.

The intent is not to chronicle my life, nor to document all of my dreams, just those things that relate to a magical friendship and the curious encounters that seem to have reached inside me like roots pushing eagerly into well-prepared soil. The appearance of an unexpected teacher, his instruction and my ongoing initiation into a world of expanding boundaries—the dreams that include my past as well as foreshadow a future, the odd familiarity of what was unpredictable; that's what I write about.

I have told and retold most of these tales so often that I remember them quite well; but worry that as I stop rehearsing them, the details will begin to fade. Consequently, I'm setting them down in the hope that they'll be provocative to someone like me who likes to sit and wonder at things. The effort to record them accurately has been as remarkable an experience as the events themselves; and like the activity of painting in my studio, has required complete devotion to an audience. How the reader ultimately interacts with this account and my reasoning—I can't decide; but the events, the dreams, I believe them to be real—at least as real as anything can be.

Alex Bigney
Smiljan, Croatia, October 2007

ONE

1
Believe and Make Believe

"What's your name? Huh?"

I watched my wooly little friend gradually advance, his steady rhythm, undulating head-to-toe-head-to-toe, inching him slowly through the grass, sticks, and undergrowth.

"Hey! Where're you going?"

"Prob'ly to that tree over there," I figured, momentarily lifting my head to check his direction. Actually he was headed for the back swamp, the one we called *the skating place*. "Or maybe the meadow once you're outta these trees."

"I could just call you Fuzzy?" I suggested. He continued unbothered as I gently grazed the hairs of his back with my pudgy forefinger.

"Or, Mister Stripy? How's that?"

Briefly, he'd stop, rise up on his stout back legs as if to sniff at something, scout around, and reach out stretching for a twig or blade of grass that wasn't there. I could hear my brothers somewhere in the yard playing, the dog barking, and the usual drone of the woods. His long journey would recommence; and I'd go back to my chatter, hoping not to be noticed there and our relations not interrupted.

"And—you're just mine, OK?"

I'm not sure how long I lay there on my belly in the dirt, captive by the deliberate progress of my larval friend across a childhood Eden, nor when I chose to leave and find more excitement elsewhere. Though I return at times, it's far too accidental when things seem suddenly so real again, too once-in-a-while and out of my control. And so, there are also times when I remember and wish bitterly through grownup tears to return to childhood, to be on my belly again by the swamp hunting pollywogs, times on warm spring evenings in a current desert of adult concerns, when I strain to hear the peepers trill again.

Children have a knack for finding Edens anywhere, caterpillars in the woods, secrets in tide-pools, anthills in the cracks of sidewalks, all accompanied by beaming exclamations. They seem to have a gift for seeing more than what there is to see, hearing more than I can hear in what is largely obvious and cliché. I struggle to remember how, too often finding grownup counterfeits in childish needs and empty addictions. Yet, still there are those times, in spite of my big self, when by surprise or luck I am able to suspend my disbelief and sophistication long enough to become a child again.

I remember falling in love to be like that, losing my newfound manhood to the silly boy in me, to the novelty of everything about a girl. After tickle fights, giggles, and oblivious cooing, I'd cuddle up in the familiar smell of her perfume, content in our confidences, and lay my head gently in her lap. She would sing to me then, combing my hair softly with her fingers and I was home again.

"And—you're just mine, OK?" I'd ask.

Oh! And childbirth—to experience the arrival of a baby and feel so helpless before the wonder of it, to see that tender tadpole of a newborn person suddenly appearing from the blood and cries of another—that is real. To witness the first breath of a small new friend, to check him out head-to-toe every inch, captivated by the unsteady struggles of brand-newness, and between my beaming exclamations, to cry just like a kid again. Then I'd sit and watch the first fragile suck at mother's breast, waiting impatiently for a turn to hold my newborn child and search the tiny angel's face for clues.

"What's your name, little one? Huh?"

It's just once in a while, and often by surprise, that I turn to see the reflection of my young self close by, the little boy standing guard over the man I have grown into. Like that morning when I heard the song of a meadow lark for the first time and ran, bursting out the back door to find myself both amazed and happy at the impulse still there; or the times I pat our family dog and feel overcome by the desire to rebury my head in the neck of a dog some forty years before. I'll smile to myself, wash my hands and get back to whatever it was I had to do. It might be the unconscious touch of a friend that unexpectedly reminds me of snuggling up with my brothers three in a bed, a monarch laying eggs on a milkweed urging me to "Quick! Get that empty pickle bottle," or the inevitable traumas of adolescence that confuse my teenage kids, calling up the image of an overgrown twelve-year-old on his mother's lap, crying for fear of turning thirteen.

I look into my lover's eyes and remember when I fell in love, then fell in love again, and again, each time seeing my reflection there, the same boyish man, but with gray hair, forever staring back at me from those same eyes.

"You look sad," she says. "Is everything all right?"

"Of course, dear," I lie, hoping she still sees the eager boy in me I want to see.

Like glances in a mirror, these events happen now and then. I turn and am surprised to catch myself gazing back, the essential me momentarily considering my changing and substantial self. In the time it takes to look again, it's gone; and I am back doing whatever it was that I was doing, but with a sense of missing someone close, an ally, a childhood friend of mine.

And growing up—I can laugh at us all now, the kind of kids it's hard to be indifferent to, dirt-streaked, freckle-faced, and precocious. Highly skilled in various classes of tomfoolery, we could have written manuals on the more creative forms of a wide range of troublemaking, from the study of trajectories, those considered in launching a diversity of materials and shapes—typical spit-wads, eggs, snowballs, and seasonally available rotten fruits or more exotic items—to the advanced methodologies of serious teasing. We were consummate rascals, masters of mischief.

But if we had an aptitude for misbehavior, we were equally versed in literature, music, and the arts. While we were out climbing trees, poling around the swamp on rafts, or playing pranks, mama was sometimes inside writing verses. We were the astute audience and critics she had patiently trained. Her request for our presence often meant one of two things: either that we'd been caught, or that she'd been writing again and wanted us to listen. The glare with lowered eyebrows meant trouble, while puffy reddened eyes meant the impending and sincere reading of a recently penned poem.

In the evening, typical conversation at our table ranged from the many complaints of neighbors to the symbology of Dostoyevsky, the ethics of Thoreau, recent readings of Chekhov, our responses to particular poets or the effects of specific works of a variety of composers. And then, "How did your violin go today?" she would ask, feigning ignorance, knowing quite well that my genius had been applied to other less celebrated artforms. We'd cast brief looks at dad hoping he was too involved in eating to have heard.

"Fine," I'd mumble hastily, and change the subject.

As often as we could, we made a pilgrimage, my mother and her unkempt brood, so many ducklings in a row, from the woods where we lived, to the city where the art museum was. It took at least an hour: the drive to Everett Station, the elevated, the subway, and the streetcar. We'd arrive and walk past the green man on a horse, a bronze Greek god in Indian attire who nobly welcomed us with outstretched arms. We stopped our endless ruckus then, slowly climbed the wide stone stairs, and passed beneath the blank-eyed gaze of a stone pharaoh, each lost in eager dreaming of the day that awaited us.

Some of my best friends lived in the museum, so first of all I paid them each a visit, just passed by to let them know that I was there. I raced quietly from room to room, by Monet's countryside of haystacks and poppies, past The Postman Joseph Roulin and his wife, by the silent mummies in their cases, down the stairs to the terra cotta bowls and urns, and tiny golden Nike flying in her earring chariot. I'd quickly pass The Sower always throwing seeds, my Man on a Rope forever hanging in midair, and then stop by Gauguin's Eve still reaching up to pick that fruit. *"They're all here and I'm here,"* I'd reassure myself, relaxing and deciding where to start my day. My path was typical, a quick check on my good friends, then on to tour each gallery, one by one, where things were always comfortably in place. I was pleased with my routine inventory, satisfied to know each time that all was as it should have been.

Then I started seeing changes. Yes, the grainstacks were all in place that morning, but somehow not the same. They seemed to glow with a syrupy new warmth I had never noticed, glistening in what looked like a mix of paint and fruit preserves. I could almost taste them, and got closer to examine their sweetness more intently. That day, from up close, I saw stray famous hairs caught forever, studio dirt stuck, brush bristles, and the fingerprints of long dead artists, all the evidence alive there in the paint. "Just what are we up to? Hmmm?" asked my favorite postman when I arrived, raising his eyebrows and almost serious. He appeared to expect an answer, sitting posed not far from bright-faced Augustine, his colorful wife holding the cord to rock an unseen cradle. She was unexpectedly crazy that day, a yellow Madonna with eyes and fancy flowers flying all around. *"But in a pretty way,"* I decided. My cool Egyptian friends, though unmoved, seemed to smile more serenely, keeping secrets. I blushed at the naked men with impressively exaggerated attributes on the terra cotta vessels downstairs as if I too were standing there exposed, as much on show as they.

I watched The Sower breathe with his work, and thought I heard him exhale hard as he swung himself around, casting seed, his boots thumping dully in his eternal plodding on the soil. And my precarious friend on the rope, nervously checking out the distance between himself and the ground, *"Hang on!"* I thought, *"You'll make it."* From that point on everything was new, the light on the hay, the Postman, Madame Augustine, the Egyptians, the handsome terra cotta heroes, and The Sower, all different every time we met.

So then, one day in front of Daumier's dangling protagonist, I looked and it was me I saw. *"I'm going to make it. Hang on!"* I remember thinking as I hung there on that rope, alone and afraid. I was standing there to look at what was clearly looking back at me. No, nothing was ever the same. I stood in front of Eve and saw her growing old, forever reaching for the fruit she'll never pick. "*Où allons-nous?*" I read up in the corner of the picture. And that was when I realized that in truth my friends were watching me. They hadn't changed at all, but like mirrors, where who I am, sees what I am becoming, they were the gentle witnesses to my transformation. I looked around at other people looking and wondered how it was for them, all sizes, styles, and colors, all of us together there, staring quietly, captives to the same images of ourselves.

"*Certainly artists are the most important of all,*" I concluded, and the boy who was a fireman, archeologist, paleontologist, violinist, and doctor at once became an artist, a painter.

After a day at the museum we'd discuss what we had seen. One evening, between horseplay and general grabbing at the table, mama asked what it was that had impressed us most. Someone brought up the little Nike earring, another had spent the day immersed in Egypt and Babylon, while I mentioned Gauguin's masterpiece, the big one with the Tahitian woman picking fruit and the questions in French up in the corner.

"Do you know what those questions mean in English?" she asked in her teacher voice.

"Yes." I answered smartly. "Where do we come from? What are we? And, where are we going?"

"Very good. But, he should have known better—Instead, I love the Renoirs, especially that dance at the outdoor café. Ahhh! You can just feel it, can't you? That Gauguin, he was a scoundrel you know, not very nice, and Van Gogh was a genius but had some problems of his own...."

Of course I had to admit the Renoirs were nice too, particularly the dancing man's half-hidden face, but we were partial to scoundrels, especially when it had to do with Tahitian women. She could hardly have given poor Gauguin a better rating.

"I think I'd like to be an artist," I said—and dad looked up.

Years later in Florence, the artist that was me sat staring out the window, watching a parade stream by. The street below was always busy. Miniature trucks and three-wheeled contraptions clattered to and from their business, piled with showy goods to fill the shops each morning. By day it was a river of people, bicycles, and carts flooding past, then flowing into evening, followed by the late trickle of voices and the gritty footsteps of a few stragglers amplified in the narrow passages of stone. At night the occasional echoes of a scooter buzzing by interrupted the silence and grew faint. *"I'm in Italy,"* I rehearsed again and again. She had seduced me, and I let her.

Each day I joined a spirited procession through the streets, hopelessly lost in the smells and music of it, anxious for something, near ready to burst with blind anticipation. Each night the tease of vivid dreams, leaving deep impressions but no memory, filled me with nostalgia for a familiar life that I had never known. *"I'm in Italy,"* I thought, *"And it feels like home."*

Once more I awakened early to the scratchy sounds of a small army equipped with twig brooms sweeping up the litter from the cobblestones before another daylong celebration. That morning I had planned my first trip to the Galleria degli Uffizi in the ancient office building that holds a good part of the Medici art collection. The piazza nearby is something between a flea market and an antique *Luna Park* of sculptures, fountains and outdoor cafés, all presided over by a full-size reproduction of The David. I made my way through swarms of tourists, by the vendors making deals, past the street performers, and joined the carnival line of people waiting eagerly to see the famous art inside the gallery.

Eventually, it was a relief to leave the rumpus outside and climb the wide stone staircase to the top. I stood a while at the entrance to a noble hall and scanned its length, watching people move quietly among the ancient marble forms there and smoothly drift in and out of several doorways. I studied the improbable painted ceiling above, and stepped inside a gallery to my left, gazing into the initial scene, feeling small and unprepared. Either the impact of the stillness was so profound that it swallowed up the noise of everything, or the volume was so loud that it overcame all interference. My inner small talk stopped. After coming so far it felt like finally arriving at the beginning of something, returning to the point of just before departing, a time of forgetting and remembering, when looking back might mean losing what's ahead, when the future I struggle to see is inspecting me, when all possibilities are briefly true again.

I met the Madonnas of Cimabue, Duccio, and Giotto, The Annunciation of Simone Martini, the narrations of the Lorenzetti brothers, so many other annunciations, adorations, crucifixions, depositions, pietàs, and coronations. Since then, they have become old friends whom I have visited many times, first as a young man, then with my wife, and eventually with our children. By now, the floorplan of the place is so well-known to me that in my daydreams back at home, I can walk the halls and corridors by heart and call on each in its location.

"It's been a while," says my favorite crucified Jesus by an unknown artist. "We should talk more."

"I know," I admit, "I'll try to make it more often."

"Too long, *old man*. Time is passing," warns the golden-hued Madonna from her fancy chair.

"Yeah—sorry. I'm so busy. I have a family now."

They have become my honest confessors whose wisdom never weakens. But, it is still the first time that I wandered there from room to room, captive to their surprising presence, that I remember best. Lippi's little angel peering out at me, Piero's pale portrait of Battista, Botticelli's primal paradise—that was when they all became my steady new companions, my loyal confidants and pals.

There before the brooding euphoria of Botticelli's springtime, I rested. A few of us, all strangers, sat on the oversized leather ottoman provided, taking turns getting up to inspect the paint more closely, then returning to our places.

The Primavera has become a platitude, the popular domain of posters, coffee mugs, placemats, and puzzles. And there it was. What I hadn't expected was the impact, the momentum of it. I searched the painting for a long time, got up to investigate the impossible looking meadow, each blade of grass, each tender flower rendered so precisely.

"But why?" I wanted to know.

It was the lush world of the woods all over again, another Eden and another Eve wanting my response. Flowers floating everywhere brought to mind the postman's wife, lemony-faced Madame Roulin. Three women in diaphanous dresses solemnly danced a ring-around-the-rosy. A troupe of planetary gods was caught in their dramatic practice, a seeming rehearsal for the ceremonious rebirth of everything.

"This is serious fooling around—and, here are the gods, like children playing on a stage."

We sat together on the soft bench, a more earthy troupe, the mundane counterpart to the progression of heavenly bodies just a few feet away. I think we represented every possible race, an unlikely impromptu family sitting there watching and dreaming together, caught somewhere between believe and make believe. Once in a while someone would come join us and we'd have to make room, or actively save someone's threatened seat. Then one of us would get up, nod to the rest and reluctantly leave. I imagined where each was from and who he or she might be; but none of us spoke.

"It's not just mine, is it?" I realized after all. I was sharing my woods and meadow now with others whom I didn't even know. I went up close again and looked for bugs and caterpillars in the grass, sure that I'd find some. I was stunned. "This isn't decoration," I whispered. "It's devotion." My gut tightened with emotion and I returned quickly to my seat turning to the woman next to me as if to share what I had found, but said nothing. She had puffy reddened eyes, yet was beaming, smiled back warmly, then got up, acknowledging the group, and went her way.

After a prolonged stay with The Primavera, I decided it was time, and glanced around to get my bearings, wondering where to go next and how many possible Edens I had missed on my way there. To get up finally, felt like starting on a long trip, deciding what to leave and what to take. I nodded goodbye to the new group, opened my little map, and stood for a moment in the doorway to the next room. Then I moved on.

2
Coming of Age

Nel mezzo del cammin di nostra vita
mi ritrovai per una selva oscura
ché la diritta via era smarrita.

In the middle of the path of life, lost in a dark wood, with no idea how he'd got there—that's how Dante began, which is after all not so odd for someone finding himself in the middle of living, whether born in the twelve hundreds or the twentieth century. In fact it's symptomatic of being alive, the recurring need to pick up your head and look around, take stock of things, and reassess the old routine.

"Hey, am I on track?"

"For what?" asks a little voice.

I guess that's the real question. *"For what?"* I repeat, confused by my lack of a ready answer. At a certain point, it's about really growing up—revisiting dreams, the ones concealed from myself along the way in deference to practicality. It frequently starts with the shock of staring in the mirror.

"*Is that really me?*"

It was the graying hair and crow's feet that instigated the resulting trips to the attic of my psyche to see what dusty hoards might be neatly tucked away and forgotten there, but it can happen to anyone at any time. And, that's exactly where I find myself, like Dante, a little lost and in the middle of things, a self-indicted late-bloomer, finally *coming of age*. Unlike Dante, however, I didn't start out intending to write anything down, so I'm not quite sure where to begin.

There was a grassy hill near our home, not a big hill, but almost tall enough to reach the treetops. My favorite trail through the woods ran along an old stone wall, by a row of long abandoned apple trees, to a small meadow at the top of the hill, where it was sunny and warm compared to the dusky chill of the woods. That's where we often spent afternoons, playing pirates or setting would-be traps for crows because we heard that they could talk. During the right season a tangle of blackberries on one side of the hill gave us enough for mama's pies and muffin-cakes. On its crest, a single pine tree grew, whose horizontal branches were accessible to the youngest of us. We could climb high enough in its strong limbs to reach the softer boughs up near the top where we would sit and sway, high enough to feel the wind on our faces and look out around us at a sea of trees and a few rooftops.

Often enough, I would escape through the woods to the top of that tree. It was a shelter, someplace to hide, somewhere to think about things—my many possible lives, my biggest house, the prettiest wife I'd marry, and the fanciest car I'd drive. From there I discovered Egyptian tombs, played concertos, painted like Leonardo, and accepted sincere apologies from the school principal. Mostly, it was just a place to disappear, to sit and dream without being bothered, up with the juncos and chickadees, a singular landmark in an inner landscape of childhood places. Eventually, an imagined little hill and its pine tree kept me company away from home. I went there in my daydreams and my dreams at night, to sit peacefully rocking in the wind, to think about the world around me and wonder who I am.

From most points of view, I'm a rather average but eccentric guy who wouldn't stand out in a crowd, any nameless neighbor, some might say a castle-builder with his head up in the clouds. I'm married and have a family, hoping like others, to travel safely with my small tribe from here to there. I'm no one really, though by passion and profession I am a painter—whatever that means.

"Oh, what do you do?"

"I'm an artist," I respond sheepishly. "But when I'm broke I get a job," I add quickly, to avoid discussion. "Yes—I'm also a consultant," I continue, which sounds more reasonable although there's a spectrum of consultable things to get paid for, from stocking shelves, or the direct sales of cleaners and cosmetics, to business plans and software design. Some consider *artist* to be less than a profession, assuming my gym bag holds a beret and bongo drums, secret pink shirts or other more peculiar props; and I admit, at times it might.

Being an artist—in Italy it's different. "*Ma lo fai proprio per passione?*" Followed by a searching expression, then admiration, almost awe. "*Bravo!*" And soon we're in the middle of an animated discussion about my work. "I've seen that! It's from the Annunciation in Cortona."

"You know the piece?"

"*Sì, certo che lo conosco*. You borrow from our artists, but change the context.... *Forte!*"

In truth, I'd like to speak to anyone who would listen. I'd like to talk about my mysteries, about my hopes of picking up the threads of various misconstrued and almost forgotten conversations. If I really get going, I might easily step up onto my soapbox and preach from Giovanni Pico della Mirandola, or quote my friends Giordano and Marsilio, citing the inquiries of restoration that prepared the way for the rebirth of all aspects of our world, the arts of thinking, of creating linguistic, aural, visual, and tangible forms—sensual events to hold ideas and experience—and the subsequent exploration of new and yet unnamed realities. For those with time enough, I'd take them to my studio and introduce them to the intoxicating smell and feel of paint, the wisdom of riddles, and finally the boy with all the questions, sitting in a pine tree.

"My uncle is an artist," many respond, raising their eyebrows.

"Well, isn't that nice—we're all related," I think meanly to myself and smile, remaining silent, and wishing to end the conversation fast.

I make pictures to mark the route of my life, to discuss visually what it is to be human, to be conscious, to be self-conscious. I plagiarize the icons, patterns, and conventions of past enlightenment, borrowing from a palette of historical art and artists the way one might use an old piece to furnish a new house, not unlike consulting a dictionary before rearranging old words into new phrases. I like the frankness of line, shape, and perspective that happens when ideas retain a sense of instinct, before they're confident and correct, before they begin to imitate themselves. It has become unnatural then for me to continue believing that art is for its own sake. To me, that's a passing thought that soon became a lie. Art is for our sakes and always has been—no matter who says what. I like to experience it as a very big discussion, a complex narrative, an overgrown chat room, not a flat timeline from there to here diagramming the past; but something always current, ready and waiting for the chatters to enter and become engaged in a free-for-all.

In most ways I am simple—a believer trying to hope in and seek for what is good and true. I like believing, as opposed to *not* believing. You might say that I believe and hope in everything: goodness and truth everywhere under a single heading, one whole thing. In other words, I understand distinctions but not divisions. I believe and hope in a greater intelligence, that whoever that is, can and does talk to those who listen. When I read them, the sacred writings and teachings of all people are holy, meaning God has spoken to, and continues to speak, to people everywhere in spite of the boundaries we struggle to keep in place. Labeling my spiritual life is problematic, as if a word is understood universally or could ever say it all about anyone or anything. Because of their desire for power and influence, I avoid most of those who profess to *know*. I question the transubstantial facts professed by science, as much as I suspect the religionists who make professions of gate-keeping spirituality. They all seem to want the audience to forget the sour notes because part of a tune sounds good. While that is in their interest, mine is to question, hope, and believe in something more. Too often, those who claim *to know,* know nothing of belief. Only those with honest hearts who listen closely, those still sowing tender seeds and nourishing the hope of fruit, those of us still wrestling faithfully with doubt, can finally believe.

Then, there are my dreams: the fanciful visions of my conscious or unconscious self, states of reverie and abstraction, the sequences of sensations, images, and thoughts that pass through my mind when I'm asleep and awake, everything transitory, vague, or ephemeral—including my aspirations—all of the above. I'm a dreamer, that boy up in a tree. I've always been a dreamer with technicolor capacity, which has been a problem at times.

In fact, once, there I was in seventh grade, some twenty thousand leagues under the sea and suddenly —"Hello? Is anybody home? (general giggling in the classroom) I asked you a question, young man! We were talking about the Hittites…." Then there was the time I was attending a museum reception in my honor, looking rather like a tall dark fitness model without my shirt on and speaking to patrons about my work, when—CLONK! The shorter less than perfect me walked straight into a cement column holding up the mall roof, which didn't budge. I'm guilty—I know. It's un-American—since dreaming has no profit center and daydreaming is wasting time, and time is money. Wasting time is wasting money—nearly treason.

But I can dream—and while I've never obsessed about it, at night I dream a lot of very vivid dreams. I refer to them as *movie dreams*, because they seem so real. Sometimes too real. Usually, I recall the events of those particular dreams quite well and have used them as gauges or markers in the flow of my memories. "Oh yeah, that was back when I had those dreams about…the Austrian Imperial Crown China saucer I threw at my brother and then it hovered like a spacecraft," or—"around the time that Spike, the family dog, and I helped us all escape from bombs falling on our driveway." It took the whole epic dream to get from the front door, through the pocked asphalt maze of craters and explosions, to the tall hedge where we all hid and watched Spike turn into a friendly giraffe. Just try going to school and keeping your mind on Math, David Copperfield, and the Hittites after that!

I've enjoyed these curious episodes since I was very young, eventually talking about them more or less freely with a few friends, party talk that happens when people are tired and the topic of conversation begins to wander to weird things like UFOs. "Hey, tell us about those skin-walkers on the rez...." It's all part of my life, and I have always assumed, a normal part of human consciousness and experience. Some of these dreams have been terrifying, involving what seemed to be those cliché beings from another planet. Other dream events were tender, filling me with a sense of intense caring. Some seemed to teach principles or reveal things I wanted or needed to know. Sometimes I was aware during these experiences that what I was seeing was a translation, an understanding of what I had no way of otherwise knowing or describing. Other times I believe that what I was seeing was very close to some kind of reality. Some dreams were symbolic, parable-like, while others seemed to be very much readable at face value. At least several experiences surrounded, or seemed to foretell, events that would take place at an end of things as we know them.

But compared to the dreams that I record here, the others all begin to fade. These are different. The recent set of nighttime stories is connected, slipping into the occurrences of my daytime—the borders between my nights and days slowly softening. I think of my relationship with an extraordinary dream mentor whose lessons have become significant to all aspects of my life, and get a little lost in my musings. It's been a while since I've stopped long enough to get my bearings, to ponder things, to imagine being high up moving with the wind again where an ocean of treetops and the sky come together. I look at who I am, what I believe, and see myself evolving. Even during the course of writing down these thoughts, I've changed. *"Is that really me?"* I worry. *"Am I on track?"*

"For what?" nags the little voice.

"The view from my pine tree on the hill, the bird traps and familiar smell of mama's muffin cakes—isn't that all part of me?"

Pieter Bruegel's bird trap sits toward the lower right corner of a homey village scene with people skating, an old wooden door waiting to drop, some feed spread under it, a flock of birds, and a rope leading off through the snow. Our comparable traps were made of cardboard boxes propped on sticks, with similar ropes that led to where we hid beneath the pine tree, watching. There was plenty of cracked corn under our boxes, but the crows never came. Perhaps we were impatient. I smile, and remember visiting La Berceuse who tended yet another rope to rock a child to sleep in a cradle—and that man gripping his rope tight, still trapped there hanging on. I look again and see my children playing pirates. For a moment everything is still. I'm more like that boy up in the tree than ever—perched here daydreaming and repeating riddles.

"Nothing has really changed at all, has it?" I reassure myself.

3
An Unexpected Visitor

July 10 – I was alone. The secret places where the treasures of my childhood were hoarded varied widely—inside folded blankets in the corner of a closet shelf, in the back of a drawer behind clothes, or under a rock in the woods. I worked rapidly, concealing the telltale signs of my activity with a patch of moss and a few dead leaves. Finally the cookie tin and its contents were safely buried beneath the large stone. I knew that inevitably someone would find my trove and I'd be forced again to find a new safer spot to hide it, but for now this would do.

The inventory of my stash was typical: pretty stones and pebbles, seashells, an old earring, a few coins, a magnifying glass, a piece of candle, a birthday card from Baba (my Ukrainian grandmother), a blue jay feather, a magnet, and a small mirror. Eventually it might also include a book of matches or a lighter, a note from a girl, a couple of adult-rated photographs, or even the coveted kind of magazine we'd pilfer during scout paper drives, tucking them quickly under our shirts. Like powerful medicine, the characteristic bundle of any would-be young shaman was carefully concealed, knowing how much control a brother or neighbor kid would have over the owner, should its location be discovered. Before leaving the woods I looked cautiously in all directions, hoping that I'd not be noticed and my cache not become the object of someone's curiosity.

"I know where your stuff is."

"No you don't."

"Yes, I do. I saw you and I'm gonna tell…."

"You do and I'll tell about you-know-what, and I know where you're hiding it."

So there was peace, *detente*, each of us fearing the other enough to leave well enough alone for the time being.

Periodically I'd retrieve the tin to add something new or to obtain an item for trading. Often I just reviewed the contents before putting it all back again, satisfied. *"OK, there's the whelk, periwinkle, limpet, crab claw, and sea urchin. Here's a new feather. And there's the pink rock, the egg rock, my zinc penny…."* I sat and stared into my broken piece of plate glass mirror, considering first the silken iris of my eye, then sticking out my tongue to examine the fleshy velvet of its papillae. The mirror was pure magic, a silver pool, a solid reflection that I could hold and endlessly explore. It was always new and different every time. Sometimes I watched the clouds and sky in it, or used it to cast the light of a reflection elsewhere. Other times I watched what was going on behind my back. As far as I could tell, the world was all there in a mirror. I held my head obliquely and got close to see around the corner; and sure enough it was in there, everything, all of it. Even things that were invisible from where I sat showed up in the mirror if I knew just how to look.

In school the teacher spoke about reflections and told us how they worked, about light taking the shortest route from A to B, but my experience was far more convincing than that. I was sure I saw a universe caught there in the glass. How could something seen so clearly not be real? I touched its surface and wondered what divided us, the world in there from the world where I sat. And, who exactly was it gazing back at me in just the same way that I gazed at him?

Perhaps dreaming is similar, springing from the possibilities concealed in the periphery of my reflections, a complementary world of what is mostly hidden within. It's like living in a mirror, a magic view just thinly separate from my waking sight. Being there is similar to being here, and vice versa—but not really. It's the almost reflection of an almost reflection, the open secret no one speaks, which is why it's so seductive after all.

Years have passed; and while my treasures and the image in my mirror look different now, the fleeting nature of my dreams is much the same. It was early morning, some time in late June or early July not so long ago, that I was dreaming an unusually pleasant dream. I still love to dream good dreams, and this was definitely one I wanted to indulge in, somewhere I wanted to linger for a long time. Slowly, almost imperceptibly, however, I became aware that the background volume of birdsong had been gently increasing. Morning in the woods, which had begun unnoticed, far away and innocently enough, was beginning to happen to me, until I knew that in spite of all that I could do, I was nearing the edge of awakening. It's disappointing to wake up before a dream finds an acceptable conclusion, and I feared that this one might be ending too soon.

"Quick! Pay attention, or you'll lose it," I warned myself.

Wherever dreams happen, I wasn't there alone. The whole of

my dream consisted of an enjoyable conversation with someone I had just met. My new friend was a gentleman, finely featured, though slightly more fragile than refined; and as I'm often more eager to know about some people than they are to tell so much about themselves, I studied him carefully as we spoke, particularly his face. He seemed to understand and generously allow my interest, although there was also a marked reserve about him. He was polished, but not uptight; agreeable, and more than that, familiar in a way that I recognized as being like a few intriguing characters I had met in earlier dreams.

First, I noticed his eyes; that they were kind and somewhat sad, revealing a benevolent nature and the sort of sensitivity that sometimes comes from solitude, or from suffering personal difficulties. I watched his lips move as he spoke, which were moderately full and flushed. The corners of his mouth turned up slightly in a gracious way, on the verge of smiling but not quite, and like his eyes, divulged tenderness and a gentle spirit. His complexion was smooth and transparent, and his skin pale, tight along the thin bridge of his nose and across the structure of prominent cheekbones. He wore a neatly trimmed moustache or goatee—oddly, I don't remember which—and was well groomed, wearing a crisp collared white shirt and a soft gray dated-looking suit with subtle chalk lines.

He spoke in a pleasingly cultivated way, clearly and precisely expressing himself, and quickly assumed the role of teacher or mentor. He was affable, but equally direct and frank, completely no-nonsense in a way that I like, which established his credibility and put me at ease. Eventually, after trying to figure him out, I remember making the conscious decision to go ahead and listen to whatever message it was that he seemed intent on delivering. Rather than trying to chase him off or force myself to wake up, as I have in the past with less likeable nighttime visitors, I trusted him.

I was so involved in scrutinizing his person that I don't recall the first part of our encounter, only that it was interesting, and that what he was explaining sounded weighty and meaningful. He had been instructing me about something rather engaging that I wanted to remember but didn't, or couldn't, which was frustrating. Then abruptly he stopped, looked straight at me and became quite serious.

"You are to carry on the work of Nikolai Tesla," he stated.

He repeated this revelation several times as if I should understand the consequence of what he was announcing and he obviously doubted that I did.

"You are to carry on the work of Nikolai Tesla," he reasserted.

I only understood the significant impression it made on me without understanding its meaning. What I do remember is that toward the end of our conversation he disclosed his identity, stating his name with an amount of enthusiasm.

"I *am* Nikolai Tesla."

I wondered that he seemed a little self-congratulatory, and continued watching him carefully, puzzled at his confidence. *"Tesla, Tesla, not ringing a bell, although it sounds like I should know him."* For all of the importance that he plainly attached to the formal pronouncement of his name, I didn't know who he was or what the work he mentioned might involve. My work is painting pictures.

Sometimes meeting someone new is like meeting someone old, like re-finding a good friend whom I've already known and cared for, even if I can't recall exactly when or where. Nikolai felt at once like someone close whom I hadn't seen in a while and our friendship as if it already was. So, to meet him was to anticipate missing him, as I knew that at the end of my dream, our friendship would also end, that he would disappear into wherever dreams live, and that I would return to my average life and never see him again. In the past, comparable dreams have sometimes seemed similarly more vital than the everyday grind of worrying about the usual stuff like a job and making ends meet. I have often wished that waking life could be more like these visions where everything is free, where I am almost always the star, and where friends seem to know each other's hearts. Finally, Nikolai did leave and I woke up. Soon after reiterating what he had said concerning his work and me, he was gone; and I was aware of myself back in bed.

I rolled over to face my wife. "There was this incredible person—I had one of *those* nights—I met this interesting guy. He told me his name was Nikolai Tesla, that I would continue his work. Strange, huh?" She was awake but didn't comment. "I don't even know who he is, and if he told me what his work was—I can't remember. Have you ever heard of Nikolai Tesla?"

In a few prior dreams I had met people who had given me their names. I remember once dreaming of a particular family whose name I later looked up in an encyclopedia to find that they were all dancers and artists from the nineteenth century. They didn't say anything much to me during the dream. I just watched them like watching a film. In some later dreams there were American Indians who told me their names: Buffalo Calf Woman, Yellow Face, and others, all on a list in a notebook by my bed where I recorded them each morning. By now, my wife is used to these odd nights when things happen. She says there's always something in the air. She can feel it. "Did you have one of your nights again?" she will ask in the morning when her sleep has been unsettled.

"I am supposed to carry on the work of Nikolai Tesla," I

repeated, somewhat amused.

"I don't know," she yawned. "Tesla? Sounds familiar. You should look him up on the Internet. He's bound to be there if he's someone real."

I was tired. It was Saturday morning when I generally like to sleep in, but I got up with some encouragement, went downstairs, and turned on the computer. I soon found that he was someone very real. The couple of pictures I saw were of the man in my dream. At that time I didn't read much about him, only that he was a scientist, an inventor, and was instrumental in developing the practical application of electrical current. He died alone on January 7, 1943, at the age of 86. There seemed to be endless sites about him and even people who thought he was pretty important, following his work with a lot of enthusiasm. Sleepy, shocked, and satisfied, I called my wife down to see the long list that came up when I searched on his name. On the Internet it was Nikola Tesla, without the final *i*, even if I remembered his self-introduction as being Nikola*i*, but it was definitely the same man. From what I could see, there was no lack of interest in Nikola Tesla.

"It's crazy," I said, between rehearsing and re-rehearsing the dream. "Me, a painter, continuing someone's scientific work? What's that about?" Nikola Tesla, whoever he was, was on my mind, as if I had always known him, a lost friend, a brother finally found, and a patient guide inspiring me to reconsider things again. *"And, why am I taking this so seriously? It was just a funny dream."* But if it was funny, it was also fun to view myself in such an unfamiliar way. *"So, what can I do to continue his work in something as foreign to me as theoretical electricity? I'm not a physicist, not the nuts-and-bolts type, am I? Just a dreamer, an artist."* In spite of the beguiling nature of dreams, I found that I was drawn to consider what Nikola had proposed, even with no idea what it meant. However far-fetched it sounded, it felt good to imagine myself as someone new and different, someone more important than an artist.

As I write this, I remember the boy back home, content to celebrate the life of his dirty-faced twin in a piece of broken mirror, or quietly admiring the empty sockets where his baby teeth had been. *"Why do I look now hoping to see someone else?"* I'm forced to ask. *"When was it that I chose to find myself not good enough?"* I think of Caravaggio's Narcissus, the tempting semblance of youth mirrored in a spring. There are so many painted images of reflected life. The Velázquez vision of Venus at Her Mirror, another ideal Eve, unveiled before herself and her audience, or Picasso's vivid personification of a Girl Before A Mirror, and Bronzino's painted picture of Pygmalion adoring Galatea, the miraculous life of his own genius; all suggesting not just the shallowness of vanity but perhaps a subtle warning to the proud and unprepared of what is hidden deeper.

I told several people about my amazing dream friend, the dead scientist whom I had never heard of before, then read about on the Internet in the morning. A few people knew about him. Others went to look him up as I had. After a week or two of talking about my experience, I realized that I had begun to repeat myself, so sadly put Tesla on a back shelf. It would pass. In fact, it nagged at me for a few days, before the normal hum of life took over and I returned again to my routine, settling back into the studio, which really isn't so bad anyway. I had been working forever on a painstakingly repetitive pattern that I borrowed from the Fra' Angelico annunciation panel in Cortona. I had been glazing on it for weeks and continued patiently applying the layers of complementary colors over and over the same small details. Soon enough I forgot about my visitor.

As a child, after not retrieving my tin for some period of time, I could forget where it was. Later, my lost cache might turn up, even in someone else's possession and we'd argue—but it was just *stuff*. We all knew that treasure could be transitory, and I'd begin again, collecting things in a large can or shoebox, starting with the basics: pretty rocks, a few shells, a lens, and a mirror.

"Perhaps living is similar to dreaming," I wonder now, "The evidence of a world concealed within me, a fleeting reflection of someplace I keep secret even from myself.

"That is, if I know just how to look."

4
A Lecture

August 7 – It's hard to describe exactly what I learn from a sunrise, what the view from a mountaintop teaches, how a waterfall sounds, how watching a moose cross a wild river at sunset makes me feel—the sometimes hurt of love, the humiliation of abuse, or confusing loss of life, these are the hardest things to talk about because I learn them all without words. A night in the desert filled with endless lightning, swimming in a spring with nothing on, seeds coming up in the garden, the excited play of sunlight on a sea all the way to the horizon—the events of my life, the things that take place outside and in—they do more than just teach or speak to me. They become me. Dreaming is like that, something I live, an event that happens *to* me and *in* me, so that it's difficult to describe verbally.

About a month after my introduction to Nikola Tesla, I was surprised to dream of him again. He came to teach me. "I am going to talk about patterns. Pay attention now. Listen carefully," he began. I've attended classes before without paying much attention, but as he spoke and demonstrated, I experienced things in ways I usually associate with sounds and smells, things my senses push into me until I feel them somewhere in my insides. Unlike a classroom where I have struggled, challenged to shepherd my own stray thoughts, to listen and respond to lessons, I felt myself transform as he taught. He described patterns from many points of view. He was thorough, comprehensive in the content he presented, describing patterns as orders, frameworks, models, roles, sequences, frequencies, vibrations, and on and on. And—he was patient, intent on making sure I understood everything that he proposed, stressing the importance of fully appreciating the concept of *pattern* if I was to understand what he intended to share with me. He was also really *good*, even entertaining, something of a performer. It might have gone on for hours more and I wished that it could have. I would have listened much longer. What was uncommon was that he seemed to know about me intimately, how to engage me in a way and on a level where I could grasp what he was teaching.

Suddenly countless spots of light scattered across a blue-black field. I wondered if I was looking at space, the night sky, or a good facsimile of it projected on a very large screen, one that felt strangely both out there and in here. I love to watch the sky at night and was immediately captive.

When we used to live where it was open, where there was nothing to obstruct the view, I'd go out on the lawn and watch for hours. I felt like a big question out there, looking up expecting something, an answer, a sign of some kind. A couple of times I awoke to find myself in my underwear standing on the wet grass in the middle of the night just staring up. *"Why am I here?"* I'd ask myself. *"Whatever it was, I guess I forgot it,"* and I'd return to bed.

"Where've you been?" my wife would sigh.

"I don't know—just out on the lawn."

I still think about the sky a lot, wonder what it means, why it seems to mean anything at all, and why I like it so much. I suppose everyone likes the sky. When building our current home, we had two large windows installed in the roof over our bed so that we could lie there and look. The sky is so much bigger than I am, but still a private thing—so far away, but close enough at times I'm sure that I can reach out and touch it.

In my dream, everything in the dark "sky" seemed to be in motion; the stars, like fireflies floating over a meadow, highlights on black liquid, sluggishly churning while I watched. I noted the alignment and realignment of specific points in the process of becoming constellations, lines, angles, fields of differing shapes becoming evident and then disappearing as others emerged. Tiny spots of silver flowed in and out of view, mixing and folding over slowly as if in suspension. I realized at once that these were all patterns and that there must be many other patterns happening simultaneously that I wasn't seeing because of my limitations. I understood that what I was seeing, or not seeing, depended almost entirely on me, my singular life and abilities, my perception tightly tethered to my experience. So, in all of my seeing, I felt unexpectedly blind.

While I was still dreaming, Tesla reminded me of a daydream, a sort of vision I had once at school while walking on a campus sidewalk and pondering the concept of mathematical points. In my mind's eye I saw a glass of clear water floating in the air in front of me. As I looked closer I noticed particles in the water swirling around slowly, being carried by the tiny currents in the glass and acting much as these star-like points were acting.

Sitting here to record this experience, I recall a time when I was very young, when I first noticed dust floating in the column of sunlight slanting into a room from a high window. I remember how startlingly dramatic this event was for me—a miracle, almost invisible, at least largely unnoticed by everyone else. The drama was happening right there in the middle of the living room and no one seemed to see or care. A golden pillar of light filled with countless lazy little sunbeams had entered our home. I stood in the light and swung my hand around noticing the interaction of myself with an agitated and colliding universe of specks. I tried to get my mother's attention so she could see it with me, but she seemed not to think that it was interesting. In my dream, Tesla helped me stop and remember related events in my life, like that daydream of the particles suspended in a glass of water, or the memory of dust floating in a column of sunlight. We'd see them together, then return to his lesson. Again, little lights glittered as they swung around against a dark expanse. I watched for some time, mesmerized by the limitless dancing patterns of sparks, a deep dome full of stars smoothly sliding in and out of formation.

"Those patterns you have been painting," said Tesla finally. "They are nothing less than the sequences I have been talking about. They are the visual representations of vibrations and frequencies." I saw the specific grid-like pattern appear that I had painted last year. I borrowed it from an early Madonna by the late-gothic Sienese artist Duccio di Buoninsegna. Nikola went on, "The light that they reflect is obviously a frequency, a vibration, but they themselves are frequencies in other senses, including graphic, musical, and mathematical senses. Likewise, your heartbeat is a vibration and has a frequency that can be expressed in many ways. In fact, all of life is a vibration, and thus a pattern, an order, sequence, and frequency."

Patterns are everywhere—night and day, numbers, flowers, trees and leaves, cells and solar systems, polka dots on lady bugs. Everything is patterns. I even look for them in the clouds—the lobster, poodle or crocodile lasting for a minute before becoming something else. *Pattern* brings to mind the frescoed walls and ceilings of some Italian cathedrals. When I sit in the middle and ponder the colorful flow of particulars that narrate the stories of saints, heavens, hells, and Edens, I am impressed. But for me, the real tale is told in the work. I try to imagine someone patiently applying the elemental overload of pigment that vibrates around me in patterns, and am overcome by the granular exactness of detail that articulates the entire space. From up close then, the stories seem to narrate the parts, and I like that.

If I had a question or seemed not to understand fully, Tesla stopped and repeated what he had said in another way. "Do not be concerned. You see, you are already involved in this work. The visual sequences you are painting are as important as any other patterns. They are vibrations and are meaningful by their very nature." I wondered then if there was some importance that he placed on these painted patterns that was beyond what I had previously thought, or what might normally be perceived. He also suggested that it's not a mistake that I am painting the patterns I am painting; that there is some meaning, reason, and order to them in the sequence of events that is my life, and thus some meaning to my life in the progression of a larger order.

"It is important to know that the most significant pattern or sequence is *one*, the pattern or sequence consisting of a single unit. Do you understand?" I thought about it for a while. "Let us look at it like this," he started. "Imagine a crowd of people milling about frantically bumping into one another." And then, we were looking together at a large crowd doing just that. While he was lecturing, we seemed to see together in my mind whatever it was that he intended me to see. It was a great lecture-demo such as I had never before experienced, right here in the theatre of me. "Notice that each person in the crowd is unique and distinct in form, dress, and attitude. Now find the people with blue eyes. Do you see them?"

"Yes," I answered, trying to pick out the people with blue eyes as they passed by.

"That is a sequence, the frequency of blue-eyed people—a pattern. Of course it is difficult to hold on to. The crowd is moving and you would have to move with it. Even then, the people would move in and out beyond your point of view, and the blue-eyed order would no longer be apparent. It is still the frequency of blue eyes in the crowd. That doesn't change; but its aspect, the shape of it, changes and shifts constantly. Let's look at the sequence of black hair in the crowd then." And we looked at the people with black hair. He reiterated what he had explained concerning the frequency of blue-eyed people, repeating what he wanted emphasized or what he thought I might be unsure of, in order to make certain that I got it. He was good at sensing any slight confusion or lack of understanding on my part. Then, without warning, there was only one person wandering around alone, and for a few moments we quietly watched him together. "Is this any less of a sequence or frequency?" he asked. "Remember the pattern and sequence of *one*. It is important to think about." Somehow I got the impression that in the future there might be things he would show me that would be based on—depend on—my comprehension of the single unit pattern.

He continued, "You understand that most ancient schools were based on repetition, sequence, and ritual. The places of ritual and worship, the temples, were understood as models, patterns. They were places of vibration, mnemonic devices suggesting something larger to the participant. You are similarly—like each initiate that entered sacred space, or every person in that crowd—a pattern, a living sequence. Do you know what a mnemonic is?" Somehow I was sure I didn't know about mnemonics the same way he did.

"You might begin to think of a mnemonic as a door or entry, the threshold to a whole," he said.

To say that I was overwhelmed by what was taking place can't possibly account for how I was feeling, as I began to realize that what he taught was both entering from without and happening within me, that it was at once *me*—that everything from the beginning of our discussion; the motion of stars in space, the crowd of people, and the ancient temple pattern—it was all me, something solid I could hold and endlessly explore—everything, all of it.

"Symbols are mnemonic in nature. You like to paint symbols, do you not?" he smiled. "Symbols, metaphors, signs, tokens, they are all emblematic, reflections of something larger, essentially mnemonics." Somewhere toward the end of the lecture I got up to go to the bathroom and he kept talking. I asked questions, conscious of being awake, and got immediate responses.

"I'm awake and this is still going on," I thought to myself. *"Weird."*

I went back to bed, and he continued, "A true comprehension of mnemonics reveals that they are not just clues for memorizing, although they are that too. Each mnemonic is a small piece whose essence contains the entire framework or pattern that it represents or brings to mind. Mnemonics are like bookmarks to whole volumes filled with endless other volumes, which may in turn be similarly bookmarked."

"Oh, like links," I thought, happy to grasp at something almost concrete that I had experienced. *"Or—like language,"* I realized. *"The pattern of letters becoming words and words then growing into sentences, paragraphs, and pages—a series of concepts developing into an arrangement of ideas—perhaps in other idioms, then possibly returning to one word suggesting the entire proposal—or a single character implying that word. Even a subtle gesture can initiate an avalanche of things, can't it?*

"Am I really dreaming about mnemonics?" I asked no one in particular.

"You will soon learn about mnemonics in that book you are reading," said Nikola. "I suggest you pay close attention and be careful as you read, to appreciate what mnemonics really are. Study it out. Think about it. That's your assignment."

I was reading about Giordano Bruno. I like to read about the Rinascimento, the Renaissance, a confusing period of exploration and enlightenment, a wild kind of game, a big tug-o-war from all directions where whoever crossed the line was put to death. I guess Bruno crossed the line, which impressed me. *"He knows about the books I read?"*

I didn't want Nikola to leave or the lecture to end, but it did. I was already eager for a next installment, hoping that there would be a next time, and fearing the thought of never seeing him again. I pulled the sheet up and stared at the clouds through the skylight. "You're not going to believe this!" I said. "Remember that scientist Nikola Tesla? He came back. He gave me a lecture last night, a real lecture, like a class in school. Don't you remember that guy who came to visit?" And I related what had happened.

During that day and the next several days, I told the same few people about the return of my friend and the lecture he gave. I had a hard time describing it to them, at least conveying the impact that it had on me. Dreams are often surprising, but I'd never had a lecture before—attended a dream session between myself and a dream teacher.

"What's a mnemonic device?" asked my son, and I tried in vain to explain it to him.

"How can I tell him about a mnemonic device? What can I say to suggest how big it really is?" I wondered. *"I don't even get it—I just dreamed it."*

"Try using a watch," came a response spoken clearly to my mind.

"What's going on? Is he still here?" Had Tesla hung around all day or been aware of my impending questions, getting reports? Just waiting to answer? Had he, or some representative, been close by and I hadn't been aware of it? *"Or is this all me?"*

"A watch is a perfect illustration of a mnemonic device," the voice continued, "A kind of compass, the image or symbol that is an entry—points to another place. A watch can be seen as a door to time, beginnings, endings, appointments and events, numbering systems—things that have happened and things that will happen—timeliness, timelessness, systems of measures, unseen inner workings, and countless lives. A simple watch contains all of history there on a wrist or in a pocket. Use a watch as an example." Then I saw a clock face in my mind as if for the first time, and felt it as an unexpectedly profound mystery.

Of course, I had never heard voices before. I had never had experiences quite like these. I thought a lot about them, where they came from and why. I wanted to find out more, talk to people about them, but feared what judgments might be passed. I didn't know who to talk to anyway. And, as I expected, after not hearing from him for a few weeks I missed my association with Nikola. I missed him a lot, and missed learning what he had to teach me. But, I neglected studying mnemonics. I tried to read about them but it was boring. No one seemed to write or think about mnemonics in the way that he did. I fretted about it some, but didn't follow through.

Eventually I began to tell myself and believe that this Tesla stuff and my emotional attachment to it was childish. *"A couple of crazy coincidental dreams, like other dreams,"* I concluded—but the night sky, a crowd of people, any look on any face, all reminded me. *"Patterns? That's old stuff, obvious and cliché."* Then a watch on someone's wrist caught my attention. *"The person, the voice I heard? Must be part of what people mean when they talk about our higher selves—whatever that means."* Not sure of anything, I began to try and shrug the whole thing off, cover it up with my own trivial graffiti; but like adding a moustache to the Mona Lisa, it didn't disguise what was underneath.

Late one evening as I listened to the music of my son's driven bow skipping across the strings of his fiddle, I tapped the rhythm with my feet, and remembered my nana from Nova Scotia step-dancing all night in the kitchen with my dad under that fluorescent ring of light with the moths around it. I thought of the broken mirror in my tin box outside beneath the rock. There's no way to repeat accurately the silent lessons that I learned from those. They are the events of my life. They are who I am. And then I got it—*"It's a door, a threshold to everywhere, and it's all me—a pattern of one."*

5
What Is a Pattern?

August 14 – Nikola Tesla was eagerly quizzing me about a peculiar visual arrangement that we had been studying. Whatever it was that we were inspecting together, he seemed to be enjoying our discussion. Sometimes during a dream when I am intent on exploring a subject, my view becomes very focused. I examine things from up close like a serious detective searching for clues through a magnifying glass. I was observing the deliberate movements of Nikola's mouth, his lips stretching, then wrinkling and tightening as he spoke. "Talk to me about this pattern," he said pleasantly, interrupting my fixed preoccupation. It felt as if I had suddenly just arrived and was struggling to get my bearings, although I had obviously been part of the conversation from the beginning. We were contemplating something together that looked vaguely like a muddy red painted surface, perhaps a Mars Purple or Caput Mortuum with some added Burnt Umber, but from a point of view so close that there wasn't enough context for me to recognize exactly what it was we were investigating.

A painting can start at anytime—in the garden, driving, or while reading a book—not yet an image, not even an idea, not a whole anything. For me, making an image is more like remembering than inventing. It begins as a shadow of something: larval, a hint, a nameless itch of a focus for my attention that I hope might lead to something, which will lead to something else, and something else, and so on and on until it reaches the end of its transformation. Initially, I'll scribble down some words or a few graphic marks in the margin of a page, or on the corner of an envelope, satisfied that they are captured somewhere.

There are so many things I want to paint. I have long lists. Sometimes a lot of them come all at once and I'll fill a page or paper scrap with hasty scribbles—and then, too often I'll forget where they are. So once in a while, I pull an old receipt out of a coat pocket, or pick up a book and open it to find a treasure trove, hidden so well that it was lost even to me. Some of it won't make sense any more. I won't be able to decipher my own odd shorthand. While some, like essential tokens of something much bigger, will expand to become the beginning of the next image I will paint. I think of these unborn ideas as visual *licks*, like the licks I've heard musicians speak of—the ticklish combinations of a few notes that will eventually suggest entire songs.

In one of my most recent paintings I reproduced an elemental marble design from the *Annunciazione* by Matteo di Giovanni. Matteo's Annunciation imitates the famous Annunciation by Simone Martini in the Uffizi, a model annunciation of Late Gothic Sienese art. As my view expanded I saw that the muddy color that Nikola and I were studying together was part of that design, borrowed from Matteo, whose was a translation of

Simone's. It consisted of two color fields, one of earthy red, the other black, separated by the wandering border between them, a graphic simplification suggesting a dark marbleized surface.

"Describe this to me," he requested.

I didn't understand what he meant and must have looked rather vacant sitting there staring straight ahead.

"Tell me why this is a pattern," he restated.

I like to live with the beginnings of a painting for a while before I begin to establish an image. I feel self-conscious around empty panels. The prospects of our ensuing relationship are so intimidating. I get to know them gradually by smearing paint on with my hands and letting it dry before adding another layer—then followed by layer after layer, to slowly build up coats of undirected color that I can wrestle with, scratch into, scrape and sand smooth. Sometimes I paint an ephemeral picture of something as part of a layer that will or won't show through the final skin of the image. This planned *pentimento* lets an eventual audience in on the underlying secrets of my work, perhaps establishing a shared sensual intimacy with the material creation of a piece. Often it allows a participant to encounter the paint with me, to see the obscure disputes I've had on my way to the eventual proposal that becomes a painting. Sometimes, before the image begins to show, it goes through many states, taking years to gestate until finally emerging as it is. I had been painting on the particular panel that Nikola was referring to for a long time before applying the paint that he was pointing at, so his request brought back a lot of memories, a confusing narrative, the musings of over ten years of my life, all suddenly current in what we were looking at together.

"Why is it a pattern?" I repeated, hoping for something more specific and easier to answer. But he said nothing.

I thought about it. *"From one point of view, it's made up of conjoined color fields that imply a circuitous border or suggested line between them. There are no distinctly repeated motifs to make this an obvious pattern. The balance between the complements favors neither the red earth nor the black in terms of dominance. The shapes here seem fluid...."* These were some of my thoughts, but I was quiet as I didn't know exactly what to say.

"I bet he knew the story and what was underneath," I conclude now, thinking back. *"He must have known how many years I wandered through those greens, reds, blues, and browns, hoping to find a suitable response to that space?"*

"How is this a pattern?" he returned expectantly.

Again my internal discussion, *"It's an irregular association between two elements, two things. I think it can be described as a pattern?*

"There are two recurring elements...," I started—then stopped. *"Does that make it a pattern?"* I asked myself. *"Recurring elements?"*

The seed of the image was my Gidu's black felt hat, the way it sparkled in the sun, the mysteries it contained, his stories of the French Foreign Legion, waking up in a house of dead men, and then the boat to America. It began with how I felt about that magic hat, a common accessory of life once-upon-a-time, a part of the wardrobe that implied a grandfather's role in my life, the walks we took, the way he carefully drew his cursive letters and numbers when he wrote, talk of the *old country*, the secrets we shared that I can't remember now.

"Tell me about this pattern then," Nikola continued. "Can we call it a pattern? What is regular about it?"

"Regular? Does a pattern depend on something being regular?" I asked silently.

"This whole thing is irregular!" I blurted out, immediately wishing to take it back.

I looked again at the visible discussion between two color fields and the meanderings of what divided them. I looked at the painted hat shape, and at Nikola Tesla, now searching my face as I had searched his, and I felt small. *"I'm not that smart after all,"* I thought.

"Is there a repeating motif or is this entirely based on singular attributes?" I half asked a question, half proposed the idea, and ended up on the verge of whining. I got quiet again.

"I sense what he wants, but I'm having a hard time saying what I'm thinking and feeling."

I have a sculptor friend who makes arrangements of things that he finds. He haunts the second-hand stores and salvage places looking for stuff that must affect him in much the same way that a nameless hint or piece of paint affects me. Before he selects something to take back to his studio, it's just what it is, waiting there on a dusty shelf. Later, he'll propose a tenuous relationship between it and another object or situation, the way the muddy red relates to the black; like a bomb casing placed beside a church hymnal, a Buddha's head hanging upside down like a plumb bob, or a plastic crucifix in a fish trap. Then together they are something else, like unrelated words suddenly becoming part of a story.

"It isn't entirely random as there are similarities or self-references, approximate repetitions in the recurving boundary between the synchronous shapes," I suggested, "but then again, nor is it regular."

"What's regular about it? That's what he asked, isn't it?"

"If I scan it straight across the horizon there is a very regular exchange between two colors. The segments along that line are intervals of differing lengths." I was pleased with myself for stating it so clearly. "I suppose that any linear slice of the design would yield a similar view of those elements turning on and off, filling each other's absence." I noted to myself that the whole view of the image was less easily definable than the smaller abstracted view, and that the definition of the limited view revealed some things while concealing others.

Tesla was encouraging, not hiding how much fun he was having listening to me explore the problem.

I remember deciding to use that marbled design from Matteo's Annunciation. I had been hoping and looking for something to support adequately the rest of a painted assortment, a proper base for the floating objects of a still life. I have always enjoyed annunciations because of the girl's gentle submission to a heavenly pattern of things. The repeated submitting of one color to another seemed the perfect foundation for the holy scene as well as for the image with my grandfather's hat.

"There is no time that the border between the two colors is straight," I said. "That means that I can predict curves along it with regularity even if they aren't identical curves happening at the same frequency." I recalled the action of the star-like points of light moving in and out of what I could identify as formations. *"But they were always in formation of some kind, identified by me or not, weren't they?"*

"And what does it mean when I'm able to associate various aspects with things?" I asked aloud. "Aren't those conscious connotations like the constellations I saw last time? Isn't recognition a response to pattern, and aren't the stars mnemonic then, like colors, or words, or anything? So symbols work by association. Like two dots and a line beneath them meaning *face*. Doesn't that imply a pattern? And what if I were to perceive this curvy interplay of two painted spaces as being the image of reflections on a liquid surface? Or the visual perceiving of a bluesy jazz composition? How powerful is my interpretation in determining things?" I realized that the counted intervals related to the possible implications of the design, creating a give and take between numbered quantities and named qualities. I was beginning to have fun.

"If what seems random can be a pattern, does becoming a pattern require my awareness of it? What is it before I see it then?

"It *is* a pattern," I said emphatically, recalling the people milling about and our ability to organize them in terms of their eye or hair color, even as the form kept changing. "There are views and properties that seem irregular at first, but it's a pattern like the blue eyes in the crowd we watched." He was still smiling. "At least I think so," I added.

These were simple questions and observations, but they excited me. The structure of the design became increasingly evident as we inspected it together. What I had initially seen as nebulous was taking shape, and Nikola seemed more than pleased. He had given me a gift and was delighted to see me using it.

Everything began to converge—those crazy eyes and wild flowers flying all around the VanGogh portrait of a postman's wife, my mother's unkempt ducklings all in a row, the rivers of people in the streets of Italy, my tenuous family of strangers enjoying the Primavera, all from different places—the pattern of our faces all different and yet the same, giving and taking, like the muddy red and black of my marble pattern, borrowed from Matteo, who got it from Simone. Our exploration of the characteristics of the painted design continued, and I awoke staring at it in my mind, feeling deep satisfaction at examining what had been so mysterious, whether or not anything I thought was ultimately correct or even significant on a larger scale. I was thinking in ways that I don't usually think, and that felt good.

"Are you awake?" I asked my wife. "Tesla came again and we had another discussion, another talk about patterns. You know, I think I really like him a lot—and it's just a dream."

"I hope you're writing these things down," she mumbled without turning over.

"Well, so far, I remember them all pretty well—I'm taking notes."

"I think you better start writing them down carefully, keeping a journal," she said.

"But, for who?" I asked. "They're just my crazy dreams."

"Even for yourself—and then, who knows who else?"

Journaling my dreams and discussions with Tesla changes things. Being accountable for communicating the scope of these events makes them seem more important to me. I suppose it's possible that someone other than myself might want to read what I write. Maybe my kids.

My experience of painting Gidu's black hat and the marble pattern, like this dream, is part of me, an event in my life as an artist, like so many events that seem impossible to prepare for in spite of all that I can do. Paintings happen to me and in me. I submit to them. Toward the center of the marble design I painted an ivory pocket sundial, an ancient watch I saw in the Poldi-Pezzoli in Milan. "Yeah—try using a watch," I laugh now to myself. The rest of the image followed, the fading layers of painted grotesques pretending to be an Italian wall, the sexy spring bulbs starting to sprout, the cloud mask tied onto a wooden bust. The meandering path of a painting's metamorphosis is similar to mine, from the hint of a nameless and preexistent itch to the wandering me caught somewhere between the reds and blacks of my life. Despite the daily chores that I so easily get lost in, I keep returning to the pattern of painting, with increasing homesickness for someplace I have never been, wondering if it's where my substance and essence might someday finally meet and become one color.

6
Comedies and Earthquakes

September 4 – Trips to rendezvous and historical re-enactments are something we have done for about twenty years. I guess it's hard to resist the chance to wear a quaint costume, take it half seriously and become someone else for a few days. Our kids grew up believing that lodges, breech clouts, fringed leathers, and life around the fire is as good as things get, while life at home is a necessary evil meant only to support such activities. They love the funny change of framework and sitting in the dirt. I love the inside of tipis, the lodge-pole spokes meeting high above me in the smoky center, the slit of sky facing east, and the fire—but sleeping on the ground in a tipi in a sleeping bag is *almost* sleeping at best.

It was early, too early for morning to begin lighting up the walls of the lodge from outside. I was half-awake, tired of tossing, and lay there thinking about being asleep, when something shook me. I was startled—a shock, a vibration, rumbling deep in the ground beneath me that I felt in my head and ears, like the low grating of hard heavy things scraping together. It seemed to have been going on for a while by the time I was aware of it. That's how dreams are sometimes. I wake up knowing that I just missed the best part. What I remember well is the last part, Nikola Tesla talking to me about our innate power. "It is in us," he repeated, trying to help me understand. "It is in us. You have infinite amounts of possibility within yourself, enough to do almost anything."

I got up quietly, checked the coals still glowing in the fire pit, added a log and went out to pee in the grass not far away. *"What could he want me to do?"* I wondered, looking up at the impossible stars and then at the village of lodges. The artful comedy of characters who travel to reenactments is diverse, like Otter and his gracious wife who look to have stepped out of Napoleonic France; Leo, a pirate of a man hawking his plunder of antique beads, a braided beard full of trinkets reaching to his waist; Grandma Grizzly passing out favors of crayon colored trade beads to passers-by from the basket on her elbow; and Leprechaun, all of almost four feet tall, a pint-sized flirt, a ladies' man—the perfect Pulcinella. The general plot was agreed upon. We all came to play our parts in an improvised drama, embellishing our roles with eccentric individuality. Nearby someone snored loudly. Our lodge was surrounded by the cluster of my family's tipis, not too far from Otter's trade tent, and Leo and Katy's lean-to where a couple of people still talked and laughed by a small campfire. *"Must be three or four o'clock,"* I figured, checking my favorite constellations and the initial hint of light on the horizon.

At night from outside, a tipi becomes a softly glowing cone. A village of them, all flickering dimly yellow in the dark with the glimmer of dying flames and half-lit snakes of rising smoke, is otherworldly. It was cold and I decided against a walk, quickly returning to the lodge in hopes that the sleeping bag was still warm. The wood had caught fire, and I slipped back into bed, dozing off lightly before the quaking began again.

"*Oh, an earthquake,*" I thought, increasingly alert to the tremors, but sleepily unconcerned with the serious nature of what was happening. Slowly, I became conscious of a growing connection between myself and the ground, a subtle affinity or melting together, the slight sinking of my body into the soil and rocks below, as if the earth had turned to liquid and I was lazily floating on my back in it. My friend Nikola had returned, and I was stunned to realize that he was causing the tremors, doing something inside himself to make the ground repeatedly shiver under us. The sudden feeling of knowing about it was strangely alarming, but not frightening—surprising at first, but eventually giving way to curiosity. "Here, I will let you feel it," he said, taking my hand in his to help me better sense what was going on. There were immediate vibrations. He was affecting things, making the earth tremble by doing something that started within him, an excitement from somewhere deep inside his chest. I felt it. He let the pulse gradually build to a crescendo before letting it release into the ground. It's hard to describe—almost as if he were submitting to the waves of earth I floated in, drawing in their rhythms in order to affect and amplify them with his own. I felt it, understood that it was happening, but didn't know exactly how.

I remembered rocking with the wind at the top of a pine tree. As a boy, I found that cooperating even slightly with a breeze would seem to magnify the effects of the wind and the movement of the tree. Like swinging on a swing, once I got the rhythm, it took very little effort to make the whole tree sway violently until it seemed that it might break or uproot. Perhaps cooperating with the natural rhythms of the earth is like that.

"Now you try," he said.

Of course I hardly knew where to start, but tried repeatedly in every way I could think of to make something happen. I breathed with it, felt my heart beat, my pulse throbbing in my feet and fingertips, gently rocked and rolled with it, and was corrected and instructed until I was worn out. After quite a while and many failures, I hoped that I was almost succeeding—or just about to. At least I could conceive of how it might feel, so I continued working at it, on the verge of making the tiniest tremble happen with his help, feeling or imagining the slightest influence over the smallest amount of dust. In my dream I was positive that, given time, I'd be able to do it. He told me to practice and that I would become more proficient. "More proficient?" I answered. "Anything would be more proficient."

"Remember that you are what initiates the process. You have to know how to access and use who you are. You have infinite potential, more than the whole planet, as much within you as in solar systems and galaxies. See how good you are already. Keep practicing and it will come." And he left.

The strange thing is that I wanted to believe what he was saying, that he was right; and I felt very, very big—huge—like a drop of water suddenly becoming an ocean, a rather average guy turning into Superman. If it is hard to describe how he made the earth shake, it's impossible to explain how deeply his final declaration affected me. *"To access and use who I am,"* I repeated. *"Me—as much potential as in galaxies."* But somewhere inside I almost believed it.

On one occasion, I watched historically costumed performers behind a puppet theatre putting on a Punch and Judy show. The public arrived in an array of everyday costumes and common roles to sit in front and be entertained. *"How curious,"* I thought. *"A stage within a stage within a stage—actors watching, re-enactors acting. And who am I then sitting here, aware of overseeing everything? Doesn't that cross the line?"* Tesla spoke of latent godlike omnipotence. There were those burned at the stake for thinking less. Maybe we re-enact things trying to remember who we are. We try on roles, masks, and costumes hoping to recognize ourselves somewhere in the familiar patterns of their parts.

I was awake, and had been on the edge of awake for most of what I recollect well enough to write down. The feeling in my gut was unusual, more than a little disquieting, both exhilarating and helpless all at once. *"I'm afraid I know something that's too much to know about, too much to hold and to be trusted with,"* I reasoned. *"What purpose can it have to share this with me?"* And I turned to tell my wife what I could.

"Did you feel that?" I asked cautiously.

"Feel what, dear?"

"The earth shake—you didn't feel it?"

It was that morning that I began to take some of this Tesla stuff more seriously. The realization of immense possibility somewhere inside me was overwhelming. I didn't know what to do with it. I had learned that who I am, coupled with a working knowledge of the patterns of things, has the potential to shake the planet. And no—she didn't feel it. No one else did either.

An earthquake is a catastrophic readjustment to what was resistant, a release, the response to built-up stress, often in the weakest places of what is crusty and rigid. My inner shake-up was no less. There we were, the whole crowd of us milling about a tipi village like big children playing on a stage. Corsets, long full dresses, bloomers, beaded buckskins, bonnets, and parasols for the women; the hairy-bottomed men in loin cloths, leggings, and moccasins—all pretending; incognito even to ourselves, trying on faces for fun until one seemed to fit. And there in the middle of that comedy I had experienced something significant. In a dream Nikola Tesla had suggested that under all of my masks and costumes, there is a singular and powerful phenomenon that is me, not a shadow of someone, but someone real.

The day progressed much as the morning. We carried water, tidied up the bedrolls, did chores around the lodge, and visited a few traders; but there was only one thing on my mind—my visitor.

"Hey, Coyote! How's it goin'?" I said in passing. Coyote Jack makes *capotes* and between customers sat plucking on a jaw harp. I grinned, still pondering my dreams, enjoying both Coyote's springy tune and a growing recognition of Tesla's spirited nature. *"I know I felt the ground shake. It woke me up."*

"Oh pretty good. How's the boys? They still playin'?"

"Huh? Oh yeah, once in a while. I miss it, ya know."

Leo was finally up. On the way back to camp I stopped to sit in the sun and look at his beads, picking up handfuls then letting them fall slowly through my fingers into a wooden box. *"From Ficino's point of view it all makes sense doesn't it? Matter is affected by exposure to the force of life, as a mirror reflects a face, or an echo the sound of a voice."* Skunk beads, feather beads, yellow jackets, chevrons, and fancies, I watched the cheery patterns spilling from my hand and clicking softly on the pile in the chest.

"That's the kind of reasoning that made the Renaissance happen, isn't it?"

"—And now causing earthquakes," I quickly responded to myself.

"Good to see you, Leo. Never made it up there last fall, did we?

"Numberless worlds in infinite universes populated by divine beings each reflecting the whole of it—that's what Giordano taught. No wonder he was toasted!" I sat entranced by the fistfuls of little planets gently slipping through my grasp. What Nikola had said about my potential continued to resonate, gathering momentum, washing over me in waves, like strange déjà vu, surprising in its natural appeal. *"Who am I?"* I wondered. *"Conscious of these revelations that seem to overcome my resistance and faults? Doesn't this all cross the line?"*

That day gave me ample opportunity to talk about my experience. In fact I talked too much. People came by the tipi to chat. I acted as if they had come just to hear about my incredible event. That afternoon I was emboldened enough to try and speak to my brother about Tesla's visit and the earthquake. In response, he rehearsed a quantum tale about someone's cat being pelted with particles because of simple awareness. He delivered an elegant brief discourse, pontificating on the true nature of everything. "So, whether you're just getting it from the morphic field, or somewhere else, it's all the same isn't it?" he finished. He was humoring me, like teasing some kind of nut. But I kept on talking, periodically entertaining a small audience, my family, a horse healer, a few friends, and various weekend aborigines who stopped briefly to listen.

"Hey, dad, be careful. Don't talk so much," warned one of my sons. But I was not very careful and began to relax and speak freely, foolhardy about what had been mostly a secret. I don't know whether he was more concerned for me, or for himself as the son of an apparent screwball. *"Do you need this kind of attention?"* I asked myself several times that day and since. In fact, by evening I began to feel rather torn and pathetic. While it's good to reflect on the whats and whys of things, I was embarrassed, wanting to disown myself and hold this all at arm's length like an odd smelly object without context. However, there is also something in me that celebrates the shared mystery of being conscious and human, gladly welcoming this as one more proof that I am more than my normally limited view.

When the rendezvous had ended, before loading the tipi poles on the trailer, we made our rounds, watching the friendly cast of characters dismantle our community. As the historically accurate set was struck, twenty-first century plastic started showing everywhere. For the most part, faces had been washed, hair combed and buckskins replaced by jeans and tee shirts as people with average names prepared to return to their average addresses. *"The world of market trends, news channels, and war is waiting,"* I remembered, glancing at myself in the rear view mirror of the packed car, confused for just a moment by the sun-burnt face looking back.

The blur that separates the states of acting and being, demonstrating and doing, can be disorienting, like the shadowy gulf between the resilience of childhood and the delicate architecture of growing up. I sat in the car, waiting for my family, and looked out at the ground where I had slept, seeing it quickly revert to the cow pasture that it was. *"How is it we let go of things?"* I asked myself. *"If that odd thesis on the cat is right, aren't we all in the process of creating what we believe or allow?"* The village of re-enactors reluctantly continued to disperse and we left for home. While the others slept, I drove and silently reviewed the comedies and earthquakes of the weekend and my life.

One of my closest friends is a painter of self-portraits. That's almost all he paints. He speaks of an irresistible urge to explore the boundaries between what is *he* and the image that appears before him in the mirror. He examines his expectations, his fears, the lure of self-recognition, and the arguments between his will and weakness, all through paint. Someday I hope to make self-portraits—but for now, I'm still a little shy. Consider Picasso's girl gazing in a mirror at someone else's image. Perhaps, like me, she coyly avoids self-incrimination; or maybe she's lost in the search for something familiar that is not herself. For my friend, it's an inner dialog of clues to things just out of sight, like the back of his ear or shoulder blade. Perhaps any painting can't help but mirror some aspect of an artist anyway, so making self-portraits is unavoidable. And maybe, after all, the world is my self-portrait.

Several weeks ago I attended an artists' seminar and saw the many stern proposals of self-expression; each artist assuming the others to be of superior enough intellect to be worthy of impressing with some authority. "This is funny but without humor," I said to the group, recalling Paul Klee's silly officers solemnly bowing to each other upon meeting. "After all, these childish scribbles, splatters, and smears of paint are really just the angst-filled impressions of adults." I wondered why we had stopped playing and become so complex and unyielding, and when it was that some had unforgiven what they had forgotten.

I follow the story of Rembrandt's many portraits of himself, from the confident caricatures of handsome youth, to the knowing tender look of an old friend. I watch him grow up, the earrings, velvet berets, and furs of success eventually giving way to a simple white cloth wrapped around the gentle gray of his hair, the final recognition of himself caught in childlike eyes that stare at me from a worn and weary face.

Hesitantly, I started reading about Nikola Tesla with fears that it might color my experience. I had been satisfied with the little I had scanned on the Internet the morning of his first visit, but figured that becoming more conversant with who he was, would better help me understand who he is. An attractive magician from far away with mythical powers—his life reads like a legend. I smiled at our shared obsession with the number 3, myself being born on the third day of the third month, and became more circumspect reading about his peculiar ability to visualize things clearly. "Not hallucinations," but "the result of a reflex action from the brain on the retina under great excitation," as he put it. The story of Tesla tuning a small vibrator to resonate at a frequency that caused a minor earthquake in Manhattan stopped me cold. He called it "the art of telegeodynamics," and said he could bring down the Empire State Building with a similar device, or on a larger scale could split the world in two.

"*That's some serious fooling around.*"

Often, to remind myself of who I am, I check for paint caught under my fingernails—Cadmium Red, Indian Yellow, Umber, and Indigo. *"I'm an artist after all,"* I sigh with relief, suspending my doubts for long enough to catch a glimpse of what's just out of sight. Sometimes I seem to cover my tracks so carefully that I can't tell how I got here. *"Oh, I remember. I painted on those clouds yesterday, and put a glaze on the trees.*

"Today—I think I'll work on the earth and rocks."

7
The Source and the Wasteland

October 17– There were times in college when the stress of my studies finally got to me and I felt the need to get away. Before escaping to the desert, I'd prepare a lunch: a sandwich, some chips, cookies, and plenty of water to take along. Most often, for safety's sake, I invited a friend. We'd get in the car, turn on the radio, drive, and talk about life, usually about the things we never talked about and wouldn't own later. We headed west for an hour or two before taking the loneliest looking gravel road we could find to follow it as far as we could go. Not much grows out in the west desert—some sad-looking sage or rabbit brush, a surprising spring flush of wildflowers on a good year, but nothing much. There's topaz out there, opal, agate, jasper, some fossils, and other stones we'd carry home in our packs; but otherwise the object was simply to relax and avoid studying for the day. We didn't talk much after leaving the car. We'd take any likely path and walk until it disappeared, listening to the gravel grind underfoot until we felt alone enough to stop and rest. After a while, I'd inevitably see a can, broken glass, or shotgun shell and decide we hadn't gone quite far enough; so we'd move on, wondering whether indeed there was anywhere left to go. Other than lizards, ravens, the flash of a coyote dashing off, or a jackrabbit suddenly materializing before bolting, we were alone. Then, just when I thought we had escaped, gone beyond the trash of humanity into *no man's land*, it seemed unavoidable to come upon a wood or metal stake driven solidly into the dirt.

A staked claim is a form of theorem, an act of faith, the prospect of what is not evident, where the pattern of things suggests eventual reward, anticipating treasure still to be retrieved and proved. So, the prospector marks the boundaries, believing there is something hidden there, describing the proposal with stakes in the ground, founding a formal basis for future exploration and discovery.

Establishing the ground for a painted image is like staking out a claim. The hope in a source that's not yet evident sets the boundaries of its eventual form. I have to believe I'll find something valuable where I'm looking, to be mined, smelted, and purified in the studio before being finally transformed. Sometimes in the tug-o-war that is believing, I lose my footing. When the irregularity of the process surprises me, when the outcome is less apparent or the prospects less common, my tendency is to doubt things, to give up and disbelieve. *"Get serious! You've never seen that before because it's not real."* And, the image fades before it finds a life in paint. It's so easy to become my own biggest heckler and heretic, and sadly watch as things begin to slip away. In the end, it's only hope and belief that get me through the unpredictability of painting, fill the quantum gaps in my perception. When the patterns are less evident, curvy, and unexpected, and I am blinded for whatever reason, it's hard work to keep my heels dug in, to keep holding on—but it's good work, something I like to do.

After a month passed without a visit from Nikola Tesla, I began again to disbelieve my experience. At best, I decided that the last dream was the finale to a distracting interlude. It was hard to take it seriously. After all, *Quirky Dead Scientist Visits Quirky Living Unknown Artist* is quite a headline, with special emphasis on the shared *quirky* part. *"Perhaps,"* I mused, *"My hesitant participation and lack of belief have caused him to pass into the ethers where he came from, to remain nothing more than an anomalous piece of my* quirky *imagination."* So the regularity of life took hold, as it tends to do, and I thought less and less about Nikola Tesla.

Finally, this morning, I was surprised by another vivid dream. This time it didn't seem to be about anything specifically related to the ideas that Tesla had previously proposed. It was a lesson of another kind, a metaphorical adventure that happened like the gradual unfolding of an epic riddle. There was a guide with me, who I initially assumed was Nikola, but now am not so sure. Whoever it was, we knew each other well. He spoke softly, from just behind my right shoulder, careful not to intrude, posing questions, giving clues, and supporting my understanding of the experience. It didn't seem necessary to look at him directly, though I was peripherally aware that he had thick white hair, was much older than myself, and wore a white shirt or tunic of some kind. He didn't lecture as much as gently instruct by responding to my thoughts and questions.

I watched myself throughout most of the experience, consciously observing and weighing my own responses to things. That's different from recent dreams, which have been more focused on Tesla, seeing him from my viewpoint with no clear picture of myself. During the dream I wore a white shirt, the wool hound's tooth dress pants purchased for my son's wedding, and white cotton athletic socks. I saw myself sitting on the ground in dry gravel not far from the edge of a cliff, in a desert, a wasteland not untypical of many western places.

The craggy scenes of some late gothic images express it best as a wilderness of dirt and stone, the dreary stage for golgothas, entombments, and limbos, a backdrop for spaghetti westerns. I sat there in a set designed by Giotto, Duccio, Mantegna, and others, taking it all in—an empty world of solitude, the lonely home of cowboys and ascetic saints. Sparse tufts of dull gray sage and some type of darker scrub dotted what was otherwise a monochrome expanse of ocher dirt and rocks vanishing into the distance. To the right, not far from my elder companion, the skeleton of an almost bare juniper seemed to make our fellowship a threesome. My guide encouraged me to look out over the drop-off to the broad plain below. So I sat there quietly studying my situation and the barren landscape that extended to the horizon.

"Do you see anything?" he finally asked.

"I see an empty plain," I responded, feeling him neither accept nor reject my statement.

"Can you see anything?" he repeated after a time, watching patiently as I considered the view.

"Just an endless world of yellow dust and stone," I answered, watching eagerly for something to happen.

From my position on the rim of a high overlook, the desolation seemed to go on forever, not unlike the west desert I ran off to like a hermit when things got tense at school. I sat and waited, but nothing happened. *"Esto loco selvaggio—what a wild place!"* I reflected, *"Why am I here anyway?"*

Then, unapparently, little by little—as if a fog was slowly lifting, my sight cleared and the rocks on the plain beneath us began to take on various shapes. It was difficult to see at first because their bodies were the same yellow-clay color as the soil and stones, but as my vision sharpened, human figures gradually appeared on what turned out to be an immense city square—individuals, couples, small groups, and large gatherings as far as I could see, reminding me of the piazzas in Italy on certain days of the week, where the townsfolk gather to do business and the drone of their chatter spreads through the streets like the low hum of a giant swarm of insects. But it was silent on the piazza below.

"And, can you see them now?" asked my companion.

"Yes, I see them," I whispered.

"Why do I resist? What good is it to doubt and end up seeing only what is obvious and unexceptional? Life within the confines of the ordinary—is that what I'm after?"

Like a panel of pigment and oil in the process of becoming a painting, the pieces of once random form and color transfigured; and the scene that had been invisible to me not so long before continued to emerge. The images below developed while I watched, becoming animated and alive. The vast site soon filled with figures going through various rehearsed motions, as if dancing an elaborate choreography. Bodies the color of an ocher wasteland moved *tai chi*-like on an endless stage, strangely unaware of anyone but themselves.

They acted and interacted theatrically, alone and in groups, intensely involved in the dramatic portrayals of what seemed like important personal events; but which, from where we sat, seemed affected and even comical. Some yelled at one another, caught in the middle of never-ending disagreement. Some were talking, discussing, or dispassionately lecturing to each other or to no one at all. There were those who laughed, while others cried, individuals screaming and alone, women giving birth, people playing out acts of love, and still others intent on killing or destroying one another. Although I expected a lot of noise from the many odd spectacles, there was none—only mouths and bodies moving in a mimed and soundless performance. *"Perhaps they're so distant that the wind is blowing away the sound of their voices and actions?"*

I watched the killers use their hands to shoot, as children do in make-believe, pointer fingers extended horizontally from a clenched fist toward the victims, and thumbs up in the air. They sneered and pulled the trigger, cocking their thumbs up and down. Those who were shot dropped as if dead; even if to us up on the cliff, it was obvious that they weren't dead at all. Some of them were shot and killed habitually, dying over and over, repeatedly succumbing to their imagined wounds. Again I noticed how serious the incidents were to those involved. *"It's like children playing. But not fun, and none of it is playful. They don't know they're just pretending."* For a long time I looked from individual to individual and group to group, guessing at the countless charades.

"That is the way it is," my mentor answered my thoughts. "Do you understand?"

The atmosphere below seemed strangely thin and stale, its virtue exhausted in empty emotion and silent activity. *"Like everything passionless,"* I concluded. *"Not real—like ideas talking to themselves. Alive but not living."*

"I think so," I replied.

Nothing they could do seemed relevant to anything beyond

their own small worlds, with no apparent purpose other than the opportunity of going through motions and acting out events. How feeble and inconsequential it all was from our point of view! And yet, how vital the performances were to them. *"I should learn to see some of my own life this way—simple occurrences viewed from a distance, as I'm doing from up here.*

"I think I've begun to understand," I reassured my guide and myself.

For some time, we continued watching the goings on in the piazza together, both of us satisfied that I had learned something. I sat there at the edge of nowhere, in the dirt, wearing my good pants, legs spread out in a wide V, and thought about the dramas happening below and my own unconscious doings. I looked down at my once white socks and started drawing with my finger in the dust, then erased it with the palm of my hand and started over—then erased it and drew again, and then again.

Disturbed by my hand, a fat old toad half buried in the dry dirt suddenly moved. "Oh look! There's Mr. Toad," I smiled, remembering the many toads I caught as a boy. I liked toads. To find one was good luck. A friendship with a toad was a powerful alliance. Images of chasing girls around the playground with a toad, while teasing about the imminent threat of warts came to mind; and I grinned, still rather pleased with myself. For a few minutes we sat staring at each other. *"I like toads,"* I reminded myself, but was surprised by my reluctance to solicit the good will of my new acquaintance, the rejection of my natural affinity for all things toady. *"Maybe it's just because I haven't held one in such a long time,"* I reasoned. Back then, I liked everything about toads, the clownish way they hopped instead of walked, their permanent satisfied expression and round glassy eyes. I really wanted to pick up the thing, hoping it might help me revisit, if only briefly, the feelings of my carefree and careless childhood; but its potential unpredictability—the frozen smirk and lidless gaze bothered me. So I didn't.

Toads once made me laugh. Shortly after picking up a toad, a clear secretion usually leaked out onto my hands, which I'd wipe off on the grass or on my pants. "What's a little toad pee, huh? I never get warts!" I was always eager to play with any newfound creature. *"So, do I want to pick you up or not?"* I was confused. It was curious that the toad had been there all along blending in so well, perfectly mimicking the color of the gravel—or, was it my inability to see things again? *"No, I think I'll leave it where it is."*

My inner discussion about the toad went on for a long time, and became uncomfortable and embarrassing. *"It's just a toad."* I couldn't understand why I wasn't able to make up my mind about the silly thing. To pick it up or not pick it up; the issue brought about a solemn face-off between the freckle-splattered stinker of a boy and the man in dress pants sitting in the dirt. The potential friend of youth was becoming my plump little adversary. The toad and I sat quietly eyeing each other. *"I better pick you up,"* I decided, *"My companion here is watching and he'll think I'm afraid. After all, you're just a toad."* Finally resolved, I leaned forward and reached down for it, but the toad was too quick. It jumped out over the edge of the cliff and fell.

"Do not worry about him. He will be OK," said my guide calmly as I turned to apologize; but I tried to imagine how it might be for a toad falling through the air like that, and how he'd be OK when he hit the bottom.

"To pick it up or not pick it up—can't or won't?" I asked myself, unhappy with both possibilities and feeling a little sheepish. I looked around for something else to focus on, trying to pretend

that nothing had happened.

Until then, the gravel beneath me had seemed perfectly dry, even dusty, but the unexpected dampness of my good wool pants from underneath suggested otherwise. *"Hey, where'd this wet come from? My wife'll be upset that I sat here in my new pants and got them wet."* I felt increasingly foolish at my mentor's evident awareness of my concerns. It was a serious dream, and I wanted to be seen as a serious student. The invisible goings on down on the piazza, the unseen toad, my fear and indecision, and now—the inability to feel myself sitting in the mud—like so many things that seem one way— *"and me, so sure of myself"*—and then turn out to be another. *"How can I have missed everything? Am I unable or unwilling?"*

"You get dirty and it cleans up. Yes, the dirt comes out easily enough," he answered my thoughts again. I felt confident that he knew what he was talking about, and curious at my lingering hesitation. "You know, life gets you dirty—but it washes out," he repeated.

"But it might not be the dirt—it might just be me," I worried.

The place where I sat continued to get increasingly wet. "This was a spring, a pool of sweet clear water," he offered as he sensed my bother at the mire that I sat in. It was sticking to my pants, caking on, and he looked almost satisfied. "No one has come here for such a long time. It was unused, and eventually filled up with debris and dirt; so the water could not reach the surface to moisten the soil. You could not tell where it was, could you?" I sensed the loss. "It has been here all along," he added, seeming to be sadly recalling other times. "It is always here, and you are the first to arrive in quite a while. But once, small fish swam in it; and there were folks who came to sit here, to care for it, to bathe and enjoy the water. This spring was the source of life to this place." My discomfort and shame suddenly became privilege and unworthiness.

"Thanks," I said. "I didn't see...."

I imagined minnows darting all around me, wildflowers, woods close by, and a spring-fed lake. The little fish scattered back and forth, flashing around my ankles as I splashed along the shore in the water that wasn't there. Then I looked out at the desert and down at my ruined pants, remembering the grubby kid back home catching toads. "The prospects of Eden are still right here, aren't they?" I asked. "Don't worry—I'll come back and start to clean it out." But there was no response.

It was a tired kind of place with uncertain possibility and future. I've worried since that I don't know where it is or how to get back. I just know that somewhere in the middle of a barren wasteland, there is an invisible and forgotten source of pure sweet water waiting to be found and cared for.

When I was nine or ten, I remember long excursions into the woods with my brothers to choose a tree for an intended tree house. Our dreams were big: three floors, balconies, bedrooms, and a lookout. After finding a suitable tree and once the project had begun, we developed a routine for working. We'd get up early, go out and scrounge around the shed looking for nails and odd pieces of wood before leaving for the work site. Often, we packed peanut butter sandwiches with a pitcher of lemonade, planning to stay out all day. I suppose as long as my mother could hear our little disagreements and the hammers banging, she knew that we were okay.

In reality, it was difficult to engineer and produce the extravagant castle of our initial vision. We lacked the tools, expertise, and materials to do so; but we worked hard at it all summer in the hope of reaping eventual rewards for our effort. One evening, tired and sweaty, as I stood back to admire the results of our work, I realized two things: One—that in the end, what we were building looked nothing like our dream house in the tree. It was simply three very shabby and unsafe platforms of recycled scrap lumber. And, two—that I was exhausted and had worked hard all day without stopping. The first realization was a given, and I adjusted my expectations a bit; but the second took me by surprise. I normally viewed myself as being somewhat lazy, usually avoiding or half-heartedly attempting my homework, violin practice, and the small tasks my dad gave me to do; but I had really worked hard and was even feeling pleased. It was good work, obviously something I liked to do.

After being gone for several years, I returned home as a rather grown-up boy of twenty-one. I walked through the woods, visiting all of the usual places where we had played: the swamp, the rope of a tire swing, a small hill with a pine tree at the top. The surprise of a few rotting boards up in a tree reminded me of the big dreams I had believed in. I stood for a while and lamented all of the hopeful things that hadn't happened, the unrealized rewards and unfound discoveries—and I wept.

Now I try to picture myself there to mentor the sad young man. "Don't worry. You'll be OK," I want to say. "It's not always a formula. It's just familiar. Look in a mirror and see who you're becoming."

I want to put my arm around him and tell him about painting, about times when I get so caught up in the vision of the thing that I forget the process. I go through the motions of mixing mediums with colors and skillfully applying them to the ground, but the outcome ends up lacking life; so I paint over it and start again, and then again. It's a hard thing to remember that I am the object of my work, the prospect of what I do. Finally, I am all there is to show.

And soon—I hope to paint a toad.

8
At the Brink of an Abyss

November 12 – There are two basic activities that make up painting; working with what is seen, and working with what is unseen. It's easy to see that I am painting when I'm holding brushes, mixing colors on a palette, or applying paint to a panel. Sometimes it's not as easy to observe what I am doing. Like when I'm just looking or thinking. After establishing a multi-colored ground of scraped and sanded paint, I'll sit and stare at it for hours before picking up a paintbrush. The unseen making of a painting can happen anywhere—while showering, shopping, digging in the garden, and even sleeping. By the time I start to craft the image portion of a painting, much of it exists already as an association of feelings, ideas, visions, notes, scribbles, and hopes. Both visible and invisible activities happen throughout the work, from its intangible conception and preexistence to the eventual decision that a painting is complete. Neither effort is more or less important. The believing and the doing are equally vital to the process, though finally, it's the more ephemeral parts of an image that give it life.

Consider the obscure sources of a Leonardo: the structural geometry, the experiments with light and atmosphere, the penumbral messages, the careful sketches, and secret notebooks filled with studies. So much that makes up a Leonardo painting isn't painted. Inspiration comes like a sudden infatuation—the lure of simple beauty, the tease of veiled whispers and shared knowing. Raphael's Madonnas are proof enough of all that. The urge to paint feels foreign to the hubbub and commotion of daily life—set apart. I look at anything by angelic Fra Giovanni, and have the vague impression of him kneeling reverently close-by. Ultimately, it's something still nameless, mostly what is not seen, that enlivens the material.

If the elusive essence of a painting remains largely invisible, what about the painter, the person? Sometimes I watch people and speculate on the part of them that I can't see; how and why they feel and think the way they do. I pick a face out of a crowd, like a piece of art, a puzzle, and try to guess what's hidden behind its public composure, the unseen context and patterns of its life. I watch the corners of the mouth, the eyes, the tilt of the head, all hints of something much bigger; and imagine wearing the face, trying it on like a mask, exploring the secrets it conceals, the fears, desires, and awareness of someone other than myself.

It was about four in the morning and I was wide-awake. I awoke suddenly—feeling caught in the middle of something significant, wondering what was going on, or what had just taken place. I don't think it's that unusual for people to wake up with a start, a little perplexed by the impression of doing something more interesting than just lying there in bed, but it feels unusual each time it happens to me. "*…ché quasi tutta cessa mia visione—the passion remains while nothing of the rest is* *remembered."* While I was at school, I took such unexpected early morning awakenings as cues to go to the living room and think, which was better than tossing around trying to get back to sleep. I'd reflect upon my being, visit with that invisible part of me, and consider the viability of my hopes and dreams. Sometimes I knelt by the sofa to talk to God, the Universe, or whoever was listening—whining a bit about things not being how I imagined them, about the less than evident pattern of my life, the unpredictable disposition of what I wished were an obvious formula.

As much as I pretend, there doesn't seem to be an immutable formula. There's no guarantee that just because I do what I believe, that life will proceed as smoothly as I think it should. In fact, often it seems the opposite—that when I'm feeling weak, I am challenged to be strong; when I don't *get it*, I get problems to solve; when I lack faith, I'm in the middle of needing some—when I want anything, I find myself in a quicksand of adversity offering only opportunities instead of answers. That's just the way it seems. Of course, there are also times when I'm positive someone intervenes on my behalf, makes sure the rent is paid, the gas tank is full, and that I'll *make it* for the foreseeable future.

Lying there awake this morning, I thought of my more youthful self in a darkened apartment, on my knees by the sofa, chatting with a heavenly Someone. *"Yeah, life has certainly been unpredictable,"* I brooded, picturing Nikola Tesla and adjusting the pillow under my neck. *"Hardly what I expected.*

"You know, I'm not really sure what's going on." I said silently, listening to the typical noises of the sleeping household, as if expecting a response. "So—what am I supposed to do?" A lazy breath of wind stirred the maples outside the window. "I hope it continues though. I'd miss him." As if abruptly tuning in to the middle of a lecture, I was suddenly with Nikola, regarding him carefully and hearing him speak, knowing just how much I wanted to be there. He took no notice of my arrival and kept on teaching as if to an entire class; yet I was aware of no other student but myself. *"Like part of me was already here listening."*

As usual, there was a lot more to it than I remember. I struggled to understand things well enough that later I'd be able to repeat what I learned and describe the experience accurately. Unfortunately, there are parts of each dream that have no apparent meaning to me, which makes them easy to forget. What I first recall is Tesla showing me a series or progression of patterns in a specific order or sequence, grid-like configurations spreading across two-dimensional planes, like very thin sheets of dully glowing graph paper suspended in shadowy space. They appeared slowly, in succession, one at a time, logically proceeding in an intended categorization or taxonomy that seemed to have meaning. I noted that some of the patterns were similar to the ones that I was painting. Others reminded me of a friend's *hoshu* and *loshu* Chinese mathematical structures which I had seen several years earlier. While Tesla and I watched them emerge from darkness, I had the thought to contact my friend and inquire about her work. One by one, the patterns became visible as if rising to the surface of a dim pool, the murky hint of each design gradually becoming more defined. Each was an endless expanse of small squares, with some filled and others empty, like an odd limitless crossword puzzle, a scrambled checkerboard or mosaic of black and white tiles—a weaving of ins and outs, ons and offs, pluses and minuses, infinite games of tic-tac-toe one against the other—in principle, not unlike hexagrams of the *I Ching*, placed close together, each running into the other, filling up my sight into the distance.

I seemed to be more aware, more able to get my bearings during the dream, able to think other things, then return and make various judgments about the experience. I recalled knowing that I had always been able to do that, but had just become more conscious of it. It felt like walking through the halls and rooms of a large building, being able to move through and around thoughts in a physical way.

Painting is like that. I extend a brush deliberately toward the palette, intent on charging it with paint. In the time it takes to move the brush through the air, that second or two between the panel and contact with the material, an entire discussion takes place. *"What'll it be?"* and I steer the bristles toward a specific squish of oily pigment. I immediately consider not just the color, but its strength, its opacity, or transparency. I imagine feeling its consistency between the brush and the painting—sticky, pasty, or buttery. I contemplate its drying time. Even the romantic appeal of a color can influence my choice. When I'm moody I seem to reach more often for my favorite asphaltum, remembering the Raft of the Medusa and other tar-rich somber visions. I speculate on the relationship of what I'm reaching for and what's already on the panel. Often I paint in complements. I'll choose an acrid-looking purple, knowing that later it will show through a glaze of Indian Yellow as vivid brown. There are times, feeling contrary, that I'll suddenly change direction and surprise myself by taking a color that opposes the effect I want, a discordant vermilion just to spite my own will and remain unpredictable. *"There! Can you deal with that?"* After any number of qualitative deliberations, the brush finally touches the paint and a quantity is pushed, or scooped onto the bristles to be mixed then with an amount of honey-like medium. Each step requires equal attention and can happen so fast that to someone watching, it wouldn't seem like much of a process at all.

The final painting that an audience can see and touch is a cue to wake up and consider a bigger view, to see something that remains invisible otherwise. How does the feeling part of paint find its way from my brush to the panel? With what eyes do I see the image before it's there? Where are those colors that I try to match in tangible form? *"You know, I'm not really sure what's going on, but I hope it continues. I'd miss it—as if part of me were gone, should it ever end."*

My dream this morning with Nikola Tesla was another lecture-demonstration. The articulated planes, filled with microelemental squares that fit together in complex arrangements, steadily multiplied as I watched. I told Nikola that I was aware of new patterns and planes being suggested by the intersections and relationships happening between the initial ones. As the number of designs dramatically increased, I realized that they would eventually fill all space. "That's good," he said, clearly pleased that I was seeing things without needing his prompts. "And they can have any number of dimensions," he reminded me. I was in fact coming to that conclusion as I watched the grids continue to multiply.

I observed the patterns for some time, their repeated appearances and interactions eventually becoming quite elegant to me. What were initially simple designs of point and counterpoint compounded, becoming deeply textured, relating to one another in flourishes and ornaments, developing momentum like a baroque fugue. Pattern-filled space intersecting and overlapping pattern-filled space—creating more pattern-filled space—I saw that there were elements in the patterns completely overlaying each other, occupying the exact same segment of space; that there were any number of superimposed elements that I couldn't see, all on top of one another like the notes in musical chords, implying infinite sequences, rhythms, or strings of components turning on and off, off and on, each filling the other's absence. Even now, as I write about it, I find myself burdened by the inability to contain it. "This is a lot for me to hold," I said, honestly feeling the weight of the idea bearing down on me.

The patterns grew from the kinship of simple singular things to complex diversity and back again. Eventually, I began to feel more comfortable, maintaining the slightest suspicion of future confidence, the hope that at some point the basics of it would become clear to me—and then the scene abruptly changed. I found myself alone and in a very different kind of place—or perhaps the same place viewed in another way; I'm not sure. It was dark but for some far-off flashes and dim streaks accompanied by the grumbling of distant thunder. I surveyed my new surroundings, all the while hearing the swelling sounds of an approaching electrical storm, soft rumbles steadily blooming into the loud characteristic booms that typically announce an anticipated show of lightning. Indistinct illuminations finally turned into glaring shafts; and I thought of those summer nights spent in the desert, watching the constant discharge of heat lightning on the horizon. I remembered my happy fear while running out in thunderstorms as a child soaked to the skin—and I waited.

As the air began to crack and sizzle, Tesla came and stood beside me, seeming more like a self-assured lion tamer than a scientist. Arcs and bolts of electricity snapped, roared, and hissed around, over, under, and above us. He looked so satisfied, a proud barker standing awestruck, impressed by his own exotic sideshow. *"He's an artist,"* I realized. *"And this is his paint."* Veins of light surrounded us in a lacey display of graceful instability, the dangerous throb of countless electrical events keeping us captive in a cold white web of charge and discharge. Tesla's work was startling, exhilarating; and I wanted eagerly to share it with others, with my wife, my family, and with friends. "It can't be just mine." I said, turning to Tesla. "But, how can I show this to anyone? *Il peregrin che spera già ridir com'ello stea*—to retell how it was. I'll wake up and it'll be gone." He smiled warmly and nodded before leaving me by myself again.

I continued to contemplate his unfolding composition, fascinated, recalling my fragile feeling of safety as a young man in a small rowboat out in the ocean, rising and falling on the dark swells that toppled over all around me. It brought to mind my initial surprise at the power of the Primavera in the Uffizi, the uncontrollable nature of Madame Augustine the postman's wife, and the solitude of a tall dim chamber draped in black velvet—being there alone, open and vulnerable to Duccio's Maestà. I was no less moved by Tesla's masterful expression, overwhelmed by its authority, feeling myself unexpectedly high, like the boy at the top of a pine tree again, floating tranquilly in the wind where the sky meets the earth. In spite of the dangerous nature of such great force, I wasn't afraid. The electricity, which would normally have been menacing and unpredictable, seemed to pose no threat at all. I was open to it, calm and satisfied by the tender sensation of being held by it.

Tesla returned, picking up our conversation where we left off. "Of course you can't hold or share it very well. This is your awareness and we are at its limit." I was gently humbled, suddenly reminded of my limitations, and a little disoriented. He went on, "This is where the power is. This is the in between place, the space between everything— between what is seen and what is unseen." I thought of my charged paint brush quickly moving through the air toward a half-painted panel; of sparks leaping across gaps and then of a person who, on hearing about my dreams, told me to ask Tesla where all the free electricity is. At that point, however, I was sure it was the wrong question. I should have asked Nikola *what* electricity is, as what I saw didn't seem as mundane as what is delivered through wires and plugs, the stuff I take for granted every day in light bulbs and toasters. In every sense, the power I was witnessing was miraculous and mysterious, perhaps as easily understood by a painter or poet as by a technician, a profound gift from the universe, which reality eludes description, definition, and measurement in the ways we pretend to own what we refer to as *electricity*.

"How can there be space in between?" I asked. "If those patterns are filling all space, where is the space between them?" Then I perceived something like the idea of a sponge, saw the would-be material notion of what it means to grow increasingly dense without ever becoming solid; the spaces in between never filling. I imagined a charged atmosphere both differentiating and relating what would otherwise be indistinct. "There's more *in between* than anything else, isn't there?" I theorized. "More space than anything—like so much dark sky holding up the constellations."

"And, we are at the edge of your consciousness," he interrupted, pointing to another kind of place, an emptiness or void somewhere beyond where we stood. "That is chaos, because you are not aware of anything beyond this point."

The electrical display passed and faded and I gazed out into nothingness somewhat anxiously. *"Here I am at the brink of an abyss, a blind world…"* I remembered Dante, picturing myself as

Friedrich's wanderer, up there musing on a veiled landscape from high above the sea of fog concealing it. *"...but to admit blindness is the threshold of seeing, the door to visions, the cusp of possibility."*

"Hey! Vincent's Starry Night isn't about the stars is it? He painted about the in between stuff!" I looked expectantly to Tesla for approval. While there with him, I seemed to understand perfectly well what he showed me, although since then, it has taken some effort to piece it all together in a clear way. I had expected that reaching the limit of my conscious awareness meant that the event would be concluding, but it continued; even if I was already filled to bursting.

"The most accurate way for you to understand what we have seen is to view the patterns as filaments, strings, or sequences consisting of basic elements." There was something definite about the way he described the filaments. They seemed most important to him, conclusive to what he had previously proposed. He wanted me to understand the patterns finally in that form. "It is all actually best perceived as filaments," he repeated. A very fine filament like a tight strand of spider's web shot across the empty space in front of me. "These vibrate in frequencies," he said, just as I began to hear or feel a faint almost undetectable hum coming from the strand. "Not unlike violin or harp strings." The filaments began to multiply regularly in the space around us, like the two-dimensional grids we had seen earlier. One by one, fine threads stretched themselves across the emptiness, becoming dense in places, suggesting eventual mass, each humming at a particular frequency.

Then, as if from somewhere inside myself, I heard what might be described as a harmonic, a haunting resonant tone that stood out against the subtle droning of the vibrations. The sound drew my attention to the place where two of the filaments came in contact or nearly in contact, where one vibration met another. As the filaments continued to become more numerous, so did the resonant intersections, the harmonics causing physical response, near palpable sound that seemed to permeate everything. Growing chords of the many resonances heard together became the sonic evidence of the overlapping that I had first only seen. *"Now I am hearing the patterns relate,"* I realized. *"Like seeing them with my ears.*

"This is like music!" I burst out enthusiastically to Tesla in an embarrassing understatement of the obvious.

"This *is* music," he answered, as the filaments continued to multiply and the resulting harmonics filled space again the way the grid patterns had filled space.

"I'm experiencing the relationships—what's between things," I thought. *"Maybe the intersections are what is most real to me—what's most evident, what resonates. Is that what constitutes awareness? Is it the associations that hold everything together?"* I have pondered since on the substantial quality of those resonant vibrations or harmonics, offspring produced from the interaction of parent vibrations, in the same way that I saw child patterns born from the conjoining of two-dimensional grids. And then, there were the ethereal chords coming from the union of those resonances—composites of composites, like one world eclipsing the life of another.

On an impulse, I got out of bed and quickly walked into the other room for some reason I forgot, and stood there a bit confused, contemplating what I had learned. *"That space in between and the chaos? Where is in between? What is the power there? And the chaos beyond…?"*

"The space in between is still at the edge of your conscious ability, and the chaos you may better understand as unorganized material that is outside your associative experience."

"*Yes, I'm definitely awake,*" I thought to myself. "*And he's still talking.*"

I lay down beside my wife again and the teaching continued, ending after a brief review of the filament concept. I looked at the clock. "*It's past seven, and light out. That lasted about three hours, and I wasn't exactly asleep was I? At least it didn't seem like sleep. Maybe somewhere in between awake and asleep?*" Again, as after other Tesla dreams, I was filled with excitement. Something fantastic had just happened—and in such an average way. I rolled over. "I had another lecture!"

That a rather ordinary person like me, just one of many in the crowd, should find himself dreaming things as purposed as these recent incidents seems surprising…something I might consider if I were reading about it somewhere, but end up questioning as part of my own life. Maybe it's all part of the uncommon conditions that include what I have supposed to be common. So I have started lowering the volume on things, turning off the radio in the car and letting the house stay silent when I'm alone. I've stopped looking at things I don't intend to see, stopped responding to what isn't important. I'm trying to listen more, to pay attention to what was there before my life filled up with so much junk.

I called my mathematical friend to talk about the microelemental patterns, which looked a lot like her work. She reminded me of the fractal concept when I spoke of the cusplike in between place, and although that seemed logical, I'm not sure I understand the nature of fractals any better than I know where that space is, or how to return at will.

It seems curious; one moment I'm dreaming and feeling so

awake, and the next, I am awake and suspect that I'm sleeping. Maybe there is a work to do? Maybe there is a real Tesla out there, or someone who wants to teach me something for a specific purpose? But then maybe, *I* am Tesla. And does it really matter? What is my consciousness anyway; the part of me that dreams dreams and then forgets or remembers them? Will my body pass it on to the dust when I die? Does the dust then dream? I think of Gauguin's worn out questions painted in an upper corner of his paradise with that Tahitian woman forever reaching for the fruit; *D'où venons nous? Que sommes-nous? Où allons-nous?*

From the urge to claim and develop an obscured source, to hours of staring—contemplating the proportions and perspective of its completed context—the veiled life of a painting, the invisible part, is always greater than what is visible. It was my mother who taught me to seek what is hidden. I remember bursting into the house, impressed by the number of pollywogs in my pail. "Mama, look at how many I got!—Why're you crying, huh?"

"Oh, I just wrote a new poem dear. Let me read it to you."

More than the poem, it was the distant tone in mama's voice, her far-off look that impressed me. I knew she had seen something I couldn't see in any way but through her eyes. She had been somewhere that only she could go, a nameless beyond place where she had been empowered, charged, struck by inspiration as if by lightning. With puffy reddened eyes and filled with emotion, she faithfully delivered the lines of her poetic message.

"Well—what do you think?" she asked coyly. "Do you like it?"

I was only seven or eight, and wondered how to like something that made my mother cry like that. I was embarrassed and soon enough forgot the poem. But I got the message. Me and my pail—and she with her poetry—it was obvious. I had tried to impress her with a quantity of tadpoles from the swamp, but she had inspired me with the qualities of what I couldn't see. The messenger was the message, glowing with passion and the look in her eyes of somewhere far away.

It's a little different now. Once in a while she'll read me a new poem, but instead of discussing Gauguins and Renoirs we discuss my work.
"Hey, mama, come see what I've done. Well—what do you think?"

9
The Empty Stage

November 27 – I am getting better at going to wherever it is we meet, unsure if it's a place, a state or something else. I have no name for it—a clear stillness I recognize when it happens, a peculiar welcome hollowness where anything or nothing might occur. Too often, like this morning, no one is there; it's completely neutral, painted in *grisaille*, gray-beige monochrome and silent, like an empty stage. So I hang around for a while, anticipating Tesla's arrival in that indefinite somewhere, before I give up and let go, relaxing into the confusing chatter of my usual dreamy nonsense.

Activity in the studio sometimes comes to a standstill. The conversation between the painting and me stops. Everything is blank. I'll sit and stare for a while, arms folded anxiously across my chest, then maybe go browse a book impatiently, or do something unrelated, hoping things will ease up—but the painting doesn't respond to my advances. Like actors without a script, we quickly find ourselves with nothing to say to each other. The image is obstinate, and the artist working in the studio just yesterday has suddenly become a stranger. I do my best to mediate, but I'm stumped and doubt starts to take root.

On the other hand, when I'm most active in the studio, life relates to what I paint rather than the other way around. I read a book, take a walk, or pat the dog, and it's all about painting. The image becomes a greedy sponge, never saturated, soaking in everything; the house, the woods, the sky, and stars. *"It's only paint,"* I remind myself, but it's hard to compete with the intoxicating smell and feel of it. *"Oil and pigment arranged on a panel, nothing else—just paint,"* I repeat. But the discussion grows, one thing leading to another, until it finally bears fruit.

I lie in bed, watching the sky above me slowly reel like a thick black whirlpool. *"Ah—but there's no window frame! This morning I'm still sleeping. This is a dream."* At times it can be tricky to tell if I am awake or asleep. "So, what's happening?" I inquire of my strange inner heaven. "These fantastic explorations with a forgotten inventor—the inner storms at the edge of nowhere...." I probably spend too much time thinking about it all, letting my pig of a brain chew and gorge on this stuff. It concerns me that I tire so easily of waking life, impatient with its relative dimness. Increasingly, the intensity of my dream world seems more engaging and immediate. *"They're only dreams, nothing else,"* I remind myself. *"Just dreams."*

It has become a pattern: to awaken, check the clock, stare up through the darkened window, and request an audience with my eccentric ghost of a companion as if he were as real as I am. Nikola Tesla has become my friend. The truth is—I really miss him when he doesn't visit my dreams. I feel drawn to what has become so much bigger and more impressive than the rest of my life, looking forward to the visits from Nikola more eagerly than I await the visits of my substantial friends. My daily routine seems dull, comparatively vague and detached from what has begun to feel so solid. I wake up early in the morning, about three or four o'clock, and lie there expecting he'll show up, wishing to talk to my unearthly mentor, straining to hear his voice—any voice, and end up talking to the stars hoping for anything in response. I watch the blue-black domeful of glowing sparks, slowly, almost unapparently rotating, and I wait. *"Not this morning,"* I must conclude often enough, continuing to track my favorite constellations as they deliberately plod around the pole star, steadily and unhurriedly tracing their habitual circuits across my window until they fade into the blue of morning.

So many times in the studio I can do nothing but sit and gaze at the paintings. Somehow my memory of holding brushes and mixing colors is veiled and I feel empty. The prepared panels and partial images tease. The muse has fled and the hero has either followed or is hiding and I miss him, examining my hands for evidence of pigment caught beneath my fingernails. Unfortunately they're clean! A skin has begun to form on the surface of the thickened oils in the little cups clipped to a palette full of drying paint. A layer of dust says no one has touched things for a while.

"Who painted these anyway?

"L'angelo codardo," I answer, somewhere between amused and accusing.

"Is the artist shy?" I tease myself. *"Maybe I'll just paint patterns in the mean time."*

I think of the overwhelming number of painted designs that fill the walls of so many Italian cathedrals and resolve to clean off the palette, add fresh paint, and refill the cups with new oil. *"Why am I so stubbornly reluctant to step forward? What am I more afraid of? Failure? Or becoming who I am?*

"I'll start again tomorrow," I decide.

Not long ago, in a dream, I struggled to identify myself. It felt like thumbing through 3X5s in a card index—"See, it's me. Look!" I told the person sitting next to me. At that moment, a lot seemed to depend on it being *me*. I had to prove it, showing my hands, pulling up the sleeves of my shirt to reveal my arms as concrete evidence, then my feet, legs, and other parts of my body. Somehow he still wasn't convinced, and I was shocked to see my extremities not exactly as I remembered, even if I recognized them as my own personal parts. *"Must be me from another time, earlier or later in my life,"* I thought. *"That's crazy!*

"Wait! I remember. I'm dreaming!" I quickly awoke to inspect my arms and legs carefully, verifying which me I was seeing and referring to here and now and hoping to conceal my temporary confusion. *"Yes, this is how I look now. How I am—just how everything was when I went to bed last night.*

"See. I am me," I asserted more forcefully to the person who wanted to know for whatever reason.

"Am I in layers then?" I wondered. *"An intersection of so many patterns? Inner and outer, from various befores and afters, heres and theres, all at once—all definitely me?"*

I reached down to feel my legs with my hands and then looked down at my feet again. "Don't worry, I'm quite sure that this is all myself here," I reemphasized loudly to whoever it was sitting beside me.

Then waking up, I looked out the window to see what the weather was doing. *"Good. Looks like rain today.*

"But wait! Wasn't I already awake and checking on a very real and physical self?

"OK. Let's see—before this I was only dreaming of waking up. Now, I'm really awake." A bit disoriented, I got out of bed and walked into the bathroom, touching my arms and legs. *"I know I am,"* I said, looking into the mirror. *"It's weird, isn't it?"*

I exhaled, focusing then on an airy image of my unlikely new friend and teacher. *"Life has certainly changed."*

In the studio I often work on several pieces at a time, four or five riddles to explore and the branching discussions that represent my reasoning concerning them. I work slowly and in layers, hoping to describe the related arguments in detail, aware that what I refer to with pigment is not a real sky, a tree, or piece of fruit, but just an amount of carefully managed paint. Later, for the audience, time will collapse. The painting will appear all at once, perhaps as something that it's not, like Magritte's pipe that's not a pipe, or the unportraits of Giuseppe Arcimboldo, his clever combinations of vegetables, shells, books and other objects suggesting the personification of intangible things—or like the millions of light-years appearing as a twinkling spot in the sky that may or may not still be out there as the star I see. As a painter, I also experience a painting as a story of descent, lineage, the image of generations, choices stemming from so many this's and that's, yes's and no's, proposals and responses, their shoots and off-shoots, the evidence of where I've been— what I'm guilty of knowing. The point is that I would rather make mistakes than do nothing—better to risk having to repent and start over than to stop. Even more than that, paintings and their associated deliberations become me, as events I participate in, places I can't return to in innocence. Like finding those people with blue eyes in a crowd—once found, I can't honestly pretend not to see them.

I've been recording my Tesla dreams the best I can. Sometimes, when I make mistakes, there are words and phrases that come to me during the day, to improve or correct my interpretation—better words suddenly popping into my head and suggesting where they belong in the flow of text. Forgotten terminology is supplied as in the case of *frequency* and *resonance* in a few places where I had simply written *vibration*. It's strange how things grumble at me when they're not quite right. A similar thing happens while working through an image. A passage of paint unexpectedly comes to mind, appearing in a way that will improve or complete a specific aspect of a piece. I do the best I can and then hope for clues, little revelations—so I don't think it's that strange to receive help from elsewhere. It happens in paint all the time. In fact my dreams are teaching me how often I've taken for granted what happens in the studio, the delicate stance between being driven by my intellectual desires and inspired by influences beyond myself.

Somewhere in the middle of the tug-o-war between the possibilities that fuel my awareness I plant a seed, nothing too big, just a *what if* that I begin to tend. It's the initial itch that eventually becomes a painting, an almost-thought that grows a context around itself—not the answer, but a peripheral world created by the question—the stage, roles, and scenery a plot can develop in.

Perhaps it's pride that makes it scary, makes me uncomfortable. "Don't do it," warns my more sensible self. "That looks like trouble!" Yet weighing the alternatives, I go there anyway, in spite of the fateful prospects.

"Why not?" I challenge, and paint the background ridiculously red to press the issue. I've been told that working through the passionate aspects of *rouge* is risky, a dramatic production bent toward tragedy, but I react. From the start I'm teased by the hope of a colorful ending, all the inevident stuff that tempts me to explore the limitations of my precarious program. I want to know it for myself.

"Make the curtains red, the roses red, the lips red, the blood red, the sky red, the fire red…I love red!" But the fruit of the red discussion turns out to be less delicious than the initial taste was. Finally, it's difficult to look at and hard to cover up. I scrape it off the best I can and start over on another panel.

"All right then, I'll try green." I nurse it along and sure enough; it grows. I paint a green garden backdrop and fill it with red roses and trees with red fruits, a woman and man with blood red lips, and a fiery red sunset behind it all. I love red, and am the wiser for my mistakes—but sometimes it's still confusing to see red by painting green. I almost wish for the restored naiveté of not knowing the difference or not caring, but the remaining residue of my experience is a reminder.

So often, early in the morning, I lie in bed and await my friend on an empty stage, wondering if it's just myself that I am waiting for, or if it's really someone from elsewhere dropping by to clue me in. Several times when Tesla hasn't come, I hear our earlier discussions repeated; "I am going to talk about patterns. Pay attention now…." And I listen carefully.

Once I played a major role in a theatrical production. The director came and found me painting in the studio. At first, I was concerned with the need to memorize so much material. The script was a book. I learned, however, that as I rehearsed the lines, the work of memorizing faded. I wasn't playing any longer. The context of the role was natural. The distinction between myself and the man described by pages of dialogue diminished in the same way that a painter transforms into the object of his paint. Like one substance magically changing into another, I had become the part and those were *my* words, thoughts and emotions. They still are.

The development of awareness is a dangerous task—that the world and I are subject to my reasoning and whims, as the soil is to seeds carried on the wind. *"Am I the garden or the gardener then?"* I ask myself, and imagine the woods back home, Monet's pastoral sweeps of paint, walks in the meadow with my Gidu, his black felt hat and the mysteries it contained, the secrets he shared that I don't remember. Carefully I retrace the diagram of my thinking. *"Wrong questions are malignant—wrong answers dead ends,"* I realize. *"This is serious play, isn't it?"* For a moment, the innocence of paradise and the confines of hell seem too similar. *"What happened when they left anyway? Was it still there—an Eden without the players?"* I continue to follow the branching lines of my logic to their conclusions and am surprised by the sudden memory of damp earth under my belly, down by the swamp again, watching rings spread out around the water skeeters' feet as they skip across the surface of a reflected sky.

"So—while doubt is human, is belief the gift of consciousness, the binder, the plot's glue? Or, does consciousness evolve from my believing?" I look again, and a freckle-faced boy mirrored on the water smiles back—that familiar uncontrollable toothy grin that always embarrassed me.

"Am I the design and image of my thoughts then—either way?"

Daily, the stars appear and disappear. I have wondered during daylight hours at the impossible sea of color above me, straining to see the invisible stars so prominent a short time before. The night sky is another thing, a velvet backdrop for a celestial theatre, marked and measured. And, there are the times when night's pale face escapes the darkness to prowl across a solar scene. I like that it gets away with that, even if the bright sun can't seem to sneak anywhere without the day tagging right along. I especially like the drama of transition, as night turns into day, and the day becomes night again, when a temporary raging palette paints the east or west. On cue, the evening sun burns hotly into the horizon and the moon's silver profile peeps above the eastern hills. It's impossible to go to bed anymore without hoping to meet my friend Nikola Tesla before tomorrow begins.

10
Butterfly Hunting

November 29 – A net to hunt insects usually began with a wire coat hanger. I'd bend it open into a hoop about a foot across, then straighten the tail—the hook part not used in forming the circle—before attaching it to a dowel or more likely to a straight branch I'd find in the woods. Removing the bark from the branch gave me a chance to use my pocketknife purposefully, sometimes taking extra care to remove the bark in various designs and patterns, including the letters of my name or my initials. When the stick was ready, I attached the wire tail from the hoop to the last few inches with plenty of black electrical tape, with string, twine, or thin wire wound tightly around the union of the two.

Usually, making nets was a group activity, which included the neighbor kids and us. The preparations were serious business as we discussed and imagined our eventual collections of bugs. Most of the time, the bags of our nets were made of pieces of old nylon stockings stitched together, then stretched and sewn carefully over the stiff perimeter of the hoop. At other times the nets were made from gauzy fabric or a piece of netting that we might find or beg from an adult. We'd sit someplace typical, on and around someone's front steps, bending wire, stripping bark, winding tape or string, and carefully stitching with odd-colored thread that no one would miss.

As the project began to near completion, talk would invariably begin to focus on the hunt. "Hey! Remember that Luna Moth? I still have it, ya know."

Really, we caught anything we could coax into our nets. If mounted specimens were the goal, one of us would have an old jar from pickles or mayonnaise cleaned and ready with a tight cover and a piece of cotton inside soaked in alcohol. The alcohol didn't work very fast, but it was easily available in the medicine cabinet and we knew it to be poison. If we wanted our prey alive, as in fireflies, which aren't much good dead, we'd forget the saturated cotton ball and punch holes in the jar lid with an ice pick or sharp knife that we sneaked out of the kitchen. Mostly, we went to the trouble of making nets when we were dreaming of butterflies, like the ones on pins in the glass-topped boxes on the science table at school.

"I bet you guys don't know what a butterfly's coiled tongue is called—It's a *proboscis*."

"Nah! Where'd you get that? That's an elephant you idiot!"

"Yeah, well I bet you don't know what a snail's tongue is called."

"So! Neither do you, freak!"

"Yes I do! It's a *radula*—from Latin. It means *scrape* or *rasp*."

"Hey! Today I'm gonna get a *fritillary*. I've seen 'em lots and never caught one."

"I almost had one once, but it got away."

So went our conversations until the nets were complete. It was an unspoken contest to see who could finish before the others and take off first for the meadow to surprise the larger more obvious specimens.

There were lots of butterflies where we lived; on the milkweed, in the vegetable garden, fluttering over and landing in the meadow on daisies, black-eyed susans, and wild pea flowers. While most young hunters were after the monarchs, swallowtails, mourning cloaks, and viceroys, I preferred the small blue nameless ones, not much bigger than a nickel. It's odd, looking back, that in my struggle to make them stay still, to own them, I was so intent on killing what I found most worthy of admiration. I remember watching them in the jar, sitting on the poisoned cotton, showing off their colors for me. Morning—evening, morning—evening; the quick open and close of two sky-blues, on the outside and surprising inside of their wings. I always hoped they'd die quickly with their wings flat open, but that rarely happened. As I got a little older and understood their sacrifice better, I sometimes tried to save them from the fate I had planned. I'd reach my hand into the jar before they were still and lift them out to freedom.

"There. Fly away now," I'd say, blowing on them gently for encouragement. "Go on. Fly away."

But they never did. My thick small fingers sometimes finished the job the alcohol was meant to do, or most often they'd just crawl around my hand and couldn't fly. I looked at the faded wings, then at the smudges of color on my guilty fingertips. No matter how hard I tried, the powder from their fragile wings came off when I handled them, which limited their ability to flutter off on the wind of my well-intentioned breath. I don't know how many times this little drama was played out before I learned my lesson; that there are some things whose tender graces cannot be examined in my normal clumsy way without diminishing their value and life.

I was impatient this morning, talking to myself and to the Universe again about my Tesla dreams. "What's the purpose of them?" I asked. "Is anyone out there listening? And—why me, anyway?"

"But—why you?" That's what most people say when they hear about my visitor. "Suppose it *is* true—why would he talk to you?" In other words, "Why not someone more important who could do something about it?" And, of course I have no answer to that.

This morning I went there, wherever it is we meet, cautiously anxious for answers and admittedly a little bold, a precocious child nagging again for something just out of reach. "So, what's going on? I've got to know. I want to understand this Tesla stuff—make sense of it," I demanded of that empty space. Once more in the relative quiet of a world still asleep I began to reflect on the extraordinary events of the last few months. *"I just want to hold everything still for a while. Examine it—claim it as part of my life."*

Then, unexpectedly, I was in a different bed, one that almost filled a small room, watching myself and strangely being myself at once, both the audience and the actor. I knew the place and the event well; my cramped bedroom of some twenty-five years before and an experience that I have retold many times. This morning it felt like a projection of some kind that I was aware of and part of, an elaborate re-presentation of a dream whose recollection I have kept somewhere set apart from the jumble of my memories. *"How many times have I dreamed this?"* I mused. *"It's so familiar. How many times must I have forgotten it in the morning upon awakening?"*

This time Tesla was there watching, prompting me to rejoin the experience. "Look again now and see if there is more," he encouraged. I felt a little shy at first, both of us observing the vivid image of myself in bed dreaming. I noted the softer lines of my face, the darker hair, my youthful wife sleeping beside me, the humble nature of our surroundings, and pondered the spectrum of circumstances that would be the future of that younger me, gently considering myself once again, asleep and comparatively innocent.

What began with a view of me in bed gradually included the awareness of my sleeping self. We watched me dreaming as I slowly felt light surround my body increasing in brightness and radiating from me in streams, my whole self somehow breathing whiteness out into the dark. The *me* watching studied myself, noting that the light was focused into a strong beam where it shot from my chest toward somewhere above. My observer self gave clues to the participant self, information from what I discerned concerning the situation from an outside point of view, while the *me* directly involved in the experience carefully evaluated and communicated how it all felt while it was happening.

"A pleasant swelling is making my chest feel warm and tight," I reported to my on-looking self.

"I see a light shooting from the sternum and streaming forcefully into space," I answered, looking up at a ceiling that dissolved into the night sky as if there were no ceiling.

Intense curiosity drew me to follow the flowing light, wondering where it might lead to or come from. Without thinking, I joined myself—that's what it felt like—leaving the *me* watching and the *me* in bed as yet another *me* began to examine things more actively. It's difficult to describe how I experienced these three selves, a knowing self from the future overseeing the remembered scene, my youthful body feeling things from home in bed, and part of both of us combined to become myself the inspector and verifier. Tesla seemed content to watch us explore the event.

Hunting butterflies, I remember stopping to watch the activities and functions of their lives, staying still in the deep meadow grass, waiting—soon sitting spellbound by a swallowtail up close, rhythmically unfolding tiger-striped wings—then, seeing it uncoil something curly where a mouth might have been, extending a long feeler to stick it into the center of each pink bloom. The startling scene on the waxy cluster of milkweed flowers was miraculous, nearly invisible, at least generally unnoticed. Within a day I had a name for the impressive secret—*proboscis*; a straw-like tube through which butterflies drink nectar. But the secrets of my dreams are different if no less startling; the closer I seem to get, the fewer names I find to describe them.

During my dream this morning, a mere thought resulted in immediate action. *"Where does this lead?"* And I was abruptly staring back at myself in bed while rising swiftly and effortlessly along the bright column connected to my chest. My interest in the glowing stream quickly pulled me higher, above the house, trees, my neighborhood, woods, towns, cities, mountains, and lakes, revealing a clear and exalted view of a vast area of earth's landscape stretched out as far as I could see. *"How beautiful this is beyond the news, above the endless images of suffering, wars, and pollution that have become daily fare filling me up until there's no room left. It all looks peaceful from up here."* So I lingered for a while, captive by the deliberate pattern of things occurring at a distance, a world miraculously unfolding despite my concerns and fears.

In the process of applying paint, sometimes my face is just a few inches from the panel for hours at a time. I use the three or four remaining sable hairs of a quintuple aught brush to leaf out the treetops of a miniature forest methodically, or to grow a field by patiently dragging strands of color off, one by one, like grass blades. I hold my breath to paint the petals carefully on tiny ray flowers about the size of a butterfly's jeweled eyes, meadow daisies small enough to fit inside the miniscule o's on this page. After a while I distance myself from the image, standing back beyond the range of little secrets. The particulars then disappear into the flow of a larger statement. The activity of the surface becomes still, while the structure of the whole begins to show. The associations of lines and shapes often appear clearer from far-off. I remember myself in front of Botticelli's paradise, getting close enough to examine the privacies of his paint, then returning to my place on the provided ottoman. From across the room the order of rhythms, patterns, and relationships formed a system, a structure that was difficult to see from up close, but no less vital to the painted creation than the meticulous details of its lush meadow full of wildflowers. Up close, then far away—up close and far away; the two singular views, when joined, made my awareness of the picture more complete.

In my dream, after stopping to consider the untroubled scene spread out below, I turned to contemplate the depth of the sky, surprisingly intimate in its immensity. *"I want to hold on to this,"* I decided before moving on. *"For when I forget—for when I think it's either one way or the other."*

My glowing current soon forked, then divided repeatedly into smaller streams. I drifted above a network of shining arteries, my light indistinguishable from others, interacting, crisscrossing, and arching back to earth here and there, like the charted circuits of airline flights connecting at various airports. I traced a few to sources in strange neighborhoods and rooms where other people slept or went about their business, attached as I was to the luminous map. Tesla and I watched me follow a beam through the wall of a darkened bedroom to stand quietly and observe a sandy-haired young man in bed asleep, the light leading directly to his chest. With Nikola, I recalled my initial reaction to the tender awareness that we were alike, the unknown young man and myself—that people from every possible place and situation were joined to us in some implicit way, our hearts sharing a connection to something beyond the reach of one of us alone.

"I'm a link," I thought. *"A door to the whole, the reflection of something much larger than myself—the pattern of one again."* And I thought on our lesson about mnemonics of several months before.

A vital arrangement, charged and circulating like the coursing vascular system of a peculiar giant, the living operation connected each of us like organs of an invisible body for what I assumed were specific roles and functions relating to a purpose or work. I felt integral to the life and success of the complex of light, seeing how many streams joined with my own. "Who am I? What part do I play?" I wondered aloud, hoping Tesla might answer. But he was quiet.

"A little toenail trying to pry information from an eye?" I grumbled to myself after prolonged silence. *"It's OK! I can be a humble toenail."*

After its first occurrence, I told my wife and a few close friends about this dreamlike event. It was remarkable enough, but twenty-some years ago I had thought it was about a possible future, that it might become important or more meaningful later. There wasn't much to do about it anyway, other than to note that it had happened—and then today, in the future, it was repeated in response to my nagging supplication.

"So how do I affect the big picture?" I asked a bit gruffly. "How important is being just a toenail?" There was still no reply—nothing.

By nature I am not a patient person. I get grumpy waiting for things and don't like depending on others. Now, that's exactly where I'm left, impatiently anticipating answers and suspecting that I'm not the least bit independent after all, bound to others in a crucial way, like a solitary thread in the fabric of things. Often upon awakening, I immediately start to dissect my Tesla experience. Lying there in bed, I chat about it with myself, trying to take it apart, to look at it logically, hoping dispassionately to tease out the facts like hidden pieces of some strange anatomy.

"Just past four this morning—they usually happen early. Not quite asleep, not awake yet—somewhere, in a place, a state where I access certain things almost consciously and others with surprising intensity.

"Yeah, it feels like arriving or suddenly tuning in—swimming out to catch a swift current.

"But sometimes, it's like standing in the middle of an empty stage.

"Then there's the talk with someone else—bigger and smarter, who tells me stuff that couldn't come from me at all—lectures."

That's where I usually decide to leave it alone, to put off thinking about it.

This morning I experimented with the experience of being there where things happen. I observed that my senses seem heightened, particularly the olfactory sense. There are times early in the morning when the strong perfume of roses, even the smell of something awful, or something cooking—burning in the oven—will awaken me. I get up and go down to the kitchen to see if someone left the stove on. But everything is off. There are no roses near my house. No one else is ever up, and I return to bed wondering what it's all about again. Most of the time the place of my Tesla dreams feels warm and comfortable compared to the immediate harsh realities of cold floors, schedules, traffic, and bills. Today I held onto it as long as I could, even awake and talking to family members. Later, I telephoned an artist friend to discuss it. I asked him how it feels when he's painting, and he answered very much as I suspected. We spoke about this common feeling, the dreamy state that happens while we're working in the studio. I think it was enlightening for both of us. It reminded me of becoming similarly entranced in focused activities as a boy, like watching the slow progress of a caterpillar, the underwater antics of water beetles or the frantic business of ants around an anthill—or making those nets, and the consequent afternoons spent hunting butterflies. Painting and dreaming feel a lot like that.

I've never lost my fascination for things up close, learning eventually that "dusty" butterfly wings are covered in minute scales, hence the name *Lepidoptera*—*lepidos* meaning scales and *ptera* meaning wings. Scalywings. And, it's impossible to forget my first look through a magnifying glass—my consequent surprise at the revealed worlds of color separations, the nearly invisible populations of tiny colored polka-dots warring for prominence, but appearing still at arm's length. In hopes of luring my audience closer, I continue to struggle with the delicate details of each painting. *"Maybe they'll get close enough to see it,"* I theorize. Devotedly I fight with just three hairs and a little paint until finally giving up to the stillness of the process. *"Up close, then far away,"* I remind myself.

"Providing free power for light and warmth to all could eliminate poverty," claimed Nikola Tesla decades before I was born. "An ultimate show of power might end all war," he theorized. This morning we saw a peaceful view of the world, he and I—beyond the range of hatred, pollutions, and profit centers, from far-off where things appear a little clearer and the structure of the whole begins to show.

My memories of butterfly hunting are as common as childhood, no more peculiar to me than dreaming. Some might see the innate cruelty of humankind in a boy's intrusive inquiries, as others might see disorders in the waking dreams of my early mornings. Value can be fleeting in the hands of clinicians like my childhood self, whose graceless handling unknowingly rubbed wonder off the wings of things. *"So much goodness clumsily fooled away, lost before lessons are learned."*

I am as sure that somewhere there are children needlessly suffering, as I am that there are children in meadows still stalking butterflies. The tender awareness that we are alike, my light indistinguishable from theirs—that people from every possible place and situation are joined to me in some implicit way, our hearts sharing something beyond the reach of any one of us, is worth the doubt and struggle it takes to keep believing. And so, I'm afraid of manhandling these funny miracles, bungling what I can't fix. I try to be more cautious now, careful not to disbelieve first or examine these dreams too roughly, fearful of wasting their color at some point, concerned that in my enthusiasm I might disregard their fragile nature and leave them lifeless or diminished.

TWO

11
Dreams Within Dreams

December 4 – I remember my mother teaching me to kneel beside my bed each evening to pray to God. "Thank-you-for-everything-and-keep-us-safe-tonight-and-bless-nana-and-grampa-and-baba'n-gidu...." It became a habit to get down on my knees and talk to Heaven before climbing into bed. "Please-make-it-so-there's-no-war-anywhere-and-help-me-be-good-in-school-tomorrow." The common repetitions of my prayers were set. Since we awoke safely each morning, my grandparents were still thriving, and there was no war that I knew of close-by—it seemed to work. The *good in school* part was the bargain I struggled to be sincere about. I'd try to behave in school if God did all the rest. Before too long, I was praying on my own and began to realize the potential. "Dear Lord, make us rich and make me just like Leonardo...." Then, it was easy to talk of being an artist *when I grow up*. I pictured the face of *La Gioconda*, the smiling angel overseeing my clever requests and was confident in my future as a rich and famous painter of masterpieces.

As time passed, my prayers changed. "Thank-you-for-everything-and-keep-us-safe-tonight-and-bless-nana-and-grampa-and-baba...."Realities developed that seemed to contradict my petitions. "Please-make-it-so-there's-no-war-here." The repetitions at my bedside eventually reflected my uncertainty about God's interests in relation to mine. "And—help us to pay the bills this month." I still tried to bargain; apologizing for things, making promises—to be more patient, more generous and to stop doing whatever it was. But somehow, in the business of living, the would-be Leonardo fell from grace and became increasingly reluctant to assume the renowned role.

"Oh, what do you do?"

"I...don't know—make trouble?" I would respond sheepishly. "Actually, I'm a software design consultant," I continued, and everyone chuckled.

Once, while working for a client, I lost track of where I was and commented on a painting hanging in an office there. "What would someone like you know about art?" came an immediate response. And I admit, at times he's right. *"Not much,"* I answered silently.

Being an artist is sometimes difficult. On the list of temporal fears and desires that were my prayers, the itch to be an artist is conspicuously different—there *per passione*, as Italians like to say, *una vera vocazione*—my initial vision, like an uncommon seed expecting some distant springtime—waiting. Sleeping there since before The Sower sowed it—before my mother knew my father, before the postman met Mademoiselle Augustine, before Gauguin painted pretty Eve reaching, before Leonardo first imagined *La Gioconda's* wistful features, before the golden-hued

Madonna sat down in her fancy chair, before an unknown artist crafted my favorite crucified Jesus, before the Egyptians started keeping secrets, before the dinosaurs—before all of the befores. That's how it feels; that in the middle of an index of common wants and worries, there is something singular about me that has always been there.

So—it was 4:50 AM and I was half-awake, once again thinking about life, about my paintings and the dreams with Nikola Tesla. On the one hand, I'm confident that creative activities and dreaming dreams with meaning and application shouldn't be anomalous to an average life. On the other, I still wrestle with the possibility of their happening so dramatically in my own life.

In the studio, while considering the aspects of any image I am working on, it's not unusual to stop and stare down at the brush in my hand, at the romantic-looking palette that I bought in Rome, at the hundreds of paint tubes greedily stacked on the cart, and then to look around my special room built just for the purpose of being an artist.
"What am I doing?"
To be honest—sometimes I don't know.
Doubt is a funny thing—not so much about what I can't imagine, but the fears and desires surrounding what I can. It is the primary symptom of the human condition, so I'd fight for the right to doubt. To question is something different. Questions lead to seeking and finding. But doubt is about disbelieving—too often built on the ruins of previous vision and belief, a non-basis for non-doing. And still, sometimes I doubt. When I'm hurt, struggling with an obstacle, or faced with something new, it's so tempting to indulge myself in uncertainty about things,

especially things as elusive as paintings and dreams.

In spite of my weakness and concerns, it has become increasingly easy to find my way to *that place*—whatever you want to call it—where I meet Nikola Tesla. I'm more observant of the process, more aware of what is now the method for getting there. My steady breath seems to release me, then slight shivers, followed by little electrical shocks and flashes through my eyelids before the eventual warm glow of arrival. It has all become familiar. Nikola was not there this time, but my vivid experience seemed similar to our previous encounters and intended as part of my ongoing instruction.

From my seat in a large auditorium, I could see only the backs of heads and shoulders of people clothed alike in nondescript white shifts or coveralls. In fact, everything was white; the walls, the ceiling, the theatre-style armchairs we sat in and the entire brightly lit hall—all white. Other than the distant presentation at a podium in front, it was quiet and still, which was unusual for such a large gathering.

I have never liked the impersonal feeling of conferences and this was no different. Although I sensed a peculiar kinship with others in the audience, I was prepared to remain on the periphery. The anonymity of the back row was comfortable, proof of my habit of partial commitment in similar situations, always leaving myself the convenience of an easy out, the quick getaway. *"But instead, what if this seat back here is an indication of my standing?"*

"No, you chose the back before the others arrived," whispered someone to my left in response to my thought. "You are supposed to be here. And—you arrived early."

As I looked around the room, studying the backs of the attentive crowd, the feeling of affinity with the assembly grew.

"OK—

"*Sure. Maybe I did choose the back row before the others got here.*" For a while I sat and watched the audience listen, increasingly impressed that we were all related in some way—not literally, but alike, counterparts attending a relevant gathering together. "*Who are they? And, where are they from?*" We seemed to be in training for a purpose or mission, each of us being considered for a specific role in carrying out some shared objective. "*I do wish I could hear better—just this time, anyway.*"

I looked to my left then to see who had answered my unspoken thoughts. He was dressed in white like the rest of us, but more bizarre; covered in a loose veil of fabric and wearing a hat from which hung another veil that fell around his shoulders. "Either it's hard to hear or I can't seem to pay attention." I confessed softly through the thin screen of fabric that concealed his face.

"*Do you tend bees?*" I wanted to ask, amused by his eccentric garb and my own wit.

The proceedings of the meeting seemed significant, but I had to remind myself repeatedly to pay attention. "*After all, I've got to write this down later.*" Perhaps I was more impressed with being there than I was with listening. The information felt slippery, hard to hang on to, even for a short time. I was frustrated by my inability to focus—overwhelmed with both the nature of the material and with the predicament of my attention deficit. What was being presented seemed to address directly a lot of personal issues and questions about life. "*I wish I hadn't sat in the back,*" I decided. My mind was all over the place—"*Or, maybe it's just going over my head,*"—wandering and wondering about things of no consequence. "*Better remember that! Oh, that's good—that's important.*" But, I promptly forgot it. "*And, what good are answers that I don't remember?*"

The curiously dressed person to my left acted as a wise coach or guide, offering remedial assistance with the discourse that I was straining to hear and remember. I quietly asked questions through his veil, and he responded patiently to my concerns, sometimes anticipating what was soon to be proposed from the front of the hall. "Now they will discuss…," he'd start, and then in hushed tones would brief me on the next topic. I could almost see his face and body moving behind the veils, but not well enough to identify him. There were times that he helped me approach difficult ideas from other points of view, much as Tesla has done during our lessons. "You can best understand *that* by considering *this*…." He seemed kind and I liked him. With his hat and drapery he was larger and sat much taller than I or anyone else in the audience—before I noticed a similarly costumed figure seated to my other side. That's how dreams are sometimes, happening *all'improviso*, unfolding unexpectedly, as I get to them.

The veiled individual to my right had been quiet and seemed to be monitoring the communications of the more talkative guide on my left—who later deferred to him several times for further clarification. Both seemed intent on coaching me, however, making sure that I understood things. I welcomed their help, feeling a bit child-like, conspicuously small seated there between them, the two large figures hung with gauzy curtains and prominently poking up from the otherwise homogeneous audience. It was odd that no one seemed to notice the peculiar overgrown beekeepers or the soft buzz of our constant chatter. *"Maybe no one else sees them? But that would make them veiled to me and unseen by others, from within a dream—which is also generally unseen."* I studied their veils to reassure myself that they were really in there. *"How many unseen layers can there be?"* I wondered.

"As many as you believe," said the guide on my left.

"Which is far fewer than there are," added the guide on my right. "And some you may believe in—are not there at all."

"Is this a game?" I asked quietly.

At that point, my two helpful friends abruptly stopped to listen to what was being presented at the podium. The speaker was not clearly visible from where we sat and hardly audible, but matters began to sound more serious. "There are many of you who have been led or found your way here, but in a short time there will be only a few remaining…." His voice shook as the man delivering the message tenderly but firmly addressed the assembly. He explained that there were requirements and specific qualities associated with our mission that were either evident or lacking in each individual. These attributes were necessary qualifications for the work. "Some will be staying…," then he lowered his voice, "…but many, perhaps most of you, will be ending your training at this point. You will not be able to continue."

I let out the breath I had been holding and my gentle veiled companions both turned then to consider me. I waited. "There are many called," said the guide to my left finally.

"So, this is what they've been preparing me for." I wanted to continue with the training and subsequent mission, but feared a lack of courage and other qualities to do so. "I may lack what it'll take," I answered timidly. "I haven't even been able to pay attention. There are many here who'll qualify ahead of me." My inadequacy was real but pride fueled a secret desire to stay. "I chose to sit in back. Remember?"

"There is work to do. This is not to satisfy your curiosity and ego," stated the veiled figure to my right somewhat flatly.

Work in my studio is a puzzling mix of questions and doubts. Each painting is a quest to make what I've never before seen appear, to tell a secret that I can't speak. Because inspiration seems fickle, continuing to put paint on a panel, to hope in something still obscure and then hold out to the end, is a struggle. Often I lack the confidence, or endurance, and become discouraged—and I put the image aside to wait for me to catch up. Or, maybe it never takes shape and eventually I paint over it. Sometimes I force myself to continue uninspired and then later, destroy the finished piece. The worst times are when my doubts shame me into abandoning, destroying, or defacing something that I believed in.

"Think back," continued my guide. "Think back and you will understand."

At once I lost track of the lecture in the conference hall and began to see images of the past; a curious event from twenty-some years before began to replay on the screen of my memory. *"Again, I am re-dreaming a dream within a dream,"* I reasoned, *"and am aware of myself from yet another point of view outside those dream worlds."*

"It is time to go," said someone I didn't know and hadn't seen before. "You must come now."

"Can't I think about it?" I begged, staring down at the table. "I'd like some time."

"There is no time. This is it," he replied. "You will find no proof one way or the other. Either you follow me now, or you don't."

"Don't do it!" screamed my scared cephalic counselor. I was frozen in place—not daring to look up at the stranger's face or to move. "Will you tell me where we're going, please?" I inquired.

"I am not able to discuss that," said the very tall man standing over me. "And there will not be another chance. I cannot return."

"Shut up!" I told my distressed reasoning as it squealed with alarm—and, weighing the alternatives, I pushed back my chair, stood up, and followed.

We flew over the red rocks, a typical great-basin panorama, a southwest kingdom of hoodoo towers and rusty castles where goblins live. Stretched out below, rows of tubby pink babushkas touched their sandstone toes, squat plump figures caught in the middle of their calisthenics, the beguilingly soft impressions of harsher realities, like mushrooms growing in the desert. In my mind's eye I was shown our destination—I watched an orange cliff glow in the reflected light of an opposing canyon wall before succumbing to the evening. We were headed for a shadowy empty socket eroded below an overhanging brow of harder stone in the darkened cliff face—but that was still a long way off. We skimmed along on some kind of platform, above the cracks, folds, and fins of rock, over lazy creeks, and dry washes.

At last my escort spoke. "Everything will be explained once we arrive—and, when we return you will not remember where it is anyway. Not yet."

"Yeah right! Se' tu quel Virgilio...?" Quite satisfied again with my own wit. "...certainly not overflowing with information; but I hadn't asked you yet."

Generally I like mysteries and the veiled nature of things. Layers of paint, layers of painting, layers of meaning, treasure buried in colorful substrata—I turned and tried nervously to enjoy the scenery—layers of rock. *"But this is too much. I've given control of my life over to a riddle."*

"What is withheld will eventually be revealed," he said.

"But the closer I get, the farther away it seems."

We traveled through the air, flying fast and low, slipping over a vast stone theatre as the sun began to set. I shivered, and briefly remembered myself at home in bed. Logic said that I was safe, that it was all a dream; but the rest of me continued to feel otherwise. The cliff face I had seen suddenly filled my view. Without hesitation we sped forward into the deep shade of an overhang and quickly passed through the darkened rear wall of what appeared as solid sandstone, but which I determined to be a projection. I turned to look back through the camouflaged opening as the last rays of sunlight cast long dusky fingers across the far end of a desert valley. *"That'll be blue and violet glazes in the shadows and some extra vermilion to warm the rest of it up,"* I thought, and we turned the corner.

The first tunnel led to a complex of well-lit tunnels and spaces, an underground warren of busy places with people and odd vehicles hustling and bustling in an orderly and efficient manner—like a port of some kind, a hidden harbor of comings and goings. After my concern on the way there, everything quickly became strange and wonderful, a refuge from the outside where night was about to happen. *"Here I am, entering the middle of an incredible secret—something I had not imagined,"* noticing the cool and not unpleasant light whose source I couldn't see. In my dream, many aspects of the world in which I live had become so ridiculous that this possible sanctuary seemed a relief in contrast.

We stopped in a large bright cavern, one in a series of connected subterranean grottos filled with activity, lined with docks and pads where landings and departures, loadings and unloadings happened. My escort turned. "There will be a briefing followed by training. You will be asked to tell no one about this—and don't worry. You will do well." He smiled and left. I walked a short distance, stepped onto a larger waiting platform, and soon was part of the deliberate rush that seemed to characterize the place.

Several other people were already on board. We left the dock, sliding smoothly in and out of the flow of odd hovering craft and passing similar floating platforms filled with people.

"Relax. It'll be OK," said a fatherly gentleman standing beside me. "Pay attention to your training and you'll be fine."

"Thanks," I said. *"Do I know you?"* I wanted to ask. *"Dad?"* I started to recognize others on the platform. *"Ernest?"* Ernest had died a few years before. The man who looked like Ernest, smiled just like Ernest and told me how glad he was that I was there, reassuring me once again that I would do well. "Yes, thanks—

"But how are you here?

"Oh yeah, this is a dream," I remembered, and everything began to speed up. The platform stopped. I stepped off. "When your training is complete, you will return home." Corridors, rooms, dormitories, baths, dressing rooms, living quarters. "Once home you will wait until you are called." Scanned in a metallic cubicle. "For now, say nothing about this place or what has happened here." I showered. "It is irrelevant to anyone else and could jeopardize things." Changed into clean white clothing. "Remember—not until then." All in anticipation of some time in the future when a *work* would commence. The dream ended abruptly before I made it to the training room. Disappointment—disoriented to be home in bed—not a science fiction superhero preparing for an otherworldly mission but a poor tired art student trying to juggle the unwieldy pieces of my life. This time, however, as the dream concluded, I was back in the white conference room, missing just a few minutes of the presentation. At once, I recognized the hall filled with people in white coveralls as part of the training that I had attended in the underground complex of that previous dream, a part of the dream I had not remembered.

"How extraordinary, that I am being reminded of a past experience now in the sequence of these events—being shown that what I'm currently dreaming is a forgotten piece from the context of another dream over two decades ago."

I glanced up at my two veiled friends. "Where is Tesla?" My conversations with Nikola had always felt caring, even tender. The conference room was feeling a little corporate; and I was on my own, not comprehending precisely what was going on—even with the help of my patient guides. "I would really like to speak with Nikola Tesla if I could?" I whispered loud enough for both of them to hear.

"He is busy," replied the guide to my left. "He has work to do and others to teach."

"But you will see him again," said the guide to my right. "He has spent a generous amount of time with you, but that is not by your choice." I wondered if Nikola was an integral part of the training and preparation in the conference room.

"Be patient," added the guide on my left. "Time here must seem quite relative. What is a short time here can pass very slowly for you." I thought of the specific durations of my visits with Tesla as measured on my alarm clock—about three hours each time. "There are other instances when time passes fast for you, while here it can be experienced as an extended period if measured in terms of events and processes."

"Am I really dreaming this all up? It's too wild...."

I was interrupted by the commotion of people moving. Many were getting up and leaving the room without returning, until there were just few of us left. A sudden thought from my mentors; "You will be staying. You are chosen as one to continue and finish the work."

"Me?" I exhaled, suddenly wishing for some backbone. Perhaps I had anticipated feeling a little smug at that point, but instead felt simple, and not unafraid of what might be expected. "Why me?"

> *The stage was set. In the quarrel between head and heart, the heart beats in place while the head wants to move. Doubt steps in and offers to end the silly dispute—a divorce, the decisive ruling to divide them, to free the lovers. The separation is swiftly carried out. In disillusionment the heart stops and the head ceases to direct things.*

"But, who am I?"

> *And, just when everything seems lost, doubt suggests they celebrate the paradox. The end. The curtain falls, and hope silently leaves the theatre.*

There was no one listening. The dream had ended.

My paintings are believed into being. Step by step, the constant back and forth of becoming, the various colorful dramas, like lives within my life, until I send them off on their own. They each play a role in supporting the intent of my work. And yet, there are so few that ever leave the studio. Not good enough, not smart enough, not pretty enough, not sophisticated enough, too light, too dark, too big, too small, too foreign, the many excuses for unaccountability, the reasons for distrusting myself. After all, I'm not Leonardo.

And these dreams—the uncommon sequences of common motifs, typical elements in a plot's pattern; meeting a stranger, going somewhere new, facing my fears, learning trust, keeping secrets, finding a purpose, and too soon forgetting what I knew—evoking my usual response of doubtful obligation; "Me? Why me?"

The studio requires that I believe in all possibilities, in the hope of revealing what I don't already see. Painting is an act of faith. To deny that would betray its intent and end the process. Likewise, to deny the possibility of informative dreaming betrays intuition, numbs my awareness, nullifies inspiration—underrates mothers' premonitions and rejects the revelations of prophets—like Joseph's visions of the sheaves, the sun, moon, and stars. To deny my dreams, is to disbelieve the prophet Muhammad, who said, "The truest dream is in the early morning." The failure to recognize the power of dreaming would reduce the role of dreams in the sacred lives of the Buddha and in The Holy Family's flight to Egypt's safety. To deny the worth of dreams is to disallow the dream of Lord Vishnu whose dream I am—so to deny my dreams is to deny myself. My own doubts are not because I question the value of visions. My apprehensions come from well-rooted self-doubt of the most mundane variety.

Early one morning, in a dream, I told Nikola plainly that I couldn't meet his expectations, that I wasn't capable.

"Can't or won't?" he asked.

"I'm doing my best, but it's just too hard." I complained.

"So you are still afraid, and not fully engaged in it," he stated frankly.

"But, I don't think I can do more," I pleaded.

"If that were true, you would not have been asked. First, you have to meet the barrier and push against it. You are not there yet. The obstacle moves when you have given all you can, at the point that you can give no more. But first, you have to meet it with all your strength."

I know a man who runs marathons. He prepares all year for an event out in the desert through the red rocks. "See—it's not the distance I prepare for. How do you prepare that way for something you can't physically do?" he explains. "The distance is what magnifies everything, but I don't go there to win or lose against the distance." He describes the long run passionately as if it were a lifetime, beginning to end, small initial decisions often deciding the outcome. "Then, after giving everything, when there is nothing left, I reach a point where I must choose either to stop or to give up my fear and doubt—the miles don't matter, it's a barrier of fear and doubt I face." He speaks of pushing through to someplace new, where he meets himself each time as a stranger, the guide who runs beside him for the rest of the way. "I would rather risk everything to take myself to that place where I have never been before, than to run predictably well to nowhere new." And I realize that the story is the same again— for runners of marathons, for artists, and for dreamers.

So, I went to bed yesterday wondering about my counterparts, the ones who left the assembly in the white conference room. *"Why was I allowed to stay? We had a mission...."* Then, last night I had a dream.

Deep in a dark cellar, I stood in front of a big door and listened to the slow twisting of a key in the lock. A turning tumbler rhythmically released the heavy bolt until the door pushed open. My companion, who had unsealed the vault-like place, encouraged me to lead the way, and I began to creep forward into a large dim chamber. No walls were visible, only piles of old boards and panels that covered the floor as far as I could see. There seemed no other way through the space but to step on the accumulation of material, which tipped and gave way slightly as we walked across it.

"Where are we?" I asked my companion as I hopped from one pile of boards to the next.

"I think you know," he answered, and we continued our slow progress across the lonely place in silence except for the soft clatter of our movement over mounds of dusty clutter. For quite a while, we traveled haltingly through the dismal scene, walking over and around the stacks of wooden panels as my concern continued to grow—but each of my few inquiries regarding our whereabouts received the same response; "I think you know."

It was a relief finally to see the hint of a wall in the distance, and we headed for it. I reached the wall first, following it to a corner where it met another wall, and I stopped there to await my friend and to investigate the hoards of drab material that filled the shadows. *"Dirty old stuff down in a vault—locked up where no one goes...."* The edge of one panel caught my eye—a bit of color in the consistent gray of its surroundings. I pulled the panel out into the half-light, then removed another from the stack, and another, carefully taking them out and turning them over. *"...wooden panels, laminate, stretched canvas...."*

"Hey! These are paintings!" I called out. "These are all paintings!" One by one, I continued unstacking and turning over panels; each of them filled with brightly painted patterns, figures, faces, and scenery. There were pieces by Matisse, Picasso, Renoir, and many others that I recognized as works by artists that I almost never consider; Egon Shiele, Emil Nolde, Käthe Kollwitz—all of that paint staring out at me. The Kollwitz work was under a large messy pile thrown against the wall. Shiele and Nolde's work wasn't far away. Every imaginable painter and period was represented, along with many works by artists that I didn't recognize—wonderful pictures leaning and heaped all over, down in a cellar where no one would see them. The more I looked the more I saw. I had walked over them. I was standing on them.

"Where is this place?" I said, too quietly to be heard.

"It's probably the bowels of a museum, a storage facility—but people should see these!" I often think *that* when I realize how much orphaned artwork museums keep out of sight, unworthy and unattended. I wondered how many small museums, galleries, and even homes could be filled by the inspiration being wasted there in the dark. *"This much art could change lives—even the world!"*

They seemed to speak to me, all on top of one another, like children who never get the chance, finally telling their tales. I looked down sadly at the pieces under my feet, but there was nowhere else to walk.

"This is a crime," I said. "Who did this? Please tell me where we are," I appealed as my companion approached. "We've got to tell someone—let someone know—get these out of here. Don't you realize how important this is? How much it's worth?" There were many pieces by well-known artists that showed something different about them; unrevealed tenderness, surprising playfulness, unexpected spirituality, the things that no one knows about them.

"Who would keep this hidden down here in such a mess?"

"But, you know this place," replied my guide softly. "In fact, you come here all the time."

"I do? I have never been here before." I stated.

"Of course you have. And yes—it's a crime, and the cost is unimaginable—to the people who leave these here and to the world. This is the place of doubt."

"Look!" I cried, both shocked and excited. "There's that scoundrel Gauguin's work, lots of it—and Vincent's—and Leonardo's—

"...all of these vivid ideas never to be known." I stood there feeling sick and confused.

"Much of this did not leave the studio," he continued. "You know about that—all painters do. Many of these were abandoned or ruined by the artists themselves. There is a whole area filled with images that were never painted at all, only dreamed of—with a large number of works by women and common laborers. A vast section on the other side is filled with art that was purposefully destroyed by others in fear and ignorance."

"Can they ever leave?" I asked.

"I am sorry. This is the only place that these exist," he answered. "They will never leave here."

Somehow, I procured a camera and spent the rest of the dream trying to figure out how to save the images—but there were too many and the light of the camera's flash made the pictures disappear. I imagine that writers might find that place filled with books and manuscripts, that musicians might hear unheard melodies, that others might find unexplored discoveries or great thoughts that have never been considered, but I saw unseen paintings and determined that, whatever it takes, my own work would be seen.

I awoke and checked the clock. *"About three hours again."* And as usual, I immediately told my wife everything, even how I had been aware during my dream that she was there beside me in bed unaware of where I was and what I was doing. *"Here we are,"* I thought. *"Two people, two wildly unapparent events happening side by side."* And I turned to watch her lying there not quite awake yet. Had she heard me?

I like to believe in things. I choose to believe, and get out of bed each day because I do, which feels a lot like loving someone—happening and unhappening until either I give up, or finally decide to push past my fears, desires and doubts. I kissed her a sleepy good morning on the cheek.

I think back, and this time it's the man who watches the little boy, standing guard over the young fireman, archeologist, paleontologist, violinist and doctor who decided to become an artist, a painter. I can see him standing there in front of Gauguin's Eve reading those questions in French up in the corner of the picture. It's strange to look back now and realize that, like the anticipated answers to his prayers, I am what he asked to be. I thought then of the dismal places I have taken him, the times I've felt like giving up.

"So, fear is what is unknown.*"*

"Though I'm not exactly Leonardo; am I who you saw?" I whisper. "Am I who you dreamed of becoming?"

"And desire is what I don't have.*"*

"Yes—I saw you, and you're still me," my heart responded.

And then I knew, "*…that all doubt is only self-doubt.*"

12
Free Falling

December 13 –"I have heard that angels fly, but I am just a toad—desperately wishing to grow wings."

I try to imagine my fat little friend, arms and legs spread wide in perfect belly-flop form, in midair, falling from the lip of a cliff up above toward the unknown below. I often feel like that while painting—rushing toward a finale that I can't quite see yet. Despite all of my carefully construed designs, I eventually come to realize each time that I am collaborating, becoming intimate with what is still a mystery.

"Geronimo!" we'd yell, as kids, leaping recklessly into comparable situations—tobogganing over embankments, jumping fifteen feet from a tree into fresh snow, or from a dock into deep water—heedless of the possibilities we refused to reflect upon—rolling boulders off the top of a high seawall to hear them explode on the rocks below, or running too fast, careening down a steep hill until our legs suddenly gave way. "Geronimo!" we hollered.

"How alike we are, the toad and I, both plunging blindly toward the inevitable and wishing to know the end from the start." But thoughts, images, and pigment assert themselves on the way. The outcome of my activity in the studio remains a murky hope until the moment I stop applying paint to a piece. It's like reading a book. While interacting with a story, sometimes a word, an idea, or a combination of things will start to shift. Reading one expression, I'll think of another and another and soon am released from the intended sequence of events—set adrift. Like tea leaves or coffee grounds left over in a cup, the type readjusts, scrambles, and melts into a blur as it settles to the bottom. Then, looking at one thing, I see something else. My eyes stop distinguishing the page. The plot disappears into a flow of associations and cabals. Things find resemblances to merge with, and I begin to read another story—not between the lines—but happening somewhere completely other than the volume in my lap. And so it happens in paint. Regardless of my attempts to own the product, a painting has its own life—but, like reading a good book, it's the seeing part of the process that I'm after.

Jheronimus Bosch, Jeronimo El Bosco was a see-er, a painter of visions and mysteries—of paradise and sensual delights, worlds on fire, chimeras, wayfarers, and flying toads—surprising views that loosen my tight grip on things. A lusty porcine abbess hoping to steal a kiss, a clay vessel sprouting legs spouts its insides—the suggestive form of bloated pink bagpipes, a blade sticking out between two tender ears, and naked lovers devouring ripe fruit from within—pictures all meant to confound and undo what I had once supposed. So I am caught unawares, like the wanderer strapped down beneath the pack he shoulders, stopping mid-stride, an accidental witness to the dramatic details of a strange countryside where nothing is just what it pretends to be.

In a dream, Nikola Tesla called me a vessel, and asked me to be more receptive, to open myself further to what he was waiting to offer. "Prepare yourself for more," he advised. "The work must go faster."

"But I study and write long hours every day. It has become my life. How can I do any more?" I reasoned.

"Let go," he replied. "Stop fearing and release all doubt."

"I'm trying," I said.

A man in gray robes and a floppy pie-shaped hat slowly shuffled toward me. "Here," he offered, pushing something forward. "Please take it." I was sure he meant no harm, but at first was reluctant. "Please. You know what it is," he continued. "And, you know what it contains, don't you?"

"I do," I surprised myself by answering. "It contains everything.

"All of it," I thought, wondering how I knew *that* and suddenly recalling an inventory of childhood treasures buried in a cookie tin. I stretched out my arms to receive the black container—a softly dimensioned cube that was not a cube at all—a vague object, a darkened apparatus, like an odd blocky radio without knobs, dials, or instrumentation.

"Now, put your hand in it," he gestured, pushing his own hand into the empty space in front of him. So I did. I reached slowly through the dim side of what seemed very dark and watched my hand disappear into the blankness of it.

It felt unexpectedly familiar—an amount of night sky, particles of light in motion on a blue-black field. I moved my hand, noticing the interaction of myself with the agitated and colliding specks. *"Like coming home,"* I thought, and the feeling of knowing grew, intimate recognition pouring into me to overflowing. I was touching, sensing—hearing and seeing everything—all at once, through my hand. "This is music," I heard myself as if speaking from far away—like all the possible notes and combinations of notes in the resonating belly of a shadowy violin, the whole in suspension, a universe of strange painted shapes—words, characters, and ideas—all floating through my fingers like little planets. "But I know all of this," I said. "Somehow, I have always known all of this." I saw the image of a forgotten spring of water in a wasteland, and little fish flashing back and forth around my ankles as I splashed along an imaginary shore. *"Like gazing into Mnemosyne's pool,"* I mused. *"So, knowing—is remembering."*

"And, it's been here all along…the source of life to this place." I repeated thoughtfully. The dream replayed itself several times until I awoke feeling full and satisfied.

Jheronimus Bosch, Jerome of the Woods, painter of dreams, images brought to life on the inner sides of eyelids. A hollow tree-man looks back at me accusingly—toads, like fig leaves, hide forbidden pleasures, and death waits at the door. A magic flute penetrates netherparts, a naked figure is strung taut across the strings of a harp, and a ship full of fools is about to set sail—like Orpheus descending to restore virtue; the reflected world of impulse first disarms and then pries open my other eyes.

Yesterday morning in a vivid dream, I listened to a beautiful woman speak of my paintings. "You are asking so much, and require preparation together with the audience you seek," she cautioned, speaking of my work and reassuring me of eventual success. "Your eagerness is ingenuous. Be patient. Just keep working, and the audience will come." She sounded direct, reasonable, and I believed her, feeling a certain closeness, perhaps as a boy might trust his mother to understand and be concerned with his optimal welfare.

This morning I awoke early again and wished to talk to the nice woman. *"If only I could meet the lady from yesterday, maybe I could find out who she is and speak with her more specifically about my paintings and about Tesla."* Then, I found myself in that neutral place walking toward a gentle-seeming woman. *"Perhaps she's a real person somewhere, dreaming about me as I dream of her."* She stood quietly at what might be described as a crossroads, like a guide or sentry posted there to answer questions or indicate the way. But, it wasn't the same person I had encountered yesterday. "Would it be possible to speak with Nikola Tesla this morning?" I asked as I approached. "Do you know where I can find him?" "You shouldn't worry so much about that," she answered. "He will meet you when you are ready. Continue on your way and you will have many chances to speak with Nikola Tesla." She smiled knowingly, and I felt ashamed for my needs, but otherwise satisfied that I would be seeing Nikola again sometime in the future.

After the two dreams, I have begun to appreciate the cultural desire for an Aphrodite or tender-hearted Madonna to intercede and take care of things, someone soft like my wife and strong like my mother. I think of the endless images of Aphrodite, from simple carved stones with vital parts but no extremities to Tiziano's Venus of Urbino, and Botticelli's heavenly apparition on half a scallop shell. And my many favorite Madonnas—the one by Cimabue, high on a fancy throne surrounded by eight angels and four prophets, or Raphael's coy Madonna of the Chair, and Ambrogio Lorenzetti's *Madonna del Latte* whose face I painted recently as a *commedia* mask. I grin, thinking of my unfinished painting of Mother Goose, and remember the yellow-faced postman's wife tending a cradle—the boy standing quietly in front of her, at the museum for the day with his mama. All of the Eves, gentle and great, *"the ones who gave to human nature so much nobility,"* looking back at me as I look at them—imagining myself coddled and indulged by so many willing Madonnas.

Citta' della Madonnina—Milan, Italy, is something between a real city and a village: home to a massive stone hedgehog of a cathedral, Il Cenacolo, the Brera, and good cheap *panzerotti* at Luini's—my lunch of choice. I was twenty when I lived there, part-boy-part-man, still losing baby fat and still surprised by the hair growing on my chest. It's been about thirty years since then—the bristling *duomo* has had a thorough cleaning and face-lift as has Il Cenacolo; but the Brera and Luini's have hardly changed at all. As an over-enthusiastic and naïve young American male, I found friends in spite of myself, so many eager Italian *mamme* and *nonne* trying to satisfy my bullish appetite for *risotto*, *ossobuco* or *cotolette*, and dessert. Among my Milanese friendships, two in particular have become more significant, only years after my departure, to the man whose furry chest is now gradually turning the same gray as the hair on his head.

One friend was a fragile woman in her eighties, and the other, an off-beat man-about-town in his seventies. The eighty-something lady wore layers of second-hand odds and ends and used a cane to get around. She lived in a hole of a flat, *un vero bucco* in a poor neighborhood, a single room on the ground floor without heat or toilet. My other friend always wore a beret and silk scarf or *foulard* and lived in a fashionable garret he called *La Bohème*, above the Galleria Vittorio Emmanuele in the stylish center of town. Both friends were painters, and had attended the Brera Accademy during youthful lives they spoke of wistfully and often.

When visiting my friend in her cramped quarters I took groceries—fresh fruit, vegetables, and greens from the *mercato*, meat from the *macellaio* down the street, a sweet from the *pasticceria*; all the things I knew she didn't usually get. I'd try to ignore her brief struggle with shame as she hesitantly accepted but delighted in my offering. Then I sat on her bed and listened as she recounted better times. "I know you'll think these too simple, but I used to paint other things," she apologized, indicating the little floral still lifes on scrounged pieces of wood and chipboard. "But, I can sell these on the sidewalk when I find frames. Don't you think a real Signora might hang one in her kitchen?" Sometimes we'd share a small meal of pasta she had prepared on a hotplate and sometimes not, but each time before I left, she'd pick up a battered guitar and sing to me—old songs, *canzoni popolari* that awakened memories. "…*torna donna ideale, tooornaaaaa…,*" she sang in tune. Her singing voice was surprisingly pleasant and strangely youthful, so it wasn't difficult to imagine a much younger woman serenading a *bel 'moroso* as the older woman closed her eyes and seemed to transform. To avoid seeing her tears, I remember staring at the window covered in plastic against the chill, and then at a few leggy plants tied up on sticks with bits of ribbon.

"*Al più presto,*" I'd say when leaving, taking her cold hand and giving her little kisses on both moist cheeks. "I'll return as soon as I can."

The life of my friend in *La Bohème* was completely different. When I visited, I'd bring my paints, brushes, and a canvas. He'd lend me an easel so we could paint together and talk—mostly about him. "I was a student of De Chirico," he rehearsed, and I nodded, impressed immediately by his confidence. "You know Giorgio De Chirico, don't you?" I looked out the window at the spires of the *duomo* and at the piazza below. "*De Chirico? Sì, certo,*" I half-lied, not quite as certain as I pretended to be. As we worked and talked, he sang lines from *La Bohème* and *Tosca*. The garret was a perfect set. Theatrical costumes and parts of costumes hung here and there on the walls, politely aged furnishings of worn leather, dark wood, and antique velvets and brocades created an atmosphere of old elegance and comfort.

"These are all beautiful," I said, inspecting a dramatic looking jacket hanging on a wooden peg. "*Sono bellissimi.* Do you collect them?"

"Look at this," he answered, "*Guarda qui,*" handing me a program from an opera and pointing at the page. "I used to sing in La Scala. Look—that's me there." I don't remember now whether he claimed to have been Rodolfo, Marcello, or Mario, but at the time it didn't matter.

"*Arrivederci. Ci vediamo,*" I'd say when leaving, giving him little kisses on both cheeks. "We'll see you later."

After these thirty years, my old friends in Milan are gone, but I look for evidence of them each time that I return. I study doors and windows in the poorer part of town, hoping for proof that my aged Mimì once lived there, and stare up at the windows on the top floor, to the left of the galleria, wishing for a glimpse of my dandy friend, the *pictor optimus*. "*But, I didn't really see them then either, did I?*" The precipitous lives of artists, reckless gamblers responding to impulse, fulfilled and unfulfilled, physical and metaphysical—pilgrims wandering down strange roads through strange countrysides on open-ended quests—I took it all for granted, waiting for the nudge of current nostalgia to help me see more clearly now what I couldn't see then, when they were there.

"Why did I take her food when I should have brought frames?" I ask myself, recalling Bosch's painting of a crucified lady. *"And maybe I could have brought both."* The pretty martyr in a red dress gazes toward heaven, stretched out on a cross in the middle of a crowd of male onlookers. Her accusers, on the one hand, watch and coldly point—but on the other, in place of the Marys, there are men who weep and faint at the sight of gentle Venus hanging there. Artists are illusionists, often painting one thing to suggest another, in the same way that some dreams seem like fantasies but uncover what is real.

Throughout my life, my dreamworld has often been the stage for tricksters. It was during a similar period of frequent dream events that I kept paper and pen beside my bed to record the names of my visitors each morning. There was a particular dream of a person with antlers who disturbed me so much that I told him to leave immediately. Recognizing my alarm, he explained that he had taken the cue for his appearance from the painted images in my studio, one in particular of an antlered man. "I am Black Elk," he said kindly. "I thought you might best see me in this way—but I will leave." I sensed his wisdom and let his intense tenderness fill me, hoping then that he might stay—but he left as I had asked, rising up into what seemed like a bright conduit receding through the ceiling of my bedroom into heaven. "Consider green as the background for that image you are wrestling with." And he was gone. The next morning I made the background Cobalt Green and finished the painting—wishing for his return.

"I think I'd like to be an artist," I said half-a-lifetime ago, hardly imagining what it would mean, and more sure today that

I still don't know. Experience outside the boundaries has taught me what it *doesn't* mean, but at a price, increasing the cost and the value of what I'm after.

This morning, after speaking with the pleasant guardian at the crossroads, I lost concentration—and the substance of the place quickly dissolved into average dreams of typically odd circumstances and props. A long awaited trip to Italy—my wife and I acting as chaperons to a group of students, assisting them to catch trains, stay off tracks, and follow schedules in and out of strange stations. *"Not my idea of Italy,"* I thought. *"Not with all these students to police. I'm glad it's just a dream."* Imaginary travels through cities I have never visited, silly concerns about my clothing being appropriate. *"Will they know that I'm American? Of course they will with all these overactive youth…but then, there are those swarms of noisy Italian school kids on endless field trips. Maybe they'll mistake me for a teacher? Perhaps from England or France?"* Then, to my complete dismay, I looked down and saw pajamas poking out from under my khaki cargo shorts. *"I guess I'm wearing shorts—not particularly Italian—and I don't own shorts like these anyway. Damn! They'll see these worn pajamas hanging down from under my pants and know that I'm really just dreaming."* I obsessed that someone might notice, so tried to hide the telltale pajamas, nervously tucking them up under the legs of my short pants. *"This is just a plain old enjoyable dream,"* I reminded myself. *"No one is interested in your shorts and tattered pajamas. No one here cares that you are really in bed asleep."* I made an effort then to calm down and indulge fully in the adventure.

In my dream of Italy last night, my concern was that some proper Milanese might stiffen at the sight of pajamas peeking out from my pants. In earlier dreams of my first grade classroom, it was the teacher asking me to do the unthinkable. "Take off your coat please," she said firmly. "We don't wear our coats in class, do we?" What she didn't know was that I had become aware upon arriving that somehow I had forgotten to put my clothes on underneath.

Recently, there were also dreams of giant snouty catfish, slimy devils escaped from a Bosch or Breugel nightmare nibbling off the scallions and gladiolas I had carefully planted around some sumps—recalling the squishy tussocks we used to hop on as children to avoid the dark mossy water as we made our way across swamps. The smell of skunk cabbage growing among the humps of spongy and unstable peat filled the air. *"How was I to know these pits are inhabited?"*

"Aah! There's the culprit!" I yelled, kicking him hard on a slippery gasping face with my foot in a black rubber flip-flop. *"Go a-way!"* Dreams, plain old dreams of the nonsensical type, effortless vacations from the stress of sensible life, are quite different from the place of mentors, guardians, and *heyokas* where I meet my friend Nikola Tesla.

"I'll change in here and be right back!" I called down the hall. "Don't worry. We'll make it to the station before the train leaves," I reassured, closing the door behind me. "I promise." I wondered what those kids were doing left alone and imagined their dangerous shortcuts across the tracks instead of using the safe *sottopassaggio*. *"Someone'll get hurt...."* The room I had entered was a tiled chamber, straight from the thirties or forties, small white ceramic hexagons on the floor with black tiles evenly-spaced between the white ones, the walls tiled half-way up and too many coats of paint above that—an old bathroom, a perfect place to lose the pajamas.

The vintage look, a white enameled cast-iron sink, a short half-window at shoulder height on my right, a gray view of the window well and a very limited patch of sky, a plate glass mirror over the sink to my left—it was a shadowy place, but not dark. In a rush, I removed my short pants and then my pajamas which I balled up and stuffed into a corner, then replaced my pants and tightened my belt. *"Check my hair now—those Italians!"* I leaned over the sink to look into the glass, and was startled not to see myself, but the black and white image of a Native American woman with a child at her side, both staring quietly back. After the initial shock, I realized that I had rushed in without warning and interrupted someone's view. *"They must be outside, looking in at themselves in the mirror."* I turned and sure enough, there they were. *"I better get outta here."* A little nervous, but pretending calm, I looked down to tuck in my shirt, then glanced up—and they were gone.

Reaching for the door knob, I stopped to think. *"This feels different from the funny dream of Italy waiting for me out there."* Coming into the old bathroom meant leaving the realm of telltale pajamas and entering another kind of place, a sober space where serious things happen. Perhaps it was that empty look on her face, or the child staring so silently. I pulled open the door and hurried out of the room, escaping back into the hallway where the crazy dream was still intact—the comical Italian sojourn with students at the station getting into mischief. "Be right there!"

I like the solemn nonsense part of being an artist, the invention of peculiar acts and situations worked out on grounds with pigments and binders—colors from curious origins held in place by seed oils, egg yolks, or tree saps—contriving views of in between, descents into limbos, visits to purgatories—as if to any street address—hells where monsters cook and eat the damned, and paradises where people holding hands can sing and dance with gods. Consider Leonardo's absurd portraits of grotesque toad-like beings, the scimian and mongrel features of men and women drawn in silhouette, the graphic counterparts to the Gioconda and other angelic faces. They all did it—Giotto, Fra' Angelico, Mantegna, Michelangelo, Arcimboldo, Bosch and Breughel, Gauguin, VanGogh, Renoir, Picasso—the Romans, the Egyptians and the cave men—all of them, serious scoundrels, provoking reflection by profoundly fooling around, "*O sant'asinità!*" stopping me dead in my tracks—clowns offering their eyeballs, to direct my eyes and make me look again.

"Aren't you coming?" called my wife from somewhere down the hall. "Is everything all right?"

One of my strengths and weaknesses is curiosity. I really wanted to close that door, lock it up tight to keep whatever was going on in there where it belonged—but I didn't. I *almost* closed the door, leaving it ajar so I could watch through the crack.

"Yeah, just a minute," I replied blankly. *"I want to know what happens when I'm not in there.*

"But the problem is—if the door is open, even just a bit—I am in there."

Thinking I could cheat anyway, I pulled the door toward me, narrowing the slit that I was spying through to the slightest of openings. Soon the mirror filled again with the image of an Indian woman, and I saw her outside looking in at herself through the small window. *"She's so still."* I noticed her chest gently rise and fall with her breath; and after a couple of minutes, she was gone. The mirror and window were empty for a short time before another woman took her place, partially in color this time with unnaturally red lips. The background was a feathery yellow ocher, textured like a photographer's painted backdrop, and the image—blurred on the edges like a photographic vignette. Then it faded and another mother and child appeared and disappeared, followed by another and another. Once in a while, one of them would move, a woman, or sometimes a child, raised a hand to brush something away or to straighten a piece of clothing. Otherwise they sat almost motionless, looking from the outside in at a reflection gazing back at them from the mirror across the little room. The pictures of women and children, appearing in even sequence, continued like a slide show—in the window, reflected in the mirror, and I watched it all through the crack in the door. *"These are pictures,"* I realized. *"Images—not real women."* Strange photographs, some of them hand-tinted, not unlike projections, but alive, conscious enough to seem intent on seeing themselves in the mirror, and to be aware of, and unconcerned with an observer from the other side of an almost closed door. After watching for a while, I became troubled. The shadowy realm of my *camera obscura* was seeping out into the hall like vapor through the narrow opening between the door and door jamb, unsettling the atmosphere of my funny Italian holiday. I hadn't tricked the system after all. Perhaps it's impossible to leave doors open just a bit, to peep at things without the effects being felt. In my dream, no matter how hard I tried, the door wouldn't close again. I couldn't stop the gradual contamination of one place with another, couldn't return to the comical dream of revealed pajamas, my wife, and the foolish students at a train station in Italy. The dusky world of the small room couldn't be stopped from finally flooding through an insignificant slit in an unclosed door. I ran down the hall and awoke, relieved to find myself in bed beside my wife.

"You've been mumbling in your sleep again," she said. "Is everything all right?"

In my studio I often sit and read, studying the associated pictures made by artists from the past. From my context, I try to pick up the threads of forgotten conversations, surprised to find them always current, ready, and waiting—Bosch's corrupted universe of strange *grilli*, Breughel's fallen angels, Angelico's beastly damned souls, the images of a pretty girl carrying her tender amputated tits sunny-side-up on a platter, the paintings of handsome youth stripped bare and stuck with arrows like a pin cushion—all the holy foolishness setting me adrift, still finding resemblances to merge with, scrambling my complacency, forcing me to readjust—until looking at one thing, I see another, the world disappearing into a flood of associations and hidden views. It's that seeing part I'm after. So, I look again, forever caught unawares, and the pilgrim has changed. A traveler, weighed down beneath the load he shoulders, stops mid-stream with a child on his back, a witness to the dramatic events of a civilized country where everything is as it should be.

"Hey! Hold still—and smile."
Once upon a time, I saw the world in black and white through the eye of a brown boxey camera—everything mirrored in its dark little chamber: our house in the woods; my dad in his pajama bottoms, sitting in the sun looking tired and resting against the scallop-shell back of a metal lawn chair; two skinny boys in a half-deflated wading pool—I sleepwalk through the pictures of my memories like a dream, conjuring up ghosts from half a life-time ago and musing on the strangeness that is so beautiful—a small Ukrainian baba with a wisp of moustache, an

old dog, faded images of trees, swamps, and fields of wildflowers that barely show up.

"Mamaaaaa—they're not holding still!"

In contrast to the typical snapshots of my inelegant childhood, the world has become more solid, a place of well-designed views where nothing is still—where things are literal, concrete, and without reflection—for their own sakes. The popular caricatures in magazines and on TV seem disconnected and self-absorbed, freed from the intangible concerns I wrestle with. How did the life of scraped knees and bloody noses become a biohazard? When did the most important picture begin to chart the bottom line? I have rehearsed and re-rehearsed the opening of that door to the old bathroom in my odd dream, my thoughtless entry into a place of shadowy possibilities that I left open just a crack. *"It was just a dream,"* I remind myself.

On the edge of a wooded countryside, at dusk, a traveler lies face down on his belly by a swamp. Eusebius Sophronius Hieronymous, St Jerome the translator, stripped half-bare and in the mud of an alien wilderness, embraces the symbol of his hope and prays. "Lord, show me mercy. Lighten my heart, for I was overcome on my way—wounded and left for dead."

"Me too!" I want to add. *"But it's just paint,"* I remind myself. *"A picture—an amount of pigment and oil carefully applied to a ground."*

Translation is the changing of one thing into another, one form into something else—the association of one view with possible others, putting into different words or interpreting in other languages—a way to explore the inside of things from the outside—the domain and gift of decoders, see-ers and artists. I imagine Jheronimus Bosch extending a brush deliberately toward a palette and charging it with color to work out the details of his namesake.

"It's unavoidable, isn't it? While plummeting toward an unseen end, that we should open other eyes?"

13
The Infinite Degrees of Santa Claus

December 19 – I lay awake and listened to the house breathe and creak in the dark. *"Today, I'll speak with my friend,"* I thought, glancing up at the sky and noting the stars in all their usual places. I closed my eyes again, in order to relax and find that neutral space, anxiously expecting to meet Nikola Tesla. It's strange to think of going somewhere without ever getting out of bed. *"Do I know where I'm going—if I'm going anywhere?"* Not really. But the temptation, sometimes verging on need, is always there—a lot like the persistent desire to make elusive things appear in the studio. Only now, I'm using words instead of pigment to deliver my visions—and more apparently, these dreams seem to be giving life to *me*.

"I'd like to see Nikola Tesla." I spoke into the stillness. "I think it's time for another lecture," I called out, not talking to anyone in particular, just the hollow stage-like place, as if T – E – S – L – A were something I could dial in or call up. Maybe I was praying, asking God again. It's just what I did.

"Oh, there you are," I said, feeling at once like a pest and perhaps a bit presumptuous. Nikola Tesla, or someone I assumed was Tesla, stood with his back to me, directly across a large dim office—dressed again as I had first seen him, in a dated gray suit with subtle chalk lines.

"Hey! I'm here!" I said too eagerly.

He was silhouetted, a dusky shape in front of a bright many-paned grid of opaque glass, facing what looked like the window of an old factory or warehouse. I watched his shadowy form against the light, and awaited a reply.

"Hello?" I offered. "Are we going to have a lesson this morning?"

No answer.

"He's probably thinking about something, but I'm sure that's him—Come on, at least acknowledge my presence."

Abruptly, emphatically, and without turning, he spoke. "If two things exist, and one is above the other—there are even greater things above them both." I felt it go right through me, entering my mind and heart directly, happening *to* me and *in* me, more an event than a simple phrase. I scrambled to understand, assuming there was more, but he remained quiet and I continued to stare at his back impatiently.

"Nothing else?" I asked after a while.

He slowly and distinctly repeated what he had said, while still facing away from me, and I became concerned. "Is that all?" Beginning to fear that I had landed somewhere other than where I wanted to be. "Are you Nikola Tesla?"

> *"If two things exist,*
> *and one*
> *is above the other —*
> *there are greater things above them both.*

"Study it. Know it. Then, come back and report to me."

"*An assignment—business.*" In spite of his self-assurance, Tesla often seems protective of his solitude. *"So, perhaps he doesn't expect my fondness. I'm sure he feels my emotional attachment, my sometimes dependence, and I have to admit that I've not been very good so far at following up on his requests or accomplishing the tasks that he has given. Then, that's self-centered—maybe he is busy, preoccupied, anxious about something else? After all, who am I to be offended by Nikola Tesla?"* Although our interaction has been satisfying, I don't think these dreams are only about my wishes. I wondered how my pleasure had become an issue at all and began to view him more compassionately—standing there alone, aloof, and definitely less interested in performing than he had been. *"I guess he's just feeling distant this morning.*

"Sure," I responded. "I'll study it. I'll read something about that today."

"Dynamism, dynamo, dynamic—dynamism, dynamo, dynamic—dynamism, dynamo…," three words repeating over and over in the background. *"I've never heard or used the term* dynamism *before,"* I realized, suddenly recalling an incident in Rome some years ago—"*Gesù, Maria, Giuseppe—Gesù, Maria, Giuseppe—Gesù, Maria…,*" repeated the prune-faced *nonna* sitting on the curb with her feet in the gutter. She was tired of standing, so sat down where she found herself and waited for the bus to arrive. "*Gesù, Maria, Giuseppe—Gesù, Maria, Giuseppe—Gesù…,*" she prayed over and over in the background, seeming invisible, while the traffic and people passed. "Dynamism, dynamo, dynamic—dynamism, dynamo, dynamic…," repeated rhythmically and inconspicuously enough that I hadn't noticed it.

I was also waiting at the bus stop, carrying two chocolate napoleons home in fancy wrapping tied with string. I had taken a bus across town to be alone and think, with the excuse of buying pastries at my favorite pastry shop. "*Gesù, Maria, Giuseppe—Gesù, Maria, Giuseppe—Gesù, Maria*...Dynamic—dynamism, dynamo, dynamic—dynamism, dynamo...." I looked down at the funny old lady dressed in black, then at my package. "*Due paste*," I said, opening the deluxe little bundle and sitting beside her on the curb. "*Io, ne mangio una. Volete l'altra Signora?*" We both sat and ate napoleons invisibly, getting puff paste and buttercream all over ourselves. "Dynamism, dynamo, dynamic...."

"*Dynamism* is a state of force, energy or innate possibility, being elementary to everything," stated a voice clearly but quietly. "A basic principle that you should become familiar with."

"*Dynamo*," I repeated silently and saw turbines spinning—the intercessors between one kind of energy and another.

"Dynamic—energetic; causing action, or change." I rehearsed.

A large wheel from a cart or wagon appeared and I became aware of the mysterious nature of the place at the bottom of its circumference where it met the ground. I watched the point, which never moved from its position, but led to the next point of contact between the wheel's perimeter and the soil. The procession of those points of contact enabled the forward movement of the wheel, and I wondered how resistance produced progress. "No reaction—no traction," stated someone I couldn't see. The wheel advanced, but the point at the bottom remained in place. I noted that the axis at the center of the wheel also remained stable, as what was up or down, on one side or the other, regularly exchanged positions as it gained momentum. I watched the revolving form interact with its surroundings, throwing off spiraling responses. *"Like the arms of galaxies,"* I imagined. It always seems surprising, that in my dreams, I should experience simple things in such intense ways—though I have no practical knowledge of them. *"That I can be so awake when I am asleep,"* and I awoke considering all of this, along with Nikola's suggestive statement.

During the day I felt refreshed, inspired; new life breathed into me, thoroughly animating my thinking—as if prompted by something outside myself. *"The discussion of greater and lesser possibility suggests comparison, implicit potential, or degrees."* In considering the nature of degrees, general opposition or complementary response came to mind, as *"what is dynamic naturally suggests action and includes counteraction of some kind."* The inner discussions of a little voice kept me busy, keeping track and recording thoughts. *"Degrees—like steps in endless progression, phases, ranges, levels, a series, stages of development, branches on a tree, rungs on a ladder, links in a chain...."* The miracle of Tesla's simple quotation began to fill me with awe, suggesting the ideas of structure, rhythm, process, counting, and basic numbering systems. It reminded me of the importance of patterns in seeing and organizing what is *out there*—points of view, stations along the way, states of being, the infinite levels of awareness, heavens, and hells—*"one above the other and greater things above them...higher, lower, within, without, bigger, smaller, brighter, dimmer—the many simple associations that I've depended on without understanding"*—all implied by the fundamental idea of comparison and the relationships between greater and lesser things.

When I walked into the baptistery of Siena's *duomo*, I was startled by the impact of the cavernous vault covered in frescoed patterns, alive with busy colors vibrating all around me—a poor scoundrel suddenly stepping into an overabundant universe. I have felt the same in many places; the Scrovegni chapel, the Brancacci chapel in Santa Maria del Carmine, beneath a sky-full of stars, in a stand of aspen trees awakened by an unexpected breeze, or sailing in the afternoon sunlight on a flamboyant Penobscot Bay—the events that seem to hold me, that cause me to feel that I'm floating again in the boughs of a pine tree, up above a sea of treetops—where I can disappear and become a child again at the edge of everywhere. "Hey! Can you hear that?" I asked my wife, humming softly until the entire belly of the baptistery dome began to resonate the tone and then throb with the reverberations of the particular note that seemed to set it off. I like that. It's how I feel when I paint—happily lost in the echoing patterns that set things off, at the brink, the threshold of somewhere much bigger than my studio.

"King me!" I shouted, smiling. He had let me win again. I knew it, but was more than happy to play along. I stared down at the checkerboard, captive to the simple pattern, the easy dark and light of two worlds touching but never meeting. "You're getting pretty good," said my dad grimly, and I believed him even knowing that he hadn't really tried. *"But, of course I am pretty good,"* I thought. I remember my cousin teaching me to play chess, but to me, it was played on a *checker*board—the place my dad and I pretended to meet on equal terms. The city-smell of taxicabs—of bodies, ashtrays, and aftershave; *a scacchi* in Italian, checkered like a chessboard, the tabletop domain of old men and cafés, the realm of grimy marble floors *a quadretti* in the mens rooms of train stations—then, in school, I played games on a torus, on a klein bottle, and other exotic checkered spaces—but it all still reminds me of home, the regular patterned board, and my dad. "King me!' my own son shouted, smiling. "Daaaa– ddeee?" I had let him win again and he knew it.

"*That something so obvious should keep so many secrets,*" I wonder now. "*A common visible pattern hiding so many uncommon and un-seeable things.*"

Dragonflies and diamonds—I broke it down into basic elements and measured their relationships before lightly drawing a grid on the panel. Red striped thoraxes, four simplified outstretched wings, black polka dot eyes, and the odd crossed diamond motifs—I had seen it several years before in a book, the pattern on a woman's dress in Ambrogio Lorenzetti's famous fresco, The Effects of Good Government in the Town and Countryside. So I traveled to Siena to see it for myself in the Palazzo Pubblico—and there she was, in a line of dancing ladies hooking little fingers and snaking through the street to the accompaniment of a singer with a tambourine. Later, back in the studio, I lay the book open on my paint cart to help me carefully plot the parts on the intersections of the grid.

The little voice kept me constant company throughout the day with intoxicating assessments of what Tesla had said. "*In the flow of things there is a tendency toward rest, but always on the verge of activity. So, what exists is dynamic, innately endowed with the possibility of reflected states, the action of one associating with the rhythm of the other.*"

"*Relaxing and contracting—the lub-dub of the cosmos,*" I thought then in response, feeling rather smart.

Some patterns are as forthright as a checkerboard; others, such as the pattern of dragonflies and diamonds, are less candid; while others, I learn to see by degrees, step by step, like climbing through the branches of a tree, until reaching the place where things open up and a view of the whole sky and countryside appears. It's interesting that what is un-seeable becomes apparent to me only as I am prepared. *"Are the patterns still there when I can't see them?"* Or does a pattern's appearance—as I'm able to associate, to count and qualify its pieces—signal its existence?

"Oh! It's that cat in the box story again…."

"Just don't try to explain anything," my brother said hastily. "That morphic field stuff is a lotta bunk anyway. You'll sound stupid."

"Well, so much for his quantum tales—

"I'm not that stupid!" I replied. *"I only feel stupid sometimes."*

All day long I entertained a crowd of thoughts begging for words; suggestions about the dynamic nature of things, the degrees of seeing and not seeing, ideas of things being and not being, and the many facsimiles of the wheel—the obvious *yin* and *yang*, barely separated by a wandering path between; medicine wheels with roads crossing in the middle; and circles of monolithic stones watching the sky spin around. I thought of hypocephali and their peculiar sun faces, of the dung beetle's brainy progress rolling balls of excrement across the desert. On my way home, I watched car tires spinning along the highway, spellbound by the common miracle, and imagined myself a dervish, whirling like a top in the middle of an expanding sphere, then disappearing into a collapsing point at its center. "I only feel stupid sometimes," I muttered, chuckling at myself. *"Yeah. Today began* there—*somewhere between asleep and awake, with a few terse words from a dream named Nikola Tesla."*

I like to paint patterns, especially the ones I borrow from historical artists. For weeks it feels like living with Duccio, Simone Martini,

Ambrogio Lorenzetti, or Fra Angelico, touching something they have touched, thinking thoughts and making plans with them, like being an apprentice for a time to someone centuries ago. I like training my impatient self patiently and repeatedly to give up, step by step, to something else—to something as humble as a checkerboard. Eventually the audience sees the pattern, the paint, sometimes without imagining the painstaking process. "Painting these patterns becomes a meditation and I have seen Nirvana," I recently told someone. "And it looks just like hell!" I added, laughing. Little by little, following patterns helps me to see, releasing me by degree into increasing levels of awareness, revealing secrets that otherwise remain un-seeable—the kinds of things that are only known by repeatedly being and doing them.

"All of this—from such little things," I mused, getting closer to examine the skin of the cathedral interior; the domed roof, arches, walls, and floors—made smooth with small tiles. A long time ago, someone had put each *tessera* carefully in place, one at a time. *"They look like scales,"* I thought, walking slowly backward from the wall into the interior of the church as I watched the rows and columns of tiny squares disappear into an articulate vision of God and the apostles. *"It must have been invisible to the artists who worked so close that all of this was just a hope."* I've learned a lot from mosaicists about persistence, patterns, and points of view—discovering once again that seeing happens conditionally, from up close where things fit neatly on a grid, to far away where the big picture is clearer and the structure of the whole begins to show. I stopped backing up and began to approach the wall slowly until the images began to vibrate again, agitated by the network of separations between single tiles—and I stood there for a while, where both possibilities appeared at once, the entire

vision tickled by the sight of its small pieces.

When things aren't obvious enough, there are some people who prefer to believe in stories; others, whose degree of understanding is built on hard facts; and still others, whose hearts suggest to them that there is more to see beyond a veil of current limitations. *"How much still remains invisible?"* I often ask myself while working on the minute details of a painting. *"How many un-seeable paths cross my own well-worn tracks?"* I wonder when I'm feeling alone and unable to discern clearly what is just a hope. *"Is it possible to see beyond my automatic responses?"*

When I was about seven years old, things were easier to figure out. It was getting close to Christmas, and we were as excited as ever with the prospects of presents and the impending visit of that magical fat man. Of course there were smarter children in our neighborhood who didn't believe, who told us that their parents had told them the truth—that it was all fantasy, that Santa was a story. Obviously, we knew that they were wrong. We knew and believed that St Nick would arrive late Christmas Eve in a sleigh pulled by flying reindeer, and that given the chance; our parents would probably fill our stockings with coal. Anyway, no one really knew. No one had seen anything, one way or the other, as we were all asleep when it happened.

"There he is! Look! There! Don't you see his sleigh? Up there! You can just barely make out the reindeer in front...."

"Yes, I see it—at least I think I do. But it's hard." I answered.

So, that Christmas, being seven years old and in the second grade, I realized that if Santa was really just my parents, he, or rather they, would have to have hidden the gifts somewhere—and I went exploring. The top shelves in the pantry? The shed in the back yard? The back of their closet? And, the last most scary place to look was the cellar. The damp smell, the cool closeness, and all those sooty cobwebs hanging—we, the kids, never went into the cellar. So I decided then, by logical deduction, that it was the most likely place to find hidden presents, the place I didn't dare look.

One afternoon while my mother was out doing errands, I decided I'd venture into the darkness beneath our old house. Slowly, I opened the door and descended the bare squeaky boards that were the cellar stairs, petrified of what I might find down there, other than presents. The furnace made those awful thumps and grunts as I quietly took each step, carefully checking above and below for imagined spider attacks. Finally, at the bottom of the stairs I turned and reached out into the emptiness, caught and pulled the chain attached to the fixture and bare light-bulb hanging in the middle of the room. *"Nothing. Nothing! Nope, no presents here!"* And I spun around and left as quickly as I could, tearing up the stairs, and then—as I turned to close the door behind me, I noticed what I hadn't seen on the way down in the dark, that above me—high up over the stairs—on the shelf—were presents, *the* presents.

But, that is the enlightened story that I tell now. What's odd is that I didn't see them then. That day when I first went down into the dark, I came back sure that there were no gifts hidden anywhere in the cellar, reinforcing my steadfast desire to believe. I didn't see the presents at that time. As I turned to close the door behind me, and glanced up at the shelf, I saw nothing. I didn't see the presents stacked on the shelf until a few years later, after understanding more fully the true nature of Santa's life. It was then that I saw what I was looking for, what I couldn't see while staring straight at them. Suddenly I remembered, and there they were. Then, in my twenties, I looked and saw more than just the packages; I saw my parents' love. Later, as a young parent, I looked and saw struggles and sacrifice on top of that. And, while that shelf is still a mystery in some ways, I've learned to have faith in its magic—though it doesn't happen how the smart neighbor kids or I once thought. The presents had remained invisible until my experience and understanding grew to include their possibility. The real miracle and potential is that the shelf in the cellar continues to fill with gifts today, so many things that I can hardly imagine—before I learn to see them.

"The infinite ways of knowing Santa Claus—which one I choose, and when I've seen enough...I guess that's up to me."

Not too long ago, I painted a snake—every single scale of its skin. *"There's a whole world inside each scale,"* I realized while working one evening. *"The colors and shape that describe its place within a pattern, the light and shadow on its smooth surface—I could spend a week on one of them.*

"It'll be my secret anyway," I thought, slowly backing up into the middle of the studio.

14
Touching the Veil

December 23 – My paintings are sedimentary, the residual evidence of activity on and around a substrate of hardboard or laminated wood. They happen in layers; layers of life and preparation, layers of intent, layers of paint, layers of painting, layers of meaning to myself and to an audience, and finally, layers of a painting's prospective history. There are often upwards of twenty layers of paint that combine to become any image in the studio. Each layer represents a specific stage in the evolution of a painting, and a point of view specific to the period of its application. Not that each layer isn't significant to the whole, but that each happens within the boundaries of conditions particular to, and most relevant to, its creation.

I mark life by paintings and the activities of painting. "Yeah, that happened when I was applying that layer of dark glaze to the forest," or "the day I was blending that huge sky behind those trees." Daily events, thoughts, and emotions also affect my work. "I just feel like painting red today," or I'm being grumpy about something and "I'm gonna scrape that all off!" So, layers of material that may appear to end at the edges of an image actually extend well beyond the panel. A painting is just the visible cue to a much larger scene, a limited view of something possibly limitless.

I awoke at four again this morning, in *that place*—if waking is what it is, and if that is a place—whatever and wherever, it's increasingly familiar—old hat. I hung around for a while, wondering what to do and where to go from there. Then someone began to speak.

"Gotta remember this." I realized immediately, repeating and re-repeating what was being said. A lot of it had to do with Tesla's terse quotation of a few days ago about greater and lesser things. Pondering that, and a few related ideas, seemed to initiate the rest of the dream.

We stood side by side where we had been before, at the edge, the boundary of my conscious awareness, beyond which was nothing, at least nothing of which I was aware. Nikola Tesla led me through our lesson this morning with systematic questioning, eliciting my responses, which in turn led to more questions. The back and forth process went on the entire time, stressing and repeating specific ideas, helping me discover things without needing to be told. Before leaving, he quizzed me once again, guiding me through the same material to make sure that I had understood.

"Do you recognize this place?"

I saw that we were at the border of a flat expanse that spread out behind us, an ordered landscape of grid patterns similar to others we had seen before, as well as some that I've worked on in the studio. In front of us, everything was dim.

"Yes." I said, silently recalling my initial feelings, poised there at the brink of myself, gently humbled, and disoriented. "This is the limit of my conscious ability to organize." I looked out into an emptiness that appeared to have no end, fearing my own unknown, and studying what I had no ability to sense in any other way than confusion.

"Possibilities," I thought, *"possibilities can mean anything."*

"Your conscious awareness is tied to experience and your associative abilities, your memory. You are you in any and all dimensions, despite the small part of you that may be apparent from any distinct viewpoint. We are standing here on what seems to be a patterned plane—but it is much more than that. From earlier discussions, you already know that we are actually in it and surrounded by it, as it is within and surrounded by us. This view represents an intersection or crossroads, which like yourself, is an abbreviated picture for the purpose of current understanding, but does not represent how things really are."

Nikola then spoke my name, waiting for a few dramatic moments before continuing. "Is it possible to remember what you have not yet experienced?"

"Remember what I haven't experienced?" I slid my hand slowly back through my hair and across the top of my scalp until it hooked around the occipital curve of my head and stopped there (as if that might help me to think). *"Can I remember what I haven't experienced?"* He knew I had no clear answer, but the idea was lodged and wouldn't let go. The question revealed as much as it concealed. The inquiry itself was a clue, but posed a hundred more questions, each of them suggesting at least a hundred more. "I don't think I understand the question," I answered.

That's often how a painting starts; sitting or standing, head in hand, propped on a fist with an elbow on a knee or on the other arm braced against my chest—gazing intently at nothing, with lots and lots of questions.

"Let's talk about that void out there," he said, indicating where my attention was still drawn, to what I had at one point, during another lecture, understood as chaos, and then as *unorganized material*. "What is out there?" he asked—another question that I felt stick and not let go.

"Again, he's making a proposal by asking a question. Obviously he doesn't want to hear that there's nothing *out there."*
"There must be something…just something I don't know or recognize, and so can't make sense of it," I guessed.
"The gift of the senses…," he began.
"But, they're so limited," I broke in, while continuing to concentrate on the void.
"Yes, the physical senses pertain to a range of physical things, the conditions particular to a limited point of view; but there are finer senses and finer matter than that."

Using traditional painting materials makes me feel a little like the man in Bruegel's brown ink drawing of an occult chemist in his workshop with crucibles, flasks, and fire (a wife hoping to sneak coins from his empty purse and children seeking food in an empty cupboard). Painting is all about the lure of transmuting plain old stuff into treasure, earthy materials into unearthly masterpieces; a peculiar undertaking, given the cost.

Before putting paint on a panel, I drag a thin coat of rabbit skin glue across it with a wide knife. The glue is made by boiling animal connective tissue, bones, and cartilage in order to release the gelatinous collagen. I buy it already made, in dried sheets or granules that I soak in water and re-dissolve with gentle heat. When cooled, it turns to thick jelly—so to apply it in liquid form, it must be kept warm. Fish glue, hoof and bone glue, hide glue, rabbit skin glue—the use of adhesives made from animal hides and byproducts goes back thousands of years. The Egyptians used it to hold furniture together; Antonio Stradivari used it to stick musical instruments together; Mantegna, Bruegel and others mixed it with pigments to paint with; and I use it in tempera and oil painting to protect an underlying support from the acidic effects of paint, to isolate and seal what is vulnerable from the impact of its future.

"How then do you recognize things? How do they become experience?" he asked.

"Is experience memory?" I answered with another question, quickly reviewing what I remembered from one of our discussions. "Experience is memory," I stated more emphatically. "Mnemonics, you asked me to think about mnemonics. This is about mnemonics, isn't it?"

"So, how do you remember things?" he inquired, calling me by name again. "How do you become consciously aware of something you now see only as blankness, something you don't recognize?"

Painting in layers allows me to grow with an image, to limit my direct activity to each step in the process, to consider its role, and pay attention to its influence upon the developing picture. After a thin layer of glue, I apply several layers of ground; a chalky base-paint made of calcium carbonate and pigment bound together with glue, oil, or acrylic emulsion.

In the excitement of beginning, anything seems possible. I'm so eager to see something show up that at times I'll add grit, or string, or seal other materials into the *gesso* to establish textures and underlying shapes. In the case of my Gidu's hat, I embedded a flattened dead snake in the foundation layers to show up later as a fossil "feather" under the paint, a secret only those who get up close will see, which even then in its new context, might not look like what it is—or was.

"What do you see out there?" he asked, still pointing into nowhere.

"I don't know," I said flatly. "What I haven't experienced yet? Things that don't relate to what I *do* know—stuff I don't remember because I have nothing to relate it to?" I was guessing again. "I don't see anything."

"That which is only possible becomes potential, then probable…," he started.

"…and eventually, must become experience and memory," I continued. *"Relate it to—I'm blind without something to relate it to…"* Again, I thought of our lesson of a few days ago and the strange passage about the relationships between things. *"…the simple associations I've depended on without understanding."*

Paint is the pasty relationship of pigments and binders. Pigments are the powdered form of colors that originate everywhere, from various clays and minerals (like Umbers, Ochers, Pozzuoli Earth, Lapis Blue, and Malachite Green) to organic compounds (like Carmine, Indian Yellow, and Asphaltum), and chemical compositions (like Chromium Oxide, Cadmium Red and Cobalt Yellow). The binders hold or glue the pigments together to make them applicable and durable on a ground. I like to work on a good solid surface, something that lets me get a little rough when I want to; sanding, scratching, digging, and scraping the paint—but sometimes I also enjoy romancing the material—adding enough oil and medium to make the paint smooth and velvety, to meeken brush marks that would otherwise be raised and sharp. I'll use soft brushes to blend wet color into wet color, or my fingers to smear and massage the paint tenderly onto the painting.

"Before it is potential, it's possibility. The void, chaos, the blankness—all of that unorganized material is possibility, isn't it?

"The discussion of greater and lesser possibility suggests comparison, potential…or degrees.

"And there must be degrees of possibility and potential." Nikola seemed satisfied at my conjecturing and I could have been self-conscious, but I didn't care.

"If two things exist and there is one above the other, there are greater things above them both."

Suddenly everything felt *all-at-once*—my thoughts rushing at me in a blur. *"Potential is a condition of unexpressed power…a state of imminent energy…innately charged…even hereditary.*

"Possibility," I reiterated. "It's not potential until *I* enter the picture."

Then comes my crazy *imprimatura*; then the *grisaille* underpainting, the composition; and then the color, the scumbles, and glazes. After every stage and in between, I step back to consider each unique layer and its relationship to the imagined outcome, so that I can make corrections and adjustments along the way to a final image that still only lives in my mind's eye.

"What is experience? And how does it happen?" asked Tesla, interrupting my speculations and restating the question. "How do you remember things?"

"Things I experience become real as I relate or associate them with other things I have experienced. Is that it?" I wondered about the very first time I painted a painting, drew a picture, or made a mark, and then recalled the first earthly breath of each of my children. "There's so much that I don't see!" I thought of the invisible gifts on a shelf above the cellar stairs of my childhood home. "As well as things that I choose not to see."

Everything points to something else, which points to something else, and something else—all drawing in, lassoed and tied, slowly pulling together until it's one whole thing. I examine what it is, taking it apart again piece by piece, until everything is exposed in a funny kind of jumble that leads everywhere— and then it starts over. Everything points to something else…. Sometimes I feel so overwhelmed by our discussion that it's difficult to stay in a dream without being tempted to turn over in the middle of it and start babbling to my wife. I want her to know—want to take her there. "Nikola, I'd like to introduce my wife…." I wish it were possible. "And, this is my good friend…." I guess that's why I'm writing it down, with the hope of including someone else who'll find it intriguing—as I do.

Unexpectedly, my vision began to blur. I blinked. The crisp edge of the plane we stood on was dissolving. I took a step back and turned to see the patterns all around us growing hazy. The indistinct nature of what was usually peripheral seemed to be spreading like a fog across the checkered landscape—as if some of the shadow from *out there* had crept into our tidy world, contaminating what was measured and clear with what was murky and unsure. Nikola seemed unmoved by the changes.

"How do you perceive and identify things?" he asked calmly.

It was difficult to tell whether my eyesight or the dream was becoming cloudy. I blinked hard and squeezed my eyelids shut before opening them again. "There must be holes everywhere," I said finally, watching the sharply focused shapes continue to get fuzzy. "It's like a sponge. Things becoming real must also be filled with uncertainty, spaces in between—dynamic because it's ongoing and hazy because it's forever incomplete." I had avoided answering the question directly, and thought about the other planes, and webs of filaments, the intersecting patterns we had seen during earlier discussions, and of the space in between that I had asked about. "There must be degrees of knowing and remembering. The process of becoming aware, seeing patterns and relationships where there was nothing—it happens a little at a time, like waking up."

At the beginning of each day in the studio, I sit and look, re-inspecting the work from yesterday, trying to think back to where I was in the process. *"Oh, I remember. I painted on those clouds yesterday, and put a glaze on the trees."* I think there's something about the uncertainty of it, the fog, the mystery of filling in blanks that are never completely filled—that's why I paint.

"So, is *real* based on my experience?" I looked at Nikola for acknowledgement, but he was still. "It's like Adam and Eve," I thought aloud. "To eat the apple or not to eat it—the act of choosing, the process of deciding, releasing them by degree from a state of inexperience into a state of remembering."

Work in the studio is all about remembering. Images happening in pigments and glues, the flesh and blood proof of my experience—separate layers of perceiving, isolated in time, but ultimately viewed together. I paint stories; visible riddles about associations, comparisons, context, and relevance—layers and layers of remembering and almost remembering things. It's the hardest thing I know how to do—so I paint.

"Of course, there are solid and pragmatic aspects to what you are exploring," he answered my thinking. "They lived in an environment of endless possibility before the opposition instigated a situation, introduced a dilemma, creating an obstacle and facilitating the development of potential—just as there are positive and negative charges whose potential you recognize as real and practical."

I looked out into the emptiness and at the softening lines of our surroundings. Without realizing it, I had been led through a response to Tesla's questions. We were discussing the generative principles of organizing what was unorganized, the conceiving and subsequent dividing of initial states, the establishment of powerful new unities and subsequent distinguishing of new complements. It had been there all along in the layers of a simple story and I hadn't seen it.

"They were enlightened by experiencing the dual nature of things," added Tesla.

Other than our voices, it was silent—there at the edge of my awareness. "That's how it happens," I responded. "It's a pattern. We do it all the time, don't we?" I imagined a bent little man high on a scaffold, painting a heroic couple on a chapel ceiling—breathing life into plaster and pigment. "Without the artist, ingredients are just ingredients." I thought then of resonance and the feeling of first-time familiarity, as when I heard strange music resulting from the harmonic relationships between parent vibrations and wondered if I had already heard it somewhere. "I think I get it." I looked at Nikola for approval. "It's unorganized out there, not unknowable—it's not *nothing*. It isn't really blank is it? It's just *before*."

"Yes, *before*. Time…time is another pattern, another practical measure." It seemed to have caught him off guard. "So then, how do you look beyond a current point of view into what you cannot see? Can you remember what you have not yet experienced?" I took a deep breath and returned to feeling slow and simple again. "Those mnemonics." he offered. "You were right. This is about mnemonics. From what we have discussed already, would they not be a way to access the rest of a pattern?" And I saw the beguilingly simple watch face that held the past, present and future.

"Mnemonic devices," I thought, recalling my son's question of several months ago—"What's a mnemonic device?"

"Are they like symbols?" I asked.

"Well, from one point of view, symbols are like mnemonics—and mnemonics can be symbolic. Symbols work by association, like magical telescopes to look out there and shed some light on what is dim, to explore what you have no way of sensing otherwise. Remember, your physical senses are limited. Metaphors—symbols, signs, similitudes, and mnemonics act as thresholds that lead outside the boundaries of your experience."

"This is such a big dream, and I am just me," I reminded myself, relaxing my shoulders and letting out my breath. *"Yeah, I like to paint symbols because they seem to hint at things beyond the limitations of my little experience."*

"A symbol is layered," Tesla began, "layers and layers of meaning seen on the surface as one thing. Symbols point past the edges of the picture, while a mnemonic is a representative model or piece of a pattern, a token through which the vast unseen portion can be accessed." He seemed content. "And—it is not a mistake that you paint symbols and patterns, thus no mistake that I am teaching you."

"Then, everything is a pattern, isn't it? Symbols, mnemonics, the words I speak—and me, my awareness and experiences; all on this side of the boundary instead of out there because we're parts of a pattern. I recognize things because I see patterns." It all seemed to make sense.

"Everything we have discussed is about patterns and vibrations—frequencies," stated Tesla. "It is about light."

"Light?" Now, I was caught off guard.

"Everything is light," he reiterated.

Of course, paintings are all about light, the way light hits a painted surface and makes its way through the effects of each layer finally to reach the ground and be reflected back. I can't help remembering the small piece of broken mirror that I treasured as a boy, the odd-shaped little pool of silver that reflected the whole world, even things I couldn't see from where I sat. For me, paintings are like that. Working in layers allows me to separate the form from the colors, to limit my focus to an amount that I can grasp at one time. The first layer is the basis and establishes the framework. It's the underlying pattern that the rest of the picture is measured by during the process of painting. The subsequent layers can be transparent, opaque, semi-opaque, dense with pigment, cloudy and turbid, subtly tinted, thick or thin; sharpening, softening, coloring and otherwise impacting past layers and influencing the future layers, that I will apply. Each pigment affects light in a particular way; absorbing, interfering, diffusing—even the blackest of blacks can be altered by seeing it through a veil of something else. The completed painting is the collapsed view, the visual perceiving of light that has traveled through the boundaries of each successive layer to be mirrored back, identified as shapes, shades, and hues, and finally recognized. "That cloud looks like a crocodile." To me, the wonder is to see so many things; forms, colors, ideas, images, times and events, joined to make one picture, and for me to play the god of that small world.

"*Light.*" I thought of the light on our meadow as a boy, the light in the woods and on the sea, the light before and after rainstorms, the light in the museum on Monet's haystacks, Italian light on David's white marble skin, the light from a colored window on the anguished but enlightened Adam and Eve on a chapel wall in Florence, and the light in my studio falling on my own version of Masaccio's vision. I thought of the lists I keep of pictures that I intend to paint someday and of the enlightenment I'll need—of course, paintings are all about light.

"So, the garden is the stage and those are the roles. Everything is based on that pattern. That's the story." I began to rehearse what I had gathered from our discussion. "I've inherited awareness from *them*." Nikola smiled patiently and let me speak.

"And, oh yes—everything is about light.

"And, can I remember what I haven't experienced?

"And—I am next to nothing," I concluded, disheartened by how much there was to understand.

"If you change a symbol, it will change the point of view," he went on, seeming to ignore my talk. "Alter a mnemonic and it becomes part of something else. Truth is a gift from experience beyond your own and is available by degree, as your heart is prepared."

It's hard to describe how small and insignificant I felt, considering all of what is beyond my own experience.

"I want you to think of light as being alive," added Tesla.

"It's alive?"

"Light is alive. It is a living thing," said Tesla clearly, so there could be no mistake. "What you call light is just the visible part of a much larger picture. The rainbow of colors that you recognize and paint with is a finite view of something infinite. To understand these limitations, consider a painting, cut through and turned to reveal its layers rather than its face to you. From examining the bands of its stratification you might see and understand a lot that would be hidden or difficult to discern from a frontal view of the image. Seeing a cross-section would better suggest the process of making the painting. We could even describe the layers of paint as a timeline of the artist's activity."

"Typically, I select a support and prepare it with several layers of a particular ground. The ground is sanded smooth before a colorful imprimatura is smeared on. Following the drying of the imprimatura, the surface is sanded smooth again. Then, I paint the grisaille foundation of the image...."

"There are before and after activities," he continued, "that are outside the visible range of the layered timeline, things we can assume from what we see—so while it is helpful for exploring some details, from this point of view the largest part of the painting is invisible, including the image itself. Based on what we are able to see from this viewpoint, we have only the faintest idea of what the painting might look like from its true perspective. Without opening other eyes, we must base our understanding of the unseen forms and colors that make up the painting's composition on what little evidence we see on the edge; otherwise, it remains impossible to see the big picture."

"You mean, without symbols and mnemonics?"

"Yes—among other things," he replied. "Light is everywhere. It is in everything; emitted, transmitted, and reflected; we are in it, and surrounded by it, as it is within and surrounded by us; we ourselves are light, but all you can see is a very small part of it. Even the darkest darkness must be considered in relation to light. It enlivens the universe and yet you have no real picture, no complete view of light, just a little cross-section, a banded diagram based on the amount that is visible to you."

"That's—without using other eyes," I suggested.

"While the form changes, light is everlasting," he went on. "From a viewpoint measured in time and events, like the cut-away view of a painting's layers, there is no way to see what is everlasting, only an abbreviated picture for the purpose of current understanding that does not represent how things really are."

"And, now you're starting to sound like an artist," I warned.

We walked together. I'm not sure how far, only that we walked an uncertain distance (that's how dreams are sometimes) until we approached a thin barrier quite different from the hazy boundary we left behind us. I could feel it ahead before I could see it—a faint familiarity, as if I had been that way before. Like the interface between two liquids that don't mix, it extended in an endless filmy glow, to either side and above us until it disappeared into the distance. We walked until we stood close enough that I could inspect and touch it if I wanted to.

"Do you recognize this place?"

"No—and yes," I felt my throat tighten around the words. "It's a separation between my world and somewhere else." Without thinking, I reached out my hand and slipped it through what parted around my wrist like a sudden tear in a sheer curtain, feeling past the strange confine into another place. *"Like what separates two layers of paint,"* I thought—but what I felt wasn't anything I could have expected. *Terrifyingly wonderful* comes to mind now as I try to put it down accurately, but it's more precise to write that it's something that can't be spoken; I can't describe it at all. "This is enough!" I cried, turning away from Nikola Tesla. "We have to stop now!"

"But, you can go farther if you would like. You can step through," invited Nikola. "And, you can return, because I am here."

"No—I can't," not knowing whether I felt joy or sadness, only that all of my emotions seemed to be happening at once. I was desperately torn, wanting to step through to somewhere else and know for sure what was there, but lacking the courage to do so. "Thanks, but not yet. I'll come back when I'm not afraid. I can't hold any more. I'm tired."

"It was wonderful!" I managed to whisper hoarsely, turning over to face the window before she could see my emotion. "Are you OK?" asked my wife. "Yeah, I'm fine," I lied. She played in my messy hair with her fingers. "Are you sure?" I wished she could have been there with me. "Of course I am." How could I tell her that I had been to the veil and touched its fabric, that I knew it was possible to reach through to something—sometime—somewhere else? It's hard to speak about, without fearing that I'll diminish it in some way, without worrying about who believes me. "Tell me about your dream," she said softly.

Writing this, I am again overwhelmed with the mood of this morning's event. *"Is it possible?"* I have asked myself repeatedly. The realization that I have no answers is a good answer. Somehow, admitting that I know less and less of what there is to know is a comforting burden, much less of a burden than to think my limited point of view is comprehensive.

In my garden, there's a short classical-looking column of molded cement that's gradually aging, by now growing lichen as it awaits the right birdbath that I have never found. I imagine the correct bowl there and birds on hot summer days splashing in its water. To me, I can already see it, catching the green light of late afternoon filtering through the leaves above, part of a picture of my perfect garden that I have daydreamed so many times. In my heart, I've wondered at myself, watched my liquid reflection wiggle on the mirror of its contents while stooping to look into the bowl of water, at its surface and what's below, one world superimposed upon the other. Sometimes I try to see both places at once, my smiling mercurial counterpart, and the fluid scene beneath his glittery face—but that's difficult, as I lose something of each when the pictures mix. In my mind, I've studied it, this peripheral place that isn't quite there, reflecting things that are. Finally, finding the right basin and putting it in place will only make it real to the birds who haven't spotted it yet, and to others who haven't dreamed of it, who don't see what I do, who only see an old half-pillar in my yard without a birdbath.

Several years ago I painted the image of a bird on a branch bent close to the surface of a pond. The bird stared down to watch a fish who had stopped under the branch to ponder the shadowy image above looking down at him. I'm going to paint it again I've decided, only this time the bird will be even closer to the water as if to whisper to the fish drawn even closer to the surface in order to listen more intently.

"How many unseen layers can there be?" I wonder, peering into the reflections that stretch and move on the surface of my dreamy pool. *"So many layers to peel away!"* I gaze down at the top of a short cement column in my garden and wait for the veil to part.

15
Like a Tangle of Something (How It Is)

My friend, at last you've bathed! Your heart's been expurgated of all that bad stuff.
You look respectable, and your back's finally clean.
Your (ahem!) part is totally disinfected.
(Nope, nothing's been left untouched.)
And, you've been sanitized from every bit of hanky panky you ever did or didn't do—or even thought of doing.
May no one forget your name, old friend.
You'll be safe here—undisturbed, until we all rise again someday. OK?

I pray someone's there to let you in when you arrive.
And, wherever it is, I hope you're happy.
But—I do want you to go to heaven.
Y'know…where you'll be with God and everyone—
living forever.
It'll be great! You'll get to see with your eyes and hear with your ears again—chat with friends, and walk around.
You'll wake up every day and see the sun.
And, no one'll lie to you.

Imagine! You can put on airs—just like you're young again.

*The Lord knows! You've got a good heart anyway.
(Golly! I feel like you're right here looking at me!)*

May your soul live forever and ever, pal.

(From *A Scoundrel's Book of the Dead*)

December 26 – A boy stood quietly by the side of a dark stone sarcophagus and looked into the two strange eyes that seemed knowingly to return his gaze—but actually stared somewhere far beyond the dirty face and worn play clothes. He had just finished reading about the man who opened Tutankhamun's tomb—and he was daydreaming. *"All that treasure!"* And the sarcophagus, with layers and layers of coffins and linens. *"All those layers!"* he marveled, *"before they got to King Tut!"*

My mother told me that the dead used those eyes to see out of the sarcophagus. Of course, they weren't real eyes, just painted on or carved in, but they always seemed more animate than I thought they should, more penetrating, wisely witnessing the world around them come and go. *"Even with no one in there."* So, each time we went to the museum, I'd try to figure them out, curious about what they saw and how they saw anything at all. Then, at home I practiced drawing them—but of course, no matter how exact they were, my copies were never as serene and smart as those eyes in the museum.

Before I decided to become an artist, I dreamed of archeology. I thought about it, read books about it, and watched the Stooges make mischief of it on TV. Then at night, sometimes I'd dream of digging in the sand to find lost tombs filled with treasure, sarcophagi, and mummies. But Egypt was far away, so instead, my brothers and I were happy to explore the woods for Indian graves. "I think we located another burial ground," I'd announce resolutely at the supper table. "And we've begun digging."

"I found a bone!" someone bragged.

"Really?" exclaimed my mother with polite intensity.

"Well—I hope—you brought—the shovels back," my dad would warn between mouthfuls, as *the boys* exchanged concerned glances.

It's an open secret that, for centuries, painters used mummies to imbue their work with actuality, like primitive mystics animating images with bits of magical substances inherent with divine significance and power. From the sixteenth to the twentieth century, Egypt Brown, or Mummy Brown, was a favorite warm dark pigment for glazing and shadows. Its composition was complex. The mummy—desiccated skin, hair, flesh, bones, and linen wrappings—rich in the preservative materials of embalming, solidified oils, resins (such as myrrh), and bitumen (bitumen is *mumiya* in Arabic)—was ground to fine powder before being blended with oils and made into paint.

Lately, I've been wondering about the material of dreams, the imagined pictures, fantastic ideas, and events that seem so real that they find meaning, often manifesting themselves in ways that go beyond what I expect; the virtual so easily becoming confused with the actuality of my life. Like the materials and activity of painting, it's mostly a problem of language, as what I paint is not often what I see, but a translation. Ideally, there's one meaning, while just the outward form changes. If that's even possible?

Mummy Brown—a favorite of Romantics, tight-lipped

painters, and secret brotherhoods, the clumsy hermetic trick of artists. "Millais, Rossetti, Delecroix, Gericault, and others—What darkness is it that engulfs that sinking raft? Could that eye really contain an eye? That severed head a severed head? Is her pretty hair made of recycled flesh and fingernails?"

"And I'm content with Bitumen Lake, Kassel Earth and Vandyke Brown."

So—they were resurrected, the power of life in a paintbrush—or, is it that thinking so makes it so? Like the transubstantive hocus-pocus of making one thing into another, while it appears the same. "Why, they burn 'em in locomotives—three thousand years old—by the ton!" quipped Sam Clemens to Nikola Tesla one evening. Virtual and actual, actual and virtual—in fact, I've stopped seeing any difference.

"Do you think I'm going nuts?" I asked a friend recently after telling him about my secret visitor and confessing some concerns.

"Well, you don't seem crazy. Not yet," he answered. "But I guarantee you—I would be, if I were you."

"Nikola Tesla? Couldn't Miss Drews have mentioned him in ninth grade science? Or was it tenth?" What is fiction anyway? To me, my dreams seem no less real than waking life.

Umbra (oom' bra) is the Latin word for shadow, as well as an English term for total shade or the place where no direct light arrives from a source of illumination. Some artists paint a shadowy background to make the foreground appear, painting the *umbra* first to establish the forms and composition that will support the image. Leonardo was famous for his dramatic use of shadow to create the illusion of glowing reality, influencing many other painters, like Giorgione, and eventually Caravaggio, and Rembrandt.

In a place caught somewhere between Bellini and DaVinci, a tired old gentleman, a sweet-faced boy and a graceful young man are gathered around a sheet of music. "Pay attention, son. Listen to your good teacher," suggests the handsome man. But the boy is elsewhere, his eyes unfocused, considering things other than singing. "You see what I deal with?" grunts the old man, grimly enlisting my sympathy. "The coddled kids of pretty cavaliers." The three men emerge out of shadow—the consuming fire of maturity, with gleaming scalp, the sagging image of heavy eyes, and overgrown nose and ears; the androgynous virtue of boyhood, tended by women, to be initiated by men; the appealing silhouette of vital manhood dressed in earthy green and gold.

Any number of plots are obvious:

> It's the skillful reenactment of a secret conversation between secret conversations, the implied association of three hidden worlds.
> Life is portrayed in degrees of awareness and the relationship of innocence to intellect.
> Wisdom seeks acknowledgment that physical beauty is not the model guide of youth.
> God the Father, dressed in scarlet robes, sent his son to teach inattentive students.
> An ideal man indicates the true nature of everything to a childlike audience.
> A father speaks of age to his young son.
> The artist bends life head to tail.

> It's just a singing lesson.
> It's a clever arrangement of lines, shapes and colors.

It's only pigments and binders applied to a piece of wood. It's simple; light hits an obstacle and is reflected back.

But then, I have learned that even *that* is a conceptualization, a limited description of things I can't see. *"What determines how real things are?"* I ponder my own reflection—somewhere between tired and vital. *"How do I measure uncertainty?"* I've always wanted the image to be by Giorgione, but no one knows for sure. *"I can't even know who painted it."* I remember watching costumed performers behind a puppet theatre putting on a Punch and Judy show, and the public in their everyday costumes and roles sitting in front to be entertained. *"Can there be innate knowledge without awareness of it?"* Reenacting, acting, being—at times, the boundaries get blurry. *"Can I remember what I have not yet experienced?"* I ask myself. *"If I am all-at-once and everywhere, how is it that I so quickly forget things?"*

"Oh! Don't be silly!" responds my over-cautious brain.

"And, what does time look like—head-on?" I have seen the painting in the Pitti many times (over the Ponte Vecchio and past the little church that hides my favorite Pontormo), but today, I study a printed reproduction of The Singing Lesson in a book. *"Is time solid or fluid? Woven like a fabric? Or more like a tangle of something?"* I think of the hopeful Egyptians being reincarnated as paint. *"Maybe it's better to be a little blind."*

There has always been magic associated with seeing things beyond the limitations of our physical eyes, and mystery surrounding the materials that make those visions appear; hidden color sources, rare pigments, and secret recipes. Umber is a natural earth pigment ranging from yellow to cool dark brown. Colored earth pigments, like Umbers and Ochers, are generally rust-stained clay containing silica and iron-oxide, which in the case of Umber, also contains manganese-oxide. Prehistoric artists simply slapped a hand covered in red mud on a cave wall to leave an imprint, or spit pigment into place around a hand to leave its ghostly form—or may have used plant fiber "brushes" to apply earth colors mixed with water, saliva, blood, or other natural binders. The same pigments used to make pictures on cave walls have been used to make likenesses throughout history and are traditional colors on a painter's palette. The colored clay is dug, washed, and ground fine, before being mixed with binders to make paint. As a typical pigment in *grisaille* underpainting, Umber is still used for shading, as it was in prehistory, to create the *chiaroscuro* impression of dimensional realism.

Shortly after *I* do, and without seeing me, a person across the room reluctantly opens his mouth and we yawn wide in unison. Like an expanding ripple on a quiet pond, I watch a wave of yawns crest across the hall, return and gradually subside as the last of us finish yawning. The kids are all wearing sixties stuff again and talk of Tesla is suddenly turning up everywhere. *"Do thoughts make ripples? Do they echo like yawns? And what of dreams?"* I look back at my art book, at a picture of three ages of men—elder, youth and adult—converging around a sheet of musical notations. *"Do dreams resonate—like music?"*

Once, I stood in the desert on the brink of nothing for hours and yelled across a wide red-rock canyon, listening for the ticklish effect of my voice returning again and again. As a memory, the scene still replays clearly whenever I think of red-rock deserts, echoes, or autumn hikes with friends. Another time, I lay on my belly watching a line of ants parade across a miniature landscape of boulders, towers, and dry washes, only to look up at the red-rocks around me and be surprised that I am also just an ant. Similarly, in dreams and paintings, it's easy to lose track of scale—to think I'm bigger or smaller than I am, feeling a bit important because of what I'm experiencing, and insignificant compared to what there is to experience.

    Bone Black is another pigment commonly used in establishing the *chiaroscuro* basis of a painting. To make Bone Black—first, fill a crucible with the osseous parts of animals: pieces of bone, horn, or scrap ivory. Then, cover it tightly, but not so tightly that smoke cannot escape the vessel, and place it in the middle of a fire of burning coals. It should remain in the fire until no more visible fumes escape and the more vulnerable and temporary material has burned away, leaving only the carbonaceous matter to be ground, washed and turned into black pigment. Or, of course you can buy Bone Black paint in tubes as I do, already made, in large impersonal batches from a modern facility. But then, it's also easy while painting, to forget that I am participating in an ongoing process, retransforming the elemental material of one kind of life into another.

    Before visiting the Cemetery of the Capuchins in Rome, I expected an antique charnel house of horrors containing the macabre remains of four thousand defunct friars. After all, that's what it is. But instead, like a dream, stimulating the fanciful visions of my conscious and unconscious self, the garlands of knuckles and vertebrae, an osseous clock, and the bony framework of arched crypts for sleeping brothers wearing the clothes they wore in life, created a virtual world that was surprisingly less ephemeral than the actual one in which I live. What was transitory and corruptible had been carefully cleared away, leaving only the essential vessels of experience.

"We were once where you are now," warned a cheery fleshless figure in the second cave-like chapel, while studying me with empty sockets. In a state of reverie and abstraction, I thought of the woods back home and my childhood Eden, of Botticelli's playful paradise—the places where time seems irrelevant. I had entered an underground stage and set where four thousand players wanted to discuss with me frankly what it means to be human—the production was a sensual event, the artful rearranging of old things into new, a complex narrative—and I made it four thousand and one. A child's clean frame, stuck up on the ceiling of the last chapel, carrying a bony scythe and scales of justice, flew above me in judgment—and I was not horrified.

I have always liked the perspective that happens when ideas retain a sense of instinct—before they're correct. Suddenly, I had the strange sensation of my bones supporting the weight of my own flesh and pushing out against my skin in places. "Yes, I think we're quite alike," I answered as I passed the same devout fellow on my way out, unsure whether time had lost or found a context there, where everything seemed so immediate. I think that's what makes traveling to unfamiliar places so intriguing, the possibility of meeting myself each time as someone new and different, the candid snapshot of a process, never too certain of whom and what I'm capable of becoming.

There are images that surprise and overtake me, and ideas that almost taste good, smells that inspire unexpected surges of nostalgia, things that ring true—rumbling through me like the swell of distant thunder, remembered confidences that reiterate themselves to my heart like reruns of private events that I struggle to remember. *"I've been here before—haven't I?"* There are things that I just have to do. *"I'm not sure why, but...."* And, there are forebodings, the premonitions that happen and change my plans. *"I have a funny feeling...."* And instant infatuations, the sudden friendships with people that I'm sure I've known before. *"Do I know you?"*

One winter evening in Milan as the sun was setting, while walking from Piazza del Duomo toward Porta Ticinese and my shabby apartment, I wandered into a gray stone church hoping to find some warmth there. I wondered how the church had escaped my attention, and noting at once that it was as cold and gray inside as out, I soon turned to leave. As if on cue, a choir of monks began to sing vespers and a column of dusky-orange light fell from a high window to make a bright patch on the previously darkened floor. So I stopped to listen to the peculiar harmonies, the even drone of men's voices in perfect unison echoing through the cold chapel. The vapor of their joined breathing hung around them in a haze as their evening cantata seemed to warm the church and me. The music rose and fell in waves. It washed through me, feeling gently amplified inside me, humming in my face, purring in my gut, legs, and arms down to my toes and fingertips. *"That something as hard as stone can be softened...,"* I thought, looking around the dull cavern for possible others sharing the experience, *"...by something unseen."* There was no one. I continued listening until I lost track of time—until the last reverberation was abruptly swallowed by the cold, and the last ray of sunlight filtered down through a colored glass window. With bowed heads, the men quietly filed out through a door in the back. The gray returned. And I left.

When I am truly awake, life is dreamlike. Or, I can awaken into dreams that are lifelike. In the studio, I sit and dream until the work wakes up inside me, and then I paint. Like painting, both waking life and dreaming are adaptive kinds of adventures. Familiar and unfamiliar combinations of things send me to the palette repeatedly for comparisons and complements—inner and outer, befores and afters, heres and theres. In life, I often work on several paintings at once, associating the parts, juxtaposing events, applying memories like opaque and transparent veils of paint one over the other—creating context, hoping to identify myself somewhere in the process. *"See! It is me!"* Now, as I recall that evening in Milan, so many other times come to mind: a dusty column of sunlight briefly excited by a child's curious hand, the night sky in motion, the imagined lullabies of La Berceuse, an unknown choir singing in the Pantheon, carols in a tabernacle in Salt Lake City, reading poetry aloud under Hamblin Arch, and my son playing slow tunes on the cello. Painting helps me sort it all out, to free the ensuing picture from what isn't important—to get a good look at things in passing. *"Can I remember what I have not yet experienced?"* I ask myself once again.

Yesterday, I was angry and swore at God (not that God is affected by my small curses). "Dammit, Lord! Why does life have to be like this?" Just the usual. This morning, I *awoke* into my dream place, not to speak with my friend Nikola, but hoping to find some peace, to think about things—find some place to disappear. I suppose I could have gone to the studio and painted, but I'm too visible there. Even in my dream world, someone came to talk to me and I pretended not to hear until he went away. Eventually, there comes a time, after the darks, that the underpainting begs for white. After a basis is established in shape and shadow, a source of light enlivens it.

Usually, before I start working on the highlights of a *grisaille* image, the places where the light is more pronounced, I put a thin milky layer over the whole painting. A semi-transparent film of white helps diffuse the intensity of the dark composition. I apply it with my hands, carefully controlling the opacity of the layer in spots by altering the pressure of my palm and fingertips. Later, I'll come back and reestablish the dark and deepest shadows, but for me, a thin veil of white is the decisive separation between the two voices. At that point, the darkest considerations are over, although the back and forth discussion between darks and lights may happen for a while before the monochrome underpainting is ready for color; first, the shadowy assertion of form, then, the response of light, before the application of color—shadow, light, color; shadow, light, color; shadow, light, color—a cycle of deliberations that continues until I'm satisfied that my work on an image is complete.

Snowflake White is one of the oldest man-made pigments, dating back to ancient Egypt and Greece. It was the most common white pigment used in painting until the twentieth century. The method of manufacturing Flake White or Lead White has always been similar; metallic lead, *plumbum*, is placed in or very close to vinegar, and the two kept warm by the decomposition of organic material. Originally, lead jars were filled with vinegar, then buried in rotting dung until the lead disintegrated into white powder, transforming what was heavy into what is light. Later, the manufacturing process changed while the basics remained the same; lead coils were placed in earthenware pots with an amount of vinegar (acetic acid) in the bottom; the pots were then stacked in the vicinity of manure until the action of acetic acid vapor, carbon dioxide (a by-product of decomposing material) and the heat of decomposition converted the lead into white lead carbonate. The lead carbonate was then washed, to remove salt and acid residue, before being ground into fine artists' pigment.

While the darker pigments of the *chiaroscuro* underpainting are relatively benign, traditional Snowflake White is toxic. Lead poisoning has accompanied the use of lead-based white pigment since ancient times, with unhealthy levels of lead found in Egyptian mummies and lead poisoning documented in ancient Greece. Stomach pain, anemia, weakness, joint pain and swelling, irritability, insanity, and possible death—artists throughout history regularly wet their brushes in their mouths to bring the bristles to a nice point, and applied paint with their hands through which lead is easily absorbed into the body (I wear latex surgical gloves to apply paint with my hands). So, as well as being one of the oldest man-made pigments, Lead White is also one of the oldest chemical toxins.

Darker pigments, lighter pigments, colored powders, and binders are the basic elements of paint, but what strange matter makes up the rest of a painting? The part that isn't seen? The part that isn't paint? The part that's more dream-like? What transforms earthy stuff into heavenly, base into fine? What part is *the art*? The need to know is why I paint. Dreaming is another matter. I'm not sure why I dream, what it's made of—or what initiated this recent chain of strange events.

But, like a painting, I'll see it through until I'm satisfied—though pictures are rarely ever finished—they're ongoing. Completing a painting is only choosing a point to suspend the discussion for a while, that's all.

This morning, I stayed in my dream for what seemed a long time, alone, paying close attention to the experience—the small vibrations humming all over; first, like a charge; then, like a warm current passing through me with more or less intensity. *"Yes, this is how it always feels."* It happened in waves and sudden peaks, depending on my clumsy attempt at controlling or resisting it, from pleasant inner stirring to physical shakes and little shock-like tremors. And, time is different there—as if by speeding up, things slow down so I can feel them more fully. I'm always surprised by the amount of time Tesla and I are together. It's relative to the event, rather than to an applied measurement—which happens when I wake up and check the clock. *"Wow! That was only three hours?"* Or, *"Over three hours? It felt more like ten minutes!"* Light and its sources are also different in dreams, seen from the inside out, emanating from everywhere and in everything. For instance, I have never seen a dream light bulb. Light is pervasive there, though sometimes, like this morning, there are sudden flashes or the light seems more expressive. I think of it as the binder, together with my mindful attention, the medium that holds my dreams together— like the mixtures of oils, resins and spirits, or egg yolks and water, the syrupy plasma that I blend with pigments and paints to shape a world of pictures. In dreams, my senses are both sharper and more subtle. The inside tunes in while the outside turns down. The result is that when I'm awake, I feel more awake. My senses have a new edge. It's something I understand from my work— after I've been painting for a while on the elements of a pattern, things often change in much the same way, even when I leave the studio. Everything resonates with the work in the studio. And the world turns on slightly, though I'm sure that it's just me finally paying attention.

 I meet people in my dreams who are alive in different ways than I am, not dead, not less material, but different—less heavily in one place. Of course, there's Tesla; and there are other guides and mentors, most of whom I've come to recognize; and still others whom I have interacted with once or twice without knowing their names. I've learned that while they seem so free, they have limitations—as there is work they must rely on me to do because of my current material status. At times now, during the day, I become aware of someone close-by, wanting my attention, speaking to me as they do—inside, which can be disorienting and leave me feeling oddly between places.

A couple of years ago, on a visit to the convent of San Marco in Florence, a poet friend and I felt the resonance of the place. As we spoke softly together in one of the monk's cells, our voices gently rising and falling in conversation, we noticed that once in a while, we could speak in such a way that our sounds would amplify, touching both the room and our insides. A word would suddenly reverberate; echo and re-echo at such a rate, and in such a way, that we heard the hum of our voices unexpectedly magnified. Though I felt it all over me, I put my hand down on my belly to explore the vibration that seemed pronounced in my gut.

"Can you feel that?" I whispered, asking the obvious.

"Of course I can," he intoned, hitting a particular note that made everything resonate with his voice.

Consciously then, we began to investigate the place with our talk, making waves of words repeatedly reach notes that changed things momentarily, until we were almost singing or chanting our communication. I noticed that it was at those brief moments of transition, between muted sound and resonance, that I felt most moved by the effects of the experience.

Yesterday, I watched my dog dreaming—asleep on the rug, face twitching, legs and paws jerking at a run. I pictured her out in a meadow playing nip-and-chase with dog friends. *"Who does she meet there?"* Or, maybe tagging along with a boy chasing butterflies. *"Which of her lives is most real?"* " Soft yips and growls signaled satisfaction. *"And, can she know the difference?"* Today, I'm in the studio and she is stretched out comfortably at my feet, snoring. In my case, to know something but not know enough is a liability, as it's too easy to assume that a current view is all there is to see, like the controlled image of myself that I tend to protect. I scan the room, stopping to appreciate a wheeled cart piled high with tubes of color and other exotic materials. Traditionally, Carmine was made from the bodies of female cochineal insects; Indian Yellow, from the dried urine of dehydrated cows fed on only mango leaves; and genuine Ultramarine Blue, precious lapis lazuli imported from over the sea, *oltre il mare*, ground and mixed with wax before being worked in a bath of lye; Egyptian Blue, remaining bright for thousands of years; Madder, from certain boiled roots; shades of Verdigris, from copper oxidized with vinegar, urine, and honey—I love paints and the secrets they contain. *"But then, she's a dog and doesn't choose the limitations of what she'll consider."* And the oils—linseed, boiled and sun-thickened, poppy seed and nut oils; the turpentines; damar gum in lumps waiting to be dissolved into varnish; mastic tears; waxes; glues and siccatives—bare and prepared panels; framed paintings and paintings to be painted over; stretcher bars; canvas and linens; and all the papers, pens, and pencils—art books and articles; all the props; shells, insects, leaves, and bird wings—stacks and stacks of stuff, my roomful of extravagant junk. *"Painting really is a strange thing to do.* (And I'm pleased.) *It is."*

I'm just beginning to understand how much the practice of painting has shaped me—and my life. My passionate attention to old pictures made of bones and poison, cow pee, precious stones and insects, perhaps a bit of someone's arm or leg; my constant consideration of values and colors; becoming increasingly fluent in the nature of associating things; participation in the subtle craft of teasing the invisible into view—finally, I'm starting to see the world I live in, the picture beyond the edges of the painted panel, and recognize myself as the image of my work. In the same way, the process of dreaming these dreams over the last several months has changed me—has become *a work* of sorts. And while I'm not sure of the mechanics of it yet, I am the object of its influence. I have realized that I am becoming the dream that I am dreaming.

16
Line and Circle

December 27 – "So—talk to me about resonance."

Nikola half smiled and said nothing. In apparent response to my request, a series of cords or strings began to appear, strung vertically, one after the other stretching across the space in front of me. I immediately thought of harp strings, but was told that they were actually warp on what I imagined must be an extremely large loom. I watched quietly, compelled, as the rhythmical advance of strings continued, one by one, in succession, lining up across the horizon.

In the process of weaving, the warp is the foundation or matrix, the initial strings or yarns that run lengthwise in a fabric, and to which the weft is added. The warp can be a solid color and texture—or it can be random, or happen in a linear order, such as in the regular sequence of warp colors that occur in checks or plaids. The final design or pattern is finished by the weft, which is woven in and out across the warp from selvage to selvage. After the warping of the giant loom was complete, extending from one side to the other with vertical strings, I began to think about the weft and the ways it could affect the disposition of what was already in place. I imagined the many potential patterns that might result from the possible ordered series of ins and outs, reminding me of those grid-like patterns I had seen with Tesla over a month before. I glanced at Nikola, who seemed intent on watching me. Somehow, I suspected that the colors and design of the weft would be added in a different way, and that my ability to experience it was being weighed.

Early one morning I awoke to the sound of rapping or knocking. *"Where's that coming from?"*

"The intervals—pay attention to the intervals," someone answered.

"You mean the silence—the in between part of the rhythm?" And the rapping stopped.

Establishing a pattern in paint, like the one I borrowed from an early Duccio Madonna, or the marbly interpretation from the bottom of an annunciation, means deciding which part of the pattern will be painted first. Will I start with what *is* or what is in between? Often it is easier to see the structure by determining *what is not*, so I start by painting one place to make the other appear. Early on, it becomes clear that what I had first taken for *what is not*—is, and *what was* has transformed into *what is not*. I have come to realize that even one mark on a panel, the smallest amount of paint, manifests equally the rest of the space—as a mnemonic suggests the whole of its universe. In fact, the process of organizing the material into counterparts begins before I touch a brush to the ground. So I reconsidered the warp, not just the emergence of the strings themselves, but in this case, the regular intervals in between—understanding that *what is not* is equally vital to the creation of any pattern. By the time the first string had appeared, the rest was imminent. An order was established. I watched the warp strings impatiently, just as I often sit and gaze at paint in the studio, eager to see the next step in the process.

As if unseen hands had begun to weave, the warp strings began to move. Seeing them against the dark in between spaces made it easy to detect the slightest motion. I decided that it was the action of an invisible weft being woven in. One by one, I saw the strings respond, each in a particular way—stretching, then returning or snapping back to an original position, as if being plucked. This left some of them vibrating—again reminding me of harp strings. And like music, there seemed to be a sequence to the display, beginning with individual strings, then progressing in waves along the arrangement of warp. Specific movement seemed related first to the quality of each vertical string, before an indication of its position in the larger horizontal series was evident. As each string of the warp was acted upon, it responded, initiating the sympathetic reaction of other strings. I watched it over and over again—starting small, like an off-handed comment sparking rumors, then spreading like gossip down the line of warp, to kindle lots of little incendiary conversations. Eventually, the actions and interactions became increasingly complex and I lost track of simple associations in a storm of activity.

The correspondent conditions between strings were not only visible—some were audible—and some strings had other relationships, which I could sense, but have no words for. The interactions seemed to occur most dramatically between strings that shared certain qualities, where I discerned similarities such as thickness, color, pitch, position, texture—or sometimes between strings that seemed complementary or opposite in nature.

Every painting, every work of art is a narrative, a story. There's no escaping that. As with the warping of a loom, there is always an initial string that gets things going. One day, it happened that while taking a pee, Marcel DuChamp looked down and had a vision—during the intimate act of micturating, the quality of *this* was suddenly divided from all the *thats*—he imagined the Madonna in the shell of a *pissoir*. A pattern was established and the rest is history. He told the story, sold the urinal for a lot of money, and a market was born. Then, there was this guy from California who became so enthused about the idea of in between stuff that he wrote music that was silent. "I've spent many hours alone, conducting performances of my silent music," he said. He had a friend who created blank canvases and called them "white paintings." He told stories too. Soon, a frustrated modern artist from Wyoming had another idea; and although the resulting paintings of drips and dribbles looked a lot like painters' drop cloths, he told a good story. "When I lose contact with the painting it's a mess," he said. "Otherwise, there's pure harmony—just paint, that's all." No illusions. The critics said he had eliminated the story altogether and liberated art from human values (but he sold a lot of very expensive drop cloths anyway, as they went well with modern furnishings). Soon, artists from all over started depending only on stories and forgot about the rest. I remember attending an art school in the sixties where the truth was all about stripes—wide brushes, house paint, and tape masking off the limits of each space we intended to collectively fill. "There's nothing else," went the commentary. "This is finally it; no self—and no plot." It's funny, looking back, that the pretenses of the plot were so evident. In fact, clever stories became so important that without them, the curtain would fall and the fairy tale end. Modern art would be nothing—paintings reverting to messy drop cloths, scribbles, stripes and empty canvases—music turning into silence, or worse, just noise—and toilets, becoming plain old toilets again. Without the weaving of tales, there would be nothing in the box. "And, that's the beauty of it," said the critics. But to me, the true irony is that something *for its own sake* should need any explanation at all.

I watched thoughtfully as the weave of warp and weft became a complex tapestry of layered affinities and correlations being woven from many places and in different ways, as if the big loom were an intersection between hidden places and other things I couldn't know yet—nameless things that I could only feel. I wondered at the distinct and diverse aspects that I didn't see from my point of view, and at the nature of other concealed views that I still can say nothing about. Abruptly, the demonstration ended, and the loom disappeared.

"No more?"

I waited.

"Perhaps he didn't understand—or maybe my thoughts are too cluttered. I'm not concentrating hard enough. I'll clear my mind and ask again.

"But—talk to me about resonance," I begged, and the vision of the loom being strung and the mysterious weft being woven into the warp repeated.

After a panel is prepared, when I begin to paint, one of the first things to do is to establish values. I make structure and form appear by deciding what is light and what is dark. The subsequent layers of paint are built on those values by adding pigments in veils of varied opacities and textures, by juxtaposing them, affecting them with colors that might change their nature—like red appearing redder in a field of green. When I get really close to any painting, I look for evidence of the activities that formed it. I remember approaching Botticelli's Primavera in order to investigate the impossible confusion of meadow-grass and flowers, each blade, each tender blossom rendered so precisely—to see the paint, the tell-tale tracks of bristles dragged through pigment and oil by another person, the proof of uncontrolled devotion to the process of painting—then, to see the worm-holed indications of history—to see my own shadow cast on that other world and for an instant, to become part of the story—one more god playing in the woods there.

Once, a long time ago, a composer named Ludwig wrote beautiful music using the rhythmic struggle and heroic triumph of notes over the silent in between; *Da-da-da-daaah*—as a recurring motif—*Da-da-da-daaah*, a simple two-measured pattern, formed and reformed to support a whole symphony. He loved the audience, but the story is—he spent many hours conducting performances of his music in silence, because he was deaf.

Again, I made the same request of my mentor, which was followed by the same vision in response, ending at the same point. The interaction of strings on a loom reminded me of a previous dream, and I was eager to experience the rest of what had been an engaging presentation, including vibrating filaments and the ensuing harmonics of their relationships. I continued to repeat my appeal for more, anticipating the rest of a great story, but not recognizing it in the image of an over-sized loom.

Then my friend spoke. "Last time, we briefly discussed Adam and Eve—and, before I propose anything further, you should begin to explore the essential qualities of the first parents."

"Oh—OK."

"How odd," I thought. *"A weaving demonstration and now this?"* It sounded as though it might require some kind of effort, unlike the wildly entertaining event that I had hoped for. The nature of these recent discussions has seemed more like work than play anyway. Nikola Tesla began to lecture. "They were brought here from somewhere else for the benefit of creation, as the principals to lead and teach, to govern and guide humankind through the process of development."

"Well—that's a story, isn't it?" I was perplexed, both fascinated and frustrated by what he had said—satisfied, but startled. Tesla didn't hesitate. In his pointed take-it-or-leave-it style, he had begun right away provoking me with extraordinary statements. I think it was the inconvenience of what he was saying that made me want to laugh.

"So, there was somewhere else to come from," I restated. "Is that right?"

I like to use plywood with birch veneer as the base for paintings, or even hardboard, which is cheaper and arguably acceptable. The paints I use are a combination of pigments, and binders to hold or glue them in place; oils for oil paints and egg yolks for egg tempera. My mediums are generally syrupy or pasty mixtures of ingredients—oils, balsams and resins, egg yolks and water—that I add to paint to alter the consistency, to achieve different effects, or to change the drying time. The miracle is that all of these exotic materials come together in my studio, brought from all over the world for the purpose of *my* making a painting.

"Of course," I answered myself tenuously. *"There's always somewhere else."* Nikola smiled a puckish smile, looking sur-

prisingly childlike.

"Yes—everything comes from somewhere else. Doesn't it?" I repeated thoughtfully, imagining olive-skinned men collecting mastic tears as they have for several thousand years, the small mastic trees in turn pulling water and nutrients from the soil—or a hen clucking with relief after passing a jumbo egg. *"Even paintings. I suppose in a world of convenient mysteries, where chicken breasts are born ex nihilo, boned and skinned, in plastic—that's easy to forget."*

In the beginning—on a panel, on a ground of chalky white, on an *imprimatura* of smeared and layered colors that I've sanded smooth, over a sketch or even a grid—I start to paint *in grigio*, in *grisaille*, a monochrome underpainting that ranges in value between the two extremes of light and dark. Traditional painters sometimes used white and black, warmed-up with a little Umber or Ocher, so it's really monochrome—think brownish gray, like Leonardo's unfinished Adoration of the Magi—but I use any lighter or darker color, often employing the values of my chaotic imprimatura to help out. Structural lines divide the space, and a scale of values suggests volume and shape—the lighter values usually projecting and the darker ones receding. It's a dialog between boundaries and wholeness, and although I'll make some changes, my choices at the outset form the basis, a context for the final image—the stage, roles, and scenery a plot can develop in.

"All right then," offered Tesla. "For current purposes, we shall call them Line and Circle if you prefer."

"No. Please go ahead and call them Adam and Eve," I answered. "I think I get it—I think—they're the embodiment of the initial values, the *chiaroscuro*, the prototypes that everything is built upon…is modeled after." We both seemed to relax and Nikola continued.

"The tendency of awareness is to grow by degrees—to progress in steps, as children do so dramatically. The complementary process is a pattern of activity in the context of a system, which tends to unwind or degenerate—as in the operation of a motor or the functions of an organism—wearing the parts down. Our first progenitors led humankind through the process of reasoning, choosing this or that, a risky path of agreements leading to understanding. Their decisions and subsequent experience give us the opportunity to participate actively in the development of our own awareness."

"The consequences were good then?" I asked.

"Consequences just are. Your choices are agreements to accept the effects of your actions. The consequences teach you to choose."

I was filled to overflowing with Tesla's presentation—something I have felt so many times before. "They came to some kind of seminal society…to teach a process? A developmental plan?" Nikola looked obviously pleased. *"Painting is like that, isn't it? I extend a brush toward the palette, and in the time it takes to move the brush through the air, a discussion takes place—I steer the bristles toward the specific squish of paint I've decided on, speculating on the relationship of what I'm reaching for with what's already on the panel—and prepared to accept the consequences.*

"But, there's a cost," I said, remembering the many failures that I end up painting over or scraping off.

"And a prize," added Tesla, "the promise that, with experience, you can become a painter of beautiful things. The relationship of opposing values enlivens the universe and enables the process of our development. Everything exists somewhere between the values of light and dark. Without both, there would be nothing."

"*It's funny isn't it? Such a fine line between story and story—drop cloths, empty canvases, silence, noise, and plain old toilets—or symphonies and masterpieces.*

"I understand. There'd be no story. But then, Adam and Eve—is that a real story?"

"How many types of fire are there?" asked Tesla.

"What do you mean?" I returned without thinking. "I'm not sure. As many as there are circumstances—and things that burn?"

"That is a good response," he said slowly. I felt him carefully studying me again. Then he said my name before posing another question. "And which fire is the real fire?"

"I'm beginning to get the idea. The initial values in a painting, boundaries and forms, the little bits, odds and ends, the binary foundation of systems, my mathematical friend's *hoshu* and *loshu* grids. The Line to divide the Circle, the I and O together, *IO*, myself, a small piece reflecting the whole—all the parent roles and patterns—I hadn't thought...."

"And which are the real ones?" Nikola interrupted. "Is that what you wanted to know? The way and the wanderer? The trajectory of an object—momentum and position? The path of a planet? Wave and particle? Or, wire on a spindle? Shall I go on?"

"I remember now—the resistant stability of the wheel enabling its momentum across the soil. So, is *real* based on my experience?"

"Yes—and not at all. *Real* to you is determined by your faith, which is more than simple belief, and in many ways is surer than experience. People disbelieve their experiences all the time." It's never about right answers with Nikola; it is about thinking through things, staking a claim—like preparing the panel, ground, and establishing layers of underpainting for an eventual image. "Understanding the personifications of these roles requires that we discuss agreements," he continued.

"This path of agreements, the process—how does it happen?" I asked.

"Agreements are necessary for any system or order. In mechanical systems the agreements are forced, built into the machinery, but in a sentient system such as humankind, the agreements are conscious choices."

"...like the vascular system of a peculiar giant—each of us connected like organs of an invisible body...

"Why?" I wondered aloud. "Machinery does something. What are people for?"

"The intent of a mechanical system is to accomplish work. The intent of human life is another kind of work."

"...numberless worlds in infinite universes populated by divine beings each reflecting the whole of it...the heresies of Giordano Bruno again....

"And—what am *I* for?"

Nikola was quiet for a while. "That—I can't tell you," he finally answered, "as it is your choice." Again, we searched each others' faces; he searched mine to know my heart, and I, his—to know my own heart. "It happens by degree," he went on. "Choosing this from that leads to understanding. The context of the system is for that purpose. These agreements enable a conscious system to fulfill its intent, and the associated parts to perform their proper functions in support of that intent."

Sometimes while painting, my current insight is not enough; I get beyond myself—suddenly unable to understand the intent of the image or to see the next step. The conversation stops because I don't know what to say. It started out fine, but unexpectedly I end up forgetting why and what it was about. So I try to view things differently, upside down, or from across the room. I play in the paint hoping to stumble onto a familiar color—I'll read a book, or go outside and stare into the woods, trying to remember.

"In terms of consciousness, participating within an intelligent system enlightens the individual," he explained, "endowing the parts with increased awareness of the whole—the order and pattern of its mechanics."

Painting what I can't see yet is a tricky proposal; it requires an agreement with the work—my renewed and increased commitment, in exchange for what I want to see revealed. Often it means retracing my steps, reviewing the pattern of my thoughts and actions in order to comprehend better how I arrived at that point—

"Yesterday, I painted on those clouds, and put a warm glaze on the trees...."

—and to submit more completely to the process.

"Wise choices support and empower both the order and the individual," said Tesla.

"That's it! Caput Mortuum! I should have seen it sooner." And I steer the bristles hopefully toward the squish of dark violet brown I have decided on.

"As much as some pretend that freedom to choose means freedom from accountability, it is exactly the opposite," he added. "Remember, choice includes the effects. Only a universe with no story is without accountability, and that cannot exist. The narrative of a system naturally includes answerability to it."

In painting, there's always more than one right color, but I've begun to consider the many choices I make without thinking, my apparent needs, the automatic responses, especially the ones that compound, as one color can require the addition of another and another in the attempt to correct or cover up a careless combination. I've learned in the studio that the best passages of paint leave me smarter, and the painting more complete, while other spots get revisited until I get them right. As I pondered the applications in the studio, Tesla continued to talk about agreements.

"In many ways these agreements are like your license to drive an automobile. A license is the permission to perform accountably, which is petitioned for and then granted after proficiency is demonstrated in the operation of a powerful tool, something that might be considered dangerous otherwise. It represents power to participate according to the values and principles of a system in an intelligent way, awarded to the licensee by someone in authority.

"There is little option to imagine or invent personal rules when operating a motor vehicle on a shared system of roads. A driver's license, the authority to act as the operator of a motor vehicle, cannot be taken upon oneself. It is a privilege, which is also lost or revoked when misused, as there are necessary limits to the deviation that can be introduced into the working mechanics of a system. The license, or agency to operate, is petitioned for and awarded by agreement. The system offers freedom of movement to those who agree to learn and comply with its principles, and would break down into chaos should its guidelines be regularly violated through ignorance, ineptness, or imagined autonomy. As public safety depends on general compliance with the values and principles governing the system of transportation, personal interpretation, consisting of more or less than those principles, usually excludes one from interaction and privilege within the shared framework. A declaration of independence from the order means exclusion from the benefits of cooperation within it."

To put it all in context, I thought back to the beginning. *"This all started with patterns,"* recalling Nikola Tesla patiently and thoroughly describing orders, frameworks, models, roles, sequences, frequencies, vibrations, and on and on. Before anything else, he wanted me to grasp the concept of pattern. *"Those patterns you have been painting…even your heartbeat…all of life is a vibration…."* He suggested that my life is not a mistake; that there is meaning, reason, and order to the events that make it up, and thus some significance to my singular life in the progression of a larger order, *"that the most significant pattern or sequence is one.*

"The pattern includes both the mechanics and the work," I realize now, recalling a crowd of people milling about and my ability to organize them, even as the form kept changing. *"Pattern means recognition. It's an awareness."*

Nikola continued. "The agreements taught and entered into by Adam and Eve were not simply contractual in nature. The idea that such covenants are binding contracts with which to bargain is a partial and arrogant view sometimes held by those not in a position to make such demands. The prototypical agreements are best understood as steps to awareness, formal interactions that represent willingness to accept increasing experience. Like a license to operate, such power is granted after proficiency is proved, and is often expressed by specific symbols or acts of compliance and humility. These metaphorical acts can inform and direct on many levels, and are oriented in a concise way toward the desired increase in awareness. They represent the requests, by those prepared, for further enlightenment and the possibility of increased participation in the work, with the understanding that additional participation includes additional accountability—which also means increased liability in terms of the potential to cause disorder or compromise. Increased license and awareness are an endowment of trust to those who qualify."

I recalled seeing one person wander around alone after the crowd of people had dispersed. "Is this any less of a sequence or frequency?" Tesla had asked. "Remember the pattern and sequence of one. It is important to think about." I got the impression that in the future there would be things he would show me, that would depend on my comprehension of the single unit pattern. Now—I look again, and the blue-eyed gray-haired wanderer has my face. I think of Adam and Eve and see myself, suddenly feeling as if a clean breath of air is blowing through me, as through an open window.

"If they already existed, and were from somewhere else, what's that story about him falling asleep and the rib?"

"We are speaking of the roles they agreed to play, *what* they became figuratively, not *who* they are," he responded. "Remember—patterns can intersect. The creation story, along with the garden drama, is about an incredible intersection." I thought of the big loom being strung, and wondered if it didn't fit in after all. Of all possible stories, this was the most peculiar, the most surprising.

"It's like me, the painter, and the process of painting—the essence of what I paint about and the pigments, the substance of the paint. The picture is the visible evidence of a story, the intersection of everything transforming together. There are so many layers to think about!"

"Many more than you can imagine," responded Tesla. "Everything and everyone existed at varying degrees of development before this—and *this* is an agreement. And, that is about who you are. The *how* of things is about the experience, the process. Part of the *how* includes division from previous unity, a veil to protect this experience and the inherent desire for oneness. The initial models and their dramatic story represent all of that. The pattern of their theatre is many layered, multidimensional, and shows up in the organization of everything—in every choice we make, in every step toward greater awareness—in painting and art, in music, in managing electrical potential, and in the stars. It applies universally to the whole, the seen and the unseen. The process was already in place. It resonates because it is about remembering."

"Paintings can start at any time, beginning as almost something—it's more like remembering than inventing; a focus for my attention that leads to something else, which leads to something else, and something else, and so on and on."

"As an electric motor operates within the limits that govern its function, perpetually rehearsing a precise dance between poles, the plot of the story describes the operating conditions that govern the development of humankind," he went on. "Yes, you are completely free to choose, but choice includes the consequences. The effects are your teachers, as I have said."

I like riddles, and quietly pondered the story of Adam and Eve, the personifications of a process, with some concern about the nature of my own life and roles. *"Essence and substance, or substance and essence—the staging of my own small drama, the odd activity of painting that I sometimes take so seriously—my choices, the agreements, the relationship between my self-determined course and the workings of a system...."* I began to ask questions.

"It is a necessary part of the framework that certain things can be shown but not told," answered Tesla.

"Yes, that's what I sometimes say about my paintings," I added.

"I can take you to the brink," he continued, "the place where that brooding emptiness confronts your awareness; I can offer you the tools to explore, but I cannot violate your exploration—I cannot foretell your choices and their effects, as those are your creations, not mine." Again, as before, we stood together at the edge of a shadow; and I peered out into nothing, hoping to see some indication of my future. "Do you understand?" he asked tenderly.

"I think I do——it's just a lot."

"I know," he offered, and we stayed there together for a time, both of us looking out into an empty view of whom and what I would become, what I would create, the agreements I would make.

"I'm afraid," I confessed.

Nikola gently reviewed our lesson several times, asking each time that I repeat back to him what I had understood. I struggled to do so, feeling still a little muddled and surprised by my emotional response. After all of our discussions, everything I had learned felt strangely preliminary. There was so much more I wanted to know, but felt confused by an unexpected inability to form intelligent thoughts and questions.

"Now, you have some work to do," he said finally. "I will be here when you are ready. I can lead you to this point but cannot do the work for you. We will be able to discuss additional aspects of resonance when you have more awareness concerning the basic pattern of things. You are again at the edge of your conscious ability and I can only give you tools to look as you are prepared to see."

I like to study the patterns of things: symbols, parables, and riddles, signs and tokens; like magic compasses to point the way, curious telescopes—the metaphorical tools to magnify what's far away, to see *out there*, to shed some light on what is dim, on unrelated things that suddenly begin to tell a story. The endless layers, the initial values of a repeating design; warp and weft, fire and water, the gods playing like children—all the Adams and Eves, Lines and Circles leaving Edens, their once gullibility becoming eventual wisdom. I like to imagine watching Masaccio as he painted the story of their sad flight on the wall of a small chapel, and have stood and smiled at Durer's coy couple in the Uffizi. I have seen them in the distance of so many Annunciations, and stood craning my neck until it hurt, to stare up at them again on Michelangelo's ceiling. They're everywhere.

In the studio I've experienced the difficulty of trying to bargain with a pattern without unknowingly changing it into something else. There is a limit to the deviation I can introduce without losing the original, to leave me painting vain repetitions, things for their own sakes.

Paintings happen to me and in me. It's difficult to know the beginning and end of them. When was the seed planted that became the image of my Gidu's hat? Was it when I became fascinated by the magic way he carefully formed his cursive letters and numbers? Or was it his talk of the old country? Did it start to grow on those walks through the meadow? Or while standing alone in front of a hat shop in Milan? Was it there when I was born? Or when he was born? Or his father, or his father, or his father? Sometimes my current insight is not enough. Even when my conversation with the substance of a painting stops, the essence continues—who becoming what, and what becoming whom, interweaving like strings on a loom. Perhaps some time in the distant future a great-great-great-great-grandson will hear of a grandfather's studio and the odd image of a hat? Or perhaps the picture will still exist as a curiosity? Maybe my children, watching me paint it, thought thoughts that will affect their lives, eventually to alter the fabric of generations? Will the funny magic of a simple black-painted shape ever die?

"*'You might begin to think of it as a door or entry, the threshold to a whole,' he told me months ago.*"

"*Yeeeeess—caput mortuum!*" And I steer the bristles toward the dark squish I've decided on.

"*Does any story really start or finish?*"

17
Talking to Myself

December 28 – Today was one of those days—the kind of day that begins as a reply to the dilemma posed by yesterday, only to end up becoming tomorrow's puzzle, a day of constant thoughts and inner chatter—similar to the proposals and responses of colors and brushstrokes that comprise activity in the studio. I've been talking to myself nonstop about my last discussion with Nikola Tesla, debating and submitting, like the busy back-and-forth of a paintbrush to and from a palette—or a shuttle shooting through warp strings, suggesting things that I had not considered, while weaving a strange pattern that feels surprisingly comfortable—and matter-of-factly transforming what I could not imagine into what I now believe.

"So—talk to me about resonance,' I said."

In spite of my continual attempts to preconceive pictures, paintings are often impudent. They talk back.

"Yeah! That's what you think!"
But, I'm used to it, and have come to depend on it.
"Hey! There's something else you oughtta know...."
Not that I believe an image has a mind and will of its own, although that's how it can seem, but that somewhere between the subtle qualities of its form and our familiarity, the material comes alive, finds expression, adding one more speaker to the exchange that becomes a painting. At least, that's what I always hope.

"A pattern, an arrangement, a body, world, or universe—a painting, the context a plot can develop in."

An actor's inner dialog, the actor and script, actor and set, actor and actor, actor and audience, the audience as actors; the numerous discussions that happen within and without—today, I was the context, the stage where the night's voices review their parts, keeping me company with endless deliberations and rehearsals of Tesla's recent discourses.

"Such a fine line between story and story. It's just not going where I expected."

But then, I surprise myself. How can I brood over a painting, enter its narrative, contemplate the nature of its process, scrutinize the layers of material and meaning, explore its composition, consider its colors—and ever doubt the conscious design of a larger system and process? How can one exist and not the other?

"Like Narcissus, seeing only his own image…can I be that blind?"

Analysis: it's what my head does, breaks things down, deconstructs—a big bang occurs. Synthesis: my heart composes mysteries, brings things together; then by deduction, I make it up. Neither operation explains the life of an image—not the number of elements, nor the magic of my imagination. Either one alone is not enough to satisfy the conditions of both structure and process that happen in the studio.

"Fortunate accident, or fantasy—for it's own sake or just because...."

In art, there's a precedent for conversation between them, the *sacra conversazione*, a bringing together of disparate ideas in one place, many points of view seen from one perspective. Years ago, I stood in front of the center panel of Fra' Giovanni's Pala di San Marco—a crowd of painted characters held together by a single frame of reference, saintly figures from diverse times and places seen on one ground, against one backdrop—*"I am the stage,"* I realized. *"I'm the viewpoint!*

"This is no lucky blunder. Clever Giovanni!" I looked at San Cosma peering out at me as if to say, "Well? Don't you get it?" And I smiled back. Ignorance and a lack of preparation had limited my understanding, obscuring my ability to see the obvious.

Then, I got it. "There'd be no story," I responded.

The boy in the museum, held captive by his reflection in the painted images there, watching his own transformation in their apparent changes—sometimes I miss him. I miss them all: the postman and his wife, the sower, the man on a rope, the terra cotta heroes, my composed Egyptian friends, and Gauguin's pretty Eve—I miss our little conversations. Perhaps I look at paintings now hoping to catch a boy staring back at me, because often enough, he's still there. And, maybe it's that paintings, unlike butterflies, can be examined and inner lives exposed, manhandled just a bit without diminishing their spirit and value.

I think of Rembrandt's old Doctor Tulp, powerless to make live what he smartly dissects, flaying the arm's anatomy so well, teasing open muscles, only to end up gazing out blankly at the mystery of it all. I catch his steady eye and look back at him with no clue to offer. "I'm not the one to ask," I have to admit. Like disciples at a last supper, they've been gathered around the table for centuries, apostolic analysts, powerless before the sacramental authority of death and life, courtiers to the sleeping *corpus* lying there relaxed and omnipotent over the scene. On the other hand, teasing out hidden parts only makes paintings more alive and no less mysterious.

"Nothing is from nothing."

Unlike my unruly palette, dictionaries keep the elemental substance of stories in order, analyzed, and arranged alphabetically—but the dictionary isn't a story any more than squeezes of paint and small tin cups of linseed oil and medium are already the image—or scales of notes are already a song, or the ingredients of recipes, already a meal. Things don't organize themselves by probability without some intrusion, without the spark, the instigation of a process. To imagine otherwise is whimsical, but without basis in the process and order of the larger system. Words can't rearrange themselves; they don't write poems and stories without the work of an author, as paints can't become paintings without the meddling of an artist.

"Nothing is from no one."

Left alone, pigments, oils, and blank panels have no volition. Without a violation of status, they'd sit there gathering dust, disintegrating, waiting for someone to set things in motion. Paintings don't spontaneously generate, any more than experiments and theorizing happen without scientists. The primordial materials of paintings await the painter to initiate a process. Often, it begins with a foundation of lights and darks, the application of one suggesting the other, proceeding in a constant dialog.

The *sacred conversation*, a Renaissance painting arrangement, exposes the complex associations, layered affinities and repulsions between distinct and diverse images; peculiar pictures of an old man holding huge keys and another clutching a book, another man with a knife jabbed into his bleeding head, another with rocks stuck to him, a pretty youth pierced by arrows, and a woman with a wheel of torture. It's an intersection between ideas and the interplay of their peripheries around the strange harmonic nature of a mother and child who are also daughter and father, who become mother and child, daughter and father, mother and child, and so on and on—

"'...Figlia del tuo figlio...tu se' colei che l'umana natura nobilitasti'... Dante; 'Gesù, Maria, Giuseppe—Gesù, Maria, Giuseppe'...a funny old nonna dressed in black; 'dynamism, dynamo, dynamic'...a dome full of stars churning in and out of formation."

—until my head starts spinning.

When I get stuck, when I don't get it, I like to think about rocks. For some reason I'm always impressed by the smart aspects of boulders on a talus slope, rugged granite masses settled into the process of rock business, sticking to their roles and what they're about, busying themselves in the gravity of their situations, tumbling into timeless gestures that always manage to look recent and animated. There's absolutely nothing about their apparent disorder that seems unconscious. Everything is always as it should be.

I imagine rocks everywhere: gray granite talus, rosy sandstone goblins, limestone columns in the dark, fist-size stones, and small pebbles—all going about their charge of being rocks; rumbling around, cracking and breaking down, crumbling, balancing, bridging gaps, dripping, building up, being molded in secret, or thrown up out of fiery holes. I envy their efficient transformations—yielding in strength, stubbornly obedient, and inclined to do just what rocks are meant to do. "Oh! To be as dumb as a rock!"

I make so many mistakes that sometimes, automatic just sounds good. Awareness seems too much of a liability. I'm afraid to move—tired of being accountable and worn out by consequences. Then, chance wields the brushes. Even the palette knows more than I do. The conversation stops, as I yield to the lure of easy ignorance and dogma, trading places with fate. (*Destino* is seldom very dependable, but our agreement is: I'll correct it later, paint over it, or scrape most of it off if it's not right.)

I study myself carefully, the man in the mirror with graying hair and crow's feet. *"I didn't start out intending much of anything by being an artist, did I?"* I confess to my silvery self-portrait. Stretching my cheek out with a finger, I inspect the teeth the dentist says are candidates for crowns, and stick out my tongue to examine its wet pink velvet. I stare into my eyes, the same eyes I saw in that broken piece of plate glass mirror—still a boy's eyes, then thoughtfully consider the parts of me that belong to a man, recalling once again the extravagant terra cotta cartoons of the guys I expected to look like. My chest and small pink nipples conceding to gravity, my belly and navel (I think of my mother), my head (I look like my father), my hands and feet, the evidence of both giving and receiving life, a fleshy dialog between functions…. "Who are you?" I ask my attentive counterpart.

But, most of me is invisible, safely buried under skin. I have to hope in those parts that I don't see; like my brain, lungs, liver, kidneys, and heart—and trust in their obedient support of the systems and processes that preserve my ability to stand here and wonder. "Who am I?"

Part of me grins inwardly and answers, "You're a real nut!"

"Concealed and nameless views, parent roles and patterns…and IO, myself, a small piece reflecting the whole. Fra' Giovanni, Filippo Lippi, Piero della Francesca, Andrea Mantegna, Giovanni Bellini, and others, the many painters of sacre conversazioni—did they all get it?"

Every painting, every work of art is a similar conversation, the proposed distance and vicinity of one thing to another, their comparative aspects and working relationships; a still life, a landscape, a colorful abstract chat, a profound discussion between values, my Gidu's black felt hat, or just another crowd of saints hanging out. I look at Botticelli's Primavera and watch it happening there with Venus and her attendant heavenly hierarchy. I catch the inviting glance of Lippi's little angel scouting for saints out in the audience. I see it investigated in Bruegel's Blind Leading the Blind past a churchyard, Picasso's sad-eyed Saltimbanques, and Kandinsky's mindful improvisations; all exploring the outer relationships of inner dialogs.

The motifs of painting are everywhere. *L'ape regina*, a queen bee holds court. The moon and sun continue to play tag. My heart and head discuss the news. My wife and I still make love—and while the chance of our coincidental loving moods can be analyzed mathematically, and the union of a particular sperm with a present egg may be described as quantum luck, the instigation of the process cannot. And so it continues, the dance of *chiaroscuro* prototypes—intersecting between universes. The resonant associations between one part and another (as many as there are circumstances) suggest a pattern, attest to a persistent design and pervasive principles—all implying the work of a real artist with something specific in mind.

"After all, nothing is for nothing."

I've been contemplating last night's discussion all day—driving to work, eating lunch with friends, or sitting in a sterile conference room examining the visceral mechanics of software. Much of today's chatter was editorial, continuing non-stop, in a torrent, spilling into all of my in between places and overflowing in a flood too difficult to keep track of. I've only written the few thoughts that pervaded and survived. Whoever and whatever Nikola Tesla is, he's part of my sleeping and my waking. My eminent friend and I, in two different worlds, but for a while anyway—sharing the same inner dialog.

"Resonance—talk to me about resonance."

18
Frequencies

December 29 – There are times when it feels as if this journal has already been written, the puzzle solved, and the picture painted—as if everything has already happened and I am only trying to catch up.

I have always been fascinated by musical instruments and the recursive mystery of music—conceived and established on a scale of frequencies—a rhythmic pattern of pitches; a beginning and end measured in notes and intervals, followed by beginning and end measured in notes and intervals, followed by beginning and end measured in notes and intervals, and so on, and so on—birth, death, and renewal until I lose track.

"Pay more attention to vibrations," counseled Tesla. "The reception of vibrations—from the earth and everything in it, from above, from the stars and heavenly bodies, and from elsewhere—is constant, as is your projection and reflection of them.

Even without trying, there is resonance between yourself and the rhythmic universe. That is the nature of awareness, that its influence happens almost automatically. Most often, you send and receive vibrations unconsciously, amplifying what passes through you like a powerful and unaccountable transmitter."

A few months ago, he tried to teach me to magnify and transmit vibrations, directing them into the earth to make it quake. I didn't do so well, and in fact haven't practiced it at all. Unfortunately, *unconscious and unaccountable* are often accurate descriptions, as I don't pay enough attention and have trouble accepting my own significance.

Tesla continued, "Vibration is ubiquitous. It is the breathing of the universe. The frequency, or the number of up and down events of a vibration that occur during the measured to's and fro's of time, relates both to size and state, quantity and quality, slower for larger things that appear still, and faster for the smallest things that aren't seen. It is wise then, to look and listen for what is still and small. Only a fool assumes that what is not sensible with common faculties does not exist."

"Ups and downs—to's and fro's; sounds like brushing my teeth," I thought. *"Several hundred times per session, thirty to forty times a month.*

"But if everything is really everywhere and all at once, what is frequency?" I asked. He looked pleased at my question and the opportunity for a discussion.

"It is more accurate to say that frequency is an important aspect of completeness, wholeness, or fullness, as in the union of harmony and melody, the concordance of notes and progression, the intersection of vertical and horizontal; it is the joining of above and below. Everything has a frequency because everything vibrates. It is the pattern of a crowd, and the pattern of one. Frequency is the music, the poetic binder that both holds things together and keeps things separate."

I remembered the resonant intersections, the harmonics we had heard, and the chords resulting from the union of those resonances—composites of composites, like one world eclipsing the life of another—but I had never thought of frequency in the way he had just described it—as I had never before considered patterns so thoroughly, or thought of mnemonics as a door to anywhere. I had never considered any of this before I met Nikola Tesla in my dreams. The nature of my instruction is becoming clearer; from the start, he has been repeating the same kind of material, talking about common things and teaching me to see the uncommonness of them. As my awareness increases, what seemed obvious enough is continuing to gain complexity and momentum, spiraling exponentially like the repetition of musical scales at increasingly higher octaves. He is training me to experience things that have been beyond the range of my sensibilities.

"It's difficult for me to understand," I responded. "I guess I thought frequency was something else."

"Yes, I imagine you have only seen it from a limited perspective, a small cross-section of something best viewed in its entirety. Vibration and frequency are everywhere and in everything. You have only considered the edge of what frequency is."

"I don't know—maybe I can hear it easier than I can think it," I apologized. "Or, maybe if I could see it?"

"The world has drawn the veil ever closer and made it into a wall. The background has become the foreground—right has become left—and up has become down. Entertainments, fashions, goods, passions; people have grown accustomed to slogans and imitations, a rhetorical veneer selling fear and desire in place of peace and well-being, making it difficult to hear and see."

"And how did that all happen?" I asked, impressed by his solemnity and the heaviness of what he was saying.

"A little at a time," he answered sadly. "But I know that you can feel things," he reassured. "In spite of the interference that fills your senses, you have developed the subtle faculties to hear and see more—that which many have grown unaccustomed to hearing and seeing. You are an artist."

"Yeah, I'm an artist," I thought, recalling my peculiar props and attitudes. I have always been reluctant to accept the title artist. When asked, I'd shrug and answer, "Well, I paint…paintings." Or, I might say, "Aaaaahhhh…I'm a software design consultant—and I paint in my spare time."

"Really? And, what do you paint?"

Then I'd be caught, because inevitably I would have to say something embarrassing that sounded as though I meant it, and they'd know the truth about me. It's kind of like a neighbor kid finding where your treasure's hidden. "Oh, just crazy stuff," I'd chuckle and change the subject.

I have noticed that when I fear, my abilities seem to shrink and I find myself at the brink of nothingness and confusion—otherwise, I'm learning to conduct potential that was once elusive, that would have been unmanageable, forces that bring me to the edge of newly expanded capacities each time. It's not that strange really. It happens in steps, by degree, the way life does. To assume my role and submit to my abilities is a difficult thing. But finally, I'm realizing that to pretend incapacity and feign ignorance is not humility—it's a lie, whose eventual outcome is my growing disinterest in a world shaped by those less able and least wise. "Yes—I am an artist," I agreed.

"Then, start with vibrations from the earth," said Tesla. "The earth's vibrations are ever-present, like many other things that are easy to overlook. But your body is part of the earth, so it isn't difficult to recognize the vibrations once you feel them. Relax now and let them fill you." And I felt them—first, a gentle charge, and then in small shocks and shivers happening through me and in me.

"The tangible world is a reflection of its vibrations," he went on. "Everything you experience is a transmission; your thoughts, your dreams, even your more solid self are all made of similar vibrating material. The spectrum that you are used to sensing is narrow, and the frequencies of that material are more or less subtle. Worlds, dimensions, realms, places…are just patterns of varied frequencies with typical characteristics."

Reference to the composition of an artwork is usually not about the tangible material it's composed of; rather, it is about the underlying patterns, the sometimes elusory substance that gives it life, the magical stuff that holds an image together—the hidden mechanics that are in broad view. The play between hues and values, the supporting structure that shows up on the surface in the relationships of lines and shapes, the repeated motifs that create rhythms and textures, the tricks of perspective that push things forward or send them back into what appears as distance— the masters used these, and more, to amplify and carry their transmissions beyond common faculties. The visual semantics of the way things grow are similar: opposing, alternating, whorled, clustered, columnar, and contorted—the directness of a pinnate leaf as opposed to the open delta of a palmate, the focus of a daisy compared to the bellflower's lack of concentration or to the voluptuous bud of a rose about to bloom—the wantonness of ripening fruit, the intellect of seeds in shells, good-natured greens, and the common-sense of roots—always in true form, all eaten with my eyes before they're touched, picked, smelled, or tasted. The natural world is generous, hiding nothing that I'm prepared to see.

"It might be said that we are each the image of our frequencies. Every person has an individual frequency signature that is particular to that person, in much the same way that the associated audible voice has a signature vibration or that the characteristics of a piece of music are typical of a key signature. A crowd operates at a frequency. Interaction with higher awareness happens within a range of frequency. You and I communicate at a specific frequency." He seemed to be enjoying his own talk as much as I was. "In the end, everything I did was about vibration, frequency, and energy transmission."

"Like music—composition, harmony, chroma, tone—the visual music of paintings...." I made a momentary trip to the museum back home, to The Uffizi, The Brera, The Accademia, Il Cenacolo, the many places that hold the pictures that live inside me, to take inventory once again. *"They're all here and I'm here,"* I reassured myself, briefly noting the distinct lineaments that characterize each image and the unique craft of its creator.

"Very good," said Tesla, containing an imminent smile. "Quickening what appears substantial enables it to function at higher frequencies, as artists throughout history have attempted to transmute the heavy matter on their palettes in order to imbue their solid transmissions with intelligence and life." I was reminded that my thoughts were available to Nikola as if I had spoken them out loud. "Musical compositions need no such transformation as the frequency of their material is more obvious."

"Maybe you should have found a musician then," I complained, "instead of a painter." It was one of those comments that Nikola tends to ignore, as he did.

"...and obviously, light reflected from a painting is frequency as well," he added, looking amused.

"Then, paintings are like musical instruments—each with a distinct song," I speculated. "And a painter is both the luthier and the composer, the receiver. Hmmmmm. The transmission happens somewhere between the solid arrangement of paint and the faculty of sight—which makes the viewer into the player." I like the sometimes ticklish nature of our talk, and that Tesla is patient with my need to chatter on the periphery of something while making room for the heart of it. "That's it! The audience has to participate in the painting of a picture or it's like un-played notes. For artist and viewer—a see-er is the one who interprets the transmission."

I laughed. At myself. At a dream named Nikola Tesla. And at a suddenly remembered spooky story of a poor cat closed up in a box. "Sure! Of course, it's obvious isn't it?" I concluded, noting Tesla's unrestrained grin.

"Then—what is a pattern?" he teased, reminding me of earlier meandering discussions.

Without waiting for an answer, he continued teaching about the conscious reception of vibrations from the earth. I learned that if I just opened up to the possibility of the experience, they were there—although this all happened in a house, in bed, and somewhere between asleep and awake, rather than on the snow-covered ground outside. (That will have to wait for spring.) If I focused on myself linked to the earth, I could feel it; something familiar, already known to me, like the sound and sight of a breeze in the woods or on a meadow, or being alone with the commotion of the sea rushing and retreating on a seashore, or taking in the dizzying view from somewhere high up. That's how it feels when I paint. Nikola suggested that after I have practiced, there are other possibilities—of consciously amplifying, transmitting and directing vibrations. I think painting must be just a clumsy way of doing that.

"Pay more attention to the vibrations from the earth and everything in it."

Working on a painted image, it's so easy to let abstractions become detours that lead away from my original intent—the qualities of a certain color combination, the enigmatic character of a passage of paint or the unexpected intoxicating effects of a particular idea. In search of the provocative, the wonder of the obvious can be overlooked. At times, distractions become so engaging that the larger composition vanishes; I lose the thread and the big picture disappears. Hence, periodically, I call in another artist to look at my work, someone who can still see what I have become blind to.

"Whaddaya think? Am I on track?"

Tesla was just reminding me to get back on track, to see something important that had become obscured—to tune in to what was lost to the noise of interference.

"…from above, from the stars and heavenly bodies, and from elsewhere…there is resonance between yourself and the vibrations you receive. That is the nature of awareness…."

"I'm in the middle," I said finally. "In between the stars and the soil."

"Awareness of who you are often begins with understanding

where you are," granted Tesla, "a perfect place of potential for a transmitter, receiver, and resonator. Becoming open to the subtle nature of earth's vibrations will teach you to know yourself, rather than just to know about yourself. The ability to have true influence in a universe of vibrations is dependent on that awareness. You either reflect or contribute in proportion to your conscious awareness and the appropriate use of that influence. This is one of many keys, which we will discuss at another time."

I couldn't decide whether to feel very big or very small, knowing my important position in the middle, and remembering my place at the top of a pine tree on a small hill, where I went to sit, up with the juncos and chickadees, swaying in the wind above a sea of treetops, to consider the world and wonder who I am.

"The you which is memory is a pattern of vibrations that happens at specific frequencies, the same frequencies that exist as you in the future. Both the past and future frequencies are the same vibrations that are the present you, who is happening now.

"Then, that means that I can…"

"…remember what you have not yet experienced. Yes. You are always at the intersection, all at once—and in the middle."

The large cartwheel I had seen with Nikola on another occasion then reappeared with the noted point at the bottom of its circumference where it met the ground. The wheel began to proceed forward as I watched the point move up, around, and down, to touch the ground repeatedly, an event that became more frequent as the cart gained momentum.

"Notice that the acceleration of the cart does not change the horizontal distance measured by the point on the wheel as it makes contact with the ground, nor the dimensions of its path.

Although its rotation and the event of a specific point's contact with the ground happens with increased frequency, the rest is constant."

I continued watching the wheel, observing what Nikola had described, curious why something so obvious should seem so mysterious. Then the point began to move gradually away from the perimeter of the wheel toward the axle. As it did so, its path became more compact; the measured horizontal distance decreased, while the speed of its action seemed to increase until it was dizzying. Eventually, the point arrived at the center of the axle, where it came to rest—where, in the middle of the motion, everything was still—no more ups and downs, no measured distance. I thought of times in the studio, when things become calm and there is suddenly no effort in the work, with nothing separating me from the image and the paint, and I looked at the wheel, relaxing and releasing my breath.

"There. Presently, I think that is enough," said Tesla.

The few rooftops of my neighborhood, my dreams and many possible lives, the world stretched out to the horizon, the whole sky, all available to a boy rocking gently in the arms of a favorite pine tree. "Why is it so difficult to believe in something that big now?" I asked myself aloud.

Without warning, I was filled with emotion. *"Go ahead,"* I coached myself. *"This world is not like the other world."*

"You know," I started. "I feel very tender—" wishing it weren't so awkward.

"Love is resonance, an effect of the coincidence of frequencies, a marriage of patterns," stated Tesla, "making their combined influence greater than the sum of their individual effects. Emotions are powerful vibrations, all with specific frequencies that affect

things within the vast range of their influence. Love attracts like a magnet, joining those who love in oneness, as a melodic progression attracts harmonious notes. Loving what you fear or lack transforms challenges into gifts, as loving your enemies turns them into friends. In a similar way, negative emotions attract negative outcomes and will ultimately void the world within the range of their influence. There are, after all, only two parent emotions—with no end to how many or how much one can love, while hate ends only when there is nothing more left to hate. Thus, one chooses fullness or emptiness—
I also care for you, my friend."

Learning to feel the earth's vibrations has helped me to recognize and love that part of me that is earth. Learning to feel what is from the stars has helped me to recognize and love that part of me from the stars. Feeling what comes to me from elsewhere has taught me to recognize and love that part of me from beyond my current perspective. So, I've begun to see part of me in everything: butterflies, chickadees, and in my dog, in trees and flowers, in rocks, raindrops, and seashores. I stare up at the sky and see myself in the complexity of heavenly events, counting my life there in days, seasons, and years. I walk down a sidewalk and recognize myself in others' faces; I see the part of me that is the crowd, in a multitude of colors and types, in the mystery of awareness reflected in a diversity of eyes and visions.

"I'm in the middle," I repeated, thinking of Daumier's friend gripping a rope, hanging somewhere between up and down. "Between the panel and the paint."

"In the place of the spark," submitted Tesla, "the place of resonance, where frequencies are reiterated, and patterns interwoven."

"Am I the loom then?" I wondered, recalling the strange weaving process we had watched a day before. "I think I'm going to return to Florence, to visit San Marco, to sing there in the monks' chambers. I want to find the notes that make them resonate."

"That sounds good," he agreed. "Thank you for letting me share these things."

"I often miss you," I responded self-consciously.

"I know."

"And, I'm more sure now than I've ever been that I'm not sure of anything at all," I added.

"Sometimes, that is the best thing to know," said Nikola Tesla.

19
Talking to Tesla

December 30 – I was fortunate enough to grow up where there weren't any sidewalks, where the paths we followed daily through the woods and fields represented the patterns of our small travels and often the habitual runs and tracks of wildlife: beside an old stone wall, along a stream, through a favorite berry patch, or instinctively hugging the edge of a meadow in wary provision for fast flight into the forest. I like to believe that treading the courses of wild animals, rather than the paved and prescribed routes in town, made us just a little wild ourselves—like the times we'd strip to nothing and run through the woods grunting, growling, and howling. It's not that we were resistant to shepherding, but we tended to identify and recognize other ways to think and do things, and regularly subscribed to those ways. We understood the nature of a clearing as opposed to the cover of a thicket, and the safety of both on different occasions—the shelter of the yard and the sanctuary of the woods. We lived between them both and knew their struggle, the brush encroaching on the fields, and the grass growing into the trees.

Tesla began our lesson this morning by reviewing yesterday's thoughts, whether his or mine, before quoting our discussion of two days ago. "Agreements are necessary for any system or order.... The prototypical agreements are best understood as steps to awareness, formal interactions that represent willingness to accept increasing experience.... They represent the requests, by those prepared, for further enlightenment and the possibility of increased participation in the work, with the understanding that additional participation includes additional accountability—which also means increased liability in terms of the potential to cause disorder or compromise. These agreements bring about the increased opportunity to act—to obey," he suggested.

"And rocks—do they obey?" I asked a bit boldly, since I've never liked the idea of obedience very much.

"Someone who obeys acts without being told," he replied. "True obedience is never enforced. It is a state of oneness where commands are not necessary."

"Like—*before hearing*," I said, remembering some high school Latin. "It fits with the idea of making agreements and seeking increased participation and knowledge. So, unconscious obedience isn't obedience at all—just a state of enforcement." I was relieved by that thought. "As you said...a state of ignorance and unaccountability. It requires awareness, doesn't it? And rocks—are they aware?"

"As always, it happens by degree. Rocks are as aware as they need to be to fulfill their requirements," came a swift reply.

"Well, that would account for all possible anomalous rock activity," I laughed. "No need to provide for that; rocks are obedient—unlike me. I suppose humans tend to explore other possibilities; make decisions to disobey, to stray—endowing us with both the capacity to cause disorder and to learn by experience. Right?"

Nikola reiterated something he had said during his first lecture months ago. "I am sure you will remember how important it is to know that 'the most significant pattern or sequence is *one*, the pattern or sequence consisting of a single unit.' I have shown you the wheel. Traveling outward toward the edge of its circumference, the outlying area becomes increasingly dynamic, but the hub around which it rotates remains stable. The trueness and constancy of the center safely contain the forces that occur peripherally during the wheel's progress. It is the unity, the stillness in the middle that supports the wheel's action."

I had learned about it on a playground, rotating an old metal carousel as fast as I could before grabbing a railing and jumping on, then scrambling to where the centrifugal pull seemed to subside—then moving back toward the edge—then crawling to the center again—playing back and forth between the forces, to feel them pushing me in and pulling me out. As the movement began to wind down, I'd sit in the middle and close my eyes, turning until I felt myself released from everything. At home, we'd do something similar in the yard, taking turns spinning around in place while gripping someone's hands until their bodies flew up and out, or whirling around alone to feel our arms flung out, our hands tracing orbits around us in the air. In my dream, I recalled my childhood games, and saw something like the eye of a storm, a picture from a weather-report, then imagined a blue screen behind a well-groomed actor moving and pointing in an unusual kind of charade. *"Pay attention!"* I warned myself, promptly rejoining the discussion with Tesla.

"…the role of the center is singular. It is the axis and focus. As Adam and Eve are prototypical, so is the Center. It is the perfect prototype, the place where everything comes together, the ultimate intersection. The position of Center has a complete view, unlike others; since all other points of view are naturally skewed, limited by the context of one side or another. The Center sees the concordance of all possible views."

There are adventures whose plot is obscured, like an overgrown path winding through the woods, unknown before it's traveled: between the two big trees, around a gray boulder, past the bog, through the ferns, across a mossy log, over the stone wall and down a steep hill. Just as there are pictures that happen without warning, drawing me into strange passages that I had not planned to paint: the unexpected image of open scissors, an odd pattern from an old painting, a stray piece of underpainting left peeking through, the painted letters of a word, or a surprising section of impressionist impasto in the middle of smooth glazes. But there are also tales whose plot is clear, told and retold until the pattern of events is known by heart, like a part in a *commedia*, the lines I never tire of hearing and those parts I can rehearse without thinking:

"Thanks, dad."
"Don't be a fool!"
"You saved my life."
"You filthy pig!"
"He's just a crazy artist."
"The mean old bastard!"
"I love you, dear."

The struggle is to recognize myself somewhere in between.

"It all happens in the garden—meaning a place prepared and dedicated," began Tesla, "within the bounds of a system and order…"

"Yeah—*l'orto*," I whispered, "*ordo—ordinis—ordini—ordinem —ordine…*"

"…that allowed Eve and then Adam to reason, to act and initiate a process. The garden is set apart for such activities. It is the place for choosing greater awareness—while the wilderness is the way of experience, the result of agreements in the garden. The wilderness is the journey back."

"I know, I know—how many types of fire are there?" I recalled before actually asking the question.

"As many as there are circumstances," answered Nikola. "There are many names for the garden and wilderness but they are always the same. Each time you return to the garden, the investment is greater; and the ensuing wilderness must be re-entered at a different point and in a different way. You choose the journey. Some are lost along the way, and others fall asleep upon returning; but the process can go on until full awareness is reached, full potential and full accountability for all that one agrees to see."

Tesla was quiet then, seeming intent but a little weary. I was thoughtful. Neither of us spoke. It was a lot to grasp, but made sense of what I hadn't understood quite as well before. I thought of The Sower in the museum back home, plodding steadily across the soil and casting seeds, and Gauguin's warm brown Eve reaching up to pick a fruit. *"It always happens in a garden."*

"Remember the pattern of one," said Nikola after a while. "The Center is the place of oneness, where deviations and forces on the periphery are corrected and the wheel held steady. It is the still place in the middle of commotion. Everything revolves around the Center." I saw the wheel rolling across the rocky ground, the spokes meeting at the hub where the axle solidly accepted the abuse and faults of the rough terrain. "Everything depends on it."

Then I saw the night sky and the stars in motion slowly revolving around a single star, and felt like a big question mark again, still waiting for a sign. *"But who am I in all of this?"*

The *me* lying in bed often considers the dream as it is taking place. *"Could this be coming from me?"* I usually ask, as if expecting a definitive response to come from the source of my concerns. To be honest though, I have never before examined anything so thoroughly, never met or imagined a character like Nikola Tesla, and never felt so awake. *"If so—is it any less wonderful?"* I always conclude, while still preferring to believe in the miraculous nature of my dream mentor and our deepening friendship.

"You choose the journey," said Nikola. "You decide who to become." For a few moments I watched a solitary figure wandering alone, and then saw myself at the edge of shadow, peering out into nothingness. "I can offer you tools, but I cannot violate your experience," he continued.

I thought of the many centers of things around which other things revolve: the nuclei of atoms and cells;
    (Considering the substance of my own body,)
all of the suns, planets, moons, stars and galaxies;
    (it's difficult to tell how big or how small I am,)
each with centers of influence maintaining the nature and order of their systems, one above the other, and greater things above them—
    (but I'm no one really…just an artist with his head up in the clouds,)
a pattern as infinitely large as it is infinitesimally small.
    (traveling somewhere between here and there.)

And I saw the wheel of the night sky again, but as a many-dimensional whole with glowing trails spiraling both in and out of its center, to and from all the star-like points of its volume, with the brightest star at the heart of its order, both radiating out and drawing everything into itself.

> *All things, among themselves,*
> *possess an order; and this order is*
> *the form that makes the universe like God.*
> (Beatrice to Dante)

"The measurements of the human body are distributed by Nature as follows...."

Around 1490, Leonardo, as a *geometer...seeking to square the circle*, described the ideal proportions of the perfect human prototype by quoting the Roman architect Vitruvius, "...that 4 fingers make 1 palm, and 4 palms make 1 foot, 6 palms make 1 cubit...," documenting the hidden mechanics, "...4 cubits make a man's height. And 4 cubits make one pace and 24 palms make a man...," the underlying patterns—the composition; "...from the nipples to the top of the head will be the fourth part of a man...From the elbow to the tip of the hand will be the fifth part of the man...," the *cosmografia del minor mondo*, a place of vibration, "...and from the elbow to the angle of the armpit will be the eighth part of the man...," the threshold to a whole, "...The whole hand will be the tenth part of the man; the beginning of the genitals marks the middle...," the human form as the embodiment of the universe—Tesla's mnemonic.

First, Leonardo must have used the generative aspect of the figure to center the drawing of the man, arms outstretched horizontally and feet held together—within a square; before using a compass to circumscribe the figure, arms and legs spread out like spokes—within a wheel centered on the navel. He drew the perfect prototype as the middle, both man and child, living somewhere between the material passions of earth and a spiritual connection to heaven.

"You see," said Nikola, "the all-encompassing view from the center requires the ultimate agreement, the complete consecration of will and self."

I knew it was important, but my mind began to wander to other things, and I found myself on strange dreamy tangents again before Nikola, with some impatience and sadness at my lack of conscious vigilance, redirected me quickly back to this fundamental lesson. "Approaching the Center requires continuous agreements and increasing sacrifice. Everything depends on it."

In my dreams, there are many things that Tesla teaches me that I cannot write about here—some things that I'm still considering, and others that can't be expressed in any way that would do them justice or pay them enough respect. I am beginning to grasp in a simple way that the hope I gain from my experiences is a gift, something steady to offset the rambling nature of my life. The surprise is that my hope is based on the substance of my dreams—or is it the other way around? I wander through a painting from the beginning until the composition is revealed and the path becomes clearer, when even misguided brushstrokes seem to support the final image. It becomes irrelevant at that point whether the paint makes the picture or the picture makes the paint. I guess it's some of both. What is important is that I am the place where the image is unveiled, standing between the palette and the panel, both the wanderer and the way.

Nikola then reminded me of the large training room in an earlier dream, where I sat between two oddly veiled figures—but from a different point of view. Once again, I watched people quietly filing out of the large hall, one at a time and in groups, until just a few remained. This time however, the difference was—I knew that it was their decision to leave. It wasn't about being chosen to stay at all. It was about choosing to stay or to leave. Then, from within the dream within a dream, I saw another vision—a beautiful tree, heavy with ripe fruit, in a clearing, in the middle of a broad landscape. I watched many of those who were seeking it eventually abandon and forget their quests, choosing to end their journeys before finding the object of their pursuits. "The liability appears too great," explained Tesla, "so they are declining the invitation to make additional agreements, finding satisfaction in less than they once expected."

I thought of my own obvious faults and weaknesses, and felt unworthy to remain, while those of greater capability were leaving. "I wonder when it will be too much for me?"

"Only when you choose," Nikola responded. "Strength, worthiness and greatness—they happen along the way."

As I thought on what he had said, an unexpected heaviness began to fill me, a crowded feeling, as if my mind and heart were suddenly overflowing with more than they could hold. I saw Nikola Tesla, sitting with his back to me, as if on a stool, slumped over, hugging his chest, and weeping. I have always preferred to avoid feeling regret, believing it to be a worthless sentiment that accomplishes little—you just paint over it, or scrape off the offending colors and move on—but without warning, I was hugging my own chest. Tesla, who had always seemed so confident and strong, was suffering the regrets of his life, and somehow I was sharing them in such an intimate way that they had become my own, hurting more deeply than I had ever hurt, for him, and for me. I pressed both hands hard against my sternum, and felt a flood of tears run down my cheeks. *"Now I know what a broken heart is,"* I thought, overcome with a profound sadness that I had never imagined.

When I get the chance to talk seriously about my work in the studio, I often describe each painting as a door, and the work relating to it as a rite of passage, a series of steps made of choices and agreements. Each painting requires a personal journey and transformation, making each picture an initiation into a new life with new awareness. "The mind of a painter must be like a mirror...," wrote Leonardo. I like to think that an artist vicariously sees and creates on behalf of the audience as well, offering the completed work as a record of the experience, accessible by degree, according to the viewer's preparation.

And then—I understood many things at once, among them, Tesla's intense desire to teach me, and his hope in my adequate preparation. My eyes were already half-open as I slipped back and forth between the light of my bedroom window and the image of Nikola Tesla—and I awoke. I left him sitting there, to find myself in bed, my pillow wet and cold, where I lay weeping silently for some time.

"I couldn't sleep. Was something…going on?" asked my wife wearily.

I turned away to hide my face again.

"Something was disturbing. I just kept tossing and turning…," she continued.

How could I answer her? How could I say anything? I was empty.

"...I don't know how to describe it," she went on. "Are you all right?"

Getting out of bed, I put on my slippers and went to sit on the hard-looking chair facing the computer. "I have a lot to write about this morning," I said softly, and reluctantly began to type—

I was fortunate enough to grow up where there weren't any sidewalks....

20
You or Me?

December 31 – Trastevere was alive early. Carts and three-wheeled gizmos piled high with vegetables and goods rattled back and forth between stripes of timid light and long cool shadows. The sudden staccato of someone hollering erupted from an alley and echoed across the piazza. It was market day. I sat on a curb and watched the production, the setting up of stalls, the *bancarelle*, umbrellas, and awnings, and noted the developing warmth on the Tiber side of the sky. After so much hesitation, it's surprising how fast the sun can rise and detach itself from the horizon, quickly polishing the smudgy faces of old stucco buildings and backlighting the laundry hanging from a tangle of lines stretched between them. Soon, shutters and windows began to clatter open and bedding appeared—blankets, comforters, sheets and pillows, thrown over windowsills and railings, accompanied by the excited cackle of *casalinghe*, Roman housewives clucking back and forth across the narrow streets.

"*Ehhh—sì che te lo giuro Signora! Non hai visto com'è?*"

It was a perfect cartoon of DeChirico's vanishing universe, filling me with nostalgia for a familiar place that I have never been. *"I'm in Italy,"* I reminded myself.

Some thirty years later, I sit and study a snapshot of my younger self in Rome, round-faced, with darker hair and a full red beard, a tweed jacket with a flower on the lapel. It's funny. There I am holding a violin in one hand and smiling. I don't play the violin any more, and I'm quite sure no one today would recognize the man in the photo as me. I'm not sure that I do.

That day in the market, the people all came: the ruddy-skinned vendors in caps, kerchiefs and aprons; the women, to fill their net shopping bags; old men, to talk business; the herds of bicycles; sleek young men preening for fleshy young women and each other; mothers with strollers; gypsies and beggars—all the busy-ness, the cries and calls, everyone clamoring for attention in the middle of complete confusion. *"Sanguinelle belle e fresche, appena arrivate!"* A heavy-set man trotted by, headed for the park, rhythmically blowing on a whistle and followed closely by a pack of schoolboys. *"Belle e mature! Dolcissime!"* I haggled over the price of a cheap sweater and scouted for a sexy *Beatrice* in the crowd… *"Sono come le donne, raggazzi—guardatele ma non toccate!"* …exploring the market and remembering the anthills that I stirred up as a boy. *"Ma cretino! Come non toccate!?"* the slender young men shouted. I watched a healthy-looking fruit vendor eating her fat noon *panino*, and noticed her petite hand holding the husky sandwich, then looked at my own hand, and back at hers as she stuffed a large plug of bread into her mouth. *"Allora bei ragazzi cosa volete?"* she crowed with her mouth full. I looked down again at my thick soft hand, at my blunt fingers with paint under the nails, then at her small but calloused laborer's hand and at the soil beneath her fingernails. I wandered off into the market, pondering our hands, hers and mine, about the boundaries between us, and the commonness of our lives.

It's becoming more difficult to know which thoughts are those of Nikola Tesla and which are my own. Sometimes, it's like a run-on sentence; thoughts come so fast and happen so naturally that they get mixed up and it's hard to sort them out. Often, and unexpectedly, I'll recall or replay parts of dreams during the day, which feels normal while working with paint in the studio, but peculiar during a meeting or while speaking with someone.

"So tell me—what do you think?"

"Oh—sorry. Yeah, would you please repeat that?"

This afternoon, I study another photograph, on the dust jacket of a book about Nikola Tesla. Professional eccentric and photographer, Napoleon Sarony, famous for images of Sarah Bernhardt, Oscar Wilde, and Samuel Clemens, must have taken it toward the end of his career. Tesla, at the height of his own heyday, sits poised and still, the image of self-assurance—a handsome gentleman, even sleek, everything that I have never been. I look at his delicate hands, posed thoughtfully on his cheek and holding the neck of a flask-shaped light bulb—the hands of an artist. *"How do I know you? How can I?"*

The tourists were long gone—as were the last of the grapes, but the oranges were finally coming in. There is something deeply satisfying about market day and its seasonal offerings, from anticipating the first wild greens in spring to savoring a slightly wrinkled apple in the middle of winter. Instead of returning to the studio, I crossed the Ponte Garibaldi and walked toward the center of town. The city felt like a prepared panel begging for paint, and I was a painter. I walked all afternoon, stopping at a few shops, eating too much *gianduia*, and too many pastries on the way to nowhere in particular. *"After all, I'm in Italy."*

Rome is a busy city, and the sidewalks were crowded as always. I enjoyed watching people hurry by, the unique body types and faces, each distinct in dress and attitude, all going places, while I walked aimlessly—past ruins, past fountains, past Saint Francis with a neon halo, and past the Pantheon, before eventually looping around to head back in the direction from which I had come. I remembered an unfinished painted image of three brothers in my studio, abstracted figures, sharing features and body parts, and I began to have some fun. *"What if that eye on the right side of her face was the partner to that on the left of another face? Whose mouth would I use? And whose nose to complete the picture? And what about that chin oddly associating with two currently estranged cheeks—that one over there, and maybe—that one across the street?"* And then it happened that everything changed, and I began to explore the fragile nature of the boundaries between the world as an empty stage, and the place held together by me— the relationship between studio and artist, market and shopper. So the faces dissolved, while the nature of their pieces and the pattern of their associations became more evident and lingered. Then it was as if everything fell into itself and the meanings vanished, just a lot of stray attributes roaming around without a purpose. And so, when I finally saw faces again, I was relieved. And they seemed clever and new. I had looked at faces all my life—I had learned to see them, but had never seen the poetics of a face. I had never seen the glue that holds the parts together until it wasn't there. Suddenly life felt like cloud-gazing, or looking for constellations in the night sky only to recognize myself among the stars.

I search the face in the photograph for clues. The glow from the oversized orb paints a theatrical *chiaroscuro* portrait, like a Rembrandt or Caravaggio. Sarony crafted it well, posing Tesla carefully to capture the dramatic image of his character. But there's no weight on that hand, lifted as if to hold up the head. The fingers tell the story, relaxed against a soft unmoved cheek. And look at the eyes, glancing coyly like a gothic saint with a slight squint, staring out but not quite at me—and that Leonardo mouth almost grinning. "How many people really knew you?"

"Do I? Do you live inside me, or do I really meet you somewhere else—in between things?"

"Yes, this is just how you look in my dreams; the self-aware hero, however reticent and humble. But how you feel at times is more like the photos of another Nikola Tesla, the skinny old fart, a tired loner in baggy suits, concerned with his mortality—when only the birds befriended you." This morning Tesla reminded me of parts of yesterday's dream that I had forgotten, and helped me to correct a few errors, and eliminate some things that I shouldn't write or talk about—making these last few events rather difficult to journal. Everything I write seems inadequate anyway. "I am sorry. I'm pleased that for a while you were happy and confident."

I would have liked to be there—to have him over for supper on a regular basis. "You became so thin!" Skin stretched over bones is all. "Come on! Eat up, Nik! Look at me!" But, nothing would have pleased me more than to help him feed the pigeons. I would have let him talk, learned his pet names for them—listened to his peaceful politics, ideas, and dreams. It's a strange place dreamers go—and who's to say we didn't meet there first in the ethers of his dream world, before I was born? "Well, my friend—it's good that you're my friend. But who are you? And why am I dreaming of you?"

I leave the book and walk over to the mirror, recalling the picture of a young artist with a violin in Rome. *"Look at you!"* The color is gone from my hair, there are creases around my eyes and mouth, and the beginning of jowls softens my jaw. I suck in my belly, contrasting myself with Nikola's slender profile, flexing the muscles of my chest and arms. *"Not so bad…."* A mirror should be a neutral place, an empty stage reflecting the will of its owner, but today—it feels like facing off with a toad. *"Nikola Tesla—how could someone seen so clearly not be real?"*

I'm working on another sketch for a painting; Tesla, as a reluctant Noah, hanging out the window of his laboratory, floating in the air above a clear-cut forest, and sending out doves. *"What divides us—the world where you live from the world where I stand?"* I hold my head obliquely and get close enough to inspect the pores on my nose. *"My personal Saint Nik…sometimes it's hard to know where you end and I begin."* Even my thoughts aren't familiar any more.

The gardens of the Villa Sciarra are tucked into a far corner of the old Roman wall toward the ridge of the Janiculum Hill where I lived. By late afternoon, I had crossed the Tibertine Island and was wandering back through Trastevere toward the slopes of the hill and ultimately to the sanctuary of what is rumored to be an ancient sacred grove—once known as Caesar's Garden. The park surrounding the villa is a haven for writers, romantics, and stray painters on their way home—a world of clean-edged gravel paths daubed with the speckled sunlight of a Renoir or Monet, exotic plants, lazy fountains, and mothers wheeling strollers and calling after children—a place where the forbidden pleasures of naughty marble fauns and entwined young couples happen within view of gentlemen hiding behind opened newspapers.

If it wasn't occupied, my favorite place to sit and think was under a small arbor dome covered thickly from the ground up in a filigree of vines. By that time of year the leaves had fallen and been swept away, leaving a bare tracery of woody lace and the rusted bones of the arbor's frame. The stone bench felt cool, so I folded my scarf and tucked it under me. I was alone. Decades of graffiti, layer after layer of deep and deeper grooves scratched into the aging stone told the tales of those whose lives coincided there with mine. Giovanna plus Fabrizio, Sergio plus Teresa, Rita ama Ugo, M plus C—instinctively, I picked up an angular pebble and patiently began grinding a heart shape into the bench partially eclipsing the love of Marilena and Elio, who had blurred the relations between Marco and Maria. After lightly scribing the initial character of my first name in the top half of the heart, I turned to watch the rhythmic dripping of a small fountain in the center of the arbor, where four nymphs carried an overflowing bowl on their shoulders. I stood, shook out my scarf, and gazed down into the mossy basin at my flickering image.

"Who is it looking back at me the same way that I look at him?"

The unlikely sound of someone practicing pop tunes on a harmonica disrupted my daydream—so I left.

When I am painting, it's easy to become disoriented, lose the thread, to forget where I am, where I entered the picture and where to leave. For all of my foresight and planning, I'm never sure what course an image might take. This unpredictability is a pattern—the back and forth meanderings of a hero pursuing a muse. Each time, I travel a circuitous path, winding my way through the ins and outs of it, only to find myself returning to the place where I started and see it transformed, not because it's changed, but because the path has changed me.

Picking up the book again to inspect Sarony's picture of Nikola, I search for things we have in common, the possible places where we reflect each other; but he is lithe and I am thick, his head is long and mine is blocky, his nose is pointed—mine is blunt, his ears are big and mine are small. We look nothing alike at all. It's the rest of us that gets mixed up, what you can't see; the part of us that likes to dream and feed pigeons, the part of us that meets somewhere in between—where our edges soften and we overlap.

"*What if Narcissus suddenly realized that the image he adored was of his own making? Would his longing be any less?*" I wonder. Then recalling Pygmalion and Galatea, "*I guess not.*"

I imagine myself under the arbor dome, back in Rome, gazing down into the pool of a little fountain. "I'm supposed to carry on the work of Nikola Tesla," I tell my shimmering twin as he mimes it back. "Crazy—huh?"

21
Black Rock, White Rock

January 4 – Asleep, awake, asleep, awake, asleep, awake—and somewhere between asleep and awake—I'm tired out by the many recent dreams. Almost overwhelmed.

"...that when I am asleep I can feel so awake."

As a result—a bit dazed, but exhilarated, and more than a little concerned that what I put down here should be adequate to convey the nature of my dreams and thoughts, I write the first entry of a new year, filled with expectations, and considering once again how much my life has changed.

"You mean *lives*," prompts a little voice.

"I guess I do mean lives—to meet myself and be surprised still feels funny, as I includes a lot more than it used to.

"But, why should it be lives? Am I not the same me, asleep and awake? Like being in Italy or being home—the same life here and there? Or the same me riding a bike or painting in the studio?" I continue to wonder and write, sometimes not sure whether to believe my own experience; then at other times, positive that there is meaning and purpose to what might casually seem absurd. But I'm an artist after all, a painter; and unless the prospects are monetary, some consider *that* absurd as well, more a peculiarity than a profession—surely not practical. At any rate, I suppose I'm not a poet. Things could be worse. And to be honest, I get tired of preaching. My real soapbox is a studio full of paintings, and for those with time enough, I'd take them there to smell and feel the paint; but in a world increasingly intent on more pragmatic ventures, there's little time for such riddles, dreams, and childish vagaries.

"Yes. I am an artist," I repeat to myself.

"Conversing with a dead scientist," adds my brainy assistant. "Talking to shadows!"

The New Year seems a good time to take stock, to pick up my head and get my bearings. Examining life on these pages, pondering the odds and ends of it, I hunt for concrete evidence; then write it all down, reaching the conclusion that at least everything seems different now. In the process, I have come to realize that I am the only proof there is; that from the outside, I look much the same as I did last year, and that my written words are just ordinary words—consequently, anyone might think this Tesla stuff is all a story. I must admit that once in a while, I do too.

Twenty-some years ago, my wife of four years and I, together with two toddler sons, lived in town, in a very small house. The typical white clapboard cottage (which has since become too cramped to serve even as an apartment for one) was our home for several years, from before I went to graduate school until two years after I had finished. It was a tidy house with a screened-in porch and fenced backyard, and though we were happy enough, our financial stability was perpetually shaky. Though I held a part-time job, the delicate state of our affairs was obviously due to my career, as I spent most of my daylight hours painting in the studio.

At that time my studio was located in the attic of a dignified old school about five blocks from our little house. The building had been around for at least a hundred years and was used for everything from high school and university classes to church functions and screening rooms; but eventually, when the grand structure outlasted its distinction and the roof began to leak, there was talk of tearing the place down. Until then, parts of the facility were rented cheap to artists and would-be artists, or became the residence of squatters and a temporary hangout for restless kids.

My studio was about twenty feet squared. Before moving in, I cleaned out piles of trash, painted the walls white, and scrubbed the old maple floor. There were no windows because the room was tucked under the west-facing eaves, the outer section of the ceiling sloping down beneath the roof. Two very large skylights, glazed with chicken-wire glass, on the slanted side of the room helped to make it either cold enough in winter to see my breath, or an oven in the summer. During cold weather, a small electric heater took the worst of the chill off and I wore a sweatshirt; but when it was hot, the best solution was to strip down to my skin.

Inspiration is neither wishful, nor scientific. It's a gut thing that I learned to pay attention to in that studio where I regularly stood with my bare belly exposed to the paint and felt the influence of a greater awareness than my own. When asked about the source of my images, I used to say, "I let the paint decide," which was a lie; and no more likely than the pigment, oil, and medium carefully arranging themselves on the canvas because they were tired of sitting on the palette. That old classroom is where I learned that inspiration comes from somewhere beyond the walls of a studio.

Several days ago an artist friend told me about a strange dream. "…and then the owl lowered his wings, holding them down in front of himself to cover his body—which was human…."

Today, my friend spoke to me again. "Remember that dream I was telling you about? The one with the owl-man?"

"Yeah—you're going to paint about it?" I asked.

"Well, let me tell you," he went on eagerly. "This morning I woke up early to take the dog out. Dawn was just starting to brighten the sky, and I glanced up as the biggest owl I've ever seen flew down to land on a post right in front of me."

"That's how it happens," I thought.

"Its wingspan was so huge that at first I almost expected to see a human body—you know, like in my dream. It sat and cocked its head to look at me; so I stood there, and we watched each other for a good five minutes…"

"In dreams, we seem to experience things in more intense ways," I said. "I think you called it to you."

"But there haven't been owls around like that for years," he returned. "Not since they tore down the old barn—and I've never before seen one that big."

I pictured the owl somewhere far off in the mountains, sensing my friend's silent call, then traveling closer each night until arriving to meet him early that morning, an unexpected messenger from another world with a wordless message to deliver. Inspiration feels like that, often a response to the heart's invocation that the head has ignored or doesn't recognize, a bolt of lightning suddenly connecting a small place with somewhere vast and distant. While the process of arranging paint happens in the studio, the secret of beginnings, the instigation, comes from elsewhere, some place still un-seeable from the artist's point of view.

"It's like painting," I said finally.

"And paintings are the only evidence," he answered softly.

"And only *the evidence,"* I reminded myself.

Another feature of my room in the old school was the closet. A door was cut into the slanted ceiling and partial west wall of the studio, which led into a cramped gable where I stored things. It was the only place in the studio that had a view, other than two squares of sky through the skylights, as a low round window let me see the street and grounds of the academy if I crouched or sat on the floor. The window was about two feet in diameter and divided into four panes by horizontal and vertical muntins crossing in the middle. There were also two small doors inside the closet, to the right and to the left, leading into the dark crawl space beneath the last few feet of roof, where the beams, floor joists and outer wall of the building all met.

Almost every afternoon, I walked from work to my studio, where I'd paint until evening. Often, in warm weather, my wife showed up with two little boys in a stroller to see and comment on my progress and then to accompany me home. I could always depend on her for simple honesty.

"Well?"

"Those hands—they make me think of salad forks. You know, the plastic ones you get at the chicken place," she said innocently. "Those part-spoon-part-fork things—*runcible* spoons." And she smiled at the kids. "I like the green?"

"Of course," I silently complained, *"...a beautiful pea-green boat!"*

"But, you're the artist. So, don't listen to me—I don't know anything. Go ask someone who knows," she apologized.

"I'll rework them tomorrow," I groaned, acting hurt and putting down the brush. "Well…that's a weird comment…*runcible spoons*!"

"But you asked, and I was only trying to help," she said defensively.

Usually, my wife spared me the pain of knowing how poor we were, but a few days earlier she had mentioned that we had no money, that the rent was well past due, and that we needed groceries. *"This is it,"* I thought.

"I don't get paid for two weeks," I answered. "And you know what that means—I've gotta give up this painting stuff." I studied her for hints. "It was crazy to begin with," I added, hoping to hear; "No it's not, dear!" But she looked serious and I could tell she had been crying.

"What do you want me to do?" she mumbled, and I smiled at the kids.

Yes, being an artist can be difficult. *"Bravo!"* the Italians like to say, but it's a passion filled with a long list of temporal fears and desires. "Just give me a few days," I said, trying to sound resourceful. "Things'll work out."

Once upon a time it was too easy to talk of being an artist, but doing it is different. The itch is persistent, a symptom that has always been there, an invisible rash or insect-bite that I can rub until it's raw and still can't resist scratching, even as the tickle becomes a sting. "Why don't you guys go home and I'll be right along? I really can't stop yet—and I promise I won't be late. OK?" So I kissed them all good-bye and stayed to scrape off the runcinate-looking hands. It's telltale when my work in the studio becomes reflex, habitual; when I stop seeing what I'm doing and start relying on what I think I know. Inspiration happens some time after that, when my own resources are exhausted and I realize how much I don't know. It was time to take stock again—of the image I was painting and of my life. *"They're claws anyway, not hands."*

In the business of living, the repetitions at my bedside can become rote, or are forgotten. I'm pretty independent even when I'm not, even when an extra tank of fuel, an unexpected bill or a trip to the doctor could ruin me—but sometimes, in spite of myself, I am forced to wake up, made to wonder that I fall so easily from available grace to end up so desperately on my own.

"Oh, show me mercy. Lighten my heart, for I was overcome on my way—and am alone…" like Saint Jerome, helplessly stuck in the mud of a strange situation. "…but I admit this mess is of my own making, Lord."

There are many times while working that I feel impressed by something outside myself and the paint. I reach for red and something says, "Try green." Or else I'm painting a sky and my brush unexpectedly adds a contrail between the clouds. Or someone shows up out of the blue and says, "Those hands—they make me think of plastic salad forks." In fact after mastering the craft, learning to paint is largely learning to look and listen to what is otherwise peripheral and unnoticed—to practice bringing things into view. So I stood there dressed as I was born, on a hot summer evening, with nothing separating me from the image and the paint; I wished and waited—for revelation about the claws that reminded my wife of runcible spoons, and for help with our larger more desperate situation.

"Dammit! How and why did I decide to do this art thing?"

After scraping off the offending paint, I picked up the brush and started to work.

I'll make them less regular. Maybe they were just too perfect—

"Dear Lord, if you're there—I really have to talk to someone."

I hadn't eaten in two days, maybe three—nothing, no food, no water—but I wasn't very hungry. I scooped up a dab of Cinnabar Green Deep on the brush and mixed it with a drop of medium on the palette.

"She liked the green, so I'll leave that—

"I know life isn't supposed to be fair, but we're in bad trouble."

Letting go of my appetites felt liberating. I added a bit of Cobalt Blue, a little Titanium White to lighten up the value, a speck of Cadmium Red to deaden the hue and a more generous three drops of medium. Color flowed easily from the loaded bristles as I touched them to the panel.

"Yeah, look! That's better now. More honest, even a bit childlike—

"I share what I have, and try not to be too greedy. You know that."

I'm afraid to let go of being an artist. I think it's who I am. The paint felt good, becoming smooth and shiny on the brush, something halfway between pasty and liquid as I applied it to the image.

"She was right—I like it."

When inspiration happens, sometimes it's subtle. I'll have a hunch or an insight that I didn't earn. But sometimes it's more than that—an unforeseen infatuation turns things sweeter, and the distinction between myself and the world around me softens—everything fuses. An entire dissertation is revealed in the moments it takes to move my brush from the palette to the image; part of me seems to dance in slow motion while the rest of me watches—simple things like a glass of water or a black felt hat find purpose, and tired clichés renew their significance. That's the addiction of art, to be surprised in the middle of the process by gifts of unimagined virtuosity, suddenly to know things that I don't know.

"Please Lord—I just want to paint. Is that too much?
"There! No more runcible spoons....
"Is anyone listening?"

Some time before, I had spent a long weekend in the woods, packing in about fifteen miles along a river to some hot springs, then soaking for a couple of days before hiking out. The last morning there, I awoke early and took one last swim, lazily floating and paddling back and forth between the warm and cold currents of the river—trying to memorize the place. It was midmorning and raining softly when I finally packed up and started down the trail to the car and home. I poked along reluctantly, as the sun peeked through in an effort to dry things off between each impending shower. Then, stopping to admire a hanging water drop, I saw rain running down the leaf toward that liquid world caught on its tip—and everything changed. I became keenly aware of all the green grooves directing water to countless other drops on countless leaf tips, each holding a pinpoint sun captive in the realm of its reflections. I watched the tiny pendant oceans all around me repeatedly get heavy—and let go. And heard their hushed patter join the rush of the river.

It was as if I suddenly understood the sucking sounds of mud, the chatter of stones underfoot, the talk of every rock. I felt the meanings of colors and shapes, the memories of every smell. That's the attraction of the woods, the lure of letting something wiser and bigger than I take charge once in a while. It's like waking up again, to someplace that looks the same as where I am—but not really.

When painting is good, it's like that, like dowsing for a source until everything changes and I tune in to something alive in the atmosphere that hums around my face and fingertips. That's how it happens. So I painted, prayed and painted;

> sitting,
> kneeling,
> standing—

I grumbled, cried, and sweat, on a hot summer night in the studio until I felt my heaviness slowly give way to something stronger than myself—like iron must feel around a magnet.

I'm not sure how it began, and don't recall now taking the first steps but I do remember stopping in the middle of the room, half-way between my painting and the closet door, to wonder at the sensations.

"But, this is how it always happens; isn't it?"

I thought about the many times I had felt that charge on my skin; listening to music, reading a poem, watching a performance, falling in love, hiking in the rain, painting paintings, or dreaming—the constant temptation and urge to experience something beyond what I can imagine.

"So, where am I going?"

Like whispers in the air joining to become a loud voice in my insides, something answered, "Just follow me."

I glanced around the studio and saw that things were still in place, but somehow not the same; the colors on the palette, a few plants in the corner, the honey-thick warmth of a late evening sunset streaming through the skylights—for a few moments I stood there considering what to do, and then continued toward the closet.

When I was a little younger, I looked for any excuse to escape to the desert; where, in the face of my insecurities, it was reassuring to witness the solitary nature of success against all conceivable odds (completely opposite to the indulgent lifestyle of the woods, where success means fighting for elbow room). I would spend days wandering around lost somewhere between a wilderness of red rock and the inner landscape of myself, staying cool in the shadowy interface between where I was and who I was. At night I slept under a sandstone overhang, sharing it with the earlier wild tenants. Life in a world of rocks, sand, and wind can be a thrifty proposal, clinging to the extremities of what is possible and necessary.

I remember walking aimlessly up a broad dry wash one afternoon while considering the conditions of my existence, and feeling impressed to enter the mouth of a narrow canyon—*compelled* to enter the canyon. And suddenly things began to shift. I was there, but not really—looking at one thing, and seeing another, the solid shapes around me quickly melting into a flow of associations. I passed between the walls of rock as if progressing through a series of staged events happening somewhere other than the place I was, and stopped along the way to ponder my life as if pausing at stations on a *Via Dolorosa*. Finally, I turned a corner to confront an abrupt dead end. It was a box canyon. That's the draw of the desert, that in the spareness of its environment, as in the poverty of our circumstances, subtle things are left exposed and my perception is amplified.

So I faced the closet door that was not a closet door, somewhere between where I was and who I was, and watched my hand grip and turn the doorknob. *"What am I doing?"* I pulled open the door and stepped into the fiery glow of the closet, set aflame by the orange glare of the setting sun. While painting, it's not uncommon to be moved by the powerful effect of color and form, but how an artist becomes that color and form is difficult to describe. I stood still, studying my skin, painted in hot cadmium hues by the evening sunlight flooding through a small round window. And that's how it happens that I can often be surprised by entering the image I am painting.

I looked right and then left at the two doors that led into separate crawl spaces. *"I could choose wrong and end it."* On impulse, I went over to the door on the right, unhooked it, pushed it open, and crouched down to enter the dark tunnel. Within several hunched steps I was just the humbled painter of ill-formed hands, black hats and other curiosities, a sweaty man sneaking through the dirt of an old building. *"Wrong way."* And I backed out of the cramped space, hoping to return to the naiveté of before my miscalculation. *"Paint can be scraped off— but, do I get another chance at this?"* I crossed the fire of the closet and entered the dimness of the passage on the other side, feeling immediately fluent again in some unspoken language. *"On my knees?"* And I began to crawl. *"Turn to the right?"* And I turned to the right, creeping slowly forward into the thick layer of dust in the tight angle where the roof met the floor. It was like trying to stay tuned to a specific frequency, setting a dial to receive communication from far away, the message being amplified within me. "Now, hold out your left hand." And I reached out into the dark with my left hand.

Revealing what is hidden is always first about grasping for something in the dark. Even my best predeterminations are tested when I finally begin to apply paint to an image. Trust in the process happens in the balance between impulse and perception, reaction and response; it's so easy to lose my way and end up putting wrong colors and shapes on a panel—and then want to get it all off, feeling suddenly exposed as a fool caught in the middle of pretending, and surprised as my belief abruptly turns to make-believe. I laid my hand around an irregular fist-sized object covered in a thick powdery blanket of disregard, the proof of decades of soot and dust from being left on top of the outer wall, between the roof beams.

"Now take it—and put out your right hand."

So I picked it up and sat back on the floor, wedged there uncomfortably in the narrow pitch of the place—

"*Heavy!*"

—and brought it in to rest against my chest, stretching out my other hand. My skin prickled lightly as I touched another age-coated object the length and thickness of a small forearm. Seconds later I was back in the studio staring down at what I held.

"*Two rocks?*" I was holding two rocks.

I sat on the floor and began to rub off the soft coat of dirt with my fingers.

"*Gold!*"

The black rock in my left hand was filled with flecks of something metallic. The stone in my right hand was white, an easily identifiable piece of stalactite with a channel running through the middle.

"God sent us gold!" Dropping the two stones, I quickly returned to the dark passage and got down on all fours again, crawling eagerly along the low wall, and checking each space between the beams that rested there. *"Nothing."* I was just a silly man prowling anxiously through the shadows of a run-down school. It wasn't the same place at all.

"I need to find an assayer," I thought. *"There must be enough in that rock to pay our bills—an assayer will know what to do."* I could hardly wait to tell my wife the good news.

"Everything's going to be OK." I said with emotion. "I told you. Look, dear! Can you believe it? This is gold!"

Of course I never went looking for an assayer, but finding the two dirty rocks got us through that month. Two rocks—and there are rocks everywhere—plain old rocks, the uncommon tokens of unseen metamorphoses. Eventually, I cleaned them up and have kept them safe for some twenty years. Once I thought of grinding them into pigments for the initial values of my pictures, the *chiaroscuro* foundation of my work—igneous and sedimentary, the manifestations of fire and water. Black rock and white rock; a tangible quantity, solid proof of what is intangible, the evidence of what is invisible. That's why I paint; it's like standing in a rainstorm waiting for lightning to strike, or praying for a sign in pigments and oil, hoping to uncover something bigger than I in the layers of my activity—the ever-present itch to go somewhere else and bring back something anyone can see and touch—to cry, "Hey look! Can you believe it?"

Sometimes retelling tales, like painting patterns, reveals things about them that aren't obvious, unveiling the fertile matter of what seemed fleeting and ordinary. Things can change. Writing about my friendship with Nikola Tesla has been like that, not that the nature of my dreams is suddenly different, but that my view of them is clearer and their substance more apparent—like the true worth of two rocks becoming increasingly evident.

And that's how it happened, that while taking stock of things, I understood that the world is just a big dirty rock—but not really.

THREE

22

Concerning My Moons

> ANY DOUBTS YOU MAY HAVE
> WILL DISAPPEAR EARLY
> THIS MONTH
>
> YUM YUM NOODLE CO.

January 17 – I watched the petite woman finally approaching our table with her usual contained smile, carrying the bill on a small brown tray along with four shell-like wafers loosely wrapped around our futures. *"That's mine,"* I thought, impressed with one that caught my eye from across the room, *"that lighter-looking one in the middle."* I could feel my fortune being drawn to me like metal to a magnet. It was obvious.

"I'll take that…," said my friend across the table, meaning the check and my cookie, cracking it open thoughtlessly, and hardly giving the little prophecy a glance before chuckling and reading it aloud. "Someday, I want a real fortune," he laughed, while wadding up the small strip of paper. But to me—that *was* my real fortune, the one I had been waiting for, the one I wanted. Because I am human, it is my nature to see patterns, to make associations, viewing things in relationship to other things, until a basis for understanding becomes a working theory. *"He stole my future!"*

That's the way a painting happens, the blank panel attracting one brushstroke, and one brushstroke attracting the next, and the next, and the next—until the pattern is complete, the meaningful association of countless circumstantial events. The growing order between the panel and paint, paint and paint, between element and element, idea and idea; like an unfolding plot attracting players, the initial itch eventually becoming an entire world proposed by the painter's supervision of pigments, binders, and ground. I think of Monet's wild application of colors exploring the providence of light on the surface of a pond reflecting the sky and filled with lily pads, while still retaining the identity of paint from another point of view.

Beato Angelico, Filippo Lippi, DaVinci, Crivelli, Bellini, Mantegna—for me, there's a certain attraction to the work of artists who understand the power of context; not as background, but as a painted system to hold an idea firmly within its framework. Consider an Annunciation without the evocative surroundings, a Madonna and Child without the effect of its setting—the event without the landscape. Take Giorgione's painting of a dandy young voyeur standing on the left side of a stream, eyeing a breastfeeding woman seated on the right, the scene unfolding beneath a sky of dark clouds pierced by lightning—or Bruegel's Icarus falling all but unseen while a farmer plows a field, a ship sets sail, and the habitual events of the countryside continue unaware. An artist knows that presenting the realness of anything means delivering all the pieces to the puzzle, the contents and the vessel—what would be lost, and what would have no purpose otherwise.

This morning I awoke a little later than usual, but decided that I really needed to visit with my friend. Don't ask why I think I can demand his attention whenever I decide I'm ready; I don't know. At first I fumbled, trying to focus—had several false starts that quickly became nonsensical dreams, but was eventually able to arrive at that empty place, the neutral stage, a blank ground—until things start to happen. It's not unlike a canvas or panel waiting for paint, but in this case…a magical theatre awaiting a production, a dramatic event. After some effort, I reached that place or state where we generally meet, and hoped that he might be there, or just happen to drop in—or however it works. (As though he's a cab driver, ready to cruise by just as I hail him?) Sometimes I'm successful in paying him a visit, and sometimes not.

Then, in an instant, without dramatics, I was surrounded by a patterned flatness, the checkered landscape that by now I have become accustomed to, a familiar place covered in a grid of microelements and their implied associations. At first, I wondered that I was alone, but felt relieved to be there, and I relaxed—feeling just a little guilty for taking comfort in the ordinary nature of what had been extraordinary. *"An artist shouldn't do that,"* I playfully scolded myself, beginning half-heartedly to seek for something more in the well-known scene.

When I was seven or maybe eight, I used to watch the hands of my wristwatch to see them move. "I saw the minute hand move!" I announced one day. "But, you have to hold still, and look for a long time before you can see it." It felt strangely good to be in the place that something not casually evident should suddenly become so plain. That's how it felt again as I watched a piece of the grid about a pace in front of me begin to rise, a row of filled and blank spaces slowly and steadily lifting away from the patterned plane on which I stood.

"Are you here?" I called out.

As it rose, I began to read it from the end like a code, *"Open, open, closed, closed, open, closed…,"* noting that back in place on the ground, sequences could be read in all directions, but that this sequence, by being separate, had become a pattern peculiar to itself. In spite of my usual impatience, it all happened gradually, at a speed that seemed not unlike the movement of a clock. It twisted and turned, like a ribbon, spiraling up in a column—although at a glance, it appeared absolutely still.

"Is anyone there?"

Curling around, it continued to wind higher until it was opposite my face, where at eye level, I noticed the same open and closed patterns within the patterns, making the filled squares only mostly filled, and the empty squares, only mostly empty; and I saw another patterned strip coiling up inside the first, introducing the possibility of additional relationships between the sequences on the two strips.

"It's alive, like a tendril—or a snake."

"It *is* life," said Tesla, standing beside me—as if he had been there all along.

"Helices…," I breathed, engrossed in their patterns and steady movement. "The code…Adam and Eve—line and circle again." I watched as other patterned ribbons began to detach and slowly lift away from the plane around us.

"This is just the visible edge," he reminded me. "Remember,

there are any number of dimensions that you cannot see."

"The serpent!"

"...and the tree. This is all part of an incredible intersection," added Nikola, sounding satisfied. I took a deep breath. "The choices between this and that, the branching discussions that represent reasoning and awareness—the agreements," he continued.

I studied the patterns blinking on and off along the ribbons, the single units and the worlds within them; and the more I saw, the more I could see; and the more I could see, the less I understood. Writing this, I realize that I can only hope to describe with some degree of accuracy what I cannot explain.

It was an annual occurrence, that when the snow was almost gone, and the woods were just beginning to hint at greening up, that on a sunny afternoon I'd take a pail with me to the swamp to look for long coiling strands of jelly caught among the weeds by the shore. They were hard to see, so I'd lie on my belly to gaze down into a world that otherwise went mostly unnoticed. The sun lit the water to the bottom, revealing a blanket of old leaves criss-crossed by recent snail travel and enlivened by the shadows of a few skeeters on the surface, and a pair of water beetles going about their business. I watched a steady stream of bubbles coming from where I imagined an old snapper must be hiding, waiting for a frog or the fingers of careless children; and I scooted away farther down the bank. You had to look for a while before your eyes became accustomed to seeing things that were otherwise unapparent, down where everything was mud-colored. Then I saw them, intertwining chains of inky gray B-B's suspended in clear gelatinous tubes, rhythmic messages, the harbingers of warmer weather and an impending amphibious chorus—serpentine parades of polka dots loosely winding through the sticks and dead grass just a few inches beneath the sky's reflection and the sun's play on the water's surface—the patterned ribbons of toad eggs.

"Mama, look what I've got!" I exclaimed, bursting through the door and presenting a brimming pail of swamp water. "I'm going to keep them—I'm going to grow them." Carefully, I put them in a gallon jar that I placed on the kitchen table, watching them day by day gradually turning more oval than round. Within a week many had tails, escaping the gelatinous coils to become a few dozen mud-brown pollywogs. I changed the water, carrying pailfuls from the swamp, and fed them goldfish food. In a few weeks, they grew arms, and then legs, as their tails slowly disappeared. I placed a rock in the jar so they could climb out of the water when they were ready, and finally released the few survivors back on the bank of the swamp where I had collected them, after some had tried to explore my mother's kitchen. I had patiently and intently watched and attended to the mystery of metamorphosis, though sometimes sitting there for hours without seeing any change at all. It happened imperceptibly, like the movement of a clock face, not visible at a glance, but seen by those with the patience to be still. The messengers were the message—life taking place as witnessed by a child—something I can describe but can't explain even now.

"It's all here, isn't it?" I exclaimed. "Everything, right here in the singular patterns of these coils. But electricity—is it here?" I asked, considering how far our discussions had departed from what I had expected several months before, and the teasing expectations of friends who know about my crazy dreams. "Well, yes—of course, this is all about what you call electricity," answered Tesla, giving me a disappointed look. "There is plenty of electricity involved.

And, in due time, hopefully you will understand what you are not yet prepared to use wisely." I felt a little stupid—and even more stupid for not knowing exactly why I felt stupid.

It was quiet then; and Nikola left me alone, there in a forest of wildly spiraling patterns which appeared quite still at a glance, pondering my impatience and pretension. Obviously, I had just failed to measure up to a standard that I hadn't understood.

Actually, there was a lot more to it than I can remember, important things I can't quite bring to mind. *"Strange, isn't it? That waking up often means forgetting."* Perhaps, as sometimes happens, it will come back to me while I'm busy brushing my teeth, eating a sandwich, or driving the car. *"...the branching discussions that represent reason...the branching discussions that represent reason...."* I'll keep repeating it until I find a scrap of paper and a pen to scribble a note to myself.

> this or that + branches = reason

"But, is that my thought or his?" Whatever the case, there does seem to be more than just a circumstantial order to my dreams, like a story told a little at a time, unfolding slowly from one fortune to the next.

Painting has taught me that things are seldom as they first appear. It's something I have learned, relearned and still need to be reminded. According to my friend Nikola Tesla, "Without opening other eyes, we must base our understanding of the unseen on just a little cross section—just the visible edge." An odd looking character in a dream twenty-some years ago said it like this; "My appearance is according to your current understanding. To you, I am who I am because of who you are."

"In other words," I realized, *"my world is like a mirror."*

"What I can teach you depends wholly on you," said the peculiar fellow, and we flew together above the clouds and visited large shiny globes reflecting the sky, which made them seem to disappear. Everything points to something else, which points to something else, and something else—in paint, the challenge is to avoid becoming too attached to or trivializing what is in the mirror. One image happens over months or years of intense personal struggle, and another happens as if without hands, reminding me that I am both integral and incidental to the process.

Dreams are common. After I started writing them down, I stopped talking about mine so much. But once in a while, there are people, who after hearing about my dreams, want to tell me theirs. It's almost clandestine—the cautious look around to see if anyone can hear what they're about to divulge. "I had this dream once…." And the secret is revealed. I can't help but smile because it's so much like how some artists discuss their work. Then there are those who have to tell me, "I never dream…," which is a lot like announcing, "I'm a terrible artist!" or, "I don't understand art."

"But, everyone dreams," "Everyone's a master of something…," or "Just start with what you see," I respond.

"Well, there was this one time…," they often admit. Or, "Really? Did you know that I collect postcards?"

I knew a man who showed more passion for his collection of matchbooks than most painters have for paint, discussing the clever cover designs, the places he'd been to get them, the ones brought back or sent by friends, and those from places he'd like to visit someday. And there's my friend who gets ecstatic describing the shapes of various mathematical proposals, and my Italian barber thirty years ago who could easily become emotional about the beauty of a haircut. "Yes, I think we all dream. Don't we? I love postcards."

I was agitated. Tesla was gone, and my mind was racing from one silly thought to the next, and so I began consciously to relax again, to breathe slowly and deeply.

"Yep, Trixy! You shor is beaut-yf-skul!" quacked Popeye.
"Oh, Popeye!" she squealed. (It was amazing how much Beatrice looked like Olive Oyl.)
"Ak! Ak! Ak! Ak! I susspposes I stares too fixskedly...," grinned Popeye (whose last name just happened to be Alighieri). Halfway between asleep and awake, I found myself grinning. *"Dante as Popeye?"* Then, giving in to uncontrollable laughter. *"Beatrice as Olive?"* And it felt good. *"Una vera commedia!"*

The fleeting image of copper wire being wound around a spool initiated an avalanche: of strings vibrating, coins being tossed, heads-then-tails-then-heads-then-tails, dervishes smoothly revolving, ribbon-like sequences coiling up as if to strike, galaxies spiraling, the night sky turning, planets orbiting, and the unseen churning of atoms—all at once, winding up and unwinding, running down and renewing—until I was spinning myself, watching the world suddenly dissolve again around a boy seeking stillness in the middle of a playground carousel. *"It's everywhere and in everything."* Then I heard Tesla's voice, "By degree, the universe, the sun's system, the earth, my motors and dynamos, atoms—and yourself—all reflect the same principles in obvious and subtle ways."

Most of the time, things act the way they look. Painted shapes within the visual fields of one another relate according to the same principles that govern the rest of the universe. Michelangelo used his understanding of these principles when he painted God's finger in close proximity to Adam's. Vincent described it in the dynamics of a starry night sky. Leonardo filled notebooks with observations concerning forms and forces that were at once academic and artistic. The arrangement of a painting's composition reflects an artist's innate sense of the mechanics that keep things in orbit; meaning that the same attractive associations that give things weight and hold structures together in space, hold a picture together. Thanks to the visual laws of gravitation, painted objects have influence on one another: a larger mass tends to weigh more and exert more attractive force than a smaller mass; horizontal forms seem more stable than vertical forms; the shape of an object affects the nature and direction of its influence; because of visual gravity, symmetry and balance tend to create inertia, while asymmetry and unbalance tend to create activity and motion. The visual kinetics of a composition depend on understanding the interaction of forms and the obvious and subtle forces they exert on one another. Conversely, the universe uses the same visual language that artists do to communicate its principles, so I can learn about the nature of many things by seeing or envisioning them—as Leonardo did.

"Yeah—it's all about the sympathetic antics of Popeye under the influence of attractive Olive." And I continued spinning, glancing down to see that I had become a rotating sphere, complete with rings and moons held in orbit. *"Like a planet! Am I Saturn?"*

"Each of us attracts what surrounds us," said the voice. "*De revolutionibus*...in the true nature of spinning...awareness is magnetic, pulling things to it as gravity does, holding things in orbit around itself"

I looked for Nikola Tesla, but couldn't see him, then looked down again at the material of my rings, noting how it sparkled like the dust particles floating in sunlight that had fascinated me as a child. "Is it good stuff or bad?" I mused absentmindedly, while inspecting my moons, one by one, and wondering how to rid myself of some things I didn't want to be associated with—the things no one knows about me, things I've tried to forget, useless things, things that awaken my self-doubts and my fears. "There seems to be some debris…."

"What you see around you, what you attract, is precisely what you want," came the answer. "More interesting than pondering goodness or badness is why you choose what you do to surround yourself. You understand—it is your own reflection that you are questioning."

I opened my mouth and a strip of pattern emerged, much like the painted messages that flow from the mouths of Late Gothic saints and angels. "And this…?"

"…is the power of your word, the vibrations that affect the world when you speak."

"And now I'm seeing it—but it happens whether I see it or not, doesn't it?" I asked, watching the strand still coming from my mouth as I spoke.

"You always see it," stated the voice of Nikola Tesla. "The effects are all around you. Even your thoughts are vibrations which have influence."

I felt uncomfortable, bothered—by the debris surrounding me, by seeing my voice, by imagining the results of my thoughts—and I awoke.

About the time I began keeping this journal, a painter friend began to paint an image. In the beginning, a painting is like something sealed in a box, something veiled. You have to look for a while before becoming accustomed to seeing things that are otherwise unapparent.

"It's like dreaming," my friend told me. "I got lost once in the desert with my son. I remember walking and slowly discovering that we weren't where we thought we were—you understand—and, everything changed."

"That's how it happens though, isn't it?" I agreed.

"It was still the desert—but not really," he continued. "We were suddenly somewhere else, and I had this experience of finding water in the rocks. I knew at the time that I was going to paint about it, but had no idea what it would look like."

Before beginning to attract future brushstrokes, paintings usually start with a few practical considerations. Shortly after returning from the desert, he chose a birch veneered panel, a square of thirty by thirty inches as the support, because he wanted something solid on which to work. He sanded it lightly and sealed it with a thin layer of rabbit skin glue before coating it with beige gesso. "After six coats of gesso, I sand it with both medium and fine grit—and then it's ready. And this time, I covered the whole thing with a thin wash of Ochre and Indian Yellow, and maybe a little Burnt Sienna—mostly turpentine."

He began to explore the composition working from stacks of preparatory studies drawn on grids, taping up the relevant sketches on the frame of the easel around his prepared panel, along with a copy of an Old Master for inspiration. He used himself as the model, the shapes and lines of his body loosely blocked in with charcoal or chalk before the value statement grew in Burnt Umber and Raw Sienna—a human figure squatting frog-like on a rock and the painting's underlying foundation of an equilateral triangle becoming increasingly discernable. I visit his studio often and watched the image continue to unfold—gradually, sometimes imperceptibly. "See what I did to this part?" he'd ask when I arrived. Or, "I worked all day on this area," he'd say, pointing.

"Wow! That's beautiful," I'd answer. But I couldn't tell.

As the painting progressed, sometimes he grumbled that he couldn't do it anymore, that he had lost his way, or that he doubted his ability. "I don't know what I'm doing," he complained with some emotion. Eventually, a picture of exposed sandstone layers appeared, pointing up and inward, above a dark pool of smooth paint that surrounded the figure. "The appeal of the struggle is in never quite knowing," he admitted. "It's almost unavoidable that the stance of the figure should keep me in between things. This painting is about *that place*." I felt like a midwife—helpless before the wonder of his wrestle with the unseen, to watch him day by day, brushstroke by brushstroke, laboring through what I could only witness. "Do you realize that I've been at this constantly for months?" he stated soberly one afternoon. "And I don't know if anyone will care." But he put his all into the image.

Making a painting can consume you. At night, you dream about it. All day, you live in it, as it lives in you, never sure whether it's worth the effort, whether anyone will notice, or whether it's the painting that you're working on, or yourself. A painter lives somewhere between painting and process, providence and coincidence. At last he announced that it was finished and invited me to come and see what he had done. I sat and studied it, looking for clues, while he stood back expectantly.

"Wow! It's beautiful!" I said finally, and meant it.

I noted the strong composition, the articulate use of paint and color, and the image of a crouching figure gazing into a blank pool, a shadowy cistern of liquid caught between rocks and staring back like a huge dark eye.

"I studied Caravaggio," offered my friend. "And his sources...." But I was lost in the painting and thoughts about my life, about the generous nature of things, about Nikola Tesla and my dreams.

"And who will believe it? I don't know if anyone will care."

Refocusing on the paint, I examined the suggestion of living stone, the edges of countless layers of red-rock, and the hint of desert varnish.

"Where do such things come from?"

A figure the same color as the rock—

"What drew this image to him, this vision of a newborn person?"

—contemplating something beyond my view.

"Is it about what lies ahead?"

And I sat there considering what lay ahead—

"The attraction is love, isn't it?"

—reminding myself that it was just a clever arrangement of paint that I was looking at.

"Love drew this to him."

"Thanks," I said, getting up from the chair in his studio. "It really is beautiful."

Since then, I have studied the painting many times. There is little reflection on the surface of the pool suggesting what it sees, and nothing revealed of what the figure sees. They gaze at each other as I gaze at them—and ultimately at myself.

"Yep! It's love's what toins it—like a wheel, Trix!" crooned Dante (who looked a lot like Popeye). "It's love what moves the sun and all them starses. Ak! Ak! Ak!"

23
The Poetics of Pegasus

February 10 – I keep waking up at four o'clock—and waiting—but no one shows up. I go there regularly, to that place, but am often preoccupied, unable to focus—or no one hears me calling out. So I stare up at the stars, reluctant to admit my disappointment and unable to find my elusive friend there—somewhere in between things. Two mornings ago I dreamed of a table covered with a fine linen cloth woven in grid designs like the patterns I've seen in my dreams with Nikola Tesla. I knew that the table was set for a banquet, though all that I could see was a round loaf of bread and a brown clay pitcher filled with water, while the remainder of the feast was hidden in a cloud. I rested there, viewing and reviewing the spare-looking still life in order to commit it to memory. Perhaps I will paint it.

"Please don't touch me!" I requested a little brusquely this morning and rolled away as my wife tried to embrace me. Almost a month has passed since I have spoken with Nikola, and I lay there feeling frustrated—just thinking. *"How does a series of notes suddenly become a melody? A sequence of notes of differing lengths beat out a rhythm? What makes coincidental notes into a chord? And how do separate elements blend to become a composition? How do colors and shapes relate? What affinity joins letters to form words, and words to create syntax? How do random things become a taxonomy—my impressions transform into experience, thoughts, and ideas? What is awareness? And how do I think? What is the process that makes a story from confusion?"* No matter how many times I explore the anatomy and life of patterns, I'm perplexed and surprised by the mysterious glue that holds the pieces of everything together.

Among the early works of Fra' Filippo Lippi is an enigmatic double portrait of a young man and a young woman. He is at her window, leaning in on the sill, his tall Florentine hat scraping the top of the casement, apparently too large to enter the scene, his face silhouetted against the window frame, and hers against the interior of a shadowy cubicle.

> *Angelica's small chamber. Orlando has climbed a fig tree in order to reach her window.*
>
> Orlando: How now, my sweet and heavenly lady!
> Angelica: Oh, wherefore art thou, most gentle man?
>
> *Enter Orlando's head from the left side, wearing a serious red hat, his hands resting on a banner laid upon the window sill. He makes "le corna" with his right hand.*

It was on a trip to New York City that I first saw the image. After pushing down a salami and cheese sandwich on a long walk through the park, I arrived at the facade of the museum and made my way through the diverse crowd gathered on and around its broad stone steps. The contents of our museum back home is felt outside, spreading quietly across the fen and city like an invisible fog; Paris seems to frame its Louvre; and the entire city of Florence is a museum—but the art in New York feels strangely captive, held securely inside galleries and the granite vault of The Met. I entered the noisy confusion of the ticket hall, reminded that in The City, it's the rush and rhythm of the subway that escapes to permeate everything else.

I am drawn to riddles (though I'm not much good at them)—the events of stories that can't be shown or told, the unspeakable parts of poems, the ambiguous beingness of things. I think it was that equivocal quality that first attracted me to Lippi's painting, immediately feeling myself held captive by the peculiar drama which begged me to identify the nature of my experience.

> Angelica: Dearest dove, hast thou become a bird upon my branch?

"Naw, that's not it at all—she's not that angelic!" I looked at the cramped place where she stands serenely gazing to the left, but past Orlando, her head-dress towering out of the picture in the upper right. Orlando seems barely able to push his head and high hat into her small vestibule.

> Angelica: [an aside] Alas, I must not encourage him.

"There! That'll do." I noted the tease in her apparent lack of expression, her heavy-lidded eye, her pale skin and rosebud mouth, then noticed that the artist has thoughtfully aligned the

distant horizon outside the far window to coincide with the line that designates the parting of her sealed lips. The details of near and far are rendered equally clear: the cherished highlights and shading on each pearl and bead, her brooch, the velvet brocade, and fur-trimmed gown, and the roof tiles and garden of someone's stucco *palazzo* on the corner. Without thinking, I began to study the countryside beyond the window frame, to imagine myself walking down the painted street—and then there were three of us.

> *Enter Me, the audience, wearing a tee shirt and dirty blue jeans—and staring out of the window directly behind Angelica.*
>
> Me: [to himself, without conviction] Aaah, com'on guys—
>
> *Me is preoccupied by the perspective of the surrounding inner space extending out of the window into the landscape, and by the image of an ancient city street, noting how much it resembles that of a modern neighborhood. Enter Fra' Fillipo Lippi, the artist.*
>
> Me: Filippo, you're crazy, man! I mean—Sei proprio forte!
>
> *Fra' Filippo looks pleased and beckons Me to follow. Exit Filippo and Me.*

Surprisingly, it was the space suggested by their opposing silhouettes that became most apparent, the emptiness contained between Orlando and Angelica like a puzzle piece, the place where heres and theres are connected to nows and thens, insides and outsides.

About four in the morning,

(Enclosed in white, surrounded by darkness.)
(Enfolded in white, enveloped by shadow.)

the regular exchange of light for shadow and shadow for light continued through my closed eyelids, then through a haze as I opened my eyes.

(Held by white, released into night.)

"But my eyes are still closed!" I argued. *"What eyelids did I open? "It's a dream,"* I reminded myself.

(Closed within white, and opened to darkness.)

What had been unexpected at first, soon became a rhythm, like day following night following day in steady succession, an order I could predict, and I began then to notice other things: the whiteness of great wings rising up around me, and the emptiness of twilight as they lowered; my skin against a horse's back and barrel like pale marble but warm and alive; the beating flow of wind and sky touching me all over, my senses awakened and in tune. Anything I could write here can't describe the sensation of being happily caught there between earth and heaven.

(Wrapped in light, exposed to shadow.)

"The universe is held together by the affection between things," came a familiar voice. "The binding power of creation is love— the resonance that makes families and crowds from individual lives, flocks from solitary birds, forests from trees, meadows from single blades of grass, oceans from water drops, and light from waves and particles. Love is the poetry of consciousness—the greatest gift of awareness."

"What does that mean!?" I blurted, provoked by what seemed absurdly simple.

"You understand that a creator loves a creation into being by bringing elements together to make unity from previously unordered things; one from many—to fulfill and name a new place that was not there; one from nothing. Love is in the union of faith and possibility, the oneness that both joins and fills."

"Where are you?" I complained, hearing the voice but seeing no one. "And, I don't get it; love is just an emotion,"

(Secured within whiteness, then freed into night.)

feeling air pushed down, around, and rushing at me.

"The urge to create is the inheritance of humankind. You make paintings based upon love."

"The desire to destroy—is that also innate?" I asked.

"Choices and actions indicate one's allegiance, trust, and even passions, but simple desire is not love. The universe is not a wishing well—faith is work."

In Lippi's Madonna and Child with Angels, he makes another polite request for me to join him somewhere between the pigments and the image, the drama unfolding on a threshold before the suggested architecture of a doorway to a dream-like place. The happy angel who fixes me with his gaze suggests that I'm an expected guest, an intended part of the picture.

Then suddenly, I was weightless—suspended for a moment

before diving down to view a patterned landscape. I recognized the gridded plane below us, but wasn't enjoying the discussion much.

"You resist what I am saying," suggested Tesla.

Then I was heavy—a weighty burden on the back of my mythical carrier…

"Because it doesn't make sense to me,"

(Buried in white, born into darkness.)

…the collective pumping of wings, muscles, and breath lifting us powerfully toward a night sky filled with stars.

"Perhaps you do not adequately understand love," he concluded.

"I'm sure I don't." I studied the darkness above me and then the patterns below, each extending as far as I could see—the rows and columns of binary elements suggesting patterns, and the random spray of stars on a darkened field variously conceived as constellations; both of them meeting in the distance at an imaginary place called the horizon. *"And here I am in the middle."*

(Warmed by light, and cooled by shadow.)

"Love is the work to which we are called," he continued. "It is the basis of the attractive associations between simple and complex things, the force that combines the elements of the universe.

"But you said that love is a gift of awareness?"

"Which happens by degree," added Nikola. "Everything is sufficiently aware to fulfill the measure of its being—from things you cannot see, to rocks, to humankind. We have already discussed the relationship between degrees of awareness and the ability to participate in the working mechanics of systems. The potential to love is relative to one's awareness. The effect of love is to bond singular elements together into unique associations."

"Like what I do in the studio?" Painting is the consummation of all that, the combination of a variety of things—materials, ideas, impressions, emotions, time; all bound together by careful attention and work. It's in the effort to fit the pieces together, to find the purpose in each part that an image happens. I recalled a time while exploring the nature of boundaries that things suddenly dissolved around me, becoming a mess of stray attributes until I consciously glued them back together. I thought of my fascination with cloud-gazing, and remembered the profound nature of my childhood realization about my painted friends in the museum.

Often, upon hearing that I make paintings, an acquaintance will begin to tell me of an idea he has for an image; "You've gotta picture it—there's this big buck, ya see, big rack, up on a hill, and behind him there's this pretty sunset…I can just see it!" I have heard it, or something similar, a thousand times. "Sounds nice," I answer. Like the time my new father-in-law quietly approached me in the hall of his house, not too long after my marriage to his daughter, "Here," he whispered, taking a small rectangular piece of cardstock out of his shirt pocket. "This is my wife." I reached out too stiffly and took the little dog-eared photo from him. "She's pretty," I said, watching his eyes begin to water. He took a white cotton hanky from his back pants pocket and wiped his nose. "Son, I carried it all through the war, and whenever I got homesick—all I had to do was look at her." I stared down at the black and white picture of my mother-in-law of forty years before—a smiling icon from a card of bobby pins. "I have always wanted to get her portrait painted just like this," he said pointing at the snapshot. "When you're ready, I hope you'll do it for me." I still have the photo, and look at it once in a while to remind myself of my father-in-law, his love for my mother-in-law, and the particular human ability to create realities at will.

"It is all vibrations," said Nikola Tesla, "frequencies and resonance—the patterns of associations between things; the sharing, borrowing and robbing of characteristics that make new things; and the charged interaction within and between everything. For humankind, the ability to affect the vibrating universe, to govern consciously through love, is inherited. The first act of reasoning sets an individual on a course of understanding that leads to increased awareness—but it is a path of choices, with many possible detours."

I have always resisted growing up; even now it seems a dangerous proposition—to leave behind the unconcerned childhood idylls of romps through the woods, of long afternoons hunting butterflies, and whole days working on imagined tree houses that might never be.

"Tell me. Why do you paint?" inquired Tesla.
"It's just something I've always liked to do." I thought back on our trips to the museum, and then saw us trailing mama like ducklings through the park where men paddled us around a lagoon in swan boats, five small Wagnerian heroes with a sense of mission. "I can hardly remember a time when I didn't wish to be a painter."
"Have you not found a purpose for that which you wish to do?" he asked. I could feel him considering me carefully, perhaps expecting a response that I could not readily offer.

"But I love to paint," I answered finally, searching the stars around me as if for answers.

"And you don't know why. Refinding innocence is a process that at some point requires dependence on a resource greater than ourselves. It is in that reliance that we learn of love, and where we discover a higher purpose for our own love. It is in that work that we begin to see our true selves as integral parts of a universe held together by love.

(Nestled in white, thrust into night.)

"That is the journey back—the only way home."
I took a deep breath.

(Embraced by light, and thrown into darkness.)

"*The way home,*" I thought, *"that place I miss, where I have never been."* The beckoning glance of Lippi's little angel, doors to dreamy places, open windows with views of somewhere else—all of them portrayed no less importantly than figures in the foreground. Behind the Mary and the messenger of Fra' Angelico's Annunciation in San Marco's dormitory there is a door leading the viewer into a darkened space where a small window is lit up by the painted image of a bright woodland in the distance. "The way home," I whispered. Giovanni Bellini makes the same kind of effort to lure me beyond obvious subject matters, beyond the essential picture plane and past central figures to meet him in a pastoral countryside. Roads that lead to villages on hills and distant horizons, misty landscapes, rivers and bridges, windows that open into heavenly skies—Leonardo makes a similar invitation to join him somewhere in between. It's not uncommon. Many of them do it. "The way home," I repeated wistfully. "That's what painters do; they offer a way to see the world from an otherwise elusive point of view, as if with new eyes. They mimic the reality of one dimension to lead me to others." Like Bellini's Coronation Between Saints in Pesaro—the image of an altarpiece painted within an altarpiece, a likeness of a likeness, a view within a view within a view.

"Only if you choose to participate," cautioned Nikola. "From the first lure and comparison of outcomes, from the initial act of reason—the path is a way of choices, awareness, and wisdom, through which we leave the ignorance of childhood behind on a quest for our true innocence."

"It's the artist's devotion that holds the pieces of paintings together," I said, remembering months of patiently using a tiny brush, some pigment, and oil, to help an audience see and feel my vision of a forest one leaf at a time—then months of painting with a few fine hairs to suggest each blade of grass, to tempt the viewer to look closer, to walk with me beneath the trees. "Yes, the work is love," I decided.

"Quite unlike what most call love," added Nikola. "It is the work through which we develop our innate divine qualities. We learn to create by participating in the oneness of things."

Again I looked out over the articulated expanse below and at the stars that spread out endlessly above. "I'm so tired of disbelieving," I said, thinking of the many images I have abandoned to doubt. "But faith and love are such hard work! And the struggle to believe is sometimes just as tiring."

"The requirement and release of energy, the push and pull of belief and doubt, is the natural vibration of faith's development. You get tired because you spend a great amount of effort resisting the process, often imagining that you might safely think your way through it—but choosing means doing. Even in your studio, the doing part of painting must be greater than the thinking part or there would be no pictures for others to see. Yes, *doing* is work."

Whether I accept the invitation of angels or remain beyond their influence seems to have everything to do with how I choose to participate in the string of events that is my life. For me, I like the idea of Lippi's kind petition—

Fra' Filippo requests the pleasure of your presence....

—suggesting that here and there connect, even overlap, and that the possibility of not being present is also a choice. My dream this morning felt similar, like an invitation to somewhere in between—where time, places, and things merge; an intersection; kind of like a painter's studio. But more than just a dream, it felt like another gift from a wise teacher, an opportunity to explore the nature of the mysterious glue that sticks the pieces of things together.

(Morning light, then delivered to shadow.)

"So—what is the binder between everything that holds it all in place? Where is the point of view that potentially includes all others? And, who is the artist, the reluctant poet responsible for making compound things appear from simple components—the see-er of patterns?"

(Wings of white, and stars of night.)
"I guess——I am."

24
A Quickening

February 11 – In the middle of winter, the woods, which I know were once flush with green, are bare and bony. On warmer afternoons when things begin to drip, I often go out to check the branches and twig tips for some sign of swelling and color, but everything is invariably dormant and gray, so I'll return to the house to sit behind the window and dream of other times—remembering what spring is like, or trying to recall when and how the darkness began—but in the middle of winter, it's hard to believe that there is any other season.

Every year there's a morning or an afternoon in August or September when things are different. It's hard to put your finger on—the light seems more oblique, the air feels strangely charged and the breeze is faintly perfumed with leaves and earth from somewhere far off. It's not obvious—in fact, it's subtle enough that I can imagine I'm the only one who's noticed, each time ending up wondering whether I felt it at all. But then, unexplained turns of nostalgia and the *chickadee-dee-dee* of little black-capped friends returning to our woods from farther up the mountain are sure signs that the season is about to change. It's the perfect time to put the leash on the dog, take a walk, and let my thoughts just happen.

Something similar occurs when a painting begins to resolve and I can suddenly foresee what lies ahead. I count the glazes I'll apply and calculate how things might finally appear. It usually happens that, about half to three-quarters of the way through, there's a quickening, when in the sadness and excitement of previewing the outcome, I hasten my work and begin to look forward to the next image. It's during that time between, when both the beginning and the end are equally in sight, a time of forgetting and remembering, that I decide to admire what I've done so far—to let go and briefly enjoy the view from where I sit.

"There is so much to teach and talk about, and not much time—not this morning."

"And perhaps not again?" I thought to myself. Something had changed.

"We have a lot to do," added Tesla, sounding preoccupied. I had the impression that he was concerned about something, perhaps circumstances he had not foreseen. "This is a simple model to understand," he stated in a business-like tone, and I saw an image of the Earth rotating on its axis.

"Maybe it's my slowness. Is he as doubtful as I am that I can do whatever it is that he expects?"

"It is a most obvious dynamo, one of the most available generators and an easy one from which to access the resulting power." I thought of a spool hypnotically winding wire around its core, and remembered the image of space spiraling in and out of a central axis. "You know that I cannot give you answers," he continued, "but I can help you to see what might lead to a better understanding of the principles." Immediately, I was watching black and white pictures of Tesla's memories: sagebrush dotted landscapes near some foothills, a series of typical western snapshots—then the color of an unreal sky; perhaps a late August afternoon; lazy clouds suspended above, evenly spaced white cotton against deepening blue into the distance, appearing so innocent until a cloudburst fills the washes with muddy torrents—the weight of the sky, straight Cerulean at one point, then burdened with a secret load, and waiting for a chance to release its charge. "I will remind you that life is vibration. Everything vibrates. It is all energy, all electrical, and the power is everywhere, just waiting to be released."

"But I don't know the first thing about electricity." I answered.

"The rudiments are best understood by stroking the fur of a cat," he suggested seriously.

"What can he want?" I remembered petting our old ginger cat curled up at the foot of my bed, and an elementary school science class over forty years ago on the electrostatic relationship of a hard black rubber rod with a piece of soft white rabbit fur. In school, I had even seen a radio miraculously powered by a potato. *"That's it—everything I know about it."*

"You have already experienced an electrical interface between dimensions...."

I quickly reviewed some of our discussions: Adam and Eve—their initial state; the garden; their choices and growing awareness; the wilderness; the hazy boundary that Nikola and I had approached together, a filmy separation between worlds; his invitation to step through—and then it occurred to me, that the way of awareness requires separation from immediate knowledge. "It's interesting isn't it, that the more they saw, the less they could see?" I reflected. "Awareness has to be earned, doesn't it?"

But Tesla was still talking and I had missed what he had said. "...it is through the basic principles of resonance that we communicate, you and I, sympathetic resonance as happens between a harp's strings, or among the filaments that I have shown you."

"So—is this your voice—or mine that I'm hearing?" I asked hesitantly, "because sometimes I can't tell." It was a question I had wanted answered for some time.

"Yes," he responded knowingly. "Good transmissions require good reception. The tuning in of the heart is so necessary, straight on the narrow band of the signal. Of course, this is our voice."

"And how many signals are there?" I wondered aloud, speculating on something I imagined to be in the air all around us.

"In everything and everywhere," reminded Tesla. "Nothing is empty and nothing is filled. You are familiar with that." He raised his eyebrows, anticipating my nod. "Access to a specific signal requires accurate tuning in to the frequency on which it is broadcast. Voice is the direction of vibration on a band of frequency. It is a broadcast, the miracle of electrical impressions transformed into sound by the expression of breath upon specialized ligaments for the purpose of manifesting realities from the dimension of emotion and thought in the aural dimension. The human body exists in many dimensions at once. The outer voice with which you speak is modeled after the inner voice with which we communicate, though less refined. The power of voice in all dimensions is the effect of an inherent resonance and harmonics on an environment."

I thought about paintings—the effects they might have on their surroundings, the many places they can inhabit, both visible and invisible. And though I'm aware of how things might be in more places at once, I have never been aware of affecting more than one place at a time while I am painting. I have always relied on the kismet of intuition for that part of my artistic activity, without much conscious consideration.

"The true power of voice," said Nikola, "is the conscious evocation of inner and outer voices together, in harmony—the intentional union of cause and effect."

"*Unlike all of my unconscious babbling, all the things I say without thinking—it's as if my voice happens involuntarily—no wonder it has so little effect.*"

"At times, you are like a child still learning to express yourself, speaking unaccountably, or even lying just a little. Voice, speech, language—these are gifts…," said Tesla.

"…that I've taken for granted. Even when I paint, I'm mostly unconscious."

"Yet, you have become skillful…"

"…at a game of chance. Most of the time, I feel like a clown rolling dice, hoping to throw doubles, to stumble onto something good accidentally—to hit the jackpot. Yeah, painting is a gamble, both a temptation and a frustration each time. It's always a leap of faith, my hope plagued by the chronic condition of not knowing anything for sure. So sometimes I blow it, I miss the mark, but I keep trying anyway." And I was overcome with confusing emotions.

"Is the sleepwalker startled by awakening somewhere unexpected?"

"I'm confused that it's a dream giving me counsel to wake up," I mumbled. "How can I be dreaming this?"

"You speak to me with your inner voice," he continued, "and see and hear me through similarly refined senses of vision and hearing. Your breath, which vibrates the fleshy mechanics of your outer voice, has an inner counterpart. Notice how you breathe while we are speaking."

"Yes. There is something different," I admitted, "a distinct kind of breathing—an inner breath, or under breath. It's difficult to describe." I was surprised because I hadn't really thought about it—the airy hum in my chest, like rhythmic sighing, a soft vibration caused by the subtle hiss of wind escaping through my tightened throat as I speak with Tesla.

"Do you remember how you learned it?" he asked.

I was reminded of what I had done so regularly as a child, without remembering how it had started, or anyone teaching me. It must have been a response to childhood fears—something I did all the time believing it would keep me safe. "One," I would count, imagining that each inspiration was made of light, filling myself full until it felt like a little sun shining in my chest. Then, "Two," as I exhaled, closing my throat a bit, which made a soft hissing sound, directing my breath upwards until it shot like a fountain from the crown of my head and fell around me in a protective field. It was a little game, which I felt compelled to practice often, a thing born from the overactive imagination of a fearful child fending off the boogeyman. This breathing and shielding became an automatic response that I stopped noticing, and wouldn't have noticed had Tesla not asked me to pay attention to it.

"No. It's just what I do sometimes."

"Then I suggest that you remember how you breathe at those times, where you place your tongue, how you direct the air, and exactly what you feel and do. While the vibrations that you normally hear with your ears are a small subset of what you are capable of hearing, and the vibrations you call light are a small visible band compared to what your inner eyes might see, your visible body is also a small indication of how immense you really are. The inspiration and expiration of breath is a powerful tool that connects you to the atmosphere. Breathing is an electrical function that charges the whole body as the whole body is a generator that charges the breath—in much the same way that the earth feeds the flesh, as flesh feeds the earth. Life depends on this recycling of energy. In all senses, this exchange is an agreement that both empowers and teaches. It is our vital connection to the whole in all dimensions."

As a child, after learning to play the game with my breath, I began to experiment with its direction, imagining my breath going to a body part that hurt, or somewhere other than the crown of my head. "What color does it want?" I'd ask, and proceed to direct ice blue light to a scraped knee or elbow. Not that the scrapes went away immediately, but that they felt better for having been attended to. Eventually, when I was older, I was able to eliminate certain hurts entirely if I wanted to make the effort, and was pretty good at lowering the fevers of my infant children when they were sick, but it has always been a curious game—nothing that I take too seriously. A couple of days ago a small bird, a female goldfinch, hit the window of our home. I heard the impact of it, quickly going out to investigate. I found her lying still upon the snow, picked her up, and cupped her tenderly in my hands. "What color does it want?" I asked, and sent a warm sunset pink down my arms and into the bird. Soon enough she was fine, standing on my hand where I stroked her feathers gently—under her chin, around her neck, and down her back, breathing light into her through my fingertips. After several minutes she flew off and I lost sight of her there with the other birds. I'm sure enough that the stunned body would have healed without my intervention, that she would have come to in the snow and flown off to rest for a while on a twig before rejoining the flock. But somehow I felt better for having attended to her, happier for our brief encounter and my participation, however modest, in the life of a small miracle. "Thank-you, my friend," I called out to her, somewhere among the birds at the feeder, for in truth, I realized then that it was I who had been healed, that she had breathed new life into me.

"Yes. Thank-you," I said to Nikola Tesla, feeling my breath spread throughout my entire body. "I think I'm beginning to understand the exchange." And then I remembered my children taking a first surprising breath, obviously startled by awakening somewhere unexpected.

"Life is an exercise of faith," said Tesla, "an agreement to give away each breath in exchange for the next. I can describe the electrical nature of the cycle; you might portray it visually; while someone else would use a series of musical notes to explore its qualities."

"My breath—I haven't really thought enough about it," I responded. "And you're telling me it's like a paintbrush charged with paint—that I can do things with it. Even if I have pretended, I don't understand the physics of what you're saying. I'm a painter and don't even get the physics of color."

"But you breathe anyway," said Nikola, stopping to study me for a few moments as he often does. "And you still paint." I always imagine that he's wondering whether I'm really the one he wants to be teaching. "In every cycle, there are seasons," he began, "and in every season—a late time, when foreseeing the conclusion and future makes events seem to speed up, when the end is invigorated by the hope of renewal."

"You mean, like Christmas," I interrupted.

"Almost like Christmas," he agreed. "Or like the half-step intervals in musical scales—the times in a cycle when a smaller amount of effort accomplishes more. That is when I work harder. If I am expecting too much from you, it is because the world is now at that point in the cycle, the time of quickening before enlightenment, and because I believe you are capable of more. Without understanding how, you have developed the power of inner breathing, hearing, and other subtle senses. You have developed your inner eyesight, which allows you to see me and what I have to show you. I too had similar gifts from the time I was young, and used them to go places, to see and experience things that many cannot understand. Later, I planned most of my work in that way; I did it all there before I did it here."

"That's how I paint! The images are already painted before I touch a brush to the panel. I'm always frustrated that I have so many paintings there compared to what's in my studio. I've painted enough there for several lifetimes."

"I think that is the way with artists," said Tesla. "They live in more than one place, and sometimes get confused. Notice how you focus while we are together." Then I saw an amount of the familiar microelemental pattern. I focused clearly on it, closer and closer toward its surface until I saw only the line inferred by the meeting of positive and negative elements in the pattern. I got so near to it that the line softened and blurred as had happened in another dream. "Which eyes are you using now? With what eyes can you see that which you are seeing?" he asked knowingly.

As I thought about it, I began to realize that I regularly use my breath and inner vision to create stillness when I dream and when I paint. It's a way to stay focused, to eliminate peripheral noise and interference, and to open up to the work completely. I recalled a morning in the museum almost fifty years ago when I got close enough to see dust in the paint, stray hairs, fingerprints, and brush bristles—when things seemed suddenly amplified and I could taste the colors. "Maybe I learned it there? Maybe it's just what artists do?"

"These paintings that you love," said Tesla, "they are yet another form of broadcast—carefully conceived electromagnetic transmissions across space and time, the direction of light vibrating at particular frequencies, to be seen by and awaken inner eyes. Yes, I think it will be a good thing for you to visit San Marco." I pictured the blindfolded *Cristo Deriso* in cell number seven, and recalled the chamber's impressive sonic resonance. "In San Marco, there is a direct relationship between inner and outer worlds, which is augmented by obvious vibration. We will talk more when you are ready. And, I would like you to study frequency and wave theory."

There were other things which we discussed this morning—a lot about the qualities of light. The best I can do to relate what I learned from the lesson is to describe light as a concentration of something—a material capable of deforming while acting solid in other ways. I am still trying to understand how solids flow, and how fluids can act solid enough to walk upon. At one point I was filled with an intense glow that I seemed both to be drawing into myself and radiating, similar to how Tesla had described my breath, accompanied by a lot of little flashes and shocks, which ultimately became a pleasant hum inside me and on my skin.

Nikola then asked me to repeat back what I had learned, a request he has made after other lessons. I rehearsed back to him what I could, noting how much I had forgotten. The notebook and pen beside the bed attest to my improvement at taking notes during our discussions, and I recommitted to writing more in the future. In the end, Tesla expressed his affection for me, and I, in turn, for him—and he was gone. I had the usual surprise of finding myself back in bed again, the sheets on my side pulled off the mattress and twisted up. And I was quickly aware of a charge that seemed to come from the light still filling and surrounding me, unable to move or unwind the sheets from myself until the light had finally faded.

For some time, I have been planning a trip to Florence in order to study some of San Marco's more curious aspects: the acoustic environment of the monks' personal chambers, and Fra Angelico's fresco cycle on the walls of the dormitories, hoping to discover some common sense in my nonsensical obsession with the monastery as a consciously designed receiver and amplifier—what Nilkola Tesla might call a huge fifteenth century mnemonic device. After his encouragement this morning, I'm even more eager to return to Italy. Nikola also asked me to study simple wave theory in preparation for future discussions. But I hardly know where to start, already finding that it's necessary to reread material several times before I begin to understand anything at all.

I'm left pondering the miracle of breath: the airy vibrations of voice, the liquid intonations of song, the needy inhalations of weeping, and the short breezy exhalations of laughter—breathing in and breathing out—the rhythmic condition of being alive. *Spiritus*, the life of little birds, the wind that moves the trees; *Ruah*, the weather of the woods and of my soul; *Ka*, the animation of inanimate material; *Ch'i*, seeing my breath on a frosty morning; *Prana*, the air's energy flowing through me—in, and out—with the regularity of waves upon seashores, like the lines of words following one after the other and flowing down this page—in, and out—the transpiring of subtle exchanges, the transport of nourishment in unseen places—in, and out—painters hoping to breathe life into painted flesh and atmospheres, the transmuting of thoughts and impressions into pigmented forms—in, and out—and on and on—the transmission of visions—in, and out, and in, and out.

   Nearly nose to nose, I remember looking straight into my lover's eyes, and seeing myself reflected there.
"Hee! Hee! Hoo! Hoo!" went our well-rehearsed puffing.
   "When was the first first breath?" I wondered.
"Hee! Hee! Hoo! Hoo!" we breathed together.
   "And how did it happen?"
"Hee! Hee! Hoo! Hoo!" we breathed.
   "Was it by chance? Spontaneous? A fortunate accident?"
"Hee! Hee! Hoo! Hoo!" again.
   "Less conscious, less loving than our breathing now?"
"Hee! Hee! Hoo! Hoo!" again and again.
   "That would be hard to believe."
"Hoo! Hoo!" we panted.
   "And no more likely than pigment, oil, and medium arranging themselves on a panel…"
"Hoo! Hoo! Hoo!" we blew.
"Hoo! Hoo! Hoo!"
   "…because they grew tired of sitting on a palette."
"Hoo! Hoo! Hoo!" faces flushed, cheeks rhythmically filling and deflating.
"Hoo! Hoo! Hoo!"
Then a door opened to somewhere much bigger than the room we were in.

"Com'on—almost there," I urged.
"Hoo!!" her eyes squeezed tight.
"Hoo! Hoo!" she heaved.
"Heeee!!" teeth bared.
A small sputter, a first gasp for breath, and then—a baby cried.
> "No!" I decided. *"Inspiration comes from somewhere else. I don't have the desire or the faith to believe otherwise."*

And then we all cried.

In Italy, the spring greens will be arriving in the markets soon and my Italian friends taking to the hillsides to gather their spring salads, *l'insalata del prato*—tender slips of *cicoria*, *arugula*, and *radicchio*—from the meadows or from small plots where they were planted last fall in preparation for this season.

"Speak what is true, and it will be true," counseled Nikola Tesla in a dream this morning—his voice, resonating inside me like a breeze across harp strings.

25
Daydreams

February 21 – This morning everything was still—not the slightest hint of a breeze. I lay in bed a lot longer than usual, hoping to remember more about my dreams, and looked out of the window at a tangle of bare treetops drawn in sketchy lines across the bottom of a dull gray sky. It's a strange feeling, to know something one moment, and as things start to fade into shadow, then not to know it. Every day, I awaken to one world while another world falls asleep and becomes memory. With each sunrise, I reconsider the knowing of things in one way, to find myself rediscovering another way at sunset.

Before they're actually painted, images change and mature. I know each one quite well; I'll sit and stare at it (wherever unpainted paintings live), or I'll lie in bed too long, scraping off and reworking ideas until I get it right. Yet, paintings are not something I can think my way through. For all of my intentions, lists, and careful planning, pictures are painted in spite of my headstrong involvement. I've learned from experience that they materialize only when my heart decides, and that often it can be a while before my heart is prepared to paint what I have worked out in my head—even years. But this morning I felt blank, like a gessoed panel ready for new paint, awaiting the *imprimatura*, without an intended image in mind—or like an empty stage: ready for the scenery, props, and players to show up, with no expectation of plot or roles. "I should get up," I exhaled like a relief valve softly letting off steam. Then I rolled over, straightened the blanket, and closed my eyes. *"I've gotta get up."*

Earlier this morning I had visited with Nikola Tesla, so was trying to review what I remembered—which was very little, as again I had neglected to write anything down in the notebook beside my bed. *"Either it doesn't really matter,"* I debated, *"or I'm being very stupid to forget so much."* Nikola Tesla is always a gentleman, but seems even more so when he is in good-humor and less obviously preoccupied. "…not long now," he had reassured, almost sounding lighthearted. "This has been for your benefit." I especially noticed his eyes and the relaxed corners of his mouth which naturally seem to turn up, at times making him appear like a bit of a rascal. "No matter how difficult it seems, you will succeed," he encouraged. "All will happen as intended." But of course, not recalling the topic of our discussion means not understanding to what he was referring.

"I will lie here a bit longer to see if I can get it back." I decided, adjusting and readjusting the pillow under my neck. *"Just relax."* And I began to breathe deeply and slowly. Most of each day is spent working in the studio, painting, and preparing to paint, and lately I've been hopeful about a new relationship with a gallery in Santa Fe. *"I bet it's about that."* Outside, the day had turned brighter, the overcast becoming a lighter gray, a slightly

warmer off-white—Snowflake White mixed with small dabs of Bone Black to arrive incrementally at the right value, then colored by a touch of Ocher, and thinned with enough medium to let the hues of the *imprimatura* barely hint at showing through. *"It could be about my lousy finances—or the general discord I sometimes feel between me and everything."* I lay there thinking, and trying not to think, tired by the tug-o-war between becauses and whys, lost on a circuitous path between the substance and the essence of my dreams. *"It could be about anything, couldn't it?"*

Yesterday morning I went to that neutral place where I meet Nikola Tesla, just to enjoy being there. Nothing happened. No one came to talk. But it felt good—to feel energized, humming again with a pleasant charge. So I stayed until the alarm went off at six, then dutifully arose to shower and to prepare for the day. But this morning it was hard to stop struggling, even against nothing—I lay still for some time, wrestling with the need to remember an illusory conversation. It was after ten when I finally got up, wandered into the bathroom and looked in the mirror at a troubled face, still caught in that old argument between my *ka* and *ba*. The dream was gone. I looked and felt terrible. Sometimes, I just don't seem to get along with myself very well.

Morning—evening, morning—evening; how easy it is for a butterfly, or for a bird, to know the way of things with the disclosing and closing of wings! But the regular rhythm of extraordinary accidents has begun to cause tremors in the solid construct of my life. Because what was anomalous now seems common, the opposite is also true, allowing me to distrust all earlier assumptions. My reluctant but growing attachment to what was once peculiar and strange has turned me inside-out.

Though I can't recall much of our conversation, I do remember that he seemed tender this morning, concerned. Oddly, during the dream, I pictured him out feeding the birds. At any moment I expected his usual lecture to start, for the business to begin, but there was none of that. We spoke as friends, about my needs and struggles—which brought to my mind his own particular situation. I wondered who had been there to encourage him when he found himself sidelined, a relic, an old curiosity, while the world enjoyed the benefits of his visions and work. I'm glad that he and the pigeons had each other to rely on. "I know. It's going to be OK, isn't it? Thanks, my friend." He smiled in response, and I fell into random silly dreams until eventually awakening to my forgetfulness, wishing to recall the specifics of our talk and his expression of support.

Not too long ago we took a short trip north, not too far, but far enough that we decided to spend the night at a friend's house before returning home. I'm not so good with directions, and it was dark by the time we arrived. "I think it's the Forest Street exit," counseled my wife. "Yeah! How could I forget?" I laughed. "Then, I think it's a left after the park with a cabin on the corner," she added. "You're sure? And the house—I hope I recognize the house," I worried. From the outside, my friend's home is nondescript, like any average house on any average street, an older home that has seen its share of remodeling. But conventions are left on the doorstep, as on the inside, my kind friend and her home are anything but typical.

"Oh! There you are!" she cackled, catching us each in a quick bearhug. "Come in! Come in!" We joined a rush of pawprints through the clearing where a living room should have been, and followed her, creaking up a steep narrow staircase to tidy rooms, where cake and cookies, chocolates, a diminutive party of rabbits taking tea from acorn cups, and cozy old beds awaited. "Yes, we love houseguests!" she giggled, gushing uncontrollably as we deposited our suitcases. "Now hurry on down and we'll chat." Returning downstairs we sat on wooden benches where a small cabin dominated the space, its shake roof disappearing up into the ceiling. "…and let me tell you what we're having for breakfast!" But I was too busy checking out things to listen: branches holding lanterns grew up and out of the walls; an enameled washtub fountain on a stump held goldfish; stepping stones affixed to the floor led to an adjoining room; and pawprints headed everywhere—the evidence of a skunk hiding behind a chair, traces of a mouse nervously scurrying beneath the window, the trail of a partridge hurrying across the floor, a raccoon heading here, and a bear lumbering by over there. I tracked a bobcat to the bedroom, a deer toward the fountain, and a wolf from the kitchen. Our friend's grin yielded as she pointed to the path of a beloved dog. "When he passed away, I took impressions of his paws for the stencils," she stated resolutely, implying her pet's continued vigilance over the household.

It was clear that we had stepped into another kind of place, where, within the boundaries of an average neighborhood, we had found an enchanted kingdom with a sheltered glade in a magic wood. *"This is how it is,"* I thought, *"that good things occur in spite of discouragement, sadness, and hardship—that great thoughts, explorations, and discoveries happen against all odds."* I have watched my friend for years and the many challenges she has faced. I've seen her stubborn faith in what smarter folk might find too simple; and her determination when facing difficulty—to be happy, to believe, and to live inside her dreams. Glancing around the room at the faces set a-glow by the unfolding fairy-tale, I wondered how many similar Edens I have missed in my life, how many likely friends I've passed without smiling, and how I lose my bearings so easily.

"Where are the fireflies? Do they still work?" I asked.

"You bet!" announced a cheery man with a jolly-sounding voice, a full white beard, ruddy cheeks, and a cherry nose, jumping up eagerly to turn them on for us. Here and there, on the twigs of a decorated branch overhanging the washtub, tiny lights began to blink intermittently.

"It sure is great to be here," I sighed, after watching the "fireflies" for a few minutes.

"We're glad you're here too," he nodded, giving his good wife a wink and a squeeze. The merry elf left, and returned in moments with a package. "Here," he said, slipping a small bundle of light emitting diodes the size of thick pencil leads into my hand. "We don't really have a use for 'em now."

We left the next day, like children hesitating before taking a first trip away from home, each clutching a brown paper lunch sack full of snacks. "Now, remember to come back," advised my friend, giving hugs all around. "We just love houseguests."

Today, I rehearsed the event to myself as if it were all a dream. *"I don't think they need a Tesla to wake them up,"* I decided, dozing off in the glow of a computer screen, my fingers on the keyboard making long lines of nnnnnnnnn's in the middle of my page. *"On the one hand I lack the faith, but on the other, I'm not really sure I want knowledge. Maybe later I'll see if I can find those little diodes...."* I looked down at my feet and shoes resting squarely on the plastic chair mat, feeling at the very brink of somewhere other than where I thought I was. I have arrived at that point so many times and then backed off, instead, succumbing to distractions. *"Am I still afraid?"* I wondered. *"What is it I'm not willing to see?"*

Dreams and paintings are the result of intimate interaction between two kinds of knowing—the heart's reflection of the head's activity, the sublimate memories of the mind's events. The art is in harmonizing both worlds in the elements of the craft, thus softening the confines between one place and another. The real challenge is to do with life what a painter tries to do with paint, what my friend seems to do so well—to live both lives fully at the same time. So, I sat at my desk, in the middle of the afternoon, daydreaming about my talk with Nikola Tesla last night, hoping my heart might remember what my head forgot.

"…I can't help it," I heard myself whine.

"But you are all that stands between yourself and everything you seek," said the familiar voice.

Then I recalled people quietly getting up and filing out of a large room.

"Whatever it takes," I heard myself whisper, looking around to see if anyone had heard my uncertain commitment.

"And now what?" But Tesla wasn't there, nor my veiled guides. I was alone, awake, and sitting at a desk.

"What am I doing here?" I asked an imaginary audience. And no one answered.

"Whatever it is, I'll do it," I called out. But I was the only one who heard.

Standing at an intersection means straddling destinations, and on occasion feeling about to come apart. I think it's just the fragile nature of the way artists live—one foot in one place and the other planted firmly somewhere else. So today I made a solid commitment to my sensitive stance; I bought plane tickets to Italy—five of them: one for me; one for my wife so she could manage the trip, and me; two for my daughters, as documenters and studio assistants; and one for my aunt so she could manage my teenage daughters. We'll see our friends in Veneto and Emilia; and visit the Brera, the Cenacolo, the Scrovegni Chapel, the Accademia in Venice, the collections in Siena, the Uffizi, and the Pitti; but our primary goal is to explore the resonant qualities of the dormitory cells in San Marco monastery in Florence—which makes no sense at all.

This time, I'm going to Italy because in a dream, I said that I would.

26
The Two Keys

March 9 – "Diddly-ump! Diddly-ump! That's what you're after. That's the basic beat," he said, taking my hand and trying to reshape it around the bones. "Hold 'em like this——There! Just like that." I did my best to hold the two seven inch lengths of cow rib in the valleys between my index, middle, and ring fingers, letting the longest part of each bone protrude toward me at right angles to my palm, and forming my hand exactly as I had been shown. Then I rocked my hand back and forth in the air triumphantly, hoping to hear the typical clickety-click, but all I got was some chaotic clacking. "Diddly-ump! is what you want," he reiterated, moving his hand in such a way that we heard the precise rhythm he had just described. "I think you're holding your hand too stiff. Just relax and you'll get it." We have replayed this scene since my childhood and I still can't make the right rhythmic sequence happen, but this morning was the first time that I remember dreaming of our recurring lesson. "I used to practice on my way walking to and from the old school up on

McLellin's mountain," he went on. "Oh, us kids—we thought we were pr'tty smart when we got it." I continued moving my hand in such a way that the bones tapped one against the other, but without the identifiable snappy series of beats.

My dad, who is from the hill country of Nova Scotia, plays the bones with both hands, and without thinking—which to me, has always been something magic, something particular that makes him who and how he is. My sweetest childhood memories include the sound of scratchy old Winston Scotty Fitzgerald seventy-eights, my dad being happy and playing the bones, while we children skipped and spun around the room. I have often wished to play the bones, as if by doing so I might reproduce the careless abandon of those times. My own sons all play the bones masterfully, having learned from their grandfather. But repeatedly, I try without success. Maybe I was dreaming this morning about my father's bone-playing instructions because my lessons with Nikola Tesla feel similar—more things that I strain to learn, things that seem so immediate, but end up being just beyond my grasp.

It has been almost nine months since first meeting my gentle friend. Imagine me, the consummate dreamer, a painter, encountering a great scientist somewhere in the ethers—to be told that I would *carry on his work*. I had expected that by now I would have learned a lot more about electricity, but my initial expectations have changed or have been replaced a hundred times, and still I don't know what to think about all of this. I have to chuckle—our talks have become an important influence in my life. To half awaken at four has become a matter of course, as has the reflex desire to explore unexpected things that continue to challenge and surprise me. Lately I have begun to study the physics of electricity, which is difficult for me to understand—both the topic, and that I'm considering it. It's odd, that most of the time, I'm able to clear my mind enough to focus on the airy work of painting and dreaming, but that simple words about electricity, whose meanings I comprehend one at a time, can combine to seem so complex. *"Patterns,"* I remind myself. *"It's only patterns."* So I read a paragraph and then reread it, hoping it might eventually sink in, becoming frustrated because I can't seem to concentrate, and feeling more like I'm dreaming than when I am asleep. *"And it's just words on a page."*

"Yes. Diddly-ump!" I repeated, hearing the familiar inflections that characterize my father's speech, the talk of "an old herrin' choker" as he occasionally refers to himself.

"You've got to hold 'em like this," he said.

I pictured a grizzly old man standing somewhere in proximity to the sea while trying to choke a small fish. "Might as well try and hold onto a spark," I snorted, watching him struggle with the wriggling little sprat. Perhaps that's what painters do—try to hang on to what otherwise might get away, hold things still for long enough to explore them, the fleeting kind of things that normally escape in a flash. At least that's what I like to think—that in the middle of work-a-day priorities and schedules there are paintings to see, books to read, songs to sing, and music to hear—the artist's fresh catch. "Electricity is a slippery fish," I advised, repositioning the bones between my fingers. It's so easy to take things for granted—and then suddenly they're gone. "But it's about the process, isn't it?"

Two mornings ago I lay in bed wondering again about my friend and his visits, which is something I often do at four o'clock when it's overcast and there are no stars to see. For a while, I argued with myself about the nature of my experience, before settling down to consider its substance, the things I think about which had never interested me before I met Nikola Tesla in my dreams. (And maybe I think too much.) For an hour or so I carried on an inner conversation about charges, currents, and the elusive power that I now believe is innate to everything. I began to ponder the existence of worlds; even my dream world and the thoughts that I think; the landscape of my body, my brain as a transmitter and receiver; all based on what I've heard and read of the thing called electricity. Then, just as I reached what seemed like the limit of my understanding, the air seemed to thicken and become substantially alive, and I knew that I was not alone. "Here are the two keys," said a voice, which sounded like Nikola Tesla from a distance, as if he were present, though far away—or maybe it was I who was both distant and in my bed at once; and I became aware of two large graphic symbols glowing in the air above me.

"These are keys, the creative principles," said the voice. "The one is vibration, and the other—direction."

I gazed knowingly at the two luminous signs, which at the time, made perfect sense. But for the last two days I've been trying to form thoughts, to describe in words what happened to me at that point. I not only saw the signs, but also experienced them as yoga-like positions facilitating my ability to receive and to transmit—to become them. I heard them. I sensed and tasted them, smelling them like a pleasant scent on my skin. It felt as if I were opened up, as if the places between the bits and pieces that are me had unexpectedly become vast spaces, as if I were spread over a large area for a wind to blow through.

So this morning, I lay in bed hoping to call up my dream of two days ago, but instead, I dreamed about my father repeatedly instructing me in the science of playing the bones. "Now watch. You see, you've got to leave the bottom one loose and hold the top one still," he explained, showing me the action of the bones and the movement of his hand in slow motion.

"The lover and the logician," I repeated to myself, *"poetry and the word,"* wondering where those thoughts had suddenly come from, if they were mine or from someone else.

"Like this...," and I saw his hand rock back and forth, away from and toward his chest in such a relaxed way that it looked easy. "It's that loose bottom rib that taps against the stiff top one," he stated gravely.

"The vibration of one against the direction of the other," I said, and the man in the dream, who was my father, stopped and smiled.

At that time, I saw and knew things, many of which I don't remember, and some of which I'm not able to write about. I recalled ideas from other lessons in a new context. *"What exists is dynamic, innately endowed with the possibility of reflected states, the action of one associating with the rhythm of the other."* I watched a crowd of people moving and milling about, and then remembered the curious image of a glass of water with dust suspended in the tiny currents contained within it. *"Like stars making their way around the sky."* And the people in the crowd began to dance, each holding a tether attached to the top of a tall pole in the center of a large square. *"Like pigments bound in medium and expressed in pictures."*

"The patterns you paint," said a voice, "are nothing less than the vibrations I have been talking about. All of life is vibration."

I swung my hand around noticing the interaction of myself

with an agitated and colliding universe, then lapsed momentarily into other dreams: a sparrow pecking crumbs from the asphalt of a parking lot; some kid rolling by on a scooter; intimate snapshots of my childhood, all similar I'm sure to what most people hold onto for self-reference.

"Light is alive," continued my teacher. "Both particle and wave—it burns like fire and flows like water."

A sudden memory: I'm walking down a dirt road bare foot, naked to the waist, wearing thin green cotton shorts, alone under a still summer sky, and trying to avoid stones underfoot by keeping to the cool dust in the car tracks—then later we all sat in the chokecherry tree eating fat black chokecherries and throwing them at each other, the blood-red of their juice mixing with the dirt on our skin, followed by inevitable tear trails running down our cheeks when the play got rough.

"Diddly-ump! is what you want," he said, moving his hand in such a way that the bottom rib freely oscillated up and down, hinged near its end in the crotch between his middle finger and ring finger, and vibrating against the top bone held tightly between his index and middle fingers. "Electromagnetic vibrations permeate everything. Light is everlasting, everywhere, and everything."

It was just two mornings ago that I studied the two radiant symbols floating over the bed and understood many important things that I have quickly forgotten, suspecting the even greater number of important things that I am not prepared to receive—then in my dream I began to list childhood mysteries, secrets, the stuff that I perceived that had no names: the images that appeared in the bending reflections on puddles; those jack-in-the-pulpits hidden among the tall ferns and dogbane where we crawled around on all fours yipping like puppies; the nights when walking down the dirt road in the dark took more courage than I thought I had, hearing unexplainable movements in the woods and the blood thumping on my eardrums; and the strange power of music and rhythm over me.

"But I can't see everything; I only perceive what I can translate into experience, the smallest part of what is reflected back—as in a mirror."

"A vision that continues to grow," added a gentle voice.

And I awoke, staring up into the empty space of my bedroom.

"Yes, I know—until I'm not willing to see more."

Dreams seem to happen in opposition to the daily grind that too often fills my waking hours—the busy bungling about, the meetings, phone calls, and white noise, the traffic of events that tries to overtake me during the day. *"I think I paint to stretch the boundaries around a bigger picture,"* I decided today, each time to see beyond the limits of the time before. It happens first with my eyes closed, where the universe is not yet digitized, downloaded, or dumped.

"Diddly-ump! That's what you want to hear," says my dad. "That's the basic beat and then you build on it."

27
Awakening in Italy

March 20 – Celadon is a transparent ceramic glaze usually applied to white china clay, varying in color between light jade and turquoise, sometimes seeming almost gray. I dreamed of myself surrounded by it, swimming in the middle of a celadon ocean. On my palette, I'd probably start with a small pat of Veronese Green, or better yet, Cinnabar Green, then lighten it up with a considerable amount of Mixed White, followed by a little Mediterranean Blue (just a touch of the brush at a time), eventually to bring it to the place of neither being green nor blue—not the color of water nor of the sky. *"The birds outside are singing,"* I noticed. *"Now correct the value with a dot of Umber."* And I relaxed again, drifting where earth and heaven meet without boundary, sinking slightly into the clear pale-hue until it began to lap over me. I watched myself from above, lazily floating on the surface of a sea as smooth as polished stone—until I rolled over, stood up, walked across the floor, and opened the window to the sudden crescendo of birdsong and the sound of busses. *"It's morning—and I'm in Italy,"* I remembered, before unlatching and pushing open the shutters.

I looked down into the garden at a terra cotta urn spilling over with geraniums, at the sunlight showing through the leaves of a young beech, at the primulas and moss overtaking the grass beneath the trees. "The way back here has transformed me," I breathed, scanning a raked path to the front steps where an old man was busy with a watering can, *"like the way through a painting, each time leading somewhere new—though I have already been there."* Spring. The gardener would be showing up soon with a couple of friends to help move the potted lemons out of the *limonaia* for the season to their places along the walk. *"The strange course through a painting—never like the time before, though always the same."* I stood at the window until the sound of children in a schoolyard began to mix with that of the birds. *"The nameless way through each painted world, at times feeling like a walk on a tightrope—without daring to look up, down, to one side or the other."*

"By now, the table downstairs will be set for breakfast," I called out.

For the next two days I awoke dreaming of the same color, though the context had become a favorite secluded cove on the Ligurian coast where I sat on a rock and let the waves wash over me, gazing out from the edge of a celadon sea, searching for the hint of an invisible horizon. "In Italian, how do you describe the humidity over the sea that sometimes makes the horizon invisible?" I asked a friend later. "*Vuoi dire la foschia?*" he answered. "Do you mean the haze?"

In my dream, there was no separation between where I sat and the sky. *"The same me here and there,"* I thought, looking out and then up, *"without boundary between who I am and whom I will become."* And I felt limitless, both terrestrial, and celestial, sitting on a submerged rock some fifteen feet from the shore and looking out toward a dreamy expanse.

"Fos-kee'-ya," I repeated absently. "Maybe that's it—fos-kee'ya."

Memories, like Theseus's string, each time leading back to the beginning, to the first layers of paint, like my favorite trail through the woods by the old stone wall—I picture myself, a dirty little pilgrim, headed off on a quest through an abandoned orchard to a small meadow at the top of a hill where a solitary pine tree grew, to be alone at the top of the tree, to feel the wind on my face, to think about things and wonder. That's the elusive path of artists—tramping through the woods, painting in a studio, or travelling to far-away places: to seek for what is most mysterious and to tell the untellable tale of it.

The following morning, I dreamed of swimming in the pale sea again, noting the evidence of brushwork on the skin of my own painted figure and the excited ripple of fine brushstrokes on a flock of Giotto-esque angels entering the space as if from behind the picture plane, their lower bodies disappearing into an endless field of faded green-blue-gray. Again, I relaxed into the satisfying concordance of one world with another, happy with the normalcy of earth and heaven becoming one place. *"Where is this?"* I asked myself, unexpectedly approaching the perimeter of a deep darkness. *"It is my eye!"* I realized. *"I'm floating on the iris of my own eye—drifting on a sea of seeing."* Then I awoke.

Painting has taught me a lot about getting from one place to another. I depend on it. Without a vision I can't seem to put one foot in front of the other; I lose my way. And yet, for a painter, there is no well-worn path through an image. Consider my friend the toad, diving headlong into the unknown—that's how it can feel leaving the safe world of sensible things to chase after dreams.

Even when at the outset, I think I have a clear picture of the outcome, typically the way reveals itself one faith-filled step at a time. Most travelers know; you don't arrive at one destination by focusing on another. It's another open secret—that you always end up exactly where you're headed. As with any wanderer's tale, the story of a painting often starts in familiar territory and by ordinary means. I have learned from experience that miracles and quantum leaps occur only after my vision and resolve are tried and tested, and that sometimes such intervention is invisible until I'm able to step back and view the finished picture. But even a completed painting is not proof enough of the process. The dilemmas and deliverance that happen along the way always seem to transform *me* more than they do the materials that I work with. It's not about my expression after all. In fact, I am the best evidence of where I've been and what I've seen. I become the image of the way I've taken. I am the expression.

Then again, in the morning, I revisited the tranquil expanse of my eye, suspended like a speck of dust on the surface of a vast puddle of watercolor. *"Where are you?"* I asked, as if expecting a different response from last time, and talking to myself as if I were someone else. *"Still right here,"* I answered, lazing into the usual tickle of flashes and tremors. I released myself fully into the spectacular wash of color, enjoying the sensation of perfect weightlessness—before hearing the abrupt gritty squeal of a tram passing around the tracks on the corner. "We have a train to catch," I grumbled, turning toward my wife and opening my eyes.

Nel mezzo del cammin—somewhere in the middle I get lost each time. Oddly, I think the possibility of becoming lost is what intrigues me from the start. It's symptomatic of painting that at some point the direct path through an image is obscured and an artist has to make a new way through. As if on cue, I begin to suspect that I lack the necessary virtues for success, while struggling to hang on to the initial vision that inspired my pursuit. It's an uncomfortable place to be, my foolhardiness becoming increasingly plain against a hope in something subtle and fleeting. Yet it's false security, the apparent easiness of the way that is the greatest danger for an artist. And though I'd fight for the right to doubt, that's when doubt can end the journey before it's really over. Then, I must discern between what I can imagine and what I will paint. That's when make-believe becomes belief—a lance becomes a brush, the cup of plenty turns into a palette, and I am armored with new confidence in myself and my endeavor.

There are times on the path when the past becomes my teacher, and when the future inspires me, but the way is made clear by simply doing; the secrets are known by being and acting in the present. As the stable point of interaction between a wheel's perimeter and the earth enables the advance of the wheel, being present enables my progress through an image. The first brushstroke leads to the last, but the painting happens in between; as asking leads to receiving, but seeking is the activity. For all of my careful premeditation and planning, I don't paint to rehearse what I already know. It's never just for its own sake. I paint to see something new.

The next day, as dawn began to happen through my eyelids, the celadon sea turned slowly brighter, becoming an endless grain field bleached nearly white in the warmth of Italian sunlight. I was wading through a tide of whispering grass, hearing the wind breathe through the heavily seeded heads of grain, and watching breezes play upon a golden ocean ready for harvest. Then without warning, the hiss of plumbing filling up with the rush of early morning showers and baths caught my attention; though I continued to dream while reluctantly acknowledging the world waking up around me. The grain field became an endless meadow of wildflowers—and again outside the window, Italian songbirds began to celebrate spring in earnest. Like the subject of a Botticelli, I seemed to hover above a blanket of blossoms, accompanied by bird song dotted intermittently with the hacking talk of blackbirds up on the roof.

I'm always plagued by the same old questions—*"What's this all about? Who is Tesla? Why am I here? And who am I this time?"* The celadon tide returned momentarily before pigeons in the eaves started restlessly mumbling, and the world of dreams finally succumbed to the quiet echo of doors opening and closing, of lowered voices and rolling suitcases passing down the hallway.

I start most images with a clear impression only to be blinded at some point by what I thought I knew. It happens often. My vision is compromised—*nella selva oscura*, and I am forced to wander for a while—*e la diritta via è smarrita*. The miracle of painting patterns then is that they offer me a map to follow when I'm lost, a regimen that I can take step by step until I find my way again. I give up my will to the pattern, to obey the repeated details that characterize its principles, eventually to be freed by strict adherence to a prescribed plan, and to take comfort in my slow and steady progress. That is an enigma of painting—that the craft teaches me the art. And that's where the transformation takes place, that's where everything changes—in abasing myself before the humble purposes of a simple-looking pattern, something that at first seems quite predictable. It's the hardest thing about my work, and the most difficult part to describe—how the literal application of paint within the format of a repeated pattern, brushstroke by brushstroke, leads to seeing what is beyond the limitations of its apparent design. It happens in the notes and phrases of musical compositions, in the reiterated elemental symbols of alphabets and numbering systems, in the reproduction of generations, in the recurrent seasons of death and rebirth, in the perpetual rotating and revolving of things— and by painting pictures. I have learned to trust that my vision can be restored, that what was veiled will be revealed again and again and again, and that somewhere along the way, before the picture is complete, the artist who set out will be renewed. That's why I paint.

I opened my eyes. The room was darker than it should have been, or than I thought it would be. My pillow felt damp and sticky and I touched my face to find that I had a nosebleed during the night. I got up, plugged both nostrils with wads of toilet paper, and returned to bed. *"Here I am again,"* I congratulated myself, satisfied, staring up at the plastic figure nailed to a wooden cross hanging on the wall above my head. In Siena, we have always stayed with the sisters of St Catherine in a hostelry they keep for pilgrims. I turned to gaze out of the window at the cathedral perched on a hilltop not too far away still lit by spotlights in the predawn shade—the dome's big belly and the tall striped bell tower. *"Patterns! Visual sequences, vibrations, which are meaningful by their very nature..."* I began to review my first lesson with Nikola Tesla while studying the cathedral wrapped in those familiar patterns. *"...patterns are everywhere."*

"Remember, it is not what you see, nor is it sight," said a voice. "Not the word, nor the language alone." The pigeons started murmuring again.

"I don't understand," I responded, hearing their worried cooing and noting the slightly blue-er sky outside.

"...neither the solitary pilgrim, nor the lonely path," said the voice.

"As usual, this is all riddles. C'mon—who are you really?" I asked, tasting blood in the back of my throat.

"I am me. I am you. I am Nikola Tesla. I am who I am. And does it really matter?" he teased. "On the long list of things that you consider important, there are just a few that really matter." I watched as the increasing light of morning slowly turned the city's ancient bricks and tiles from dark umber to rusty red. White – black – white – black – white – black – white – black—I counted the alternating layers of stone from the bottom to the top of the tower. *"...18, 19, 20, 21..."*

"The power is in the dynamic association between the two—the wayfarer and the way," continued the voice.

"...39, 40, 41, 42..."

"The one is vibration, and the other—direction. That is the pattern."

"...81, 82, 83, 84...that's a very tall campanile. Perhaps I should put it in a painting." The bells in the bell tower began to ring. *"Time to get up."*

Siena is a city of patterns. Everything there seems to be articulated with the geometric and flowing business of filling up space, which is somehow comforting to my overactive reasoning, keeping it busy so the rest of me can take in other things—like watching tourists, even if I am one. Italy is filled with tourists, people who are out of place, a little lost on their way. It's like watching old-style animations, colorful, often predictable, and usually good for a chuckle.

"Doo'-ay," the man said slowly, distinctly, and louder than necessary, as if the proprietor was hard of hearing and unable to count the two fat fingers wagging in his face. "Doo'-ay jell-ah'-toes. Doo'-ay. Two. Two—ice—creams," repeated the man, holding out the "creeeaaams" an extra two beats and grinning.

"*Guarda, c'è un'altro cretino americano.*" The proprietor returned a patronizing smile and motioned to a bored looking girl with a tantalizing *scollatura* who mechanically went to wait on the customer.

"Van-ig'-lee-ah and choc-lee-eh'-toe," said the man, obviously pleased.

"*Mamma mia!*" mouthed the girl silently, turning to scoop the *gelato* onto two cones. There were similar scenes happening all around. Tourists clucked, croaked, and barked, all hoping to make themselves understood.

"Doo jeh-rah'-to…jeeh—rraah'—to. Doo. Doo!" The man held up two fingers.

"*Non! Non! NON! Deux! Deux glaces!*" The lady waved her hand around impatiently.

"Du'! Eh! Gel! Aaah'! Toh!" the man ordered, reading authoritatively from a guide book and jabbing two fingers into the air.

"*Mamma mia!*" the voluptuous girls all mouthed silently, turning to scoop the *gelato* onto the cones.

In the piazza I watched a swarm of tourists relentlessly chasing a large daisy held high on a stick. Here and there, Italian youths sat passionately nuzzling, while slightly older males stretched and primped, vying for the attention of unsuspecting young travelers. Vendors unpacked and packed up wares. Yesterday was St Joseph's and Via Dupré still looked festive. We bought some of the creamy-centered rice fritters, *fritelle di San Giuseppe*, from a makeshift stand and crossed the crowded Campo, headed for the Palazzo Pubblico while we snacked.

We spent the day exploring the elaborate patterns of Sienese art: colorful, faded, layered, peeling, some in the process of restoration, some reduced to nostalgic hints of the past. In the Palazzo Pubblico I visited with mentors and friends—Simone Martini in the Sala del Mappamondo, and Giudoriccio da Fogliano, clothed in complex patterns to match those of his richly caparisoned horse; Ambrogio Lorenzetti in the Sala dei Nove, and the orderly pattern of well-governed life, my lady friend dressed in dragonflies and diamonds and dancing in the street. Then—the cathedral; the trompe l'oeil universe of the Piccolomini Library; the resonant baptistery, the tales of saints and heroes framed in grotesque flourishes, zig-zags, and waves; and the Museo dell'Opera del Duomo with Duccio's view of God's life arranged in a grid of small panels. All day the spell of details, of particulate worlds caught in suspension, bound by the articulate language of patterns, begged me to reconsider the illusion of what is real. I especially noted the many painted images of roads—leading through towns and countrysides, from castles, and to mystical cities, everyone and everything travelling down roads to everywhere and nowhere, all of the roads at last becoming one ubiquitous road leading into the distance—the road I'm on, the very road that led me here.

Finally, I went to bed tired by the overabundance of the day, an artist filled to bursting with the patterns of a loaded universe, feeling joined to others by the common nature of our individual efforts to describe our passage—to name a nameless way.

"Your active participation as a receiver in the charged medium of the universe regenerates the universe, which regenerates you," said Nikola Tesla.

Somewhere between the sea and sky without a horizon, the cares of my life washed away. Solemnly the bells in the black and white tower began to sound and somewhere far off the birds started singing.

"The interaction of conductive material with a magnetic field is a pattern," he continued. "In greater and lesser scale, in greater and lesser universes, the pattern is pervasive."

I noticed my breath—breathing out, and breathing in, like waves washing up on the shore of me. "I think I have felt that," I answered softly, trying to sink deeper into the sweep of liquid color.

Flashes, twitching, and little shakes.

"I'm floating on the source of visions, swimming in the ocean of my eye."

And then I thought I heard the hushed babbling of pigeons in the eaves. The gentle wrestle between asleep and awake had begun once again.

28

Music and the Bonfire

March 26 -- It's hard to avoid the monastery of San Marco when I am anywhere near Florence. The corridors, cloisters, and galleries are familiar, constant, like the lure of home. My attachment has evolved into something of a *vocazione*—my mission: to memorize its passages and contents, to explore its secrets so thoroughly that when I'm not there, I become one more ghost haunting its halls.

Each visit, gentle Fra' Giovanni instructs me in the same catechisms, leading me through the reflections and meditations that I have come to expect.

"Devotion is the key, *sapete*.
Pray before you work each day.
Avoid straying from the way.
Sacrifice and study.
Don't be afraid of what it takes,"
he preaches matter-of-factly.

"*Business as usual today,*" I noted, and watched him busily shuffling about in his *tonaca*, hoping that perhaps we had become friends by then. "But that is pride isn't it?" I was reminded. He was as direct as always, though strangely aloof—unlike Fra' Filippo across town, who seems far more affable and aware of his own prodigious abilities. Fra' Giovanni's celestial preoccupation is obvious, forever marked in the distant gazes of his messengers, the painted mediators from somewhere between here and there who populate his views.

I was on a pilgrimage of sorts, *un pellegrino* traveling on a road to discovery, and feeling like a hungry question mark, *il peregrin pensoso*. I think of myself back at home, standing on the lawn in the middle of the night, staring up at the Milky Way, wandering though a field of stars, hoping for answers or a sign of some kind. So I arrived at San Marco again, prepared to commune with the unknowns of the place in order to return and report to my mentor, Nikola Tesla.

The Sala dell'Ospizio is the original hospice for travelers, accessed from the fifteenth century cloister of Sant'Antonino. I passed the lunette where Fra' Giovanni has painted a fresco of two friars welcoming Jesus disguised as a wayfarer, like me—though not in dungarees and t-shirt. Part of why I've come is to inspect the painted pattern on the image of drapery behind the enthroned virgin and child with saints in the central panel from the *Pala di San Marco, St Mark's Altarpiece*. The Sala dell'Ospizio is now the home of most of Fra' Giovanni's panel paintings.

Each time, it's like visiting family. *"Yes, there's Cosma looking a little lost again."* I smiled. For over thirty years Cosma and I have been chatting about life. Since my last visit, I have painted the peculiar pattern on the drapery behind him into one of my pieces. I noticed then that the photograph I used as a reference back home lied to me, omitting certain subtleties that I left out. "So, what now, my old friend? Do I return to do penance and repaint it?" Disheartened, I stood gazing blankly at the peculiar palms in back of the hanging textile. "But—as a sad attempt, my work is honest and accurate. To humble me, I think I'll leave it as it is," I concluded. "That is wise," agreed the friar from over my shoulder. In return, I wanted to tell him that Cosma still seems confused and that his palm trees look like asparagus stalks, but I have always liked them that way.

I took my usual path from the altarpiece of San Marco to the *Deposizione* at the end of the hall—the cooperative effort of Lorenzo Monaco, who left it unfinished when he died; and Fra' Giovanni, who later completed it. I looked at each figure carefully, at the two ladders leaning on the arms of the cross, then studied the crucified figure being gently lowered—his body draped diagonally, his head fallen back horizontally. I can never get enough of any of it. Then on to the chairback decorated with heaven and hell, and to the series of small furniture panels with white banners painted across them to hold related inscriptions. Last year I used a similar banderole and text in one of my own paintings. I spent some time there in the galleries, particularly noting several images where the rope tied around the waist of the Madonna's robe is let down from above, offered as a means of transcendence, recalling the ropes of my childhood friends: the rope in the hands of the pendant person painted by Daumier; Breugel's image of a rope tied to the supporting stick of a bird trap; and the rope held by La Berceuse, the postman's wife. *"That a simple rope should be so omnipresent!"* I realized, suddenly seeing them all as the same rope—from heaven, to the man hanging on, to the hidden boy with a bird trap, through the hand of VanGogh's yellow-faced Madonna, and to the cradle.

Eventually, I left the place of strangers and wayfarers to climb the stairs to the dormitories, instinctively prepared for the drama of the *Annunciazione* appearing from above, the vision of it growing gradually on my approach with each step up. I understand that the staircase may not have always been in that position, and that seeing the Annunciation in that way might be due to the restructuring of the convent at some point. In fact, it wasn't visible to a public audience at all until the second half of the nineteenth century when the monastery became a public museum. Until then, it was still the private haunt of Fra' Giovanni and generations of his humble brothers.

There are places where I was physically reminded of the layered nature of my experience, shown the exposed *budella* of the building, encouraged to peep through glass panels in the floor down to previous floors and walls that were in place before Michelozzo imagined this instantiation of the friary. *"Yes, this is Italy, isn't it?"* I remembered, *"in the constant presence of the past, where the present becomes transparent, repents, and falls away, revealing the underlayers of things—a protection against forgetting. That's why I like it."* I've come to believe that where time is relative, it becomes more obviously relevant. So, what happens when a place destroys the evidence, or remodels the past in such a way that people have no reference? The Italians have no such luxury. They try, but there's too much constantly resurfacing. Juxtaposing chic and sleek with dated and irregular only makes the timeworn seem more timely. I took in the Annunciation briefly, reassuring myself that I'd be back to study it before leaving.

Because I am a true child of the Sixties, conventual life seduces the *Fratello Sole* in me. *"If only…,"* I have said to myself so many times; the notions of a brotherhood chanting vespers together with a little reverb, of gardening barefoot wearing nothing but an old blanket, arouse my true mendicant heart. After all, gardening is just another form of painting. *"Good. We're the first ones here this morning so we'll be alone—almost alone."* (Including Giovanni.) We headed for the cells, finally to accomplish what I told Tesla I would do.

Most of the forty-three monks' cells are similar—cozy, whitewashed, vaulted chambers, each decorated with a fresco. In each room on the outer wall of the building there is an arched wall painting a few feet from a small arched window. *"Window-in-window out. Clever."* The inner and outer always in the context of each other, the essential in view of the substantial, the creative and receptive joined within the awareness of the chamber's inhabitant.

I love the first cell, and entered with the usual anticipation—not to be disappointed. *Noli Me Tangere* is one of my preferred themes. *"Still here, these two—still frozen in place."* The gardener with a hoe over his shoulder and the beautiful woman kneeling by him on the flowery meadow—she's been reaching and he responding for centuries, even before God reached for Adam on that ceiling in Rome, both images forever eliciting a *will-they-ever-touch* response. She is of the earth, open-armed, glancing coyly upward, forever expecting and extending, and he, standing above her, *contraposto* as if to walk away, a tender-faced but reluctant bridegroom. And so they never meet. I studied the folds of the fabric in their robes, hers sweeping dramatically up and his lyrical, and watched his pale feet move across the grass. *"Hey! Didn't I see him really move just a little—same as I did last time?"* I have always thought that if I couldn't be a painter, I'd be a gardener instead. Or the soil is pigment, or the pigment is soil; under my fingernails it's all the same—plants in rows and paint in patterns, the mindful direction of light, and hoped-for cooperation of outside forces. I tried to imagine the gardener holding a paint brush and palette in place of his hoe.

"You've got the tuner?" I double-checked. It was why we were there so early, before the tourists came, to intone, to sing and identify the notes that resonate the chambers. It's a large part of why we went to Italy, to explore the magic of resonance in that familiar context. My daughter produced the electronic tuner from her large purse and clicked it on.

"I'll start, and then you. OK?" The cell naturally echoed my voice, but I knew that there would be one note to make it vibrate like the body of a musical instrument, amplifying the tone beyond an echo. I slid my voice slowly up and down the scale a few times hoping to hear what was expected. And I did. "There! Do you hear that? What's that note?" I asked with some excitement. "Write it down! Write it down!" My wife, waiting with a pencil and pad to record the results of our research, took down the note. I sang it repeatedly as if chanting my matins, feeling the note vibrate through me. "This is how it must have sounded. This is what they heard and felt multiplied by the number of cells and voices!"

("Nikola, this is Fra' Giovanni. *Caro fratello, questo è il mio caro Nikola.*")

I looked up from the tuner to the fresco, but from the new perspective of seeing, singing, hearing, and feeling C sharp, and remembered the resonating filaments I had experienced with Tesla almost a year before. I felt myself begin to readjust, my doubt giving way, my gut reverberating with the impressive connection between the vibration of my vocal chords and the structure of a monk's cell—and the implied relationship between myself and something much larger beyond the small room. I intoned C sharp, on and around the edges of the note, together with my wife and daughters who had joined me in C sharp and various attempts at harmony. It was a resonant agreement with the whole building, its foundation, the city of Florence, with Italy, the world, and with the solar system. We were interacting directly with The Pattern, knowing then that nothing would ever be the same. We had touched and affected the Universe with our voices and our insides, amplified by the resonance of the chamber and the image of a kneeling lady and a gardener.

("Thank-you, but we have already met," said Nikola. Giovanni looked serenely pleased.)

When I was young, playing the violin was an enforced privilege. Reluctantly sitting in my room to practice, I would often take long rests, stopping between songs and scales to explore, to try and see into the darkened interior of my violin through a curlicue shaped slit cut in the soft wood of its top. For years I read and reread the name of the man who had made the instrument, the date that he had made it, and pondered the meaning of an enigmatic stick of wood stuck between the ceiling and floor of the empty little room. "I'm one year older than you," I'd boast, and then apologize to my wooden side-kick. And although I never did master the violin, we spent a lot of time together and she became a confidante of sorts, a kind of counterpart. I took her with me everywhere, to college and home again, and to and from Europe several times, but gradually I played her less and less, spending far more time just sitting and looking. I'd take her gently out and examine her, carefully turning her over to see myself reflected in the polished maple flames of her back, then turning her around again to try and peek inside the shadowy arched chamber of her belly.

I don't know what I was looking for. But the mostly hidden world through an *f* hole, like the top of a pine tree where I retired so often as a child, became a landmark, a constant place where I could spend time thinking and dreaming. "Hello," I would whisper, my lips brushing her varnished face, speaking into the dim space of my violin's hollow insides as if expecting a response. I really didn't—but I always thought that my voice should echo more in there than it did. I think it was like speaking to the part of me that never happened—the practice that never was, my parents' wishes, my own daydreams, the futures that I didn't live, the perfect life that isn't.

I sang C sharp and looked at the gardener, then down at his lady friend, and recognized them both—the eagerness of my yearning to unite with my being, and my reluctance to accept my earthy part until I see myself as heavenly. Once in a while, I hear my son or daughter playing my violin, but it has been years since I have picked it up. I'm a little embarrassed for the secrets spoken into it as if some day they might escape to incriminate me. *"How much easier it would be to have faith,"* still shy of accepting the circumstances of my own life, *"living within the resonant expressions I'm trying to imagine resounding through this chamber and the pigmented plaster bodies of this hesitant gardener and his pretty companion."* (Had I missed the point?) "But wait! This is the after, isn't it?" I rushed out of the cell to stand again in front of the *Annuciazione*, staring at the antecedent. "And this is the before!"

The Annunciation is arguably the most famous image in the monastery. I recalled another of Giovanni's Annunciations in a chamber we had not yet visited farther down the corridor, and yet another in Cortona, both equally important works—but the fancy wings of the Gabriel in the Annunciation at the top of the staircase are hard to compete with when it comes to popularity. I am drawn to all three images for different reasons.

"Before what?" my daughter asked, arriving close behind.

I inspected the two figures— another heavenly being and a different Mary, portrayed under a *loggia* as if on stage, each visually contained within the boundaries of a painted arch, not unlike the shape of the arched frescoes in the cells, and reminiscent of Michelozzo's library down the hall and the architecture of the cloister below. "Be it unto me as thou wilt," I watched her answer the angel resolutely.

Their arms are folded tenderly across their hearts as if to protect and emphasize their separation, unlike the relaxed open attitudes of the two figures back in the cell we had just exited. "Touch me not," the *giardiniere* tells the other Mary, though both of them are open-armed. The intentional relationship between the two pictures is undeniable. "You see, it's the same flowery meadow— that enclosed garden, and the woods beyond the fence. And the doors—this one, leading back into an inner space and through a small window into those distant trees; and the other, an exit from the underworld into the space of the composition." Each image contains two figures—one earthy, and one heavenly, captured there in acts of communing, reciting lines, playing parts that their bodies seem to belie—two narrations, suspended in pigment and lime.

"This Annunciation is a prequel and the scene in the other room is the sequel," I said while continuing to study the picture. "They're like the prologue and epilogue…." I explained that, besides the fresco we had just seen, the Annunciation at the top of the stairs is the only other place in the cycle of San Marco frescoes where that particular meadow appears. Then I walked around the corner back into the hall in the direction of the first cell. "...making it seem to extend invisibly through the space of this corridor and into the other room." Instantly, the air where I stood felt palpable. "The two doors suggest the rest, the intersecting of events joining here with there, the before and after connecting within the dimensions of our responses." Then I turned toward my daughter who was studying me rather than the fresco.

I remember seeing inside a violin for the first time, opened up and layed bare; which wasn't as interesting as I had expected. It was just the inside of a curvy wooden box. Although I could finally see everything—the parts were all there and the strings could still be plucked and stroked with the horsehair of the bow—without the mechanics all in place, the magical voice of the violin was dead. It reminded me of periodically finding a lifeless bird in the meadow or in the woods—still beautiful, but unable to move, sing, and fly.

"*Ingenious Giovanni,*" I mused, recalling some of the more clumsy modern conceptual pieces I have experienced. "We're the theatre he has chosen for this drama to unfold in. It resonates within us," I stated. "We bring it to life." And I hoped that she had understood.

We traveled down the corridors of the dormitory, studying the frescoes and patiently intoning the resonant note for each chamber—C sharp; B flat, the other Annunciation in cell three; C sharp; B flat, a Nativity in five; C sharp, the Transfiguration in cell six. Our singing and the succession of painted conversations set me adrift, like so many other images throughout history that string ideas and events together, loosening my uptight attachment to where, when, and who I think I am—like threads in a virtual chatroom. We stopped, settling into cell seven where the fresco depicts an all-seeing God blindfolded and enthroned on a red box placed upon a raised platform.

"Riddles." Sometimes, you have to close your eyes to see the picture.

As seasons change, there are times in the woods when the wind whips the angry treetops while below it is still. I'll look up and wonder how the weather above doesn't seem to reach the ground. Those are thoughtful times, when from the shelter of my position I am safely able to sense the uneasiness of the world around me. So it is—that my head can be filled with commotion while my heart remains quiet. I inhaled the morning chill of the cell, then let it escape slowly, releasing all of my usual concerns. "Is this it?" I exhaled, opening my eyes. "Is this where you show us the way?" Among everything else, paintings are often expressions of homesickness. Artists are unlikely heroes—travelling alone, in the dark, and fumbling ahead on missions of uncertainty, lured by a hope in something elusive. So frequently they leave a string behind to indicate the path they've taken, hoping someone else might follow—or to help in the return. It stands out like an unexpected sign with an arrow that reads, "I went this way."

Several stray hands, a head, a comet's tail of spit, a stick—strange objects in vagrant orbits painted on a field of green-blue-grey are the intended backdrop for an unseeing subject. Two still figures, a woman and a man, seated in the lower right and left corners of the implied foreground make an equilateral triangle with the same subject seated in the middle ground. *"The artist is a tease."* The background and middle grounds collapse and the trajectories of the peculiar planets collide with the head of the subject. The foreground and middle grounds flatten to form a pyramid of three sun-like orbs. I stood there open-mouthed, staring at the hint of facial features showing through a white band covering the subject's eyes. "My dear brother…," I began, but Giovanni was gone. A celestial tone filled the chamber and my gut began to hum. "C sharp," sang my daughter.

"Storm above and calm below," I noted, looking again at the image to see God become a sightless juggler, and still wanting to see a brush and palette in his hands. Like cloud-gazing, I watched the centuries old tableau painted on a plaster wall pass in and out of view, the intended backdrop for prayerful repetitions becoming a stationary pageant for wandering troupes of players in a museum. In the lower left, the picture of a monk sitting poised and still, his delicate hand posed thoughtfully on his cheek, changed into Nikola Tesla. "I choose the journey," I repeated under my breath. "The shape of things continues to change and shift, while the substance and essence remain the same," I heard him respond. What was once obvious was suddenly no longer apparent.

"Did you get that?" asked my daughter. "It's C sharp again." We all intoned the note while my wife wrote it down. And we returned to the hall.

"I am the view—in and out, seeing or not seeing, hearing and not hearing. I'm the place in between where knowing and unknowing meet—where the meadow and woods meet the sky. What happened in there, happened in me."

"Yet some things you may imagine—are not there at all,"

reminded a voice.

"But how can I know?"

"First, know the pattern."

"I understand," I responded silently, recalling an image of a single person wandering around alone where a crowd had once been. "I am the pattern."

This time, re-entering the hall was different—like entering somewhere else. I looked up at the rafters of a high roof that I hadn't noticed far above the tops of the monks' chambers—and I felt small, and then big, and then small again, and so on, and so on. *"I am the pattern,"* something I had learned from Nikola Tesla during our initial lesson. But this time, I knew that I knew it in a different way from before; it was the first time that I recognized it spoken so clearly in my own voice.

More cells, notes, and frescoes—a Coronation, and the Presentation of an infant; we turned the corner to confront a brooding heaviness at the end of the corridor.

"What's down there?" my other daughter asked instinctively.

"Girolamo Savonarola," I answered, remembering the painted chairback downstairs; one side of it depicting an angelic host in a pastoral paradise, holding hands, singing, and dancing in a flowery meadow; while the other shows monsters cooking and gnawing on the damned in a fiery hell. "He lived at the end of this hall."

Living, dreaming, and painting are precarious activities, undertaken in spite of the risks.

"What were you thinking?" demands my intellect.

"I'm not sure. I thought I saw something over there."

"Well, whatever you do now—don't look down."

"Thanks. I'm afraid of heights," I reply, peering down into the darkness.

It's often like that. Before realizing what I'm doing, I get out in the middle of things based on a vision and pure enthusiasm, caught somewhere between up and down, and one side and the other.

"But there was something over on the other side," I reassert. "I saw it."

"Not likely," counsels my brainy advisor. "Next time, just ask me."

Unexpected events can challenge my perception. My hope is sometimes overcome by fears; I focus on concerns and forget the destination. Dreams can abruptly turn into nightmares.

"I have walked to the horizon…," said someone whom I couldn't see.

"…and stared at the stars," I responded.

"I have been to the horizon…," rehearsed the voice.

"…and stared into the sun," I recited, relieved to have recalled the passphrase.

Then things became dark. The dream turned. I looked into two round eyes, shiny black, and insect-like, and was startled awake. The clock said three thirty-one. I got out of bed and went outside. It was raining lightly and I heard a deep hum in the woods.

I have watched films where what seemed innocent was unexpectedly exposed as menacing; I've paid surprise visits to friends who weren't home; I stopped for a view and then my car wouldn't start; I fell in love to end up arguing with my lover; untimely death still shakes my belief; I turn each page of a book not knowing what is on the next—I understand it best in paint, where the darks simply add dimension.

We studied his portrait, the stern birdlike profile, his hooded silhouette floating in a field of shadow,

"Who was he?"

like the man in the moon staring silently ahead,

"He was one of the first reformers."

the shape of an up-turned blade reflecting a face against the black of night,

"Oh."

A solitary flame in darkness. In another small room we considered his scratchy flax and horsehair girdle, the tools of mortification, and a piece of singed-looking black robe,

"I don't understand."

the sober reminders of ardent sermons and strict renunciations.

But I didn't answer her.

We were quiet as we viewed a painting of him hanging from a gibbet above a bonfire with a couple of devout friends, a Gothic event in the middle of the Renaissance piazza, just one more rehearsal in the square that day, among the many dramatic portrayals of life on an oversized stage—of all the vanities he had set ablaze, at last it was his turn. Some folks continued doing business; others passed by on horseback; a few carried fuel to the fire; groups and individuals caught in the middle of playing parts, many of them strangely unaware of anything out the ordinary, went about their day.

And we forgot to sing.

Most of the remaining cells contain depictions of Saint Domenic kneeling beneath a vivid Crucifixion, each with bright red rivulets running down the cross onto the suggestion of barren ground. "D," sang my daughter, as columns of sunlight streamed in to warm the monk's chambers and we began to hear the muffled sounds of restless traffic coming from outside. "So vespers must have been a different note from matins," I concluded. "The pitch changes while the process and principles remain the same. Naming the specific resonant notes that vibrate the cells is not as important as coming here to sing them. I guess that's what he wanted me to know." Soon the halls were filling with visitors and we hurried to finish our musical tour of the dormitories. A large group of tourists clamored up the stairs as we descended. Leaving San Marco, I felt torn—between compassion for zealous Fra' Girolamo, and my passions, appetites, and vanities, my too many self-directed indulgences. Then the dream abruptly ended as we stepped out into the noise of a busy street.

Creative activity is always an exchange between worlds—inner and outer, higher and lower, unseen and seen. When we were still having babies, I remember looking at my wife's belly as she lay in bed, inspecting the expanding pale dome that temporarily housed our child, the context of our combined creative and receptive expressions.

"Do you think it's Sam?"

"Well, I don't have a girl's name picked."

"Will you be disappointed if it's a boy again?"

"Of course not! Silly."

Each time, we looked forward with anticipation to meeting our new friend. For months I was awed by the growth and activity of what we had begun, and wondered at the increasing awareness, as evidenced by the responses to my gentle pokes, of what had started with our shared enthusiasm and a couple of cells. I watched her belly gradually develop and tried to imagine who its inhabitant might be. "What's your name? Huh?"

We tried out names until one seemed to fit. We pondered the

state of the world and dreamed about the future of the life we had created.

"I'll be twenty-eight years older than you. I hope that's OK?"

"Which means that when he's twenty, I'll be forty-eight!" I exclaimed (thinking that to be quite old).

And he or she became a confidant of sorts, a friend in a hidden world, an unseen intercessor between here and wherever it is that awareness lives before this. "Hello," I'd whisper, my lips brushing against my wife's soft skin, then placing my ear against her as if expecting a response from within—though I really didn't. But I knew that we were interacting directly with a mystery much bigger than ourselves. We had touched and affected the Universe, and nothing would ever be the same.

That day in Florence, I thought of my friend who runs marathons and remembered his telling me that the distance didn't matter. He said, "The distance is what magnifies everything, but I don't go there to win or lose against the distance." He speaks of pushing through to someplace new, where he meets himself each time as a stranger, the guide who runs beside him for the rest of the way. "I would rather risk everything to take myself to that place where I have never been before, than to run predictably well to nowhere new."

Later, I wrote myself a note:
> "And now I know for sure, it wasn't San Marco I came to see, or the tones I came to identify—once again, it was me I came to meet."

In fact, I have decided that in the discussion of cats in boxes and points of view, within and without—I might be the box.

29
Pietà and Compianto

April 8 – Art museums are strangely wonderful places—wonderful for offering the communal family somewhere set apart to re-enact the experiences of artists, to assimilate the vicarious provisions of art; and strange, like zoos for paintings, sculptures, and fine crafts, where what was once alive in a natural environment is objectified and confined, roped off, protected by intricate security systems, and sometimes behind thick glass barriers. As museums go, the Accademia di Venezia feels less antiseptic than some—more like the art museum of my childhood and the Italy where not so long ago I could view things from up close without too much interference. I go to the Accademia for a comfortable day-long odyssey through Venetian painting, to wander through a labyrinth of halls and adjoining rooms housed in an attached network of old Venetian buildings—a school, a convent, and a church. It's where some of my favorite pictures live; works by Tiziano, Lotto, Giorgione, Giovanni Bellini, Mantegna, Cima da Conegliano, and others; where the influence of Leonardo's sojourn in Venice still feels fresh. This morning, I went to renew my acquaintance with a few old friends, to review my affinity for paintings I try not to miss when I'm in Italy.

I watched people enter and leave, one group after the other—filling, then emptying the small room where I stood: about twenty Asians crowding around a short woman waving a plastic orchid corsage taped to the top of a tall dowel; whole busloads of noisy French-speaking students shamelessly courting and touching each other; and ten to fifteen elderly Americans yacking and acting ugly. For the most part, they passed by without much interest in the paintings, arriving in successive fronts like bad weather—grumbling storm clouds audibly approaching from the larger exhibit hall, then bursting noisily into the modest-sized gallery where I was busy studying a favorite painted image. "Art's just not my bag," I heard one old bird crow to another, gesturing toward the walls, scowling, and leaning close in mock confidentiality. And then the Germans arrived, coughing out their throaty dictums, as if to cue the exit of the Americans who scurried off, before a few Italians strolling arm in arm and gossiping *sottovoce* about the tourists became the hushed closing act to a tempestuous script.

"Must be the morning for tours," I realized, turning to resume my musing on the Pietà by Giovanni Bellini, which felt more like considering the tender features of an aged face, thinking on what power held me there captive to its unassuming dimensions and character. *"Yeah, Italy's so full of visitors anymore."* Periodically another unchecked stampede would enter the room and loiter for a few minutes before leaving, on the way to spaghetti lunches, gelatos, and probable gondola rides. So I'd stop my review of the painting for a while to watch them pass and ponder my own devotion to the place. *"When did I first discover the layers? When did I first sense life happening in a bigger*

way than what can be observed in passing—each world eclipsing another and seen together in one view?"

In truth, I'd like to speak to them all, to anyone who would listen, to talk about the mysteries of painted scenes, about the visible threads of almost forgotten conversations, citing the inquiries of restoration that prepared the way for the rebirth of what has since become routine. (We accept the benefits without acknowledging the source.) But they'd move on, and with the return of quiet, each time I'd re-enter the peaceful landscape proposed by a generous host almost six hundred years ago where a gentle woman cradles the still form of a man relaxed across her lap as if asleep. *"Maybe they all forgot what to do—or how?"* I searched the lady's expression, reminded that it was only fading pigment arranged to suggest her image. *"And perhaps I just never stopped—never managed to grow up all the way?"* Their surroundings are rendered in such detail that I am drawn to reconsider, to look elsewhere than in obvious places—toward the horizon and the ancient walled city of Vicenza, and past that to the suggestion of mountains, the distant Dolomites disappearing in *sfumatura*.

By the standard of impressive size, the picture is small enough not to stand out in a museum filled with grand paintings, but I can't help staring at it, at the two lonely figures suspended in the middle of a complex backdrop—and me feeling strangely pregnant, an expectant character lost in a painted countryside, shuffling down a dirt track in search of the plot and author, fixed on the heroine and hero of the setting, and stopping where I was to scrutinize the two strangers—the three of us stranded together in a field of particulars in ochers and earths.

How is it that we know when someone is watching us? A tickle on the back of the neck? An odd sensation on the scalp and skin? Turning, I caught the curious gaze of a woman who had approached to stand just a few feet away to watch me watch the painting. I tried to smile, and thought of telling her about my studio, the intoxicating smell and feel of pigments and oils, about my dreams, the wisdom of riddles, and the reasons I was there. I wanted to explain that, while the pictures in the museum are centuries old, the experience and ideas are as new as today—right now—each a personal invitation, a magic ticket to somewhere far-off right there under our noses; but she quickly moved on, so I continued my dialogue with the painted image. "Is it you or is it me?" I repeated, looking at the Madonna supporting the man on her lap. "I know—it's us. That's what *he* says." Actually it was her robe, clouds of billowing lapis and indigo that seemed to hold the man drifting in a patch of night sky. I continued to study the specifics surrounding them. And I missed Nikola.

The people passed by. The museum guards looked bored. And I remembered a typical discussion about my work which I have had many times:

"It's just about what ya' see, right?" My involuntary response is a puzzled look.

"I mean, it's whatever you think it is."

I'm always at a loss. *"Does that make me a giraffe because you think so?"* I want to shoot back defiantly, but remain silent.

"It's up to me—isn't it about what it makes me feel?" In fact, I often paint clouds into pictures for that purpose, making them almost resemble angels, ducks, or crocodiles floating above an exact pattern, to give the audience someplace peripheral to imagine, to feel what I am proposing.

"Anything goes. That's the point, isn't it?"

"I guess—if you say so."

"Like, did you know that cloud looks like a duck?" While it's true that visual perception is related to personal experience, for me, it has become a game to see how well I can predict that experience.

"Artists are all a bit crazy anyway," he proclaims, winking and nudging the person next to him. And—I leave it at that.

I refocused on the painting by Bellini and recognized my own assumptions, recalling the boy in a museum suddenly seeing himself reflected in the pictures, and my more recent discussions with a wise teacher who spoke of my limitless potential, only to remind me of my limitations. *"Some things you may imagine— are not there at all. Remember, it is not what you see, nor is it sight—not the word, nor the language alone…Active participation as a receiver in the charged medium of the universe regenerates the universe, which regenerates you…"*

For all of my pretenses of contributing to humanity through art, sometimes my discussion with the audience might as well go like this:

"It's just about whatever, isn't it?"

To which I would respond, "Sure, whatever."

To which he should respond, "Yeah, whatever." Then both of us could grin, wink, and turn to people standing close by for approval.

"It's that damn *whateverism*," complains an artist friend frequently. "It destroys everything." Or, I could just paint white canvases.

So—there is another discussion that I would rather have with an audience:

"It's just about what ya' see, right?"

My involuntary response is a puzzled look.

"I mean, it's whatever you think it is."

"Well—first, it's paint, the elemental material of the vision, a literal amount of powdered colors and oils carefully crafted and arranged on a prepared ground, and in Bellini's case—pigments often mixed with an emulsion of diluted egg yolk. Second, after you have studied the paint—it has nothing to do with the paint at all. Lacking paint, he'd have used dirt and spit, berry juice, or blood; consider the visual arrangement, the composition. Paint is only the material used to suggest the composition, how things relate based on the visual laws that govern the image and the rest of the universe, a pattern or system of principles, the key by which a thing is measured and deciphered. Third, the arrangement, or composition, suggests a world in the likeness of the viewer's understanding—the set, roles, costumes, and script that happen somewhere between the life of the artist and that of an audience, the artist's shared experience with an actor who has just entered the stage—a singular point of view, which is yours. It's like a reflection, but not really."

"Egg yolks?"

"They're full of fat that binds the pigment as it dries, and based on all of the colorful paintings still around centuries later, like some of these Bellinis here, it's pretty permanent. Did you know that the collection and preparation of pigments was the realm of alchemy? Scientific, artistic, philosophical, and spiritual expressions were often the same expression. And it's just paint. Then consider this—the stratified paint reveals the artist's activity, tells the story of the process that resulted in the painting. The particulars of each layer contribute something vital to the final picture you're looking at. It's amazing how things that seem solid, like paint, can unexpectedly be so undefined. And there's the ability to see—to receive and interpret electromagnetic vibrations travelling though time and space in selected frequencies from reds to violets and invisible colors you might only feel, the translation of that light into electrical impulses by specialized color receptive cells on the retina, and the subsequent transmission of those signals to the brain by neuronal relay—even just the ability to see the colors of the paint is worth stopping to ponder."

"I didn't know any of that."

"I think it's about remembering what we knew before we had to think about it. Maybe that's the magic of art; it can happen to us without the interference of what we imagine knowing." I looked at the Bellini, some paint applied within a rectangle. "And then there's the painting that begins to escape the frame."

"What do you mean?" asks my imaginary student now seated on the floor to the dismay of a dozy museum guard.

"I mean that, what can be measured is the threshold to places that can't—the effects of that small location (pointing to the painting) on everything else are what I mean. For example—on a page in a book we can count and name the letters of the alphabet, but the instant we start seeing words, the letters begin to escape the page. The prescribed character sequences we call words; their relationships, rhythms, and repetitions; the rules of language that dictate their structure in a sentence; lines and paragraphs; chapters—those are patterns that are not measured, only described. Even before we start exploring the endless potential for meaning, letters and words begin to escape their boundaries. They are evident on a page and can be counted, but they live here (pointing to myself). And a lot of it is already here (still pointing to myself) before I even see the page. In fact, like pigments to an alchemist, letters themselves have meanings and interpretations; they already imply other dimensions, such as sonic dimensions. So they escaped the limits of their finite forms before words came into the picture or the page was even imagined. Most of the time we skip all of that understanding before we jump to the meanings of words; but in pictures, the effects of elemental structures are tied to the meanings of the image and must be considered."

I look at the student and see that he still seems to be engrossed in my lecture. "You're a good student," I tell him. And he grins.

"As we begin to explore the quantity of paint that is a painting, the qualities of its arrangement become apparent; the vocabularies of color, line, shape, value, and texture suggest any number of dimensions beyond the picture frame—the patterns of balance and symmetry, harmony and contrast, proportion and perspective, rhythm and repetition, geometry and chaos—that's how the paint escapes the painting, by transmuting into something living and breathing, as part of the image comes alive in the experience of the viewer."

I look down at the student again who is looking up at me in much the same way that I look at him. "What's your name, huh?" He's a stocky kid, and in spite of his apparent bravado, a little self-conscious—a round face, blue-green eyes, freckles, some premature graying around the temples, pretty average—not someone you'd notice in a crowd. "Where're you from?"

"Please go on," he says. "No one has ever talked this way about it."

"It's like a door," I continue, "an entry into…well, it's about mnemonics. Do you know what a mnemonic is?"

"I'm sure I don't know about mnemonics the same way you do," he answers.

"Symbols are mnemonic in nature—symbols, metaphors,

signs, tokens, they're all emblematic, reflections of a bigger view, like special telescopes to see out there into nothingness, into the dimness that hides what you can't yet comprehend. In a way, to experience a symbol feels like remembering the future. It's not a formula, but that's what paintings can do—the literal paint leads to the rules and rationale of structure and composition, the configuration of pattern, which leads to a metaphorical place where you approach the artist and begin to understand some of what he hopes to say. In fact, you can begin to see yourself as the artist, holding the brushes, choosing the colors, thinking Bellini's thoughts—and time stops existing in the same way because everything is happening right now. We respond by seeing ourselves related to the artist's experience—the first-person painter and first-person participant in us. Have you ever been surprised by a particular tone in your voice that resonates the space around you and you feel it in your insides? Entering the metaphorical world of an image is like that. We find the notes that resonate the painted world we have entered, to feel them resonate within us. It's about the creator's direction of vibration and the individual's ability to tune in to those frequencies.

"The harmony of a musical ensemble comes from each musician knowing his part and the role it fills in the overall sound of a musical composition. Musicians understand the limitations of interpreting the notes. Too much interpretation and an arrangement can become a different melody. To interpret is to stand between places as a mediator, a negotiator between the known and the unknown. To enter the world of Giovanni Bellini, like approaching the creation of any composer, you've got to be ready to negotiate between his intentions and your own references. For instance, there are symbolic elements that show up regularly in his work. The equilateral triangle, the Great Tetractys of elemental and spatial dimensions, is suggested here by two overlapping figures, one point—the intersection of vertical and horizontal, one triangle, one head positioned at the apex; two points—the two directions, two figures, two equal halves of the triangle, the visual association of his and her left shoulders; three points—the three points of the triangle, and the alignment of his right shoulder, his right hand upon eclipsed creative sources, and her hand cradling his knees—and so forth…the ten counted dimensions eventually becoming infinite. Then there's the polled oak, God's tree, the *axis mundi* cut down for the purpose of regeneration evidenced by the young shoots that will be branches in a future season, the door to everywhere; and the mullein plant, *verbascum*, from *verbum*, the word, the name, logos; then the road, and the city on the horizon. We could continue, but the real free-for-all starts only after you do your homework. I have learned that even stripes tell stories beyond their obvious edges. You see, nothing is ever *whatever*."

My discussion with the strange student reminds me of discussions with my mentor and friend Nikola Tesla, where I meet him, out there somewhere, in a different kind of place, and I wonder when we'll meet again. "A great teacher of mine taught that artists have the power to shake the planet."

"Really?" responds my young friend, obviously entertained.

"I'm sure they must practice," I chuckle. "You know, he said it's in us—infinite possibility, enough to do almost anything."

For a few moments we're quiet, standing and sitting, both of us studying the other. "Of course, perspectives can differ," I add, "you, down there seeing it from where you sit, and I, from up here at the level of the horizon. Points of view are individual. Acknowledging *that* is the key to understanding our own points of view, which frees us to experience the artist's point of view. I learned about the power of perspective at the Brera in Milan, standing in front of a work by Bellini's brother-in-law Andrea Mantegna. A Compianto, a *"weeping together"*, a shared lament, is another model, a pattern or paradigm like a Pietà. Mantegna's Compianto exemplifies the artist's invitation to a viewer to participate in a communal drama between the characters portrayed in the image and the artist himself—a conversation between diverse perspectives, worlds, and ways of being. Mantegna uses forced and eccentric perspective, much like the quasi omniscient vision of the Cubists centuries later, to draw us into and around the scene. To be fluent in the language of perspective is to see beyond the surface of our awareness, to explore outside the boundaries of appearances, and become wiser in translating our impressions of what is still unknowable.

"From the tangible *what* of paint, to the visual *where* of paint (which opens our eyes in preparation for opening our minds and hearts), to the meaning and *why* of paint—the key is to hang on until we're ready to meet the artist on his terms, the *who* of the painted image. Exploring a painting is like climbing through the branches of a tree to reach the top where the view suddenly opens up."

"Where'd you learn this stuff?" he asks while shifting his weight.

"In there," I tell him (pointing to the painting). "It's all in there." He shrugs and I go on, wondering when he'll tire of my long-winded litany.

"Quantities, qualities, similarities—and fourth, the mysteries of the paint. If we endure, eventually we uncover the secrets of the artist. That's when everything transforms, when the will of the participant and that of the artist become one. The awareness of the viewer meets the awareness of the painter. Bellini's intent becomes our intent. And what was concealed is at last revealed."

"How can that be possible?" asks my ingenuous protégé from down on the *terrazzo*. "Is it true?"

"I don't know," I state firmly. "But I sure hope so."

"*Signore! Signore!* No sit on floor—*non si può!*" scolded the guard who had re-entered the room before a group of tourists quickly surrounded the man seated beneath Bellini's Pietà.

"So—you can choose to view a painting however you'd like, temporarily, because ultimately it may not have a basis in the reality of a bigger picture." I stood, calmly dusted myself off, and nodded to my unexpected audience. "But remember—nothing is ever just *whatever*!" Then turned back toward the image to take leave of Bellini and the two painted companions.

"*Madonna! 'Sti americani!*" sighed the guard.

I looked to the resolute face of the woman and then at the man asleep across her lap, at his closed eyelids and relaxed mouth, and remembered kneeling by an open casket where my Gidu lay sleeping in a good suit, touching his cool hands, and wishing he would wake up. Then I wandered out of the room.

"Did you see that Pietà back there?" asked my wife when I met her later.

"I've returned three times," I replied. "And I'm going back a fourth before we leave."

They continued to pass by in noisy waves, filling, then emptying the small room where I stood, all of them trying to be heard above my thoughts—but the humbly proportioned image on the wall finally silenced everything around it, and like veiled acts hidden behind the curtain of an empty stage, the drama began to unfold. And I missed Nikola Tesla.

30

The Rudiments of Electricity

April 17 – It was almost noon. I looked down at the canal from my perch in the open window, watching the high tide measuring the foundations again. "Higher than yesterday," I noted aloud. The familiar green-blue-grey of the water bloomed in the sun that had at last reached down between the walls of dissolving brick. I strained to see through the murk, guessing at the secrets that almost appeared from beneath the glow... An old crate? A fallen piece of stone? A rotting length of rope? ...accompanied by the sound of water softly licking at the steps that led to somewhere down below everything else.

This morning it was with some difficulty that I found the place that seemed so approachable just a few months ago, recognizing my eventual arrival as I felt the charge, the little shakes and prickles that I have come to expect. And I spoke to the space, "I know. You want me to understand the rudiments of electricity before we can continue, but I didn't do my homework. I haven't studied, and don't know where to begin. I'm just a painter—at least I thought so."

"There is no rudimentary way to understand what is called electricity," came the reply in a familiar tone. This time, Nikola's voice described his face. I felt him close but didn't see him. There have been other times that I have interacted with a voice, as well as the many times that I have had a clear vision of my mentor. I'm not sure what the difference is and why it happens one way or the other, but it does.

"Remember, that which you seek requires another way of thinking and being. The potential we are exploring is a gift from outside common experience, a proof of what is unseen and unknown from a mundane point of view. What you call electricity comes from beyond the edge of your awareness, a power which can be a threat both to your physical and cognitive well-being."

I thought of the startling electrical display of several months ago, recalling my fears and exhilaration while confronting the easily imagined danger of such power. "I understand the physical threat—but cognitive?"

"Things are veiled for many reasons, often because the awareness of those outside the veil is too fragile, unprepared to view what is within the veil. Veils can be lifted when understanding and wisdom become sufficient to see more, when the viewer's awareness is great enough to participate safely in what was seen as a mystery."

Brief updrafts of garlic, fish, fancy perfume, and sewer, and the smoldering glitter of sunlight in the growing shade spreading across the Rio di Verona held my attention. I had been sitting there for hours hoping to soak in all I could of Venice and Italy on our last day as the water slowly transformed from luminous satin to a band of white highlights slipping around in the umbra like the cool glisten of snakeskin.

"This is not about a list of terms and definitions, or even a series of complicated concepts to be memorized," advised Nikola. "At best it is a loose set of properties, a different kind of idiom, an unusual grammar, an organic pattern of attributes, like a language of constellations that continually move in and out of form. This new way to see and experience things is what I have been hoping to transmit to you since we began our discussions. Without realizing it—it is what you have been learning all along. There is really nothing you could have studied as a foundation for what I want to teach you. Yes, you are an artist. And I chose to teach you for that reason."

I stayed there all afternoon drifting in and out of the pleasant canal scene until the glow was gone and polished black gondolas powered by grown men dressed like schoolboys in tight pants and straw hats with ribbons began floating by at regular intervals. Soon, the damp brick resounded with *Santa Lucia* sung repeatedly by over-zealous tenors to the requisite accompaniment of accordions, over and over and over like the needle of an old record player stuck in a groove.

"Now, imagine a crowd of people milling about," said Tesla, and then we were looking together at a large crowd doing just that. "But this time, notice that the crowd consists of two types of people that characterize two unique classes of attributes." Then there were just two men standing as if on a darkened stage: a tall slender fellow with white hair parted in the middle and swept back sleekly, wearing a crumpled off-white linen suit, a white shirt, an off-white silk tie, white cotton socks, and canvas shoes; and a shorter thick-set guy with a close-cropped brush of gray hair, dressed in a gray flannel suit, a black shirt, a narrow black tie, black transparent hose, and shiny black oxfords.

"Do you see them?" asked Tesla after a couple of minutes.

"Sure! It's you and me!"

"Oh. Is that whom you see?" he responded.

Then the two images began to multiply until they were a crowd, the linen suited Teslas on the left and the gray flannelled me's on the right, before they began to move and mingle to become one blended group of two men, two distinct sets of properties in form, dress, and attitude.

At dusk the nearby piazza filled with the chatter of the community. I could hear it before arriving, like the buzz of swarming bees getting louder and clearer until the words became distinguishable. "*Sì, sì, sì, lo so benissimo Signora. Hai sentito che lei…,*" one voice or another rising momentarily above the rest. Sometimes I wish that I could slip unnoticed into the babbling stream of communing that echoes through the narrow tracks of Italy each evening. I speak the language. I understand the words.

"An understanding of electricity begins with an understanding of two elemental kinds of material that perform complementary roles, acting like the two likenesses of what is reflected in a mirror. The two characters we are watching represent agents of those two roles."

"So everything is either one or the other?"

"Well—no, not exactly. The one is explosive or emanating influence, while the other is attractive. The universe exists in equal parts of both, the one expansive and the other contractive. The two function together pushing and pulling everything in and out of being, or more correctly, in and out of presence in a dimension. They represent an elemental view where scale becomes irrelevant, where everything is forever coming into and leaving one place for another. Rather than matter, it is best to refer to these roles as energies or even principles. Watch the two men carefully and tell me what you see."

As I watched, I saw that while they were in constant motion, they were also passing something back and forth between them, the light-suited men always interacting only with the heavier dark-suited men, and vice versa. I strained to see what it was that they were passing back and forth, but could see nothing. Then Nikola Tesla spoke my name, "Everything exists between these two potentials in the likelihood of being thrust away and drawn toward what can be called conditions, realms, loci (places), or dimensions."

"But I hope I can understand it all," I said, looking to Tesla for some assurance.

"You already are, or you could not be watching our two friends. Please describe to me what you see," he repeated. And I rehearsed what I saw—a crowd made up of two men, one in a light linen suit, and one in a dark flannel suit, moving in and out without touching, and passing something invisible back and forth. I noted that it was like an odd dance.

In Piazza Santo Stefano they huddled in groups waving arms and hands ceremonially, some of them eyeing me with suspicion, guarding the privacies of their exchanges. "*Comunque, sapete che lui m'ha detto così…?*" She started to whisper—then steadily raising her voice, eyebrows, and arms in unison, became a great conductor. But I'm not one of them, still unprepared for the rite of *due chiacchiere*. And, the chorus responded, eyes widening and narrowing, mouths abruptly set in motion, expressions and postures immediately animated.

I stood still, hands in my pockets, looking on as the conspiratorial game of Simon Says spread from one side of the square to the other like a grass fire—and I thought of the view of Venice from the taxi headed toward the airport in the morning when they'd all be asleep.

"And if the two men were to become suddenly invisible...," and at once they disappeared, "...all you would see is the likelihood of presence in one place or another."

"It shimmers!"

"Yes it does. Fundamentally, that which you see as solid reality constantly shimmers. And here, language fails us. You are witnessing the to and fro vibration of possibility and the potential of direction, the evidence of electricity. Distinctions in what is present are only differences in frequency; otherwise everything consists of the same elemental material."

"And electricity? What is electricity?" I asked.

"Electricity is an elemental attribute, a blended set of properties or principles, each consisting of other distinct sets of properties or principles. The ancients called it *electrum*, the god-power, which falls from heaven and is in everything as was evidenced by the silver-gold discharge of sparks from amber as it was rubbed with soft fur or fabric. What you call electricity, that which is delivered through wires and plugs, what you take for granted, is just a show of readjustment, response to what was resistant, often in the weakest places. You are seeing electricity as a shimmer. In fact, that shimmer is the evidence you observe all around you of what you think of as solid matter. What you commonly perceive visually is just a shimmer—the magic that makes things visible. You might think of it as the silver interface of a mirror reflecting electromagnetic transmissions. Again, your language is poor when it comes to these subjects so we use symbols, metaphors, and mnemonics to suggest the rest. You are watching electricity happen, but the truth of it is beyond your awareness."

Every time I leave Venice, I take pictures from the back of the boat—the spreading V of the wake, the city growing smaller, the silhouettes of lopsided bell towers gradually shrinking against the early light—past a silent barge piled high with gravel, a few fishermen heading out, the seagulls standing like sentinels on log pylons lining the boat lane, and a solitary clam digger standing out in the lagoon on a sand bar and waving, all of them up that early to see us off. I hold on to the images as evidence of what is beyond a current reality—the shimmer of one place while I am in another.

"But if it's beyond my awareness…," I began.

"That is where painting patterns becomes important," said Tesla, "as a means of transmitting what cannot be spoken. I cannot tell you everything, only what can no longer be withheld—that which you are prepared for, as you can only comprehend and live according to the rationale and structure of the place where you are. Pay close attention now."

Then I saw a familiar figure, a solitary person dressed in my dungarees and t-shirt wandering alone through the shimmering field.

"Do you see him?"

"It's me again."

"Awareness is a singularity," stated Nikola Tesla with emphasis on each word, "an intersection; a discontinuity in the regular weave of the universe; like a seed with properties, structure, and life peculiar to itself, and surrounded by soil. It is the pattern and sequence of one."

I studied the lone figure wading through the array of shimmering conditions which closed around him with the glimmer of brooding water, and noticed his influence on the activity of the liquid field which became increasingly excited in his immediate vicinity—like silver highlights on dark ripples, or a school of shiny minnows encircling him. I remembered the spiraling patterned strips slowly growing up from a patterned matrix, and recalled a child standing in a column of sunlight delighted by the interaction of his hand with an agitated and colliding universe of dust specks.

"A singularity changes the nature of space around it. As the energy of a wheel can be expressed by central forces, the properties of a singularity include both the push of radiation and the pull of gravity." Again Tesla called me by name, "You are a pattern, a living sequence, the intersection of sequences which are intersections of sequences—a singularity."

I imagined myself walking through a painted field, the causal singularity of the place, drawing the paint around me into the patterns and passages of an image with the help of colors and a brush. "That's how paintings happen." There are times while working in the studio that I feel impressed by something outside myself and the paint. I reach for red and something says, "Try green." I can spend hours wishing and waiting for revelation about the picture until finally the distinction between myself and the world around me softens. "But how does it begin? What causes the cause that sets off the chain of events?" I wanted to know.

"Please continue observing your good friend." And I watched my image move through the flickering expanse while seeming to ignite the fluid conditions around him. "Let me repeat," said

Nikola, "the power of awareness includes its innate ability to transform surrounding circumstances." Then once more, I saw my image disappear, leaving just the shape of where it had been, the gleaming form of a man's body interacting with a dimly luminous field—and the field grew to become an atmosphere, and the vision receded into the distance until my image was just a twinkle, one star in the middle of a crowd of stars, like a view of the milky way on a very clear night in the mountains.

"If two things exist, and one is above the other—there are even greater things above them both. One star is a planet; another—a sun; yet another—a system of stars or a galaxy—stars within stars within stars, even universe within universe. There are greater and lesser singularities, greater and lesser awareness. The potential quantities and qualities of awareness and their power and influence are infinite."

"You mean, because I am—"

"Yes, exactly. Remember, the discussion of greater and lesser possibility suggests comparison. It is a process. So there are degrees of awareness, like steps in progression."

"Like climbing up through the branches of a favorite tree," I added. "I'm afraid I know something that's too much to know about, too big to hold." And for a while we were quiet. "So, Where did you learn this stuff?"

"It's all there," he said (pointing to the stars), "in the mirror. Study the mirror."

"But how can that be possible?" I whispered.

"I must leave now," said Nikola Tesla (even if I never wanted it to end).

"Thank-you," I replied. Then deliberately he leaned forward and kissed me as a parent might kiss a child—and as if it were only yesterday, I remembered playing with a piece of broken mirror that I had buried in the woods. And I felt like a child.

Talking to Tesla has been a process, changing me by degree, as if exchanging each part of me—my head, my heart, my hands, and feet, for new ones—completely renewing me. Exploring the mysteries of things like electricity has required me to leave my tired self behind, to find my new self thinking unexpected thoughts with the mind of a boy at play again.

Often it seems to take a few days for me to catch up with my physical self as I slip back and forth between one place and another. So I awoke early this morning with my eyes already open, staring out the window into a dark sky full of stars, confused, then saddened and relieved to find myself back home in my own bed dreaming of Nikola Tesla and yesterday in Italy.

31
Of Compound Things and Complexities

May 23 – Paintings can happen in many ways; it's never quite the same or they would all look alike. Sometimes I plan an image meticulously beforehand, practicing on paper or on a smaller panel, starting with an underlying pattern or composition. Other pictures occur internally first, originating with a need to explore and provide shapes for my emotional or intellectual scenery. Some paintings are about faithfully reporting on the distinct visual aspects of things—the blush on a piece of fruit, the structure of a flower, or the poetry of a face. Still others are complete revelations, beginning with an impulse that I paint to identify. And once in a while there is a painting that surprises me in every way, happening as if without thought or effort on my part. The certainties are that, in the end, a painting is due to a mix of things; that it's never predictable; and that while the look and occurrence of each image may seem dissimilar, the core process is always typical. It begins with a shadow of something, a clue that I hope will point to something else, and something else—an urge leading to a color, a color to a brushstroke, to a texture, to a passage of paint; and so on and on it grows in response to itself, to myself, expanding as I approach it, finally to fill the whole ground.

I have noted recently that my lessons with Nikola Tesla have changed, that as he teaches, the larger part of discovery is left up to me. He introduces a topic for study, orients my thinking, and some time later—a few minutes, a day, or even weeks—I return with a report of my inquiry, my understanding, and relevant questions. Last night, he also spoke of this journal, encouraging me to be attentive in order to insure the accuracy of what I write. It is increasingly obvious that he is no longer interested in entertaining me, and that, whatever the purpose of our discussions, it does not include my amusement—although it still feels exhilarating to awaken into a fantastic dream where he is waiting.

"Before we continue, it is important to review the nature of compound things."

Slowly I grew aware of something floating in the air above me—several characters, a word, glowing like a neon sign—first dull, then bright white against the dark background of the unlit room. *"Idea,"* I read it to myself and then repeated it aloud, "Idea." Oddly, it was as if it had always been there, I-D-E-A, and I was just getting around to noticing it. (The truth is that at first I was confused by its common nature and wished it were something more exotic.) During some dreams, I seem to be aware of myself in two places—in bed, and watching myself in bed; so I both saw the word, and saw myself seeing the word.

As with a quantity of paint applied to a panel, it was obvious that the four letters were about much more than what was immediately apparent. Equal parts of I, D, and A, supporting an emphatic E, bound together in a particular poetic construct and suspended importantly in the air; a sequence representing spoken or internal sounds and thoughts—vibrations; the association of object, context, and awareness—meaning; the fulfillment of cognitive instinct—an opinion; from one point of view to another—a message. I watched it for a while, exploring the word and my response, while Tesla remained silent. Soon enough I began to realize that, given time, the simple pattern, an arrangement of distinct aspects read together as a single manifestation, was an entire language whose substance and essence suggested yet larger patterns: a word to a phrase, a phrase to a sentence, a sentence to a page, a page to chapters, books, and libraries. *"Mnemonics again,"* I thought as I decided to relax and enjoy myself. *"This could fill universes."*

I feel less dependent on Tesla now, though more secure in our friendship and confident in his guidance. He suggests a path in the form of experience and related proposals, allowing me the challenge of weighing myself against an objective, leaving me free to make errors and adjustments. What I learn with Nikola develops integrally, as part of my life. Fortunately, my friends and family have been patient with my associated activities, which have become something of a compulsion, taking up a good part of each day. So while I am still eager for his visits, I often hope that he'll give me time enough to study, reflect, and write, before he returns with new material.

Then an identical series of characters appeared to the right of the first, shortly before a plus sign became visible between the two words. As with most things that I experience with Nikola, it began to unfold only upon my active investigation. The closer I looked, the more I saw, peeling back impression after impression, context after context, meaning upon meaning. I gazed at the incandescent equation until I could see no more; painfully aware of how much I must have been missing, but feeling closer to the heart of it. It looked something like this:

IDEA + IDEA

Then another word appeared, and another, always the same sequence of letters, the same word in a lengthening formula. It happened very much like the graphic patterns that had multiplied as I watched almost a year ago. A very long string of the same glowing word stretched across the air above me until it eventually formed a horizon of **IDEA**s. The plus sign between the words, however, was replaced here and there with a minus sign, a division or a multiplication sign, an equal sign, a greater or lesser than symbol, and various other symbols representing relationships, many of which I didn't recognize. Then another row of the same word separated by mathematical-looking symbols appeared under the first, then another, and another, one at a time, followed by more symbols to relate the words vertically. Soon, similar lines of the same word separated by symbols began repeatedly to appear above the first line, followed by another, and so on, and so on. Lines became regularly visible above and below until a flat grid of words and connecting symbols was created, not unlike the microelemental patterns with which I am now so familiar. Instead of the associations of white and black, open and closed spaces, or places filled with various colors, these were patterns of the word **IDEA** relating and filling a plane, representing any number of implied components and their associations. The grid was readable in all two-dimensional directions, suggesting countless linear paths. I was allowed to view the plane for a period of time before it began to reproduce itself in layers above and below, forming the beginnings of a matrix or sponge, navigable in all directions within its three dimensions—words made from letters, which became lines, which formed planes, which created space.

"You have already learned that order is born from disorder through awareness, but you are only now beginning to believe that perhaps you can actually participate in bringing things into being that were beyond your awareness—which power is called faith."

I began to trace various routes through the matrix and was reminded that having any number of dimensions suggests a multitude of other dimensions, greater and lesser—some readable from within and without, while others remain beyond discernment. I thought of the conceptual basis for Fra' Giovanni's fresco cycle in the San Marco dormitory; the inner and the outer, hidden and apparent points of view carefully designed to reveal themselves as I am prepared to see them.

"Think of the loom," said Tesla, "that intersection where different places and perspectives come together to weave a single fabric. This is a similar intersection. The power of participation is in the gap between what you can conceive and what you cannot. The spark happens at the soft edge of awareness, leaping from the palette of possibility to the picture of what will be. Faith is the conductive material that makes the arc possible. Like your brush moving through the air between the paint and panel, everything happens from that stage of in between, in the interval between what is imagined and what will become the image. We have spoken of this many times"

"The artist wields the brush," I said half to myself and half to be heard. "The artist moves the brush."

"In fact, a painter directs vibration; emotions, thoughts, and light; organizing them into a picture. You do it all the time, usually focused on the end result, and without thought to the process."

"I do," I agreed, continuing to follow the chaining associations through the matrix: **IDEA + IDEA > IDEA = IDEA / IDEA - IDEA**... and noticing that the paths I had followed each seemed to leave a trace, an amount left behind, the hint of a string running and twisting through the array of words. Soon, the strings that I had followed began to relate, until another kind of pattern became evident, one made up of my compounded wanderings; crisscrossing, aligned, and separated; a tangle of branches and stems; a system of circulation uniting in places to form limbs, which converged finally to suggest a dense trunk of thinking. *"This is a view of choices: heres and theres, befores and afters, all at once..."* Again, as I often do, I considered the colossal amount of painted designs that articulate the walls of so many Italian cathedrals. *"...a lineage, the image of descent, generations of this's and thats, yes's and no's, odds and ends; the evidence of where I've been, a diagram of my thoughts, the plotting of a story...."* I watched the action of my thoughts continue to pulse in procession through the paths that I had followed, flowing through the luminous trunk, like water and nutrients through the xylem and phloem of a living tree.

"This is the picture of a painting!" I exclaimed.

The activity of painting can be exhausting. There are times, when I'm tired or stuck, that it's best to intercede, to facilitate the struggle and progress of a work by letting it alone, leaving the studio—to take a walk, to eat some chocolate, or to lie down briefly and forget an artist's concerns. Or sometimes, I like to take a shower—just letting water, like thoughts, brushstrokes, and colors, fall on the back of my head and shoulders, looking at it slip snakelike down the skin of my biceps and chest to pool in the hollows of my arms folded across my torso. I watch the pools filling up, then spilling over, and listen to the water slapping near my feet. I stand still and let the water do its job until it runs cold. *"What is it that makes me want to climb a tree for the view? And what is a view but a bigger picture of the tree itself?"*

"Yes," answered Tesla. "It is another way to see a painting and many other creations."

And so, I was encouraged to ponder the nature of the glowing tree as it proceeded to grow, identifying the gentle streams and knots of **IDEA**s as various thoughts—the beliefs, theories, languages, designs, fantasies, and nonsense of my ramblings. The trunk thickened and grew down away from the treetop as the branches eventually found conclusions and terminated above. In time, I noticed small buds forming at points along the branches, then swelling and slowly opening into leaves; and I saw that the veins and structure of each leaf resembled the branching form of the whole tree, but flattened and in miniature.

"From up close and far away—it looks the same. Isn't this an image of the process?" I asked glancing at Nikola, who, as usual, was paying particular attention to me.

I watched the tree continue its regular progress until I thought that I had seen enough, and wished that it would stop. But it didn't. The ends of branches grew large buds that gradually paled, whitened, and bloomed into waxy petaled flowers. I watched as the blossoms wilted and browned to reveal small green fruits that expanded, became heavy, and ripened. And I felt the quiet presence of seeds asleep inside them—each seed, within each fruit, containing the infinite potential for new generations of my radiant tree.

"I think it's enough," I suggested tenuously, imagining painters on high scaffolding tirelessly painting interminable patterns on moist plaster. "It's so much."

"And this is only the beginning," responded Tesla as the tree steadily grew. "Yes, this is also the process."

I suspect that at least a few of the many assistants, who prepared and detailed chapel interiors for their masters, tired out once in a while and decided, "*Basta!* That's enough!" Some of them went on to become masters themselves, turning the details over to their own apprentices. But some must have spent the rest of their lives painting endless patterns, and perhaps at times feeling just a bit overwhelmed. Whenever I start to paint a newly borrowed pattern on one of my smallish panels, I try to imagine how it must have felt to stand before the expanse of a new blank wall and silently proclaim, "It's too much!" Yet for me, as for all apprentices, enduring what seems tedious, confronting and eventually welcoming what looks to be beyond my capacity and vision, is just part of the process.

While the treetop leafed out, flowered, and bore fruit, the trunk proceeded to reach down to where earth might have been, where there was only an empty matrix of **IDEA**s and no soil. "Is this tree my awareness?"

"Among other things, it is also a picture of your awareness," answered Nikola.

I watched the trunk begin to divide, then subdivide; dividing again, and then again; shoots and off-shoots happening with counted precision, like a musical composition predictably growing variations from a simple theme.

"This is a way to view the design, nature, and life of many things," added Tesla.

What had first appeared as roots soon began budding and sprouting leaves to become, in time, a branching and fruiting reflection of the tree above it. "Tree above and tree below…," I noted, as two new opposing trunks began to grow horizontally, midway between the upper and lower trees, followed by another two horizontal trunks at ninety degrees, each developing similar networks of leafy branches. "…and trees between." Trees continued to grow between trees, always equal but counter to their twins, and I was pleased—like the way I feel when it becomes apparent that a painting is on track. At that point when a painting starts to come together, when I begin at last to know the outcome, work in the studio seems to speed up; although I find myself standing back more often just to look, to enjoy the ticklish sensation of clearly foreseeing what will soon appear. And so I looked at my miraculous tree and was satisfied.

I'm not sure how to define joy, other than to refer to the times in my life that I have felt it: on my wedding day, at the births of our children, watching soft clouds morph and move against a blue sky, or running through a summer cloudburst—life proving to be so good that I am forced to expand in order to hold it. Unexpectedly, that's how I felt, watching ideas string together in thoughts that entwined to form a trunk, a tree; then two, then six; then looking like a lacy snowflake of branching cerebrations; and ultimately a thriving convergence of intelligence and reasoning.

"To be endowed with the capacity to think and reason is godlike. It is an inherited gift for which I have reverence," stated Nikola. "Now, watch closely."

I examined the matrix that hosted my thinking and was filled with wonder at the magical view of my own developing awareness. **IDEA + BODY > IDEA = OBJECTIVE / IDEA**. Slowly, the word, which had made up the medium on a cellular level, was being replaced by other words. **FRAME - MECHANICS + PARALLEL < IDEA = DREAM X IDEA**. The possibility of infinite specific meanings was being added to the existing possibility of infinite conjunctions, resulting in the possibility of even greater complexities. And then—I saw the floating tree that I had painted in an image over two years ago, an uprooted fruit tree from an imagined paradise; plucked up from behind the garden walls of painters like Leonardo Da Vinci, Ghirlandaio, Baldovinetti, and others; almost bare-rooted, drifting over that pattern from a Duccio Madonna, the pattern Tesla had referred to during my first lesson.

"It is all in motion and difficult to grasp," said Nikola, "You have to move with it."

The branches seemed to catch a breeze; meanings and relationships in constant flux within the matrix of the tree; my painted tree and my thought tree—the representation of all possible trees. "But the essentials do not change," I responded, and he seemed pleased that I had understood—that over time, sequences of ideas are replaced by new ideas with new associations, while the process and form remain the same.

"This is something that you already knew," he said, "which has now found life within you."

"It feels like the beginning all over again," I answered, my gaze still fixed intently on the tree suspended in a painted sky filled with clouds just as I had carefully positioned it, a symbol of enlightenment hovering above the borrowed pattern from a Gothic Madonna. "Thank-you."

"But it was already yours."

"And I didn't see it."

From a distance, what had begun as one word, one thought, one tree, had grown to become an indistinct texture, developing in ways too big and too small to be immediately apparent—leaves and branch tips growing new opposing branches which grew new trees, which in turn grew new branches and trees, and so on, and so on. The simple four letter association had become an increasingly compound expression that I thought of simply as *the tree,* although it eventually consisted of many tree-like parts. "What is the basic pattern—the motif?" I asked. "Is it the word? The **IDEA**?" From up close, each part continued to look like the other, the near mirror image of its counterparts. Each side of each part was the near mirror image of the other side, the furcating pattern being reiterated in gross constancy and in finely scaled repetitions—the geometry of it becoming the evidence of a recurring series of events, a nearly predictable routine.

"Remember, a crowd of people is not just a frequency of blue eyes, nor that of black hair," he responded without hesitation. "Of course, it is both—among many other things."

"But I don't get it. What is the shape of the whole thing? And what's the smallest part that is a whole view?"

"What you see depends on what you are looking at," he answered.

Paintings happen somewhere between the irregularity of thought and emotion, and the regularity of a routine; in the interaction between the matters of my life, and a sequence of material events in the studio—a painting is the revealed pattern of my relationship with paint under various conditions during any given period of time, much like the intervals of a line measuring what at first seems chaotic.

"Certainly parts of the tree resonate, echoing each other; and surely there are implied centers where trunks and branches intersect. Perhaps there are other trees that I don't see, growing invisibly in nameless directions. And maybe there's still a grand center somewhere in the middle of everything where it all began. It is *like a painting—*

"Is it always my reflection?"

"Even the individual letters of the initial word are reflections, as is the word itself, the line of **IDEA**s, the grid of **IDEA**s, the matrix of **IDEA**s, and their relationships—it is all a picture of the way you see things, which is like, and unlike, the way anyone else sees the same things."

"Though the essence is always typical," I repeated. "But is what I see real?"

"As real as anything can be," said Nikola.

"Then, what I'm really painting, is myself," I stated, as if for the first time. "An artist can't help but paint self-portraits."

In the grayness of early morning I got out of bed and stood in the open balcony doorway, looking out into the shadowy treetops of the woods. A small stick snapped and I stared hard into the murk for evidence of the culprit—a dog, a deer, or a fat skunk. Down where it was neither dark nor light, I watched for a shape to solidify somewhere between what I could see and what I could imagine. After a few minutes, I heard another branch break farther off, and I turned away from the door, and went back to bed.

"Harness the spark," said Nikola, but I didn't understand what he meant.

Of course I continued to consider *the tree* and the extraordinary kinship between its parts, generalities, and intricacies, noting how unity leads to division, how parent thoughts lend life to child thoughts generation after generation. I pondered the pliant nature of what I call *real* and let my mind wander, watching the tree, and imagining honeybees, like busy little angels, drifting from blossom to blossom. And I wondered at the endless potential for regeneration within each fruit. "Is awareness neverending?" I asked—but at some point, Tesla must have quietly left me alone with my fantasies for there was no response. Then I remembered my grandmother knitting, rhythmically knotting and passing yarn from one needle to the next; and I lay awake until it was light, just thinking, and watching her knit.

Scale is the ratio or relationship between the proportions of one system and another, a measurement of similarity. A scale is a series of divisions at regular or graduated distances used to measure, a means of connection between higher and lower, larger and smaller, lighter and darker, greater and lesser, farther and closer, and so on, and so on—the infinite degrees of transcending or transforming in phases, ranges, levels, stages of development, rungs on a ladder, one above the other, and greater things above them in endless progression. I thought of the branches of my tree, of trees within trees, and felt part of a great mystery, that my potential awareness is all of that: the standard of evaluation, the means of comparison between things, the quantifier of qualities, and qualifier of quantities, the key to order in the gap between dimensions.

In the Galleria degli Uffizi, in the same room with Botticelli's paradise, there is a possible counterpart, a large triptych altarpiece that has always demanded my complete attention. It was painted in the late fifteenth century by a Flemish painter, Hugo van der

Goes, about the same time that Alessandro di Mariano di Vanni Filipepi (Sandro Botticelli) was at work on the *Primavera*; and like many other paintings in the Uffizi, it was commissioned by a prominent Florentine family to be displayed in a local church. Scenes of the Portinari family and associated saints appear on the left and right wings of the altarpiece, which are hinged to a central composition containing depictions of the Holy Family, angels, and adoring shepherds. It is complex. While Botticelli's company of gods rehearses for a springtime renaissance over my left shoulder, I watch a somber procession in a chilly landscape of bare trees arrive to surround a newborn baby. "Go ahead, pick up the poor thing!" I complain each time, though no one ever listens—all frozen in place and gazing intently at the child. "Well, don't leave him lying there naked in the dirt of a barnyard!" But the red-faced shepherds, a whole flock of angels, and the rest of the entourage don't move a muscle. "Hold still!" I hear the artist complaining to his models. "Hold still please!"

Painted in the distance on the left wing of the altarpiece, two tiny figures, what looks like a man and an expectant woman, carefully precede a donkey down a rocky outcropping toward the central gathering. *"Will they meet themselves?"* I muse, feeling strangely omniscient. On the right wing, an even smaller group of shapes suggesting figures on camels travels through a familiar landscape of painted hills and villages. What is extraordinary about the depicted incident is the unusual space it occupies; over fifty figures are gathered together from a variety of perspectives to participate in one dramatic event. The relative size and placement of each figure describe a compound picture plane fractured into a diversity of circumstances, times, and places: micro, meso, macro, mega, younger, older, higher, lower, before, after, here, and there—all appearing mystically in one inspired intersection of colorful branching logic.

In the center foreground of the wintry scene two vessels appear filled with bouquets of irises, lilies, and columbine, as if just picked from the vernal meadow across the room. Automatically, I check my hands for stains of green chlorophyll and feel curiously compressed, standing there between the paintings.

"The artist moves the brush," I remind myself.

32
Birth and Rebirth

October 21 – I am always amazed that paint can have so many aspects, the same ingredients arranged and rearranged in an endless diversity of textures and shapes, suggesting an infinity of themes and views. As a painter, I wander through my work as if through a neighborhood, seeking the usual landmarks that tell me I'm on track. Then, once in a while like a surprising dream, the activity of painting takes me somewhere completely new.

"But—where are you going with that? It doesn't look at all like you...."

And the unexpected detour through a strange countryside suddenly becomes my new way home. Each time it happens, I arrive to find that I'm an outlander, someone to meet again, a foreigner who needs an introduction, speaking a language that at first, I don't even understand myself.

Frequently, that's how it is approaching the prospects of another artist's domain—I'm pleasantly disoriented by feeling at home. I recall my immediate recognition of Monet's gentle scenery, and remember gazing knowingly at the intimate curves of Gauguin's Tahitian Eve, and later, exploring the familiar woods and meadow of Botticelli's Eden, or basking in the comfortable ordinariness of long shadows cast across De Chirico's empty piazzas—all of the paint that I can identify at once as someplace new within me.

It felt much the same way as we boarded a bus bound for Rijeka, and eventually another to Gospic, the pleasant rat-tat-tat of open-mouthed Italian quickly giving way to the breathy escape of sh, ch, and zh between the teeth and soft explosive kh and gh of the Croatian language—like the sounds of leaves and twigs underfoot.

The bus passed through a dreamy landscape of storybook forests, pastures, small gardens, and stone farmhouses, reminding me of a time some ten years before—a pleasant walk through the Italian countryside, a long line of school children on a fieldtrip holding hands, and the unexpected deep clatter of black helicopters flying low over the slope above us. *"La Guerra! La Guerra!"* screamed the children breaking ranks and pointing up at the dark shapes overhead. Yet, there was little obvious evidence of that war as we made our way, village after tidy village, through the idyllic scene toward our destination in the interior of the Croatian highlands. *"Like paint—the most recent layers leave little evidence of the struggle it took to get here—just a layer or two of paint and life starts over. I think I could grow to understand a place like this."*

In 1856, in Smiljan, in what is now Croatia, in a simple white cottage behind the Serbian Orthodox parish church near Vaganac stream at the foot of Bogdanic hill, Nikola Tesla was born. He arrived as lightening flashed—at midnight between the ninth and tenth of July during a thunderstorm. I don't remember exactly when I decided that I would travel to Tesla's birthplace. I suppose it was just a passing thought that quickly grew roots until I knew that it was real. *"So, here I am,"* I thought, looking out across the rough upland. *"Where I dreamed of being not so long ago—and here I am."*

It's always a shock to find myself in the middle of painting something new in a new way, attempting things with my brush that I had not yet considered. *"Look how that red speaks to the green! And if I add a bit more medium, see how smooth the surface can become!"* Soon enough I can find myself far away from where I started, headed for places that I had only briefly imagined, if at all.

In Gospic, Croatia, Nikola Tesla is everywhere: in the names of things, on the fronts of buildings and the covers of brochures, in a restaurant on a television screen, in the expressions of a sweet-faced couple with a stroller who led us to our hotel from the bus station.

"Taxi?" the girl at the front desk laughed.

"Yes, you know—a taxi," I repeated slowly.

"Here? No, not here," she continued, concealing a smirk with her hand. "Why would you need a taxi?" I explained that we had come from America to visit Nikola Tesla's birthplace. "Then, I will take you to Smiljan," she answered flatly. "Tomorrow morning."

The next day found us walking down a narrow lane in a late autumn landscape of faded velvet worn through in patches to reveal a bony underneath. "I'm here, Nikola," I whispered, pulling up my jacket collar against an icy wind. I pulled out my camera. Empty stone foundations, an old well, a lonely steeple far across the hay fields, and a few balding hills rising up like big stony craniums; *"But I don't know who I am here,"* I realized, snapping a photo of an old man on a heavy blue bicycle herding a half-dozen cows. The momentary shadow of a small boy playing beside a nearby stream caught my attention. "This is *your* woods and garden, isn't it?"

Memorijalni centar "Nikola Tesla", reads the sign.

"I told you I would come."

After a time, what was new becomes old. I can forget everything then—where I am, when I arrived, and how it happened. At that point, I tend to overlook what I once saw clearly and begin to take for granted that my brushes and paints know exactly what to do. I am learning at last that it's during these periods of feeling too secure that I am most lost—an apostate painter; that knowing something often means losing the faith that supported the first brushstrokes, the initial quantum leap that instigated the painting process.

That night, I awoke. I shook and shivered trying to relax deeper into the hard mattress, then glanced at the clock. *"Three forty-five,"* repeatedly entering and exiting a flickering dream where I saw him waiting, seated near the foot of my bed as if patiently attending to a child.

"Sometimes, when you cannot find me, I am here," he said at last. Immediately I had the peculiar sense of being at home in a strange place, exactly where I was supposed to be, when I was meant to be there. "Now that I know, I'll come more often," I offered. "I too had someplace to go once—but I've almost forgotten it."

"I know you did. And I left this place behind," Nikola began to reminisce, speaking wistfully of his home and family, his mother and an older brother. "I return now when I want to think. It has become my point of view as much as the place of my birth." I reached over and picked up a pad of lined paper and a pen. "I see the world best from here," he continued. I closed my eyes again as it was too dark to see anyway, and began to write our conversation, calling up the view from a treetop on a hill back home where I went to dream about life and the world.

"At times, I wish I could go back," I said, "—or come to where you are."

"But you still have work to do," he countered good-naturedly. "As a child I often floated between my observations of life and my experiences with something beyond. How I longed for what was past the horizon! I think I first gained a gift for seeing while I was very sick. For days I lay in bed while playing in the stream outside, or climbing our hill to sit and wonder at what seemed so far away. In time, I learned to go there to think—to view the world. After Dane died, I retreated to my place more often until it became, for a time, a most real part of my life. I suffered from the appearance of these visions, often accompanied by flashes of light, as they were sometimes disadvantageous to seeing my immediate surroundings. You understand—they were pictures of things which I had really seen, not things that I imagined."

I nodded in agreement.

"Painting is not something that is imagined—you make it real," added Tesla.

"Yes, I paint in hopes of making something real."

"And now, I return to Bogdanic hill, to sit and think, to look around me at a sea of fields and woods—and I wish to go back. At times I can almost smell the cabbage browning in the fat of small pieces of meat—it was one of my father's favorite things to eat, so mother made it often."

That night, in my dream, I returned to Smiljan and approached the small white house, an older version eclipsing the newer one I had seen during the day, like a slightly washed-out double exposure; though the pitch of the roof seemed less steep, the cottage more welcoming, and the church had a different steeple than the restored place I had visited. I lay in bed half asleep; smelling fried cabbage and the ever-present sweet and sour smokiness of wood fires, hearing the gentle commotion of children, and watching a small family scene—a woman in a dark dress, a larger church, images of Gospic, and pictures of a boy with his mind elsewhere all playing through my eyelids.

"Tata never knew what to think of my abilities and dreams. He saw them as an affliction, which often seemed to set us at odds. At least I know now that it must have worried him. And yet it was my ability to see that allowed me to explore and understand the invisible nature and power of things, including what is called electricity."

Becoming a stranger means giving up control—it means intense participation in a *patria* whose native inhabitants can tend to be complacent, blind, and indifferent to their habitual experience, language, and country. It happens occasionally, when work in the studio becomes rote, that I must distance myself from what I thought I was painting, to review my initial intent and start again with restored perspective.

"But it is not about paintings and electricity, is it?" he went on. "First, it is the source that makes things possible, the vision we tend to take for granted; which vision is the pre-existence of everything. Then, being happens in the doing, the fulfilling of the initial spark and observations."

I thought of the will, the endurance and hope it takes to make an image from what was just the hint of an idea, and remembered imagining a small boy by a stream fashioning crude waterwheels from odds and ends. I recalled a few rotting boards nailed to a tree, the evidence of dreams I had believed in, and a dark cellar where the products of doubt gather dust.

"Artists must be makers as well as schemers and observers," stated Nikola to conclude our discussion.

In the morning the waitress in the restaurant downstairs brought *strudla* for our breakfast. Later, a puree of sweet ripe peppers showed up on our supper plates, *slatka paprika*, bright red against the fried potatoes, sausages, and pale cabbage salad. "*Kvala*," I thanked her with the first Croatian word that I had learned. "*Molim*," she returned, seeming pleased. All day I watched it try to snow over the nearby half-clothed hills—

"I'm here. I really came, Nikola."

—as fleeting images of a Tesla Coil's scalp sprouting a vivid halo of electric blue hair appeared and reappeared, bringing to mind my day at the Tesla Memorial. Again at night, Tesla seemed to be sitting by my feet, waiting for my dreams to happen.

"Niko?"

"Yes."

"You know—you changed everything. You lit up the whole world. Talk to me about that, about how you came to understand electricity and how you knew what to do."

"Perhaps I made things worse. They use it for making money. Some use my work for increasing their power over others—for war. That is not what I foresaw, not what I intended. Sometimes I think my life was spent foolishly. And now I wish to make things better from where I am."

"So, why speak to me? Why am I the one here in Gospic taking down these conversations in the middle of the night?"

"Because, if there is a chance, I cannot risk not taking it;

because you paint patterns; because artists do things without consideration of constraints and cost; and most important—because you came."

"I did." It was still hard to believe.

Then, as in so many other dreams with Tesla, I saw the gridded landscape appearing all around me, the place I know so well. "The patterns are everywhere—and yet they cannot see them," he reflected. "Everything is in plain view."

"But I can see them," I gently asserted, "and don't know what to do about them." I remembered that sketch of Nikola Tesla at Wydencliffe, the basis for a painting. I had been planning and thinking on it for more than a year, the compound shape of a strange tower and brick building floating ark-like in the air, casting shadow over a clear-cut scene of stumps; and Nikola hanging out of a window and releasing a dove into a field of sky-blue paint. "It's not your fault, you know."

"There is no blame," he responded. "I had something to do—and there is still something to do. The work is unfinished."

There are paintings that take a long time to bring to a place that I can let go of them, like that of Gidu's hat. The work of establishing the true picture of it followed a rambling course, became a series of events, an unfolding pattern happening to me and in me. In spite of all that I can do, it seems impossible to prepare for such images. I struggled with the painting of my grandfather's hat for years, layer after layer, committing and submitting until I was satisfied that the material had reached the end of its transformation.

"You're an artist too," I said finally, and Tesla grinned like a little boy again. I think I felt even closer to him then than I had felt before—if that is possible.

"Did you know that I had the unique distinction of being a champion crow catcher in this region?" he asked after a pause.

"But the crows never came," I complained. "I tried. There was plenty of cracked corn. I hid beneath the pine tree on the hill and waited. Was I too impatient?"

"I believed that what I had discovered would make things better, that progress would change things," he explained. "I was impatient. Eventually, the intellect of humankind will govern the motion of the stars. We are divine beings, each of us reflecting universes. Of course, we are impatient." I recalled the faces, the rosy cheeks and noses of the kind young couple that I would never see again, who had led us out of their way to our hotel, just because they are good. "Yes," I agreed.

"In the meantime, there are wars. As we struggle to grow up, we fight. See—I am both a Serb and a Croat, and feel no enmity within myself. My blood and my homeland are at peace within me, so I am impatient with senseless things such as war."

"Do you know," he said after some time, "that Mr. Einstein's work was not completely correct. $E = mc^2$ is incomplete—unfinished."

"No, I wouldn't know that." It seemed that Tesla had unexpectedly changed topics. "I'm just a painter."

"But, that is why you do know. You affect the working of Einstein's simple theorem all the time and you take it for granted. As a painter, you hope and act as if there is no such thing as immaterial energy, including the energy we call thought or awareness. That is what an artist hopes, is it not? To affect the matter of the universe in ways that Mr. Einstein might call spooky. You see, he described the mystery from an observer's point of view rather than from that of a participant. A real painter knows that the outcome is also relative to an artist's more curious genus of participation, the material influence of awareness."

I felt the idea plant itself inside me and immediately start to grow.

"I am speaking of divine influence, however immature. To be fair, I must admit that he was right, though not complete. Nothing can stand independent of our awareness. The inert observer does not exist. Mr. Einstein ignored the physical phenomenon of the conscious mind and will, and left out the equation's most powerful element—himself."

"Then if $E = mc^2$ is incomplete, how should it read?" I asked, feeling like an eager child on a very important occasion, impatient, and small.

"*Energy* equals the *mass* of an object times the *speed of light* squared; all of it qualified by *individual intent*—the emboldened *i* miniscule." As he spoke, the equation appeared clearly in front of me. "**E** equals ***mc*** squared times *i*."

$$(E = mc^2)i$$

"The *i* is part of another equation which I will teach you, that of possibility affected by intent, **?** + *i*, but that will wait for another time. Intent changes the picture considerably. So while Mr. Einstein was not exactly incorrect, his assertion is not completely correct. The intent of an aware individual affects everything. Pure intent, pure vibration, ever-increasing awareness is how divinity happens. Remember. By degree—one thing greater than another, a step at a time. His theory is relatively static in the face of divine awareness, which is dynamically and universally influential. Awareness animates. Awareness is kinetic. It is the wheelwork of nature. The creative power of *i* is the transforming influence of the universe."

"*Of course, that's it!*" I realized. "*But can it be true?*" I felt like a traffic jam—filled with so much all at once, my thoughts going in all directions. "*That would mean that—*" It had happened before while speaking with Tesla. "*Then, am I the whole story?*" The image of brushes, paint on a palette, a clean ground to work on, and a strong desire to fuss with layers of painted details… "*Or, are we the words that tell the story?*" …one color over the other, developing the patterns that support the rest of the picture. "*And who is the author then?*"

Nikola began to speak, and again I experienced what he was describing as a real event. "Imagine standing on a platform and watching as a train approaches the station on the nearest track. Abruptly the air explodes with the heavy rhythm of iron wheels on rails and rushing train cars. The train soon becomes a blur—and you blink. For a fraction of an instant, in the time it takes to blink your eyes, you see the side of a train car, a train car window, and a stranger's face staring out at you—before the blur suddenly returns and the train continues to speed by, passing down the track until it recedes into the distance. That is the vision of an observer standing on the platform. In the middle of the blur, someone else may experience only the impression of a train, or miss the train altogether. You might decide to participate by running with the train to feel its speed and to decrease the blur—but the influence of awareness has the power to slow or stop the train. Awareness amplifies the experience. It offers greater vision in increasing stillness—'coolness in the middle of fire.' What Mr. Einstein did not guess, what I have always known since childhood, is that I am the train. Inert observation does not reveal the magic of it; that the person in the train car window is a reflection—yours, mine, or Mr. Einstein's. You understand—

children and artists become the train. In all of our wandering, the important thing is not to forget what we once knew—how to be children."

In my studio, I paint through the events of my life hoping to stumble upon something to suggest the start of a pattern, a vision in the blur. *"Where are you going with this?"* I inevitably ask myself, gazing at the work of a stranger on my easel. *"To be honest, I don't really know,"* I reply. *"At this point, I have no idea where it's leading, only that it feels right, like starting over again from the beginning—but not really."*

I looked at Nikola sitting quietly by my bed and remembered my old friends in the museum on the day that I learned that they were my reflections. I thought of the broken piece of plate glass mirror in my treasure box, my toothy smile on the surface of our skating pond, and the view from the top of a favorite pine tree on a small hill. Gradually my heart gave way. What had seemed muddled grew clearer, like transparent glazes of different colors combining to form a bright new hue. "There's the landscape, the station, and the tracks," I began. "Who is—"

"To know the author, you must become an author," preempted Tesla before I could finish.

I briefly recalled a peculiar dream of several years before—a crowded sidewalk filled with people of every age, race, size, shape, and social class; and the eventual realization that everyone had my face. For a while, it had a deep impact on how I tended to see and treat people. "Nikola?" I began to reason. "Does that mean…"

"…that, I am you?" He completed my uncomfortable proposal.

"Over a year of lectures and conversations and we're nearly back

to where we started—the pattern and sequence of one, the hero's journey, the garden and the wilderness, vibration and direction, particle and path—the i. But what does it all mean?" I pleaded, feeling my voice beginning to tighten and reveal my frustration.

Like a sketch for an important painting, the groundwork was in place centuries before artists and thinkers began to distance themselves from traditional icons to investigate beyond the habitual boundaries of prevailing dogma, each hoping for a better view—from studios and lecterns, towers and telescopes, from Mounts Ventoux and Subasio, like the boy Nikola who regularly climbed to the top of Bogdanic hill to see outside the confines of St Peter and Paul's parish.

"How many times can you rebuild on the same stones?" I wondered, considering Tesla's new old house and church, while inspecting the dry-stacked foundations around them that indicate a small community which has disappeared.

"The world is a mirror," Nikola answered calmly, "enlivened by an extraordinary power, a part of which is referred to as electricity. This enlivening force is in you, in me, in everyone and everything. I cannot tell you more without violating the terms of an agreement. What you do with that knowledge will eventually reveal its meaning to you. That is the limitation of observable proof; it has no context or meaning. Without the application of *i*, fact is just fascinating argument. Only an author has true authority. And to know what an author knows, you must do what an author does."

In my studio, I have begun to recognize and accept the recursive phases of my effort: the self-assured explorer who loses his

417

way periodically to become a vagabond; my subsequent experiments and quixotic dabs of wishful paint; and the hope in yet another beneficent favor from somewhere beyond myself and the studio, wishing for the sun to show me the right road—for wings. I make pictures to mark the route. The cycle has happened often enough that I grow a bit more sure of its outcome each time—the eventual renewed dispensation of undeserved inspiration and the return of my confidence, the dreamer's deliverance, my re-arrival home, to look around and see everything as if for the first time—"to rebehold the stars," wrote Dante seven centuries ago.

"I feel the thinness of our separation here," I said, breaking the silence.

"That happens when you grow too big to fit where you are," he responded softly.

I studied the gentle structure of Nikola's face; the delicate features and apparent refinement of his bearing, not just familiar now, but known to me—his kind eyes, the soft shadows in the up-turned corners of his mouth, his pale complexion, the narrow bridge of his nose, and prominent cheekbones. I began to review our many adventures together, and feared as I often do, that this time he might finally disappear at the end of our discussion, never to return. *"But my life hardly seems average anymore, does it?"*

"Tell them—write that we do not really die," he interrupted my musing. "Our *i* cannot be dissociated from the plot, nor can our agreements and accountability. Our divine intelligence is matter that does not pass away with flesh any more than it is born from it. The covers of a book contain the words—but not the story."

"As a frame contains the paint, but not the image or the artist," I pondered aloud. "Without *i*, the materials have no context—I

do understand. It's the association with *i* that gives meaning.
"My good friend—how can I care so much about someone who is just a dream?"

"Continue to work, and I will continue to visit as it is required," he concluded in a business-like manner. "But the room number could have been better," he advised. "The 9 is adequate enough, but 210 next door would have been divisible by 3." We both smiled at our shared habit of counting things: the number of breaths, stairs, or steps. I remembered kneeling to pray that evening and automatically beginning to count, "1, 2, 3, 4, 5, 6, 7…13, 14, 15, 16, 17…," before catching myself.

"And I'll return here often," I reassured both of us, reminded of my Gidu's secret counsel concerning numbers.

I awoke, quite sure that I had been speaking some other tongue than my own, feeling my mouth distinctly forming strange words—sh, ch, and zh escaping between my teeth with the soft explosive sounds of kh and gh snapping here and there like leaves and twigs underfoot. Outside, it had finally begun to snow in earnest. We finished repacking our suitcases and left in the dark, silently walking from the spell of one glowing streetlamp to the next, from light to shadow and then to light, retracing our path back to the Gospic bus station. I watched snowflakes briefly fall under the radiant influence of electricity and then disappear, and thought of the boy Nikola Tesla leaving home on a pilgrimage almost one hundred fifty years before. I looked for him in the faces of the handsome young men boarding the bus. "Breath is time, and that is life," Nikola had said. I sat down in the bus seat, stared out the window and began to count—inhalation, exhalation; inhalation, exhalation; inspiration, expiration; the recurring sequence of remembering and forgetting; dreaming and awakening; the endless rounds of seeking and discovery transforming what was obscure into what is manifest—breathing in, and breathing out. After coming so far, it felt odd, not knowing whether I was returning or departing, both possibilities suddenly seeming true.

   I watched it snow against the windshield,
     "*Galileo, Giordano,*
wanting to sleep until we arrived in Rijeka.
     Nicolaus, Leonardo,
Condensation ran down the inside of the windows, the bus driver repeatedly wiping off a hole to peer through with a wadded page of news.
     Marsilio, the Giovanni's,
Due to the storm, the four hour trip stretched into twelve, plus a night in Rijeka.
     the Francises, and Nikola...."
The next day, on the way to Trieste, we all filed off the bus and lined up waiting to enter a small office at the confine of Slovenia.
     "*Documents, please.*"
I handed over my passport which he quickly slid through a reader. Thump! He stamped a rubber seal down on an inkpad. Bump! He stamped it on a back page to record my passage.
     "*It's just that easy.*"
I double-checked my passport photo.
     "*Yup, that's me.*"

   In De Chirico's painting, The Joy of Return, the train leaves its habitual place on the horizon to enter the heart of the city. And so, eventually I arrived home, eager to enter the studio and see some evidence of pigments reappear under my fingernails.
     "*Loss and restoration, birth and rebirth,*
It has been too long since I've refreshed the paint on my palette

in order to start a new picture.
like winter and then spring,
Among other things, I have been thinking about depicting the insides of a clock, the kind with a face and a pendulum.
when everything is remade, 'as new trees—renewed with new foliage,'
I want to paint an image of the main spring, the part that drives the mechanics of a clock and depends on someone to rewind it periodically.
de revolutionibus meum,
In fact, I'm almost ready to pick up my brushes and put on my paint-smeared apron once again.
myself wearing the imprint of the seasons."

Then, a few days after my homecoming, I visited with a friend who shared an experience—

"I have to tell you about something that happened to me the other day—something that changed everything. I was looking at a Rembrandt portrait, a picture in a book, and suddenly I wasn't looking at the image anymore. I became it!"

"I understand," I offered, recalling myself as a boy standing in front of paintings in a museum.

"But I was just looking…"

"That's why painters paint, isn't it?" I interrupted.

"…then I started seeing everything differently. It was me I saw."

"It's the *commedia* again. The artist gave you everything you needed to play the part, to assume the role impromptu."

"But I was the image!" he insisted.

"—*times i*," I thought, and smiled.

33
Where All the Stories Come Together

There's just something about this place. I try to hold it, but it moves away—like what happens sometimes with wild things; I reassure them that, "I'm okay. I won't hurt you, you know." But still I can't seem to get close enough. Maybe it's the smell of too much soap on me, or the plastic, or my combustion-powered lifestyle. Or maybe it's my need to own things that frightens them.

I came by the grace of credit cards and hours spent consulting, on an urge, a sudden inspiration about six months ago, to sit here where so many stories seem to come together; to consider my life, and to bring this chapter of my own story to a conclusion, here among my friends—Cimabue, the Lorenzettis, Simone Martini, Giotto—in a painted world of intersecting narratives and endless patterns. I have imagined and rehearsed this many times—and yet, I'm unprepared, dazed, overcome by the power of the place. In spite of the grand cathedral filled with pictures and hues, there is something else here that I did not expect.

(From notes written in the Basilica of St Francis in Assisi)

November 15 – Outside, it was pouring. The narrow sidewalks were a war of umbrellas. The streets had turned to streams and the air smelled of wet stone. The clouds hung solid over the untroubled scene below us, a heavy ceiling above the grey olive groves, over the patchwork of plowed clay soil and red tile roofs and towers that surround Mount Subasio. I arrived three days ago to end this part of my adventure, surprised by the emotions that sprang so easily to the surface as I stepped off the bus, and then in the hotel room, and again and again sitting in the cathedral for two days watching the painted stories happen around me on the walls, sitting for hours and hours gazing up into blue vaults of gilded stars (and even now, as I review my notes, my feelings are so close, ready to spill out onto the page in what might seem like hyperbole.)

> I'm drawn by something familiar—not the kind old city as much as the mountain, the stars, slopes, and grottoes, and the lingering residue of an idealistic youth, another rascal traipsing through the woods in search of something bigger, rejecting the popular view and asking hard questions.

(From notes written in the Basilica of St Francis in Assisi)

Walking through the Basilica of Saint Francis in Assisi feels like moving through the layers of a painting—starting with the final enlightened image or narrative, then down through the colorful underlayers of paint, to end underneath at the shadowy foundation and prepared ground of the piece. I entered the main nave of the upper church from the Piazza Superiore toward the bottom of Via S Francesco, immediately confused by the weightiness of what I saw, every surface of the cavernous interior painted top to bottom with the particulars of extreme designs and plots; the light on them streaming down through more tales told in colored glass. Adams and Eves; gardens; seas filled with strange fishes; men with wings and carried on clouds; flying chariots; devilish creatures flying with bat wings; buildings in strange perspective, like faceted jewels, tipping and tumbling in fish-eye views; and patterns everywhere, rosettes, crosses, checks and curlicues, ropes, knots and grotesques—all of it begging to be seen, all at once, and me, as if out of breath, hardly capable and patient enough to stop and take in the smallest detail. So I found a bench and sat down.

> I have just entered a fading world of common miracles, of pale ghostly images, of painted memories like my dreams with parts missing or forgotten, motion and emotion caught in midstride, a *trompe l'ouile* reality within a real fantasy. I sit here and stare, thinking of my studio back home where I can sit for hours before I feel the authority and wisdom to make a mark, to add or change a color or shade—and then it always feels borrowed, beyond my limits, something I don't merit, a spark of grace from elsewhere—and here I am in the middle of elsewhere, surrounded by the work of true *cantastorie*. I clear my throat and it echoes for a moment or two before joining the pervasive mumble of tourists and pilgrims swelling and subsiding like the distant rolling of musical thunder.
>
> *(From notes written in the Basilica of St Francis in Assisi)*

Not so long ago, an earthquake collapsed parts of the painted ceiling which has been in the process of restoration ever since;

specialists sifting through the clutter of painted plaster to put it back together flake by flake. *"Like me wishing to pick up the threads of past conversations to make them new again."* I thought of my Trevisan friend who lovingly resurrects old Alfa Romeos. "I don't care so much about owning the finished cars," he told me once as I admired his work. "My passion is restoring things—bringing to life again what had life before." In Smiljan, Croatia, I visited Nikola Tesla's reconstructed childhood home and church, which had been destroyed during a war, noting that the new construction was almost true to the pattern of the old, but lacking in some important aspects. "The Pravoslav-looking steeple was not replaced," I said innocently. "Because it must reflect *our* tradition, as this is *our* homeland," stated the tour guide firmly.

Eventually, I stood up again to wander slowly around the perimeter of the nave, walking from episode to episode of Old and New Testament accounts and the popular chronicles of the life of Francis. I got up close to inspect the application of pigment on the plaster, the carefully managed effects of restoration, and the layers and layers of initials, names, and notes scratched over centuries deep into the plaster and up the walls into the images as far as one might reach. Then I backed up toward the center of the church to see the painted parts in context, letting the graffiti recede into the bigger view.

I started at the east end of the church by the main entrance, and proceeded west along the north side of the nave toward the transept. *"Poor Cimabue, the ugly ox"*—his work has all but vanished there, oxidized, dissolved, and pulverized by seismic activity; while his student Giotto's work, though washed with time, is largely still alive. *"In painting Cimabue thought he held the field, but now it's Giotto's—as the other's fame has been concealed...."* I wondered how fast it took invisible time to begin to take advantage of the visible material, and when it was that Dante must have walked the same path that I was walking to compare the shadowy dreams of the one with the pale visions of the other. Then passing along the south wall of the nave to return to the east end, I stopped finally at a faded fresco of Francis talking to a flock of birds—and for an instant I saw Nikola Tesla feeding flocks of pigeons. *"Giovanni di Pietro di Bernardone—Saint Francis—San Francesco—who are you anyway, that I should know you in my gut and in my stinging eyes?"* And I found a bench, and sat down.

> Years ago, I decided that the view of art is symptomatic, or even prescriptive of how I see myself—or perhaps how the world sees itself. From that point on, everything was new; I remember the changes: the new warmth of light on Monet's haystacks, the colorful life of a postman and his wife, the secrets of my Egyptian friends, and the passions of my exposed terra cotta counterparts, a common laborer breathing life into the countryside, and myself hanging above the uncertain depth of my future. "*Où allons-nous?*" I remember reading up in the corner of Gauguin's Eden. That's when I discovered that the world is watching me, like a mirror, a witness to my transformation. I knew that I was looking at what was looking back. "How powerful artists are!" I realized. So I became a painter. And now I'm forced to recall once again, that like a painting, the world is a reflection. I sit here knowing that it's not the world that has changed, but that I have changed. I look around at others, the lives coming and going, all of us together here, some sitting quietly with bowed heads or staring silently, and some merely passing through to talk about where they've been.
>
> *(From notes written in the Basilica of St Francis in Assisi)*

After deciding that an image is complete, I sit back just to look for a while—for hours, days, or even weeks, taking breaks for eating and sleeping, but otherwise fully engaged in the activity of seeing what I've done, adding little touches of color here and there, and adjusting the strength of transparent glazes to help moderate the discussion, subtly pushing some things back to emphasize others. I live with the painting until I'm satisfied that I have done all that I can do to make the statement clear. So I sat and reviewed the upper nave for a while, panel by panel, until I was content that I could see no more.

Entering the lower church felt like entering the deep woods, the overarching painted vaults and ribs like leafy branches mitigating the effects of the sun, the air becoming damp and heavy, the colors darkening in the perpetual dusk of the place. I quickly pulled up the zipper on my jacket as if against a chilly night though it was just afternoon. *La basilica inferiore* is the same basic **T** shape as the church upstairs; the intersecting directions of Francis's *tau*, a symbol for life and renewal, and the fulfillment of revelation, joined at the top of a tree where I stood to take in both the east and west wings of the transept and the length of the nave. *"Of course—the tree is the door…,"* I mused, heading back to the south side of the transept to begin studying the frescos, *"…the key to hidden wisdom."*

But as the sun began to set, and before I had finished my tour of the lower church and crypt, I was strongly encouraged to leave by the vigilant guards. *"So I'll return tomorrow,"* I decided, following a small crowd out of the church from the great side door, stepping out into the rain and Piazza delle Logge lined with colonnades, then climbing back up Via S Francesco to our hotel.

"Hello? Are you Saint Francis?" I asked, feeling a bit intrusive.

"I am certainly not who you think I am," he answered in a tired voice. "You are late."

"I'm sorry. I am here looking for Saint Francis and I thought that you were he."

"Yet you have found just another person like yourself with faults and frailties," he replied. "And, you have missed the better part of the sunset." I looked out over the valley through a deepening haze of dusty gray violet which turned to Raw Sienna over hot pink where the sky seemed to burn above the western hills and the sun lay on the horizon like an orange egg-yolk.

"But are you Saint Francis?" I repeated.

"I suppose that I am not—and that I am," he confessed.

"Then tell me who you really are."

"If you are looking for the legendary hero of so many tales—that is not I. If you seek the rebellious idealist whose regrets are often like a prison, here I am."

"Aren't you a saint?"

"That depends on how you define *saint*," he sighed. "Let me explain that after these many years I am still thoughtful about the events of my life. Certainly there were, and are, plenty of things to rebel against, as well as many things to live for—and an abundance of mistakes that even saints make."

"But I admire you," I stated. "I'd rather focus on your goodness than regrets."

"What you mean is that you have admired the folklore surrounding me."

"Well, maybe you could try and live up to it," I responded bluntly. "You know—when I paint an image, I miss the mark all the time, and then have to readjust, sometimes starting over and over again—but I think most painters understand that eventual success is often the result of all the mistakes it takes to complete a picture."

Saint Francis tried to smile, perhaps softened by the prospect of someone to share a conversation and the evening, and most likely entertained by my ingenuous advice.

"A true artist learns through experience to see everything in the context of a final image, when the sum of all the errors and corrections looks beautiful," I went on, feeling more than a little shocked to hear myself preaching to a famous saint.

"Then, I will teach you about becoming a saint. Yes, I believe that being a saint, good brother, is a lot like your struggle with colors and a brush; for a true saint, like a painter, is not declared by others for his or her worthiness, but by a personal declaration of willingness to participate in the process that finally renders him a saint. Willingness is the highest qualification for artists and for saints, as none of us is sufficiently talented or worthy."

"So every time I paint, I end up realizing that I am the real work," I admitted, "that each image is of me." The partial smile spread warmly across Francis's face.

"And becoming a saint is not determined by a number of miracles," he continued, "for each saint knows that miracles are everywhere…in the sunrise and sunset, in birth and death, in the clouds and in the rain, in living water from a source, in the renewal of our sister mother by the craft of each season. It is not through the occurrence of miracles that we are made saints, but in allowing them to happen through our faith."

Distant laughter followed by the audible peaks of a woman's animated voice attested to the proximity of a house, or perhaps a not too distant town. In the shadows, the powder gray of evening was deepening to blue gray. "Woo-hoo! Woo-hoo!" sang a bird toward the edge of the meadow.

"Once I used to dream of good company, good women, a pretty wife, and a house bigger than my father's," he began, "but now this open place is my shelter, where I come to think and to pray—out here with the birds. And even when I am not here, I return to this place in my dreams and daydreams, to sit peacefully, to ponder the world and wonder who I am."

He was leaner than Nikola, if that's possible, though broader across the shoulders and not so tall. In fact he seemed small, and had a worn carefree look, even if his eyes divulged softness and gentility. Francis didn't look much like the images of Saint Francis I had seen in the basilica and elsewhere; as his face was more angular, his beard thicker, and his hair longer. He seemed to be wearing a dark loose tunic full of patches and that was all.

"Have you ever watched the night arrive?" he asked. "Have you ever lain down in a meadow just to see the sun vanish and the stars appear? When others would be eating and ready to fall asleep, I would come here to study the sun melting once more into the horizon and to witness the moon finally finding her way up over the hill. And each time, I could feel a world waking up within me."

"I've spent lots of evenings outside," I answered, followed by the muffled chirp of a single cricket close by.

"I mean—taken the time to welcome her moment by moment?" added Francis in a hushed tone, as a bony-looking doe stepped out from a thicket and began grazing on what grass was left, her hide dull and sucked up tight against her ribs. "Winter approaches, but she has given her strength to someone else," he whispered as a healthy fawn followed close behind. "I learned to know myself by knowing the sky, the wind, the weather, the trees and flowers, the birds, and the deer. Once escaping the temptations of fleshly comforts, it seemed to me that in birth and in death only humankind can live and die unfulfilled. Thus, by seeing the divinity in the world and her creatures, I found the divinity within myself." And so we sat, watching the deer, and witnessing the color of the scene gradually change to deeper blue and the blue to indigo. "What colors are these, brother artist? For I don't believe they have names."

"You must be right; I don't know how I'd describe these exact shades to someone who hasn't seen them."

"Today I saw the tired dragonflies trembling for the last time on the ground, so I believe this may be the last warm night. Spend it here with me and we shall talk about the shades, from sunset to sunrise—and then about the colors of the meadow and of the sky." But we remained quiet until the world around us was all shadows and silhouettes, attentive to the slow advance of a dark cloud above a smudge of rain moving across the valley to arrive in a cold steady sprinkle, and I followed Francis under an overhanging rock to sit on a bed of dry leaves.

"Remember, like painting, faith is an active principle; as fruits and flowers arrive after seeds are sown, watered, and tended; these woods and meadows, gardens, your paintings, and miracles depend on faith. A saint knows that every breath is a resurrection, and that the miracle of our earthly bodies depends on the transformation and support of our brother and sister elements through our participation—for are we not all born as images of holy gardeners and creators? No, little brother, I have learned through experience that a saint is not a title that others can bestow, but an agreement to live by."

The night became a texture of afterimages and dim suggestions, a mix of sounds in the dark—the light patter of raindrops, the huffing of the wind, a branch breaking in the woods. I yawned and pulled my extremities in closer, tucking my hands under my armpits, and hunching my shoulders.

"You're not who I expected," I said after prolonged silence.

"Praise be for brother wind," he sang softly, "for his breath across the hollows of our ears," as a chill breeze blew across the hillside, "and for the air and clouds and every kind of weather. Nor are you."

Morning came too soon and I awoke (more or less), showered, brushed my teeth, dressed quickly, and ate in the room—some juice, a hard roll with some local cheese, and a pastry we had purchased the evening before on our walk back to the hotel. My wife and daughter planned to visit other sites in town while I returned to the cathedral. *"My whole life is like my messy studio,"* I grumbled, ambling down Via S Francesco and nodding to a few shopkeepers out tending to their storefronts. "*Buon giorno!*" The slopes above us had been dusted with a trace of snow and my breath puffed visibly as I spoke. "*Buon giorno!*" Somehow, I had experienced a shakeup overnight and was struggling to put the pieces back together. *"Dammit! Here I am on this silly dream quest—!"* I recalled an evening some thirty years ago, playing solitaire until the middle of the night, when I began to win again and again and again. Seventeen times, until I became afraid and put the cards down. "*...giorno!* " And remembered the restoration of a Veronese mural in the Accademia, watching a man and a woman on ladders working from a palette of colors painstakingly matched to the painting, and carefully applying touches of paint that magically disappeared into the image. *"...with absolutely no disposition for sainthood! And here I am a painter? HELL! I don't even know* *why I'm angry—Buon giorno!"* Upon entering the basilica, I looked around at the fading story of a young man experiencing the poetic nature of himself as the context of all good things. *"But of course I'm an artist. What else could I be?"* And I found a bench where I sat for a long time and wept.

I retraced my path, starting again in the northeast corner of the nave, standing before the painted vision of Saint Francis divining water from a rock. I looked above on the north wall to see yet another water scene; this time, the water being poured into vessels at a nuptial feast. "Miracles are everywhere," he had said, "not a violation of nature's laws, but the evidence of our humble knowledge of them...." I headed west along the north wall, reviewing again the scenes I had studied the day before, and was saddened once more by the pale impressions of Cimabue's masterpieces in the transept. A small stairway to the right of some choir seats and the apse of the upper church led to a similar staircase that brought me to the north transept of the lower church, where I stood at the branching of the **T** to get my bearings and to decide where to begin.

> There is something reassuring about places like Assisi—walls, roofs, streets, and piazzas, all built from native materials; the borrowed stones and clay that surround the town rearranged here by genius and industry to form this nest of churches, towers, homes, shops, and barns. It feels like being inside clockwork slowly ceding to time, winding down, to be rewound again and again, the inherent cycle of disintegration and rebirth evident on every corner, the careful re-placing of original elements back into original patterns. I think that's part of what makes the images on these walls so compelling, the striking contrast between the comfort of what feels predictably

local and the surprise of what seems other-worldly.

(From notes written in the Basilica of St Francis in Assisi)

I stayed down in the lower basilica most of the day, first taking in the panels on the perimeter of the church, then visiting each side chapel before returning to study my many favorites. I spent extra time in the chapel of St Martin admiring Simone Martini's sense of color, his elegant draftsmanship and intelligent composition; paying particular attention to the panels in the entrance arch from which I borrowed a simple pattern of hexagons and triangles a few years ago. Later, in the south transept, I contemplated the work of Pietro Lorenzetti, his strange associations and the homey details of fourteenth century Italy applied to the portrayal of daily life in ancient Jerusalem: boys climbing trees to gather boughs, a servant washing the dishes after a holiday meal, a lazy cat by the fire, and a dog licking individual plates clean. There is even the image of a pet monkey climbing along the balustrade of a pavilion where the man tied to a post is being scourged. Of course I revisited the painted allegories by Giotto and his workshop on the presbytery vault several times, and thought better than to lie down on the altar from which I could have viewed them more comfortably. I remember wishing for a similar set up in the Sistine Chapel where I left with a very stiff neck. After one last look at images by Simone Martini and Cimabue in the north transept, I went back to the upper basilica to walk slowly around the outer wall to take leave of my friends, confused at the prospects of finally departing from the church. One last time, I found a bench and sat down toward the east end of the nave, and looked over at Giotto's image of the back of a crucifix, feeling again like a secret witness to the scene—a stage, within a stage, within a stage—and prayed for my return.

> In the theatre of painting, in the dramatic interactions and relationships between exotic elements and circumstances, there are times when something beyond the boundaries of the studio transmutes pigments and shapes into something else, when the paint disappears and a new world is born, giving life to the image, and renewing that of the painter; offering the audience the vicarious opportunity to enter the context of the experience—to become the artist. So today, I sit here in the middle of this, and suddenly today is forever and everywhere, seven hundred years ago, and seven centuries in the future, here and there, all at once. The discussion is always the same.
>
> (From notes written in the Basilica of St Francis in Assisi)

I watched the sun burn passionately into the western hills, igniting the edges of steel-gray clouds in electric shades of yellow, pink, and orange, as if it were trying to get in a last flamboyant display before relinquishing the stage.

"*Dominus regit me, et nihil mihi deerit—in loco pascuæ ibi me collocavit…*"

Across the meadow, the starved-looking doe and her fawn grazed unconcerned with five other deer. Francis was singing.

"*…Super aquam refectionis educavit me—animam meam converti…*"

"What's that?" I asked.

"Poetry—words for the humble, in the language of the proud.

"*…si ambulavero in medio umbræ mortis, non timebo mala…*

"A true saint sings, brother.

"*…quoniam tu mecum es….*"

His singing voice was pleasant, sweeter than I had expected from his rough appearance. "I have wished to sing," I said, "but the only ones who've really heard me are my children as babies, when I sang to them each night as they fell asleep."

"A saint sings," repeated Francis, "not because his voice is in tune, but because his heart is. How sad that a well-tuned heart resists rejoicing." So I tried to hum along though I didn't know the words.

While he was finishing his verse Francis pulled out a dry hunk of bread and began throwing crumbs to a flock of waiting sparrows that greedily went after the larger pieces, sometimes stealing them from each other's beaks. Again I saw the fleeting likeness of Nikola Tesla casting feed to waiting birds in a city park.

"Are you ever lonely?"

"Only when I think too much of myself—and then I find someone or some creature in need and I forget my own concerns." A repeated rustle in the leaves beneath the underbrush produced a small finch which flew up to sit near the end of a branch above us. "Besides, there are so many brothers and sisters here who are willing to keep me company," he smiled. "Loneliness is fear—and what have I to fear?" I looked at his skinny body, his thin legs poking out from under the patched tunic, and couldn't help but consider my own well-fed proportions.

"Do you ever miss home?" I asked.

"But I am home. Wherever I find myself is home. Loneliness is fear," he repeated, "and what have we to fear?"

"I suppose I fear a lot of things—like going hungry, for instance—or being cold, or having no money." I studied his gaunt face and recalled the roundness of my own face in the mirror. A dog barked from somewhere down the hill and another answered, which seemed to set off a chain reaction of distant barking.

"Fear and faith cannot live together in the same heart," he counseled. "Hunger, cold, and poverty—once you meet them, you no longer fear them. Even death teaches us of life."

While we talked, the shadows had arrived. A sapphire glow in the west was the last evidence of the sunset as the first hesitant stars began to appear in the darkening bowl of heaven. "A few days ago," he began, "while collecting wood for my fire, I found a dog wandering in the woods—starving, cold, and afraid. And he stalked me at a distance until he followed me here. So I offered him my supper of bread which he had been seeking from the moment he arrived, and thought that he might sleep then by my fire for a while." Francis was a good storyteller. As he spoke, it was as if I saw the events happening, similar to how it is with Nikola Tesla when he's showing or teaching me something. "Then I placed my supper before him and backed away, but fear defeated his hunger and it took a long time for him to trust enough to come and take my bread, after which he greedily ate so fast that he could not have enjoyed it, still wary that I might want to reclaim my meal. Eventually, he did come and lie down not too far from the dying fire and me—and he slept until morning when he ran off into the woods. I thought, how like the dogs we can be—lost and hungry for something, but too filled with fear to take the meal placed before us."

Then we sat still for a long time watching the evening, and I dozed off to wake up with a thin cover placed over me and a small fire making shadowplay under the overhang of rock. A cold breeze blew and Francis sat beside the fire humming a tune. "Follow me," he said softly once he realized that I had awakened, indicating a place in the center of the grass and walking out into the meadow where he lay down on his back motioning me to do the same. As I lay down beside him, I marveled that he seemed able to accept the chill while I needed the cover. And we stared up into a dark vault filled with stars.

Francis spoke. "We have watched the sun set and the stars appear; we named flowers and animals; then left the wilderness to lie here in the garden—but we have moved in stillness, for it all happened within us." The shade in the woods and meadow seemed to deepen and spread as I watched the black sky fill my vision until that's all there was. It was like gazing into a dark pool that encompassed everything, as if I could reach out and touch the surface of it, causing ripples that would spread out from where it had been disturbed.

"But how?" I inquired.

"That star is the center," he answered; pointing toward the seven stars I call *the little dipper*, "the star at the end of the great dog's tail. There is always a center, a still heart. That is where I look when I begin to fear, when I get lonely, or lose track of who I am. Though everything around it moves—the center is always still. That is where I look to see myself, to acknowledge the saint in me, the creator, the artist. To be a saint, good brother, means to see myself as a reflection of that role." We lay in silence as I had nothing to say, both of us flat on the ground in the damp grass with our hands clasped behind our necks, watching the sky slowly spin around. I thought of myself, the boy, gazing into a broken piece of mirror, admiring my own image. Or was I gazing out of it? I can't tell. "We discern first with our physical senses, then with the senses of our minds, our hearts, and spirits," said Francis finally. "We live in a world that lives within us."

"I don't think I understand," I owned, sure that I was missing most of what he meant, and surprised by my voice escaping as an airy murmur.

"We are each the work and glory of creation," he stated solemnly, "singular living sequences; each of us, a complete example of the pattern. Even the angels know our individual names."

"Mnemonics," I mumbled, remembering a lecture from an eternity ago, "…a door to the whole."

"There is no way to harm creation without harming ourselves, and no way to harm ourselves without harming creation," continued Francis.

"Where'd you learn all of this?" I asked while shifting to try and get comfortable under the cover.

"There," he replied, (pointing to the heavens). "It is all there." And we were quiet.

Some time later, I remember seeing the moon, an icy eye finally beginning to peep above the glowing mountain, to cast long thin shadows across the meadow. Nothing moved. Even brother wind had stopped his restless venting, and the stars began to pale as the whole sky turned a silver gray. The world that had disappeared into darkness hours before reappeared as a cold image of itself. Francis began to speak of his life: of work as the remedy for doubt; of his desire to renew things, to restore a pattern; of hungry wolves; of mothers and sons; of love and his regrets; and I believe I heard him quietly weeping at least once. "You can sleep," he offered. "The dawn will not be here for a while and I will awaken you before he comes."

"No. I want to stay awake with you," I replied, and continued listening to him talk as I watched the shadows drawing in toward their sources and the moon begin slowly to cross the sky, wondering if she'd make it to the western hills before the sun arose.

"Wake up, brother artist!" he whispered. "I did not mean to rouse you so soon, but he is brightening the east now and you will want to see his arrival in its entirety."

"But, I didn't want to sleep!"

"It was not long. The flesh is weak and you must have needed rest." The moon was not half way across its course and the eastern sky was already tinted cyan. Roosters were crowing at various distances. After my eyes adjusted I saw that color had begun to return to where the night had been. I pulled the thin cover up, which uncovered my feet, then pulled in my feet. "But how can I fall asleep while I am dreaming?"

"The same way you fall asleep while you are awake," he chuckled, stirring the coals and adding a few twigs to start a smoky little fire, "and in the same way that many stop living before they die." The blue spread out above us overtaking the gray while the hues of day continued to flood the shadows. I stood up to stretch; and the deer, which had spent the night in the meadow and were grazing close by, hardly lifted their heads before springing off into the woods—first one, then two, then four. The stars were fading fast and the grass, trees, and air were filled with the twittering, peeping, and chirping of little lives.

"…at that hour close to morning when the swallow begins her melancholy songs…."

"What is that?" asked Francis.

"Just some poetry." I grinned. "Thank you, kind friend. I think that I have been your stray dog tonight."

"My friends and I would say that I have been your mother and you, my brother son," corrected Francis returning my smile. As if on cue, a first ray of sun lit up a few oak leaves on an overhanging branch where a little finch began to chitter. "Remember, we are nothing before we are each who we are. The rest does not matter—for I am not a saint and you are not an artist while we are sleeping. It is the *i* that makes the difference." And the boy who was a fireman, archeologist, paleontologist, violinist, doctor, and painter, at once became *me*. So I awakened, watching the sheer curtain in our hotel room swell with a breath of air, to feel a chill, and pull in my feet.

December 3 – During the last few days that I was in Italy, I entered every church I could, to see if there were real wax candles rather than the electric ones that are becoming typical. And if there were, I'd leave a generous offering, light a candle, and place it in the bank of candles with the rest. *"Here's a wish for my kids, for Nikola Tesla, and for Saint Francis,"* I said to myself, pondering the nature of the burning hopes surrounding mine and thinking on whose hopes those might be, and how long I'd be represented there after I was gone. *"Who knows? Perhaps tomorrow when I'm home this candle might still be burning here."*

Then at home, I awoke each morning somewhere that I didn't recognize—in a hybrid place between here and there—my familiar room, an Italian hotel room, and a meadow in the woods on a mountain side. *"But the stars overhead are the same—like on Mt Subasio."* It is similar to what happens after a good dream, or when I've been painting on an intricate pattern for a long time and then leave it to do something else. I end up feeling stretched between places, not quite where I thought I was.

December 13 – Today, before getting into the shower, I stood in front of the mirror and studied myself—*"a rather average guy; too soft, too white, and too mature…"* I leaned forward over the bathroom counter getting closer to the glass. *"…that unmanageable gray hair, those little creases that have shown up leading from beside my nose toward the corners of my mouth, and the embarrassing few stray hairs growing straight out of my ears…."* I thought back a few years and recalled my similar dissatisfaction well before the signs of aging started to show, and tried to look ahead and imagine the old caricature that I will one day become. I smiled at myself, and my eyes began to water—those emotions again lurking just below the surface. *"At least I don't care anymore about that. It actually feels good—and I'll feel better after splashing some water on myself."* I stepped into the shower, comfortably back home, though less attached to the place. *"Maybe I am the place now."* Turning on the water and stepping back to wait as it warmed up.

Paintings are always filled with surprises. I can begin with a clear picture and end up crafting an image that looks exactly as I had foreseen it, only to find that it's not what I had imagined although it looks the same. Last night I dreamed of Nikola Tesla. I told him of my trip to Assisi and reported on my discoveries and speculations. "It is about subtle differences in frequency," he reiterated several times, referring to thoughts, ideas, emotions, and places. "Alter your frequency and you alter everything, including where you are. Frequency is all that separates things, even things that seem quite solid."

"And I think I'm beginning to know something about electricity," I nearly bragged. "I've seen it, felt it, and understood it, though I have no words to describe it yet."

"Then come with me," responded Nikola. "Please, follow me." And we made our way through a darkened wood thick with undergrowth. After some time, I thought I saw a dim light far ahead, which, as we proceeded, grew in brightness to become a flame, and then a small bright campfire where four men sat, huddled in dark tunics with firelight shining on their faces. As we approached, the closest man, with his back to us, stood up, turned around, and began making his way toward us through the brush.

"Brother Francis!" I called out. He responded with that same warm smile. "Brother Francis! It's me!" I shouted, rushing forward.

"Now, open your eyes," said Nikola Tesla firmly.

"But I don't understand! This is a dream and it will end!"

"I said, 'Open your eyes.'"

A Final Note

"Is that all true?" some have asked after hearing of my dreams.

"As true as any poem, melody, or painting," I have replied. Or, "That's what you must ask yourself," I often say.

"...but he's been painting for years," I heard my wife respond the other day, "and no one's ever asked him that before. They've always been true!"

As the real work of painting an image magically happens beyond the walls of a studio; so the work of our awareness happens beyond the limits of our tangible and temporal experience. While I can't explain the need to paint pictures any more than I can explain my dreams—where they come from and what they might mean, my hope is to have painted, on these pages, not just the portrait of an artist as a middle-aged man, but a clear picture of this painter's mind and heart—for the purpose of exposing the creative being—the artist in each of us.

I have struggled to report these events without distortion, to portray them as faithfully as I would any image on a ground, but with the colors and values of words instead of paint. Then I sat back and reconsidered it all; changed a few words here and there; played with punctuation; and fine-tuned the emphasis of things, pulling some into the foreground and pushing others back toward the horizon. As with every finished painting, I am satisfied that the picture is complete now—my best to this point. Tomorrow, I will clean and dust the studio, scrape the old paint off the palette and fill it with new colors.

Peace and all good things.

Acknowledgments

First of all, I must thank my wife Marilyn, without whom I would not have started, nor completed this adventure. Her belief, commitment, and patience have been constant.

I want to thank my children and family—especially my daughters Falcon and Miriam, who with their mother, have endured countless readings and rereadings of every page of this book—for their devoted support.

I am also forever indebted to Kent, Marilee, Alice, Elizabeth, and Toni for their steadfast support and encouragement.

To the members of my team—Kent, Jack, Alice, Tammy, Marilyn, and Gavin, who have worked selflessly to see this book happen; to old friends and new who have believed and contributed in so many ways—and to Mark, Bryan and Holly, and Jack and Betina for their eagerness to contribute in tangible ways to make this book become real—"Thank-you."

Ultimately, I offer my deepest gratitude to The Source of all inspiration through whom all is possible.